C000261307

First
We Met

CR 2016

the First Time We Met

JO LOVETT

bookouture

Published by Bookouture in 2020

An imprint of Storyfire Ltd.
Carmelite House
50 Victoria Embankment
London EC4Y 0DZ

www.bookouture.com

ISBN: 978-1-83888-965-4
eBook ISBN: 978-1-83888-964-7

To my amazing sister Liz

PART ONE

Chapter One

Izzy

December, fourteen years ago

'Smile for the punters,' Izzy's boss Terry hissed in her ear as he squeezed his way past, a little too close for comfort.

Izzy scowled. You'd have to be superhuman to still have a smile after two hours of boiling in a too-small and over-revealing Christmas elf costume, serving Full Englishes and builder's tea to total letches, with another eight hours of your shift to go.

She was going to kill the next man who told her that he wouldn't mind finding her in his stocking. Apparently the average frequenter of Earl's Court's 'Number One Greasy Spoon' (No Free-Range Here! No Green Veggies Either!) didn't know that in the twenty-first century there were laws against sexual harassment. Unfortunately, Terry didn't seem to know either, so there was no help coming from his direction and, even more unfortunately, Izzy was desperate for cash but could only work Saturdays round her speech therapy training, and this was the only Saturday job going.

'Your baps look perfect to me, love.' The grinning middle-aged man – seriously, he had to be older than her father – was looking straight down her top from over the counter. 'Do you come as a side order?'

'Hil-ar-ious,' she told him, trying to lean backwards so that her cleavage was less visible. 'Never heard that one before.' She pushed her elf's hat back onto her head – annoyingly the dress was too small and the hat was too big – and dolloped a spoonful of her earliest-cooked, and therefore coldest, baked beans (The Only Fibre We Serve!) onto his plate, hard, because she wanted to slap him. She dolloped too hard. Some of the juice splattered off the plate and onto the bodice of her dress. Excellent. *Excellent.* Now she'd have to have it dry cleaned, because she couldn't risk washing it again and shrinking it even more. Marvellous. The dry-cleaning bill would probably be more than an hour's pay. Fantastic. She took a quick glance at her watch. Nine o'clock and already she had The Rage. Most Saturdays she managed to make it to at least nine fifteen, if not nine thirty, before wanting to murder someone.

She shoved the breakfast towards the grinner and yelled, 'Next,' reaching for another not-that-clean-looking plate; Terry should really get the dishwasher fixed.

'Morning. Full English, please, as it comes, and a black coffee.' Wow. The next customer had an amazing voice. Deep. Gravelly. Rich. And it sounded as though he was smiling as he spoke. Nice accent too. Izzy *loved* an American accent. She was pretty sure, from extensive TV and film watching, that he was from New York. You could hear a lot from one sentence.

'No problem.' Izzy switched the dirty plate for a clean one and added the two eggiest slices of toast to it. Everyone loved extra-eggy toast. She always gave good portions to nice customers and rubbish ones to not-so-nice customers. Completely fair. Café karma. The only bacon left in the tray was grim – grey and flabby looking. She added some more rashers to the griddle and looked up at the man to tell him that it wouldn't be long.

And wow again. She found her eyes actually opening wider. His face matched his voice, in a way that almost never happened. Normally the ones with the nice voices *really* didn't do it for her physically. And vice versa. Last week, for example, she'd had a customer who'd been one of the most amazing-looking men she'd ever seen, until he'd spoken. And then something about the way his mouth moved, in conjunction with his very high and whiny voice, had made her skin crawl, and very much not in a good way.

But *this* man, again, wow. He had wavy, dirty blond hair, olive skin almost the same colour, a very square, stubbly jaw and dark-brown eyes. *Smiley* eyes, with little lines at the corners already, even though he only looked about mid-twenties. And he was tall with wide shoulders, wearing a faded Eagles t-shirt over a very solid chest and under a battered leather jacket. And she was *staring*. Well, whatever. It wasn't like there were a lot of advantages to this job other than the fact that it was hers and it paid her (a small amount), and he wasn't a regular, so, really, who cared if she looked a bit nuts.

And then he smiled. And everything around them slowed down and then disappeared, like it was only the two of them left in the world. The smile was making his eyes crinkle exactly as she'd thought they would and his mouth had gone slightly crooked. Izzy's stomach actually physically lurched, as though she'd been hit by something. She had no option but to describe it as love at first sight. The kind that no-one sane believed in. The kind that *she* didn't believe in. But she knew. She absolutely knew. She knew that he'd make her laugh. She knew that he'd laugh at *her* jokes, however bad. She knew that she'd never get bored with him. She knew that he'd treat people, including her, well. And she knew that if, when, they kissed, she'd actually melt. She *knew*.

'Hi.' She was smiling right back at him. He was looking at her like he knew things about her too. Like he was feeling what she was feeling. The same thunderbolt. Electricity. Fizzing in the air. 'I'm Izzy.'

'I'm Sam.' His smile had grown. He was *definitely* feeling what she was feeling. She could *tell*. Sam was a good name. It suited him.

'Well in, mate,' shouted Greg-the-Groper, from behind Sam's shoulder. 'I've been asking her name every Saturday for six months and she always ignores me.'

'That's because you regularly try to grope me.' Izzy dragged her gaze from Sam to Greg with extreme reluctance.

'Izzy. Over here. Now.' Terry had his arms just about folded over his stomach, across his truly disgustingly dirty, greyish-white t-shirt and apron. Izzy took a couple of steps towards where he was standing next to the swing door to the kitchen, really not wanting to move too far from Sam. Or too close to Terry.

'Yes, Terry?'

'If I hear you being rude to customers one more time, you're out. You're only *here* because the punters like you.'

'I work really hard,' Izzy said. If she was going down, she was standing up for justice as she went. '*That's* why I'm here. No-one else would put up with all of this.'

'It's alright, mate,' Greg hollered. 'It's all part of the banter. She'll give in one day.'

'Off you go.' Terry unfolded an arm and moved it towards her as though he was going to pat her bum. Izzy leapt out of the way and back to her place behind the counter. Greg was leering at her. The contrast between his face and Sam's was huge. Red veins and bloodshot eyes on a pasty middle-aged face versus dream-come-true gorgeousness.

'Piss off,' Izzy mouthed at Greg so that Terry wouldn't hear. Greg guffawed.

'On the one hand I really want to speak to these men on your behalf and on the other I'm thinking that you're dealing with them better than I could,' Sam said.

'Yeah, on the one hand I'd love you to punch them and on the other, you know, feminism... I'll sort them myself.'

'Sounds like you love your job?'

'Oh, yes. The aching feet, the smell of grease in your hair that lasts until at least Monday, the costume, obviously, and the delightfully chivalrous customers. Not to mention my wonderful boss. It's actual bliss.'

Sam smiled at her and then his expression got a little more serious as he leaned in closer. Was he, could he possibly be, maybe, actually going to *kiss* her? Across the counter? No way. Please way. Izzy was fairly sure that she couldn't breathe at this moment if you paid her. He was leaning further. If everything and everyone else had seemed far away before, now it was as though they were in a different universe, all to themselves. Although he wasn't looking at her, he was looking at the counter. Shouldn't he be focusing on her eyes and lips, like she was on his? He had lovely long, thick, dark eyelashes.

'Bacon's on fire,' Sam said.

'Shit.' Izzy stopped fantasising about what would obviously have been an earth-shatteringly amazing kiss and whipped the bacon off the griddle and into the bacon tray. All the congealed fat in there caught fire immediately. She batted at it with the tongs. The fire just grew.

She chucked a full jug of water over the tray just as Sam said, 'Tea towel.'

Izzy stared into the tray. 'A tea towel would have been better,' she said. 'It would have cost a lot less to replace than all this bacon.' There was no way any of it was servable now.

'Izzy,' Terry yelled. 'That's coming out of your wages.' Seriously. He was apparently blind to all sorts of things that happened where she could have done with a bit of help, but the second she made a mistake, he was on it. So annoying. Terry didn't exactly source his bacon from high-end, ethically run local farms – it was definitely all from battery-reared, antibiotic-fed, miserable pigs from the furthest corners of Europe – but there still had to be at least three hours' pay worth of bacon in there. It was a big tray. That plus the dry cleaning was going to mean a whole morning's work that she effectively wasn't going to get paid for. Izzy carried on staring at the bacon and thought about resigning. No. She really couldn't. She really needed the money.

'Hey.' Sam only raised his voice a bit but everyone, including Terry, stopped talking and turned to look at him. 'That was my fault,' he said. 'The bacon. You can't take it out of Izzy's wages.'

'Someone's got to pay for it.' Terry was sticking his chin out, as though he was squaring up to Sam. He was standing well back from the counter, though. Without the counter as protection, he'd probably have been running, or waddling, for the door. Sam didn't even twitch, Izzy was pleased to see. He pulled his wallet from a pocket and took out a couple of notes.

'Forty pounds to cover the bacon,' he said. 'And I'm sure it's worth a lot less than that.'

'I can't let you pay for it,' Izzy said. She really couldn't; it wouldn't be right. But forty quid. Bloody hell. Forking out for that would mean a whole week of surviving on beans on toast. Terry was already stuffing the money into one of the back pockets of his low-slung jeans.

'Really not a problem,' Sam said.

'No, honestly. I don't actually have forty quid on me right now, but I'll pay you back. Do you live nearby?' Please let him live nearby. It would be easier to see each other if they didn't have to travel. Although it didn't really matter. She'd go anywhere for him.

'Just moved in round the corner.' Sam indicated with a nod of his head. 'Although why am I telling you that? You absolutely aren't paying me back.' So generous – they were *definitely* meant to be – and a huge relief given Izzy's current financial situation. She'd make it up to him in the future.

'Thank you so much. I owe you big time.'

'Holding the customers up, Izzy,' Terry boomed.

'Sorry.' Izzy didn't look round. She really didn't want to stop talking to Sam, or looking at him, drinking in his face, the way he held himself, the way his accent rolled. He was smiling at her again.

'I should probably eat my breakfast,' he told her. 'Busy day ahead.'

'Of course. Here's your coffee and here's your no-bacon Full English. I'll put some more on the griddle and bring over a couple of rashers in a minute.' She'd given him the three most nicely done sausages, instead of two, to make up for the lack of immediate bacon.

Sam took the plate and mug from her and put them on one of the café's delightful stained plastic trays. He had very nice hands. Very strong-looking, very capable. Good nails. Not bitten, but not long. No jewellery. Perfect, in fact.

'Thank you.' He smiled at her again and then took the tray over to a table close to the door and sat down with his back to her.

'Full English please, love,' said Greg-the-Groper. He leaned in with a leer. 'Izzy.' Marvellous. She glared at Greg. Her name sounded a lot better on Sam's lips.

The whole time Sam was eating, Izzy snuck glances at his back. It was really hard to concentrate on the other customers. Sam had taken his jacket off to eat. His forearms were amazing. She could see the muscles flexing in them as he used his cutlery. When his bacon was ready, she was going to go over and have another chat. Definitely.

Bugger. The bacon wasn't cooking because the gas under the griddle was off. The water must have spilled over and put it out. Never mind. She flicked it back on. It should heat up quickly. She looked back at Sam. If she craned her head slightly, she could see his profile as he ate. He had an intelligent face. A nice face. Very nice.

She was feeling physically sick with nerves, like she had before she gave her uni presentation the other day, although in retrospect that hadn't been such a big deal; this was way bigger. The conversation they were about to have could be one of the most important of her life, *their* lives – the start of something big.

And then Sam finished eating just before the bacon was ready. He pushed his chair back, shrugged his jacket on, stood up and made for the door.

As he reached it, he turned towards her, gave her a little salute, which, from anyone else, would have looked ridiculous, but from him looked exactly right, and said, 'Goodbye. And good luck.' He accompanied the *good luck* with a little eye roll and a smile. Izzy laughed. What she actually wanted to do was cry. He was leaving. Walking out of her life. She'd been just about to go over and speak to him but he'd gone.

The café's tinny radio was blaring out Noddy Holder, the last few bars of 'Merry Xmas Everybody'… the soundtrack to Izzy's horrible, sinking feeling that the love of her life was walking away from her.

Although, maybe she didn't have to let him walk away. Maybe she should go after him, seize the moment. She pushed her way out from behind the counter and through the café, ignoring Terry's shouts.

She registered a shock of cold air hitting her as she burst out of the heat of the café into the December day, and then she saw Sam at the end of the road. She started running. There were shopping-bag-wielding and Christmas-accoutrement-holding people everywhere, in her way, most of them meandering. Clearly, nothing really important was happening in their lives at this moment. Izzy ran faster, weaving.

'Sam.' Her panting shout sounded pathetically quiet against the traffic, but he must have heard because he stopped and turned.

'Izzy.'

'Hi.' She came to a halt in front of him.

'Hi.' He was doing a very attractive lopsided smile, one eyebrow raised combo. An 'I'm pleased to see you but a little surprised' look. She should say something instead of standing here smiling foolishly at him.

'So, I was wondering—' she'd never actually asked anyone out before '—would you like to go out this evening? If you're free? I mean I know it's the Saturday before Christmas so you're probably busy.' She was actually busy herself this evening, but she'd cancel. This was more important. But maybe Sam had plans he couldn't cancel. 'Or tomorrow evening? I mean any time you're free? I owe you for the bacon. And, also, it would be nice to go out? If you're free?' Okay, she was sounding ridiculously desperate. But this was important. And when you were asking The One out, who cared about sounding desperate. They'd laugh about this when they were in their eighties and reminiscing. Izzy suddenly had an image of herself in a wedding dress and Sam in a suit in a gorgeous country church. Maybe in a couple of years' time. Maybe a winter wedding.

'Izzy, thank you so much but I'm afraid I can't. I'm getting married today.' Sam's dark eyes were serious, looking into hers. Izzy sensed him move his hands towards hers and then drop them back to his sides.

She couldn't speak. She was stunned. This was just awful. She couldn't work out what was worse, the mortification or the misery. *How* could she have been stupid enough to read the signs so badly that she'd asked someone out on their *wedding day*? And also, he was *her* One. Except he obviously wasn't. He was getting married to someone else. Today. He loved someone else. It was actually really hard to process the information. It was so wrong. She took a deep breath and wrinkled her face, trying to get her mouth to work and form some words.

'It's my wedding day.' He said it very gently. 'The wedding's this afternoon. I was having a pre-wedding, calm-the-nerves, greasy spoon breakfast moment to myself. You know.'

Izzy nodded. She didn't know. But she could imagine. Ish.

'Congratulations.' It was surprising that she was managing to work her voice now. 'I hope it goes really well. Nice weather for it. No rain forecast.'

'Yes. Thank you.'

'Okay. Well.' Weirdly, she didn't want to end the conversation, even though it was truly gut-wrenching *and* embarrassing. She didn't want to break the contact. But obviously she should. She shivered, suddenly aware that it was really bloody freezing and she had no coat on, just her tiny elf costume. 'Congratulations again.'

'Thank you.' He was looking at her like he knew what a terrible moment this was. Tears were pushing hard against her eyelids. She needed to walk away right now.

She nodded and, with a big effort, turned round and started to retrace her steps back to the café. This was so bad. So wrong. So awful. In the same way that she'd known that he was The One, she knew it was going to take far longer than it should do to recover from this. And not just the humiliation. Which was ridiculous. She'd 'known' him for the length of time it took to be served and eat a large breakfast at normal speed and walk the length of an averagely long road. She knew no actual facts about him other than his name. But she honestly felt truly bereft.

Terry was yelling and gesticulating at her from the door of the café. Izzy bent down and picked up her elf hat from the pavement. It must have fallen off as she ran. She plonked it back on her head and carried on trudging towards Terry.

Chapter Two

Izzy

Eleven months later

Izzy looked at her watch. Yep, just about time to grab a Pret sandwich before her first afternoon appointment. The last one had run on beyond its scheduled finish time but when you were helping someone with a stammer, hurrying them was obviously not the way forward. Wow, the temperature had dropped since this morning. She wrapped her scarf more tightly, huddled into her coat and pulled her gloves out. And then stopped dead in the middle of the pavement and dropped the gloves. Someone behind her bumped into her and she apologised on autopilot.

Sam, actual Sam, was walking up the steps into Chelsea Old Town Hall maybe fifteen feet in front of her. So close to her. She'd be able to cover the distance between them in seconds. It was definitely him. She'd thought about him so much, fantasised, compared – negatively – every man she'd met since then to him. She'd imagined several times over the past few months that she'd seen him in the flesh, but it had never actually been him. But this time it was. No question. He was dressed a lot more smartly than he had been for his wedding day greasy spoon breakfast: charcoal grey overcoat, suit and tie, smart shoes. Presumably his working uniform. She wondered what job he did.

Izzy's heart was going unbelievably fast, thundering in her ears, and her scarf was suddenly scratching her neck and making her feel claustrophobic. She'd been imagining this moment for so long. She should do something. Say something. Go and speak to him.

No. She shouldn't. She *really* shouldn't.

He obviously hadn't been fantasising about her, measuring every other woman, unfavourably, against her, wondering about her for eleven months. He was *married*. Probably very happily. He probably didn't even remember her. Actually, he might do. It probably wasn't normal for a girl you didn't know to ask you out on your wedding day. But he certainly wouldn't have remembered Izzy's name, or thought about her again.

Yup, she should just walk on past. He was nearly at the top of the steps now, about to go through the double doors at the top.

And then he turned round. And looked right at her. Properly at her. They locked eyes for a second or two. Sam hesitated for a fraction of a moment. Izzy was sure that he recognised her. And then he dropped his eyes, turned his back on her, pushed open one of the doors and took a step forward.

And he was gone. Just like that. Either he hadn't recognised her, or he had and he had no interest in talking to her. Well, of course he hadn't. They didn't know each other and he was married. Izzy was, frankly, a complete loser to have been hung up on him, on an *idea*, for nearly a year.

Okay. This was it. She needed to move on. It was beyond sad to have been thinking for so long about someone she didn't even know. It was worse if that person was married and utterly, utterly off limits. And even worse if thinking about him prevented her from living her own life properly. She needed to become a new woman. A new woman who dated properly, fell in love, lived her life.

*

Izzy took one step inside the club and immediately wanted to turn right back round and walk out again. It was your classic sticky-floor, sweat-dripping-off-the-ceiling, dive venue. Total meat market. It looked like everyone was already pairing up with strangers, and it was barely 10 p.m. She could murder a good night's sleep. If she left now, she could get the bus and wouldn't even have to fork out for a taxi.

'Remember—' her best friend Emma spoke very firmly into her ear '—you're a new woman. Goodbye Sam, hello the rest of your life.'

Izzy sighed and then nodded. Emma was right. As of this lunchtime outside the town hall, she *was* a new woman.

Bloody hell, the music was loud. She was going to have a headache within about five minutes.

'New woman,' Emma instructed again.

'Yes, I am.' Izzy slapped a smile on her face. 'I'll get the drinks in.' Everything would probably feel better once she had a couple of very alcoholic cocktails down her.

Obviously actually buying the drinks was easier said than done. Everyone else around the bar was so bloody *tall*.

'This is going to sound like a really bad chat-up line, but for someone so pretty you've got very poor bar presence. I'm Dominic. Can I buy you a drink?' Dominic was good-looking in a classic, boy-next-door kind of way. If he were American, he'd be preppy. He wasn't American, though, and Izzy was not going to think about Sam.

Dominic actually had a very nice smile. Open. Pleasant. It wasn't doing anything tingly to her, but that whole love-at-first-sight thing was obviously total crap, and she was a New Woman. As far as she was concerned, Sam might as well not exist. Dominic did exist and he was right here, and he might well be the perfect man for her. It felt like a little piece of her soul was shrivelling up and dying, letting go of Sam. But she'd never had him. And never would. Maybe that part of her had to die so that she could actually live like a normal person.

Izzy gave Dominic her best smile. 'I'd love a drink.'

Chapter Three

Izzy

March, six years later

Izzy heaved herself and her shopping out of the supermarket. Why did people like being pregnant? Why did people talk about pregnant women blooming? Izzy was not blooming. She had bags under her eyes from nightly 4 until 6 a.m. insomnia. Her skin was stretched unpleasantly taut over her water-retention-huge feet. She was wearing flip-flops even though it was only about five degrees, because her feet were too fat to fit into any of her shoes. Her toenails looked like total shit because she'd tried to paint them herself when she realised that she was going to have to wear flip-flops but she couldn't reach properly and then it had felt like too much hard work to reach down there to remove it. She couldn't breathe because the baby had its feet up, squashing her lungs. She needed to go to the loo *all the bloody time* because its head was on her bladder. Nine months was an eternity.

Her right flip-flop caught on the corner of a pavement stone and she tripped, in weird slow motion. She was going to fall right over. Or drop her shopping. She let go of the bags and put one arm out to catch herself on the wall of the shop and the other around her stomach to protect the baby. It might get hurt if she fell. No, panic over, she was still upright on her uncomfortable feet.

She looked down. Her bags were not upright. Her groceries were scattered all over the pavement. Bloody hell. Now she was going to have to bloody *bend over*. Like that was possible.

'Hey, that doesn't look good. Can I help?' The man was already gathering up her shopping, working about a billion times faster than she could have done. He reminded her of someone. The man she'd once asked out on his wedding day. Sam. Same dark-blond hair, same wide shoulders, same gorgeous New York accent. He looked up over his shoulder at her and smiled. 'All done.'

It *was* Sam.

He was still stop-the-traffic handsome. Despite being a happily married woman, she might even still fancy him a bit if she weren't too pregnant ever to have or even *think* about sex again.

'Hi, Sam.' Now that was an example of speaking without thinking. He wasn't going to remember her. He was going to be completely freaked out that she knew his name. Think she was some kind of insane stalker. She should just gloss over it. 'Thank you so much. Really kind of you. I'm not great at bending down at the moment. Thank you.'

'Hi, Izzy.' He remembered her name too. Wow. *Wow*. He must have a freakishly good memory, given that she'd clearly meant nothing to him. His smile was still gorgeously infectious. Her own lips were widening in response. 'Not a problem. Can I carry your shopping somewhere for you? Where're you going?'

'That's actually a very good question.' She hadn't thought things through when she'd gone into the supermarket. She'd come out to wander around the shops for a bit, because when your husband and all your friends were at work and you were too unbelievably fat and uncomfortable to do, or enjoy, anything you might normally do, maternity leave was actually extremely boring. She'd finished work ten days ago and was now having to kill time every day. She was actually looking forward to the week of intensive ante-natal classes that she'd booked for Monday so that she had something to *do*.

The gooseberry yoghurt had called *Buy me* to her from its shelf and she hadn't been able to ignore it, and once she was in there she'd realised that there was a lot of other food she needed, and now she had to carry it all. But she didn't want to go home yet because it was only about two o'clock and Dominic wouldn't be home before seven, at best, and she might actually die of boredom sitting on her own in the house for five hours *again*. Okay, she was going to go to a café and read her book for an hour or two with a cup of uterine-wall-strengthening, labour-shortening raspberry leaf tea and some cake. And then maybe get a cab home because she was never going to be able to carry all her groceries.

'I'm thinking a café,' she said. 'Are you sure you don't mind carrying my bags for me?' It was okay being a pathetic accepter of male bag-carrying help when you were eight and a half months pregnant. 'It's just round the corner on Kenway Road.'

'Definitely not a problem. Late pregnancy always looks like very hard work to me. How long do you have to go?'

'You think I'm *pregnant*?' This very weak, it had to be said, joke was the best bit about late pregnancy, possibly the only good bit. Sam did some serious eye contact avoidance before squinting down at her tummy again.

'Erm?' he said.

Izzy waited a few seconds before sniggering. 'Sorry, bad joke. Obviously. It's fun winding people up though. On behalf of pregnant women everywhere suffering from the "You're huge, is it twins, ha, ha *ha*" and "Eating for two *enormous* ones, I see" type comments.'

Sam laughed. 'You got me good. Genuine moment of panic there. So how long do you have to go?' He bent down and gathered the bags up.

'Thank you very much.' Izzy gestured at the bags and started walking in the direction of the café. 'One week and six days until my due date. Not that I'm obsessively counting down the days or anything. I mean, I'm very pleased to be having a baby but I'm really not enjoying my third trimester. Do you have kids?' He probably did. He'd been married for over six years. Sadly, the date of his wedding was engrained into Izzy's mind pretty much as strongly as her own. She should really have managed to forget it by now.

'Twins. They're nearly six now.' His wife must have been pregnant on their wedding day.

'Wow. That must be hard work.'

'Yeah. They're amazing but yes, definitely also hard work. But worth it, you know. Obviously.'

'The café's just along here.' Izzy pointed. 'Why don't you join me?' Yes, she'd embarrassed herself hugely in front of him several years ago, but it had to be obvious to Sam that she'd very much moved on given that she was married and pregnant, and he seemed very nice, and Izzy was *bored*. 'I owe you for the bacon.' Oops, stalkerish again. Though surely she could be forgiven for remembering. Unless, of course, she looked like someone who'd ask so many men out that she'd forget if one of them had been getting married that day. 'If you remember. Forty quid. That'll buy you a very nice coffee and I could even throw in some cake.'

Sam paused for a second and then smiled and said, 'Yeah, great, why not. I'm working from home today and I awarded myself a lunch break, which I never normally get in the office. I can do coffee.'

'Fab. I've got to be honest. My own grumpy-pregnant-woman company isn't that enthralling. I'm starting ante-natal classes next week but until then pretty much every single person I know's at work.'

'Pleased to be of service.'

They'd arrived at the café. Izzy pushed the door open with her back and held it for Sam while he manoeuvred her four full bags-for-life inside. The café was on the ground floor of a Georgian townhouse and there was a log fire at one side of the room, which was always appealing. Today Izzy was desperate to sit in front of it, to start to defrost her feet. It was extremely physically unpleasant when your top three-quarters was boiling to the point of under-boob sweatage, while your bare lower legs and feet were freezing. She made straight for the sofa next to the fire, thank goodness it was free, lowered herself down onto it with difficulty, took her coat off and stuck her feet out. The warmth on them was *good*. Her nails looked atrocious, but whatever. It wasn't like the rest of her looked great. And Sam probably wouldn't notice. It probably wasn't normal to study other people's toenails.

Sam arranged her bags in the corner of the room, away from the fire. 'What can I get you to drink?' Bugger. Izzy was going to have to stand up again and go over to the counter so that she could pay.

'I'm buying.' She put her hand out to support herself and started the process of rolling herself off the sofa. It was far too squishy to get out of easily. Maybe she needed to roll left instead of right and use the sofa arm to hoist herself up. If she, specifically her backside and tummy, carried on increasing at the rate she had recently, she'd need a crane to get out of a comfortable seat by the time she actually gave birth.

'I'm already on my feet. What do you want?'

'Okay, thank you very much.' Sometimes you had to admit defeat and let a nimbler person do the walking. 'But you have to let me pay. And you have to let me buy you lunch. They do some great sandwiches.'

'Deal.'

'I'll have a raspberry leaf tea, please.' She took two twenties out of her purse and gave them to him. Their hands brushed as he took the notes, which felt a little stomach-droppingly weird. 'A cheese and onion toastie. And a slice of lemon drizzle.' She could get a brownie afterwards. Or maybe some carrot cake. Maybe both.

'And if they don't have raspberry leaf?' Evidently he wasn't finding it weird that they'd touched hands, because he obviously hadn't thought about her like she'd thought about him.

'They do. I've been here quite a few times.' She'd been here a *lot* during her pregnancy. They did very good tea and even better cake. 'It's quite a fancy café.'

Izzy studied Sam's back as he waited for their drinks at the counter, sharing a joke with Delia, the very lovely middle-aged owner. He had a very nice laugh. Rumbly. Was she in danger of finding him attractive again? She was, and she wasn't. He was definitely now firmly in the past. A memory. The man she'd asked out on his wedding day and who had then featured heavily in her dreams for months. In a few decades' time it might even be an anecdote that she could bear to tell someone other than Emma and Rohan.

Now, the present, in her actual real life, she had Dominic. She was very happy with him. They were friends. They had fun together. They had some shared interests. They had good sex. When she wasn't massively pregnant. She'd fallen in love with him gradually, rather than on the spot, and it wasn't always mega passion, but that was real life, wasn't it? Real life was *not* seeing The One, getting together with them on the spot and living happily ever after. Real life was mundane.

'They'll bring it all over.' Sam folded himself into the armchair opposite her. 'So you're on maternity leave. What do you do?'

'I'm a speech therapist, specialising in stammers.'

'Interesting job. And so worthwhile.'

'Yes, it really is. I love it. As you say, both interesting and worthwhile, and there can't be a lot of jobs like that. There's a lot of variety in the people I see, and it's so good when you can truly help someone, because a stammer can be so debilitating. And it shouldn't be, of course. Society should accept people the way they are. Sorry, I'm sounding militant. But you see children being bullied for it, or people with so much to say losing the confidence to communicate effectively, and so on, and that's so wrong. So, anyway, yes, I do love it but at the moment I'm struggling to imagine coping with both a baby and work, but I really don't want to give up my career.' Realistically, Dominic wasn't that likely to be able to be a very hands-on dad, given that he was extremely work-addicted.

'It can be done. If you can't work part-time, you can still manage as long as you're lucky enough to have family help or be able to afford childcare. You just have to forget about non-essential things like sleep, you know.' He really did have a very nice smile. His upper front teeth were perfect, but the ones further back and his lower teeth were slightly uneven, the kind of imperfection that Americans didn't usually put up with, unlike their crooked-toothed English counterparts. It was actually more attractive than fake-looking total perfection.

'So does your wife work?' Was it a bit weird to ask about her? Hopefully not. It was the obvious follow-on to what he'd been saying.

Sam's smile dropped a little. 'She. No. She didn't.' The hairs on the back of Izzy's neck prickled. It was immediately obvious that this was not a good line of conversation to have brought up. Something very bad had happened. She could tell. Maybe they were divorced. Sam's smile had vanished and he was looking down at the table instead of at Izzy. 'We lost her nearly a year ago.'

'Oh my goodness. I'm so sorry. That's awful. What happened? If it's okay for me to ask?' She wished she knew him well enough to give him a huge hug to say how sorry she was. The laughter had gone from his eyes and he suddenly looked very tired.

'Cancer. Breast. Metastasised.'

'I'm so sorry.' Shit, Izzy felt really tearful, and it was *so* inappropriate to cry on behalf of someone who you barely knew and when they were being completely stoical.

'Yeah. But you know. I'm lucky. I have the children. Liv and Barney.' His smile was back, but not a real one that reached his eyes; it was like a mask. 'And they have each other and me. So, you know. We're good. Could be worse.'

'But could be better,' Izzy said.

'Yeah. But we're doing okay.' Sam took a long sip of his coffee, like he didn't want to make eye contact.

'Here you go.' Delia put a laden tray down on the table between them. Izzy gave her eyes a quick wipe while Delia was hiding her from Sam.

'Thank you so much.' She smiled at Delia.

'So you like onions in your grilled cheese?' Sam looked like a man who really wanted to move the conversation on. Understandably.

'Yes, I do. It's the only way. I love caramelised onions.' Izzy picked her knife and fork up and then moved her knees apart so that the baby could squish down between her legs so that she could lean in. She had a serious point to make. 'I do *not*, however, like cheese and onion crisps. I actually hate them.'

'Now that is interesting. I, by contrast, like ham in my grilled cheese sandwich, essentially a croque monsieur, and I like bacon chips. Sorry, *crisps.* I think it's all wrong if your crisp tastes don't follow your sandwich tastes.' Sam's smile was reaching his eyes again now.

'But bacon is not cheese and ham. Would you like bacon *and* cheese crisps?'

'I think I would. I think anyone would. But I don't think they exist. We might have hit on a business idea here.'

Izzy nodded, pleased. 'Yes, I think that's got to be a winning flavour combo. Something for me to research while I'm wallowing on a sofa until the baby comes.'

'How much maternity leave are you planning to take afterwards?'

'I think in total the full year that I'm allowed. And then I'll maybe just go back two or three days a week to start off with, see how it goes. Work have been fantastic about being flexible and my husband's been cool too, so, yeah, I'm going to take full advantage. Try to have my cake and eat it.' Why did it feel weird mentioning Dominic to Sam? Izzy took a big bite of her toastie. Munching was a good cover for awkwardness.

'Sounds perfect. What does your husband do?'

'He works in banking. You know, finance.' Izzy loaded a token bit of side salad onto her fork. 'I don't really know, actually. Bonds. Fixed income. Trading. Those are the words I hear but if I'm honest I'm not really sure what they mean.' This did not feel right. Telling the man you'd spent nearly a year thinking of as The One that you had no real idea what your husband's job was. It felt a bit disloyal. 'But he enjoys it, which is cool. And his colleagues are nice.' They'd been fine on the few occasions she'd met them. Maybe a little bit keen to talk only about work-related stories, maybe a bit keen on flashing their large amounts of salary around, maybe too keen to be *extremely* patronising about her career, but fine, really fine.

'A lot of jobs are remarkably difficult to define,' Sam said. 'Like my own. I'm a corporate lawyer. My own mother would struggle to tell you more than that, and she bores all her friends with constant stories about me. I'm the only son out of four siblings – something of a novelty. She can recite pretty much every one of my achievements – including winning my first-grade field day sack race – and she'd still be doing all my laundry and cooking if she had her way. She's one of those great, adoring mothers, but any time I've ever tried to tell her what I do, she just glazes right over.'

'You know what she needs to do? She needs to watch *Ally McBeal*. I used to love that in my teens and as a result I know exactly what corporate lawyers do.' Izzy pointed her fork for emphasis. 'They wear pencil skirts and amazing heels, and cry in the loos a lot.'

'Totally right. You're literally the only person I've ever met who knows exactly what I do at work. This is where I've been going wrong. I should have pointed my mother in the direction of Netflix instead of trying to use my own words to explain.'

'Exactly.' Izzy smiled at Sam and took another mouthful.

'Just going to get us a couple glasses of tap water.' Sam stood up and ambled back over to the counter. Izzy thought about him as she chewed. And about herself. All that time when she'd imagined seeing him, meeting him. And now she had met him, and they were chatting, and it was lovely. And he was widowed with twins and she was married to Dominic, who she really did love, and about to give birth to Dominic's baby. So when they'd finished their coffee, she'd go home and forget about Sam. And that was that.

Chapter Four

Sam

Sam watched Izzy lug herself out of the room towards the restroom. Small-to-medium-sized woman, gigantic baby bump. Bigger than Lana's had been, with twins, but Lana had been supermodel tall, close to six foot, so she'd had a lot more space to accommodate her bump, and the twins had been tiny at birth, probably no greater weight in total than a single baby.

Izzy's red hair clashed beautifully with her orange dress. Sam was pleased that she was wearing orange. He'd had a sense that she'd wear bright colours when not forced to be an elf and it was satisfying to be right. He realised that he couldn't remember anything about what she'd been wearing when he saw her on the King's Road outside the town hall, when he'd been going into the library; all he could remember from then was her face. And his own shock. And guilt.

He took another slurp of his second cappuccino and looked around. This was a lovely coffee shop. Cosy. Classic, tasteful décor. Very British. Was it odd that he was here with Izzy? Maybe. He'd thought, known, when they met in that excruciating way on his wedding day that they'd get on well, given a chance. And he'd been right. He pulled his cuff up to check his watch. Woah. That had been a long lunch break. They'd been talking for just over two hours. The time had flown if he was honest.

He drained the rest of his coffee and held the cup with both hands in front of him, staring into it. Now Izzy wasn't here to distract him, he realised that he should probably get going.

Had Lana lived, he would never have cheated on her. The guilt he'd felt when he saw Izzy that morning outside the library had been horrendous. And, as he was reflecting on how easy their conversation had been today, the same guilt was creeping over him.

He hadn't felt guilty when Izzy asked him out. Maybe because he hadn't been pretending anything to anyone at that point, or certainly not to himself, anyway. He had felt helpless, and pretty pissed to be honest. It had definitely been a bit of a body blow to discover, on the day that he was marrying the fairly new girlfriend he'd drunk-proposed to because she'd got pregnant, that the whole 'love at first sight' thing existed. Obviously, it didn't really. Obviously, he'd known nothing at all about Izzy then. But if he'd been single, he'd have ditched any plans he had for that evening in a heartbeat and gone out with her. And they'd have had a fantastic time. He'd been pretty sure of that at the time, and now he knew. She was warm, sarcastic, very funny, clever, *nice*. Not to mention pretty fricking gorgeous. And managing to make eight-month-pregnant crabbiness very cool. What wasn't to like?

In fact, if he'd been single and they'd gone out that day, maybe she'd be pregnant now with *his* baby.

Except then he wouldn't have the twins, and they were everything. Plus, really, love at first sight? Instant, easy happy endings? Doubtful.

And Izzy was probably very happy with her husband.

Yeah, she had a husband. And Sam had his honour and, if he was honest, he'd enjoyed her company way too much while they'd been talking. He put his cup down on the table and stood up. It was definitely time to leave. He should wait here, standing, so that when she got back into the room she'd know that he meant to leave so that she a) didn't waste energy getting down onto the sofa and back up again, and more importantly b) didn't feel embarrassed in demonstrating that she might want or expect the coffee to go on for longer than he did. She'd be able to take her cue from him. He really didn't want to cause the same, very nice, woman to feel humiliated or silly twice.

How long was she going to spend in the restroom? Probably a long time. It was probably very difficult to go pretty much anywhere quickly when you were that heavily pregnant. He turned his attention to the fire. The flickering flames were making patterns against the green vertical stripes of the wallpaper. You could happily stare into a fire for a long time.

'I love a fire.' Izzy had come back into the room surprisingly quietly. The door must be well-oiled. 'I can watch them for hours.'

'Yeah, me too.' Sam picked his jacket up from the chair, fast, so that she'd get the signal that he was leaving. 'It's been great to see you. Wish I could stay longer but work calls.'

'Yes, it's been really nice. I'm going to get going too.' Izzy reached for her coat and then looked at her shopping. 'Actually, I'm going to call a cab.'

'How far do you live from here?'

'Three roads away. But I have a lot of shopping. As you know. And normally I would never be a princess in a taxi with all my shopping bags, honest, but I'm a little out of bag-carrying condition at the moment.' She lived three roads away. Extraordinary that they'd been living so close to each other in the Earl's Court area for so long. They could have bumped into each other any time.

'It isn't really worth waiting for a taxi to travel three roads away when I could carry your bags for you. My good deed for the day. I have time.' He could catch up on his work this evening, when the twins were in bed.

'No, I couldn't. And surely you're good-deeded-out on the carrying bags front today.'

'Seriously, not a problem. I don't want to pressure you to walk if you don't feel like it but if you do, without the bags, I'm absolutely happy to carry them. Little bit of fresh air.' Izzy studied him for a long moment. Sam realised that he actually did want to carry the bags for her. It felt too abrupt to say goodbye right now. And if he was carrying her bags, there was nothing to feel guilty about, right? No, wrong. The guilt was still there. He smiled at her, just in case she could read his mind, to try to assure her that he did really mean it. She smiled back.

'Okay, well, thank you very much. It's very kind.'

'Oh my goodness, it's freezing,' Izzy yelped as they emerged into what was now a very grey and icily drizzly afternoon. 'I'm going to get actual frostbite on my toes.' Sam looked down at her flip-flopped, scarlet-toenailed feet.

'Would it be rude to ask what the rationale was behind your choice of summer footwear on this beautiful, sleety day?'

'My feet are too fat for any of my other shoes.'

Sam looked more closely. She had to have painted her nails, and quite a lot of her toes, herself. A huge tummy in the way had to be the only explanation for them looking as though they'd been done by someone blindfolded. He turned his head away, worried that he was going to laugh.

'Are you *smirking* about my badly painted nails?'

'No, I am not,' Sam lied.

'Hmm. Men are so lucky not to have to be pregnant.'

'That's very true.'

'And you get to wee standing up.'

'Yup, the world's a very unfair place.' It really was. If it was a fair place, he'd have been free to go on that date with Izzy, all those years ago. Immediately, he felt more guilt, as though he'd just wished away Lana's existence, which he would never do.

It was easy, walking along with Izzy. Companionable. They actually didn't need to talk that much. Although, equally, they seemed to have a lot to talk about, like they could make a conversation out of anything.

Which was lucky, because she was slow. Remarkably slow. She had to stop on every corner, plus at least once on each of the few roads they walked along, for a rest, each time putting her hand into her back and leaning back on it, the classic uncomfortable pregnant woman stance.

'So this is me.' Izzy had led him to a flat-fronted terraced house.

Suddenly, the moment was awkward. And it was a long moment. Izzy spent minutes fumbling through her ridiculously large bag until she found her house keys while Sam stood next to her, still holding the bags.

She had the keys out and the door open eventually. Sam wasn't going to offer to carry the shopping right inside, definitely too strange. As he deposited the bags just inside her hall, keeping his feet on the step outside the threshold, Sam got a glimpse of dark wooden floors and tasteful greige walls. Not very Izzy, he'd have thought; must be her banker husband. Maybe it had been his house first, and Izzy had added the flashes of purples and reds he could see in the cushions, curtains and pictures.

'Thank you so much for helping me with my bags. And for keeping me company.'

Sam smiled at her. He knew that they weren't going to exchange numbers, or email addresses, or anything. It wouldn't be normal for a happily married woman who was planning to stay happily married to suggest staying in touch with the man she'd once asked out on his wedding day. And it wouldn't be appropriate for him to suggest to that happily married woman that they stay in touch. And, really, he didn't want to.

From the moment he'd purposely sat with his back to her in the greasy spoon, to squash his conviction that he'd just met the woman for him, fighting his desperation to turn round a) to see her again in that ridiculous elf costume, get another look at her face, her eyes sparkling with humour, her smile, and hear her speak again, and b) to see if she was looking at him, he'd known that it was a bad thing that he'd laid eyes on her that morning. He'd struggled not to think about her occasionally over the years. Which had been bad enough before Lana's illness, and terrible after it.

Yep, he was absolutely not going to suggest exchanging details. This had to be it. This was like the library steps all over again. The longing, the temptation and the knowledge that it would be very much the wrong thing to do. And the guilt that he wanted to do the wrong thing, was even thinking about it. He'd only been at the library because they'd just got Lana's diagnosis and he wanted to look at physical books instead of typing things like 'breast cancer prognosis' into his laptop and leaving a virtual trail that she might find when he was trying to be upbeat for her. And on that terrible day, when he should have been entirely focused on Lana, he'd seen and thought about Izzy. So wrong. Yep, he needed to go now.

'So goodbye then.' Maybe he should go in for a kiss on the cheek. Or maybe just an air kiss. No, no kiss. 'Good luck with the baby.'

Izzy smiled at him, a wobbly smile. 'The birth'll be great. Like shelling peas.' He couldn't stop talking, wanting to take one little extra bit of conversation.

'Yeah, I've heard that. It'll be a walk in the park.'

'Exactly.' Right. Really time to go. It felt sad, but it shouldn't. Izzy was obviously happy now. Married to a nice man. About to have a baby. All good. 'Okay. Bye then.'

'Bye.'

It was really hard to keep on walking to the end of the street without looking round.

PART TWO

Chapter Five

Sam

May, seven years later

Sam loosened his tie, undid his top button and rolled his head and shoulders. Then he stretched his arms. And did another head roll. Nope. It wasn't helping. Nor was the view out of his fancy floor-to-ceiling windows. All well and good having a thirty-fourth-floor office with a stunning Manhattan skyline backdrop, but if you spent your whole life in that office, the view just reminded you of the life you weren't out there living. No amount of head rolling and Central Park panoramas were going to make spending yet another evening in this room any more palatable.

Fricking clients. Seriously. So damn unreasonable. And so damn paying his fees, which paid his bills, which meant that he had to pander to their unreasonable damn demands, any time of day and a lot of the night. Unfortunately there was no halfway house with this job. You couldn't just scale back, work half the hours, for a fraction of the money.

Sam adjusted the volume down on his phone. Jim Buck, his newest and biggest client, by fees and by ego, had been barking out suggestions and ridiculous demands for over an hour now. Sam had himself on mute and was working on his desktop at the same time, but it was hard to concentrate with all the shouting. How the hell was he going to put up with this man dominating his working life for the foreseeable future?

Finally, yes, Jim had stopped talking. Probably had an eighties throwback dinner featuring a lot of champagne, fat cigars and exploited women to get to.

'Not a problem,' Sam told him. 'I'll have that with you by noon tomorrow.' He didn't even bother to attempt to inject warmth into his voice.

He pressed the red circle on his phone and took a breath. Now he had an even more unenjoyable phone call to make, which he needed to do immediately. He swiped and pressed green.

'Hi, Daddy. Are you phoning because you're going to be late home?' Liv didn't sound annoyed or reproachful, just resigned. And very unsurprised. Perfectly pitched to make her father feel like crap.

'Got it in one. I am so sorry.' It was torture knowing that his kids were upset, and that it was his fault. 'But listen. I have a couple things I need to do in person in the office but once I've done those I'm coming home to see you and I'll finish my work once you're in bed.'

'Have you forgotten?' Seriously, she'd make an excellent parent with her ability to convey quiet disappointment.

'No?' What had he forgotten? Not a physio appointment, please. He'd made every single one so far, but it was a constant worry that he was going to mess up and miss one. Surely the next one wasn't until next week.

'Our pizza and ice cream date? At Mariano's?'

'Wasn't that Thursday?'

'It is Thursday.' Damn. *Damn.* He spent the whole time letting them down.

'Liv, honey, listen. How about we do Mariano's next week and this evening I order takeout when I'm on my way home and it'll arrive just around the time I do?'

'Do you think Mom would have forgotten?' Liv had kept her tone so sweet, it took Sam a second to register the passive aggression in her words. He was still trying to form a reply when Barney spoke.

'D-d-d-d-dad.' Barney's stutter was always more noticeable when he was upset. Liv must have had the phone on speaker. 'You're a liar.' It took him a long time to get the word *liar* out. 'You promised.' Even longer to say *promised*. And then the phone went dead.

Damn.

Sam needed to stop letting his children down. He also needed to make some progress on finding the right speech pathologist or therapist for Barney. And he also needed to read through and comment on this contract because without his clients he probably wouldn't be able to afford Liv's extortionate health insurance, Barney's extortionate therapist fees and all the other extortionate things in their lives.

He had great kids, a great family, great friends, a great apartment, a great job. A lot of great things. He was very lucky. He just needed to find some extra hours in the day to take advantage of any of those great things other than the job.

*

'That was fantastic pizza.' Sam stood up to get the ice cream out of the freezer.

'Almost as good as Mariano's.' It took Barney a lot of attempts to get his words out.

'It's okay. We're going to Mariano's next week instead. It's nobody's fault that we had to postpone again.' Liv's words and tone of voice were saccharine. But the barb in there was definitely intended. Clearly it was Sam's fault. Did she blame him for everything? He was beginning to think that he didn't have the emotional agility to deal with a complex teenage girl. Especially given how busy he was. It had taken extreme willpower to avoid looking at his watch during this meal. He just didn't have the time for a leisurely mid-week dinner with the kids.

'I'm so sorry about messing up this evening.' He gave the twins an extra scoop each. If only you could buy teenagers' happiness with ice cream like you could with toddlers. Barney scowled at him and Liv smiled at him suspiciously angelically. Neither felt good. Sam smiled back at them anyway.

He glanced down. If he nudged his cuff against the edge of the table, maybe he could expose his watch face, unnoticed.

He had so much to do tonight. A phenomenal amount of work, plus he owed return calls and messages to his mother, two of his sisters and his best friend Luke, not to mention the woman he was currently dating, Melissa. And he needed to get back onto doing something about Barney's speech, underlined by Barney's stuttering anger this evening. And he should probably be thinking about Liv, too, trying to break through the barriers she seemed to be erecting between them.

'It's 9 p.m., Daddy.' Liv's eyes had flickered to where he'd inched his cuff back. Her smile was bland and wide and didn't reach her eyes. Yeah, he should definitely be thinking about how she was doing emotionally. Not right now, though.

*

The kids in bed and hopefully sound asleep for the past three or four hours, none of the calls or messages he owed returned but the contract work finally finished, Sam checked the time on his office wall clock.

Just shy of 2 a.m. He could go to sleep for four and a quarter hours or he could spend some time researching speech therapists and sleep for half an hour less. At least either way he'd be so tired that he wouldn't dream. The nightmares were a killer. Last night, yet again, he'd woken at 4 a.m., bathed in sweat, his mind replaying images of the accident.

He was so unbelievably exhausted. But Barney's confidence was so unbelievably diminished because of his stutter. And getting worse. And in just over a year's time he'd be entering high school. Things needed to improve by then or he'd have a very miserable few years socially.

Sam was going to have to do the research.

He was good at his job, a lot better than he seemed to be at parenting teens with issues. Maybe he should approach this as though it was a tricky business problem. To which he would no question find a solution.

So. He needed to think outside the box.

Everyone and everything they'd tried so far hadn't worked. To date, they'd just done a very good job of proving that you couldn't solve every problem by throwing enough money at it.

He'd tried a lot of options, including therapists in far-flung states. Maybe he should go big on his outside-the-box thinking. Maybe he should look at speech therapy methods used in other English-speaking countries. Australia, South Africa, the UK.

England. Speech therapy.

Izzy. She'd been a speech therapist specialising in stutters.

He hadn't thought about her so much in recent years. She'd occupied his mind a lot when the kids were younger. How old must her child be now? Probably about seven. It had been a few months before he and the twins moved back to New York that they'd had coffee.

Suddenly, the idea of speaking to Izzy again was very appealing. He'd spent, what, just two or three hours with her, several years ago, but those hours had felt precious. Comfortable. As though that was where he'd been meant to be. He'd had the same feeling that he'd had on the morning of his wedding day, that, another time, another place, and she could have been The One.

Maybe he should contact her, ask for advice.

No. This was middle-of-the-night loneliness talking. The wee hours were always the worst, when the rest of the world slept and you were up worrying, watching over your children, or working, all while nearly out of your mind with sleep deprivation.

Although, maybe Izzy *could* help. What harm could it do to ask? Tonight he was out of any other concrete ideas.

He didn't even know her surname. And at work was she Izzy? Isobel? Isabella? He needed to drink another very strong espresso and get googling.

Twenty minutes later he had alarmingly blurred vision but also Izzy's work details and email address. And a genuine little heart flutter when he looked at the speech therapy website photo of her with lanyard around neck and that dimply smile, bordering on cheeky. The heart flutter would be the middle-of-the-night factor again.

It really couldn't hurt to email her. At worst, she wouldn't reply, or she'd be unable to help. At best, she could help Barney. And perhaps she and Sam could chat again, and he could get a hold of that comfortable feeling again.

Chapter Six

Izzy

'I need to wee *now*.' The key was never going to fit in the lock. Izzy was going to *burst*. 'My bladder isn't what it was when I was younger. Childbirth ruins you.'

'And also you've practically drunk your own bodyweight in margaritas and haven't been to the loo all evening. Give me the key, you daft mare.' Emma wrestled it from Izzy and got it into the door first time. *First time.*

'You're an actual key-using genius.' Izzy kicked her shoes off, hooray, they'd been *killing* her toes, ran past Emma and Rohan, and went straight upstairs to the bathroom.

The *relief.*

When she got back downstairs, Emma and Rohan were in the kitchen, Emma plonked on the two-seater sofa next to the garden doors and Rohan at the sink filling three glasses with tap water.

'Probably not going to make much of a difference to how you feel tomorrow, but worth a shot.' Rohan handed their glasses to them.

'Thank you, lovely Rohan.' Izzy squished herself into the sofa next to Emma, only spilling a bit of her water as she sat down. 'And thank you both for organising this evening. Two best best friends ever.'

'Our pleasure. Happy birthday again.' Emma clinked water glasses with her. Some slopped out onto Izzy's knee.

'I've had a really lovely day today.' It had been one of those birthdays where pretty much everything had gone well. Izzy was mixing work-from-home and holiday all week, because it was half-term, and Emma was deputy head at a local comprehensive and on half-term too, and not working today or tomorrow. They'd done girls' lunch and cinema on nearby Kensington High Street with Izzy's seven-year-old daughter Ruby, before Ruby went to her best friend's for a sleepover. Nearly everyone who should have remembered Izzy's birthday had done so. She'd had some great presents. 'Thank you again for your wonderful gifts. I'm really looking forward to them.' And she'd had a couple of weird ones. 'Just remembered that I forgot to tell you what my mother and Veronique bought me. Beyond strange.'

'Straight to Oxfam?' asked Rohan.

'Yes, but no. In that, yes, I'm getting rid of it immediately, and no, there's no way I'm taking it to Oxfam.'

'Is that why you couldn't tell me in front of Ruby?' Emma was sitting up straight, looking delighted. 'Was it something *adult* themed? Sexy underwear? Sex toys? Like your wedding present?'

'Yes,' Rohan scoffed. 'From her mother and her wife. For her birthday. When she's single.'

'Emma's basically right. I will never complain again when they forget my birthday. Which they have of course done every year since I was thirty. First present in literally six years and they bought me—' Izzy paused for effect '—only the *Kama* bloody *Sutra*. And some other sex books. Basically a whole set of Female Sexual Empowerment genre books.'

'Noooo,' Emma screeched. 'I was joking.'

'What, really? Where are they?' Rohan looked over at Izzy's bookshelf, like she'd have stuck them on there between Mary Berry and Delia.

'I hid them inside my biggest casserole dish.'

'Would you classify the *Kama Sutra* as Female Sexual Empowerment? I'm not sure. We need to read them. Which cupboard?' Emma was already trying to get herself off the sofa and onto her feet.

'Eeew, no.' Izzy shook her head so hard she saw stars for a couple of seconds. 'I don't want to read any of it, and definitely not with you two. I don't think any of us need to know what the others have or have not done.'

'You're very, very right.' Rohan was looking horrified.

'Not tempted at all?' Emma asked.

'So very much not. My mother and stepmother bought them for me. Surely *no-one* should buy books like that for you other than your own partner? I mean, grim.'

'Yeah, fair enough.' Emma nodded. 'Wow.'

'Full marks to them for originality,' Rohan said.

'I think it's a hint,' Emma said. 'They must think it's time for you to move on.'

Rohan gave Emma a massive nudge. 'And that's the drink talking. We really don't need to do this this evening. Shut up, Emma.'

'She's probably right,' Izzy said. Dominic had obviously moved on. He hadn't sent her a card or even a message. Which was fine. *Totally* fine. Not at all hurtful. On *his* birthday she'd bought him a present from Ruby, a too-expensive-for-her-budget pair of Mulberry cufflinks, because he loved a double-cuffed shirt, and the latest Ian McEwan book, which he wouldn't read, but would enjoy keeping in his sitting room, and got Ruby to make a card for him, but there was no reason he should do anything for her birthday. That was the whole point of being separated; you weren't in a romantic relationship any more. Izzy should absolutely be moving on. Although she would not be reading Sexual Empowerment books, especially not ones purchased by her mother. 'This evening was fab, wasn't it? Good to know that we aren't too old to do the macarena.'

'Never too old.' Emma nodded. 'Can't beat cartloads of cocktails and a group dance.'

'Yep. A very good evening. A lot better than last year.' Splitting up with Dominic two days before Izzy's birthday the year before had not made for a festival atmosphere on the day. It had just been so *sad*. They'd grown apart and Izzy knew that it had felt inevitable once they'd decided, although she couldn't even remember *how* they'd decided, other than that it had been precipitated by his secondment to Milan – maybe they'd never been fully joined and just hadn't realised initially – but when you had several years of history and a daughter together and you didn't actually dislike each other, it just felt unbearably tragic to finally acknowledge that you weren't going to be together for life.

Izzy had spent a couple of days after their decision full-on ugly crying and then a lot of time crying in an 'I will be brave', eyes always nearly brimming over, way.

It hadn't been attractive. Looking at herself in a mirror on the evening of her birthday last year, she'd seen that most of her face had looked remarkably pasty-white and puffy, while her cheeks and nose were very red.

Oh, crap. Now she was feeling sniffly again.

'Yes, that was a *bad* day.' Emma glugged some water and then worked her arm round Izzy and gave her a big hug. 'But it was the right thing, wasn't it, and you're in a much better position now.'

'Ably assisted by the *Kama Sutra*,' said Rohan. 'Position? No, sorry.' He shook his head. 'It was funny when I thought it, but out loud it didn't work.'

'Time and a place for shit jokes, Rohan,' Emma said.

Izzy and Rohan had met on the back row of a history lecture at the beginning of their first term at university and had instantly clicked. There'd also been instant clickage between Emma and Rohan when Izzy introduced them, and they'd always got on well until they'd become flatmates for a few months a couple of years ago. Since then, there'd been a lot of bickering between them. The bickering was sometimes funny, sometimes not so much.

'It was totally the right thing to say and I am in a good place, or *position*, now, and I love your jokes, Rohan. Most of them, anyway.' Izzy downed quite a lot of water to hide her face in the glass while she waited for the hovering Dominic-related tears to settle down. Bugger, she'd drunk the water too fast. Now she felt sick. It *had* been the right thing to split up with Dominic, of course it had, except it did feel wrong that Ruby's father lived in Milan, and occasionally she still missed him. Not in an 'I want to have sex with you' way, or an 'I want to tell you that because it would make you laugh as much as it made me laugh' way, because sex and laughter hadn't featured highly in their marriage in the last year or two; but when you'd been together for so long, there were small things you talked about that you wouldn't really mention to other people. Although to be fair, she had Emma and Rohan, and her other friends. She talked to them about mundane things all the time. She did not need Dominic for that. They could have a mundane conversation right now, without Dominic.

'Not to change the subject but I need a new dishwasher,' she told them. 'Which I can't really afford. But I hate mine. It doesn't wash dishes. You have to wash them up yourself first. Always been like it.'

'You wash your dishes up and *then* put them in the machine?' asked Rohan. 'Why would you do that? Why don't you just not put them in if you've already washed them up?'

'Because I like them to be perfectly clean.' Dominic had liked them to be perfectly clean too.

'Right.'

'Appliance issues are shit.' Emma nodded. 'My washing machine doesn't spin properly. I need a plumber. Everything comes out sopping. Driving me bloody insane.'

'Please tell me you don't wash all your clothes twice,' Rohan said.

'No, I don't. That would be weird.'

Yeah, no, it wasn't the same. Izzy was in many ways closer to Emma and Rohan than she'd probably ever been to Dominic, if she was honest, even on their honeymoon, but he'd agreed with her about the dishwasher. Things were a lot sparklier if they'd been through the machine. Obviously *she* was nearly always the one who put them through that machine, but that was a separate issue. Maybe if they'd worked harder on agreeing on other household matters, they'd still be together. That was what it was all about, wasn't it, living together, being able to agree on small things. It wasn't about sex and laughing, it was about the dishwasher and whether or not you'd have salmon or chicken that evening, and enjoying the same box sets.

Why hadn't Dominic sent her a birthday message? Would it have been better if he had done? Was it better that he hadn't?

Her father hadn't remembered her birthday either. Not surprising that a man with one fiancée, three ex-wives and seven children wasn't too hot on family birthdays – not Izzy's anyway – but still hurtful. He probably also didn't like to be reminded that his oldest child was nine years older than his fiancée. But still hurtful.

Okay. No. She wasn't doing this. She was *happy*, she'd had a really lovely birthday, with her extremely lovely friends, she was in a very good place now, and she was not going back. She hauled herself off the sofa and walked over to the fridge. 'Water isn't doing it. We need a glass of rosé, some chocolate and *Erin Brockovich*.'

'I'm going to love you and leave you.' Rohan stood up. Emma was staying with Izzy for the night.

'Do you really love me?' Izzy asked, fluttering her eyelashes at him. Ow, she'd hurt her eye. Could you dislocate an eyelid? 'Owwww.'

'Will anything bad happen to me if I say yes?' That was the legal-caveat-loving barrister in Rohan.

'Will you take the *Kama Sutra* and the other books and get rid of them for me?'

*

Izzy dragged herself out of bed and staggered into the bathroom.

Last night had been worth it for the memories and the feel-good factor, because you couldn't beat late-night drunken film watching with your best girlfriend, but this morning Izzy was actually going to die. It hadn't been a glass of rosé; it had been a bottle. It was like someone had a vice all the way round the front of her head and was tightening, tightening, her mouth was *so* dry and tasted disgusting, and she had some serious tinnitus going on. On the upside, it was the Friday of half-term and she had the day booked working from home to catch up on paperwork.

On the even greater upside, Ruby's friend's mother had just messaged to ask if Izzy would be happy for her to take Ruby with them trampolining this morning, followed by a pizza lunch. Happy? Izzy would be absolutely bloody ecstatic. Obviously she adored Ruby, but there was a time and a place for seven-year-old shrillness.

There was no sign of Emma from Ruby's bedroom. Izzy downed two paracetamol and a pint of water, crawled back into bed and turned the pillow over to find some lovely coolness. Another hour or two of sleep would help a lot.

She turned the pillow over again. No. She couldn't sleep. So annoying.

Her phone pinged. Dominic.

Happy Birthday for yesterday. Hope you had a great day.

Well. That was normal. Totally normal. Drop your ex-wife, the mother of your child, who you weren't even properly divorced from yet, a very casual birthday message, and no present, one day late.

Anyway. Now Izzy had the answer to whether or not she'd have liked him to have messaged her yesterday. No, she would not. It did not feel good that he'd remembered; it felt shit all over again that they weren't together any more. Even though she *knew* now that their relationship hadn't been working. She shoved the phone under her pillow. Hopefully the two blue ticks accompanied by no reply from her would mean that next year he wouldn't bother with the birthday wishes.

Maybe she *could* get back to sleep.

The doorbell rang, twice. Izzy got out of bed and looked between her curtains. It was the postman, holding a parcel.

The sprint downstairs really hurt her head but at least she got to the door in time.

The parcel was from Dominic. He'd sent her a birthday present after all. Izzy's eyes pricked. She should probably go and open this in bed, in case Emma got up soon, so that she had time on her own to work out how she felt about it.

He'd bought her a baking recipe book that she already had and a Hermès silk scarf that she'd never wear. Well, maybe she would, if she ever turned into a well-maintained, tweed-and-pearls kind of sixty-year-old. There was also a birthday card, with a mango on the front, very sweetly thoughtful of him, because he'd always thought she loved mango, and him buying her mango-related presents had been their thing. She actually hated mango. Sickly sweet with a horrible after-taste.

Izzy sniffed hard. So many reasons to cry, because of one parcel. Dominic had got the book exactly right, because he knew her well, except he didn't know that she'd already bought it for herself, because they didn't live together any more. And he'd got the scarf exactly wrong, because he *didn't* know her that well, despite eight years of marriage. And the mango card really summed the whole thing up.

And now the tears were coming. No. She was not doing this today. Her head was already too sore. She'd do something else now to take her mind off things and send a thank you message this afternoon when she felt calm.

She folded the paper and put it and the card and presents on top of her chest of drawers. She was going to do half an hour of work to take her mind off Dominic. Nice and slowly, sitting in bed with her laptop on her knees, with the lights off. Then she could maybe have a little rest later.

She had lots of mundane work emails. And one from a sender whose name she didn't recognise, with an intriguing first line: 'Sam McCready: Speech therapy advice: Hey Izzy, You might remember me from when we had coffee…'.

Izzy's stomach lurched slightly. It couldn't be *Sam* Sam. Though, what other Sams had she had coffee with? But… really?

The email had just arrived. She clicked it open.

From: Sam McCready
To: Izzy Castle
Subject: Speech therapy advice

Dear Izzy,

You might remember me from when we had coffee a few years
ago. I gathered up your groceries and we went to a Georgian
tea room with a lovely fire.

I hope you'll forgive my having hunted down your email
address. I'd like to ask your advice on a speech therapy issue
if I may.

The reason that I'm writing is that I remember that you told
me that you were a speech therapist specializing in stutters (or
stammers as you probably call them), and I could really do with
some help in that department right now.

My thirteen-year-old twins were involved in an accident a
few months ago. For background: my daughter was seriously
injured but is now doing really well, with ongoing physiotherapy.
My son, Barney, wasn't physically injured but he was severely
traumatized, we think both by the accident itself and by the
aftermath with his sister, and he developed a stutter. The stutter is
severe, getting worse, and fairly debilitating. We've seen a lot of
speech pathologists and therapists and have made no progress.

We live in New York now and we seem to have exhausted
all options here.

Do you know of any speech therapists specializing in stutters that you would recommend, or do you yourself undertake
private work?

Obviously if you're no longer working in speech therapy or don't feel able to help, please ignore this email. Otherwise, I look forward to hearing from you.

Best
Sam McCready

Woah. Full-on stomach lurching now.
Woah.
Weird.

Over the years, Sam had become one of those memories that seemed almost like a dream. A pretty amazing dream, granted, but a dream nonetheless. She hadn't even known his surname. McCready. Sam McCready. It suited him. Like a New York private eye from a black-and-white movie.

She didn't actually want to think about Sam today. Today, she was aiming to focus on the fact that she was in a very good place in life, albeit hungover, with very good friends, and totally fine about everything, including Dominic. She did not want to think about Sam, because remembering that coffee had always made her feel uncomfortable, especially when, like today, she was thinking about what went wrong with Dominic.

Looking back, their relationship had had tiny cracks in it almost from the day they met and, obviously, their split had had nothing whatsoever to do with Sam, who she barely knew. Except, it hadn't helped that just before Ruby was born Izzy had spent an amazing two hours with a man who wasn't her husband. She and Sam had talked for hours, and they had made each other laugh. A lot. Dominic didn't always get Izzy's jokes, and he didn't often make jokes of his own. Not ones that Izzy got anyway.

And from the way Sam had spoken about his children then, it had been obvious that he was a fantastic, hands-on, caring father. Borne out by the email he'd just sent her at silly o'clock New York time. A lot of single fathers in well-paid jobs like law would have hired round-the-clock nannies. Dominic adored Ruby, but he'd always been more than happy to leave the majority of the childcare to Izzy.

She still missed Dominic's dishwasher empathy though, and the fact that she could bang on for hours to him about Ruby's achievements and milestones.

This was bad. Izzy did not need to go here *again*. She needed to close Sam's email and ignore it and move on from all past negative thoughts. She could totally ignore it. From the way he'd worded it, he almost expected to be ignored. He was just a slightly desperate father reaching out to every person he could possibly think of who might be able to help. He'd probably written to dozens of different people.

She pressed the cross on the top right of his email and clicked open a message containing a completed questionnaire from the mother of a little boy she'd seen last week with a severe word-blocking issue.

*

'Mmm, that is *so* good.' Izzy took a large mouthful of American-style pancakes with blueberry compote, maple syrup and crème fraiche. She was so lucky to have this café just round the corner. 'I think I'm genuinely going to be feeling quite human after this.'

'Yeah, you can't beat a good carby brunch for a hangover.' Emma pulled open her free-range pork and spiced apple sausage sandwich on seven-grain wholemeal bread, and dolloped in some home-made tomato ketchup. 'Also, when it's hangover food, you can eat millions of calories without putting on any weight.'

'That is *not* true for normal human beings.' Emma was tall and lean and ate like a horse without ever putting on any weight and could not empathise with mere mortals like Izzy. 'But I really don't care.' Izzy took another to-die-for mouthful.

'We need to decide on our city break. What about New York? I know it's hot in August but maybe less touristy then? I googled. Lots going on that Ruby would like.' Emma took a big bite of her sandwich and moaned loudly. 'That is sooo good.' The two smartly suited men at the nearest table both looked over and goggled, as they might if the very beautiful Emma were orgasming in public. Emma glared at them. 'Just enjoying my sandwich.' Izzy was pretty sure that at least one of them would ask for Emma's number before they left.

'New York's actually a great idea.' Izzy thought about Sam, now living there. Would it be weird if they bumped into each other? Obviously they wouldn't. New York was a big city.

Wonderful, now she was thinking about Sam again.

'Speaking of New York… I had a weird email this morning.' Why was she even mentioning it? It wasn't a big deal. She just wanted to ignore it.

'Mmm?'

'It was from Sam.'

'Sam who?'

'*Sam* Sam.'

'*Sam* Sam?' Emma did some suggestive eyebrow raising and eye swivelling while she swallowed a mouthful. More goggling from the suited men. '*Sam* Sam?'

'Yup.'

'I didn't know you emailed each other. How did you get each other's email addresses? When did you start emailing?'

'We don't. I mean, we don't know each other. At all.' Izzy realised that she hadn't ever told a soul about those few hours she'd spent with Sam.

She hadn't told Dominic. That had felt awful, like having a secret; well, it *had* been having a secret, but it had felt too complicated to explain why her first, very brief, meeting with Sam had been so memorable, and why it had subsequently, six plus years down the line, seemed normal and fine to go for coffee together. It was just easier not to tell him.

Strange that she'd never told Emma about it, though. In the nearly twenty-six years that they'd known each other, when Izzy had moved in with her grandmother and joined Emma's school, she'd told Emma pretty much everything, barring the more intimate details of her sex life. She'd even told her about how infrequently she and Dominic had slept together in the last months of their marriage. And in the nearly eighteen years since she'd met Rohan, she'd told him most things too, but not this.

'What do you mean? Why did he email you then?' Emma asked.

'Basically, he remembered that I was a speech therapist and his son has a really marked stammer; he's tried a lot of therapy, none of it's worked and he wanted to ask my advice. They live in New York now. He hunted me down on Google.'

'He remembered from a short conversation with a stranger on his wedding day a very long time ago that you were then a trainee speech therapist and managed to find you on the internet?'

'We bumped into each other once and had a quick coffee.'

'*What?* When was that? I can't believe you didn't tell me. That's *huge.*'

'It was when I was on maternity leave and you were living in Munich. Just before Ruby was born.' Hooray for the Munich excuse. 'It was just a quick coffee. But I told him about my job then. He was a widower with twins. He mentioned that the twins are thirteen now.' Izzy would have known without Sam telling her almost exactly how old his twins were given that she still remembered the dates of his wedding and their coffee, and how old the twins had been then.

'Wow. And how was the coffee? Was he still gorgeous?'

'Yes, still gorgeous, obviously, but I was a good eight and a half months pregnant and very grumpy and desperate for the loo the whole time. It wasn't a long coffee.' An Oscar-worthy piece of lying there, if she said so herself. It had been, frankly, the best coffee of her life, with the most attractive man she'd ever met, still memorable seven years down the line.

Emma nodded. 'Yes, you didn't love late pregnancy, as I recall. Is he still gorgeous? Have you googled him?'

'Nope. Didn't occur to me. I'm incredibly restrained like that.' Izzy rolled her eyes. 'Of course I have.'

'And?'

'I think the photo must be quite recent because he looks older. In a sexy George Clooney, grey-at-the-temples kind of way. He's a partner in a New York law firm and he specialises in corporate law. There's a paragraph describing what he does, which is a lot of words that you understand individually but which make no sense when strung together.'

'Show me?' Emma took Izzy's phone, where, obviously, she still had the website up, and zoomed in on Sam's photo. 'Wow. Not surprised you fell for him on the spot. I mean, what first attracted you to the handsome, chisel-jawed, rich lawyer? Who, as well as all the client stuff, lectures a course at Harvard and does some pro bono work. I mean, God's actual gift. I would.' Yup. Izzy would have done too. In the past. Although what had actually made her fall for him had been his smile, a one-off sense of connection. And his voice.

'He was even better in the flesh. Great sense of humour.'

'Not surprised he was already taken when you met him. The good ones always are.' Emma shook her head regretfully. Izzy was definitely not going to mention that he'd been single the second time they'd met. And that to her shame she'd wondered a *lot* during her maternity leave what might have happened between them if she hadn't been married and about to give birth. 'So what was weird about his email?'

'The fact of it is weird. It's a weird thing to send an email of that nature to someone you hardly know.'

'Not that weird? If you're a desperate parent?'

'Hmm.' Izzy did not want to speak to Sam and revisit how their second meeting had made her feel.

'He must have put quite a lot of effort into finding your email address. Did he know your surname beforehand?'

'Probably not. I didn't know his.'

'There you go. Effort. Could you take him on as a private client?'

'Yeah. There's a mutual recognition agreement between the UK and the US for speech therapists. I got my US certificate when I did my six months in Seattle.' Izzy and Dominic had been newly in love when they'd done their US stint. A long time ago.

'There you go then. Another coffee?' Emma smiled at the waitress.

'Yes, fab.' Bloody hell. Obviously, Emma was right. Izzy was going to have to reply to Sam. After all, what kind of person would she be if she ignored a desperate parent?

Chapter Seven

Sam

Sam hit the Refresh button on his personal email account for at least the tenth time today. And no, still no message from Izzy. It was 6 p.m. in New York, so 11 p.m. in London, i.e. she almost certainly wasn't going to reply this evening. Maybe she wasn't going to come back to him at all.

He'd hoped that he'd have a response waiting for him when he dragged himself out of bed at the crack of dawn this morning, and he'd carried on hoping all day.

He didn't know why he was so keen to hear from her. Because, really, was she going to be any better than any of the other therapists they'd tried? Well, perhaps. Perhaps it wasn't so much about the methods. Perhaps they just needed to find someone that Barney would connect with. Hard to imagine Izzy *not* connecting with someone.

However, if he was honest, maybe the reason that he wanted to hear from her so much, especially now that he'd seen the photo of her smiling face, was that he'd just like to talk to her again. Silly, really. She was essentially a stranger.

Right, he was going to re-refresh one more time, leave the office, arrive home at a reasonable hour for once, spend a quality hour or two with the kids, and then meet Melissa for their date.

*

'Daddy, I've been invited over to Chrissie's apartment this evening for a pizza movie night. Can you pick me up at like ten?' Liv had obviously been desperate for him to arrive home. Her face was sparkling. Friendships had been a little difficult for her since she'd missed so much school after the accident. 'Her mom's going to pick me up now if that's okay?'

'Sure, honey. Could any of your friends' parents drop you home?'

'I don't want to ask.' Her smile was dropping. 'Can't you pick me up?'

'Sure. Of course.' This was an opportunity to avoid letting Liv down for once. Maybe he and Melissa could just have a quick drink this evening, and dinner next weekend. And, yes, Liv was smiling again. Barney wasn't, though.

'Are you going out before that?' Barney's stutter was highly pronounced, again. Sam looked at his beautiful, anxious son who'd had exactly zero social life in the past few months, since the accident, and whose sister was now a lot more popular despite her own friendship issues, and whose father had been about to consign him, on his own, to a Friday night babysitter, while he went on a date.

'No, I'm not.' Snap decision. Would Melissa be sympathetic? Probably not, especially since it would feel disloyal to Barney to explain to her that he had to stay home because he didn't want his son to be what the British might call a Barney No-Mates. Whatever, he had no choice. 'Now that Liv's going to be out, I'm thinking that you and I can grab some tacos and shakes—' Barney loved Mexican food '—and watch some junk TV?'

'Cool.' The word came out easily and Barney smiled. Sam realised with a jolt that Barney didn't actually smile that much any more.

*

'You take the last one.' Sam slid the taco box across the sofa to Barney. His housekeeper would be furious if she could see them but a) she couldn't and b) he was pretty sure there was no grease on the bottom of the box. 'You're a growing boy.' Barney grinned at him and took it. He had a great smile. 'You want to watch some more basketball?'

'Yeah, cool.' The effects of one-on-one parenting and two evenings running of junk food. Noticeably increased confidence in speaking. 'Do you think I'm gonna be tall enough to play professionally?' Still pretty fluent.

'You never know. Your mother was nearly as tall as me, so you could end up several inches over six feet.' Over Sam's dead body would Barney attempt to go down the professional sportsman route. A much better life policy to be a successful amateur and then do something sensible, like law or medicine, but now wasn't the time or place to mention that. Barney was smiling again.

It was good having father/son bonding time. They should do this more often. Specifically, *Sam* should do this more often.

His phone rang. He took it out to look at it, in case it was Liv. It was Melissa. He carried on looking at it, unsure whether or not to press the green button. He should answer it, because this was obviously her reply to his message about postponing until next week, but he didn't want to ruin this moment with Barney.

'You should get that.' And the stutter was back and the smile was gone. Sam put his phone down.

Obviously, if Izzy or any other competent therapist of any kind witnessed their home life, they could diagnose a fair number of things. In particular, Sam should carve out more quality time with his children. That was true, clearly, but Barney still needed coping strategies for when he was upset. Not every child whose father worked over-long hours or dated had a stutter. Sam was increasingly sure that Liv wasn't happy with him either, but the unhappiness didn't manifest itself physically.

Was Izzy going to reply to his email?

Another call. Still Melissa. Sam pushed the red button on his phone and picked up the remote. 'So how about you show me how to play one of these video games?' It was more than worth it to see the look of delight that lit up Barney's face.

Melissa sent a hostile, and, for such a fastidious woman, surprisingly coarsely worded text a few minutes later. Yeah, it wasn't likely that she would have been sympathetic about Barney. She was good company, though, which was the best you could hope for from a date.

But not as good company as his son, actually. This was genuinely turning out to be a fun evening.

*

Saturday morning wasn't so good.

During breakfast, Sam had to field a call from his mother, who was disappointed that he was going to have to drop the twins with her and his father and then go into the office instead of staying for their family Sunday lunch tomorrow. He adored his parents and his sisters and he didn't know how he and the twins would have coped since Lana died without all their help, but right now he could do without their nagging in his life.

He then had to take a couple of lengthy work calls; cue stuttering fury from Barney and glacial politeness from Liv.

Straight after a lunch cooked by his housekeeper, which he'd eaten in his home office during a conference call, Sam decided that enough was enough on the weekend. He lied to Jim Buck that he was going to be at a funeral in the afternoon and insisted that Liv and Barney accompany him into Central Park for a walk.

It was ice cream weather. Sam bought huge double cones for the three of them, blackcurrant for Liv, vanilla for Barney and salted caramel for himself, and they strolled along one of the paths into the middle of the park. It was great. Harmonious. Proper family time.

Liv's walking was dramatically improved compared to even a few weeks ago. Her physio was delighted. She hardly needed her crutches any more, and it was easy to believe now that in due course she'd be back to sport in the way she was before the accident. The first thing Sam had allowed himself to hope for in the immediate aftermath of the crash was that she wouldn't be permanently disabled or disfigured. And now he was hoping, almost expecting, that she'd soon be fully recovered. A few months ago, he'd have paid any price to get to this stage.

Now, he'd pay any price to get Barney to the same stage of recovery, and to work out how he could ever begin to make up to both of them for what had happened. It was harder to see mental injuries than physical ones, but he suspected the children still blamed him. Rightly so. He still blamed himself.

'Hey, aren't they your friends?' Liv indicated with her ice cream toward a group playing ball.

'Yeah.' Barney turned his body away from them slightly. Heartbreaking how different he was now from how he'd been until the accident, always the kid who'd run over and join any group playing ball, whether he knew them or not. Liv had been the quieter one, always a little in awe of her brother's lack of shyness.

'Aren't you going to go speak to them?' Liv should have been watching Barney instead of the other kids. She'd have realised that she should stop talking.

'Why don't we head off this way?' Sam started to walk in the opposite direction from the group.

'Hey, Barney,' one of them shouted. Sam looked round. The kid was waving. Sam looked back at Barney, who hesitated and then raised his arm.

'Want to go over there?' Sam was almost holding his breath.

'Maybe.' It took Barney a long time to get the word out.

'Go, dumbo.'

'Liv.' Sam did a zip-it signal behind Barney's back. 'Why don't you go?' He gave Barney his best encouraging-dad smile.

After a long moment, Barney nodded and started walking over to the group. He stood awkwardly at first but then started to speak a little. But not fluently; the breeze was carrying some serious stuttering to Sam. And then one of the boys laughed. And then another. And suddenly it was a group of kids, some of whom Barney had been good friends with for years, laughing at him. And this was Sam's fault. What an idiot. He shouldn't have encouraged Barney to go over.

'Nice one, Dad.' Liv's sneer was impressive.

Sam opened his mouth to reply, but Barney's need was more important at this point. He turned away from her and strode over to the group and said, 'Barney, sorry, dude, we need to get going.' His voice came out more loudly than he intended. 'Boys.' He nodded at them. 'Barney'll catch you later.' They did at least stop laughing when Sam spoke. But maybe that was even worse. When he was younger, Barney had commanded respect amongst his peers on his own account.

Sam slung his arm round Barney's shoulder as they walked. He opened his mouth to speak and realised that he needed to wait until his voice was steady. After a few seconds, he managed to start a fake cheery monologue about baseball. There wasn't a lot that could make a grown man cry but, witnessing his son be humiliated, Sam had come seriously close to tears. He still had a lump the size of a watermelon in his throat. He was going to get back on the speech therapy hunt that evening.

*

A watched inbox never pinged. Sam had continued to wait for an email from Izzy all weekend. And then he'd accepted that, while she might be on vacation, or not answering emails outside working hours, there was also a good chance that she wasn't going to reply to him and he was going to have to research other options, which shouldn't have felt as disappointing as it did.

Early Sunday evening, Sam finished yet another call and typed 'private speech therapy pathology recommendations New York' into Google. As soon as he finished making changes to the latest Buck contract after the kids were in bed tonight, he was going to make a new list of therapists to contact tomorrow.

As he stood up to join Liv and Barney in the snug, his phone signalled that an email had arrived in his personal account.

From: Izzy Castle
To: Sam McCready
Re: Speech therapy advice

Dear Sam,

Good to hear from you. I do remember our coffee – so kind of you to pick up all my groceries and help me home!

Apologies for the late reply: I've been busy with work and my daughter.

Could you give me some more details about Barney's stutter and about what you've tried so far? I don't know if I can help at all, but I can try!

All best,

Izzy

Sam found himself smiling at his phone, genuinely pleased to hear from her.

Dear Izzy,

Thanks for getting back to me, especially at the weekend.

Not at all—it was nice to see you again!

I understand, from the various speech therapists that I've spoken to and from what I've read, that there are various types of stutter. Barney gets stuck on the initial letter of words. There's no question that it's worse when he's stressed, upset, embarrassed, etc. I think that's all fairly classic. It definitely dates back to the trauma of the accident. The therapists that I've spoken to agree that he needs strategies to cope when he's in a situation where he starts to stutter, but so far none of them have come up with any strategy that helps. I'd be very interested to hear whether you had any suggestions. The stutter's really starting to affect him socially, and I'm concerned that that will only get worse as he gets older.

Best,

Sam

He *could* have mentioned how guilty he felt, how hard it was to see Barney suffering, how pleased he'd be to speak to Izzy again, but he was a potential client, not a friend. Funny how he thought of her as one though.

And funny how often he continued to press Refresh for the next couple of hours, until he realised that it was well after midnight in London and highly unlikely that she would be replying until the next day at the earliest. Was it his desperation over Barney, or something else keeping him glued to the screen?

Chapter Eight

Izzy

Izzy held her arms out as Ruby hurtled towards her.

'I missed you, Mummy, but I had fun.'

'I missed you too, gorgeous girl.' Understatement. Izzy scooped Ruby up into a lovely, close cuddle. Dominic returned to London religiously every other weekend. As time went on, would it become easier to cope with Ruby's fortnightly Sundays with him?

And would it become easier to talk to Dominic when they did their handovers? It was always so stilted, too polite; there was the sense of unfinished business hanging between them. After more than a year of separation, they should probably have made an attempt to talk about actually divorcing.

'Ruby will have a lot to tell you about the London Aquarium.' Dominic smiled at them both. Izzy's heart clenched a little.

'You're so lucky,' she told Ruby, setting her down. 'I didn't realise you were going there. What was your favourite fish?'

Ruby talked with extreme enthusiasm and detail about aquatic creatures while Izzy and Dominic watched her and exchanged a few awkward smiles. Eventually, she finished.

Before she could start talking again, Izzy dived in with, 'Say goodbye to Daddy, Rubes. We need to get you to bed. Back to school tomorrow.'

'Can Daddy come in?'

Izzy waited for Dominic to reply. Normally, when Ruby asked, he said he had to go.

He said nothing.

'Um,' Izzy said. She wanted to stay on good terms with Dominic. Her parents had, to the best of her knowledge, only been in the same place at the same time once since they'd split up, and that had not gone well. They had also always ignored Izzy in favour of their new families. Izzy knew that she and Dominic would always put Ruby first and hoped that they'd always be polite to each other, and she didn't want to be rude to him now. But she also did not want him to come in.

Apart from anything else, she had some things out in the hall to go to the charity shop, and she was fairly sure that the baking book he'd bought for her birthday was on top of the pile. So she definitely wasn't going to invite him in, even though he was now smiling at her and showing no signs of wanting to leave.

'It's really late, munchkin,' she said. 'But definitely next time, if you get back a little earlier.'

'That sounds like a plan,' Dominic said. Izzy had always liked the way his eyes creased when he smiled. 'I'll look forward to that. Have fun at school tomorrow, Ruby.'

Ruby put an arm round Izzy's waist and reached out with the other to Dominic.

'Hug, Daddy,' she said.

Dominic hesitated for a moment and then stepped forward. Ruby pulled him in too, by his waist, so that he was standing only inches away from Izzy. This was about a billion times more awkward than smiling at each other while Ruby burbled about the beautiful queen angelfish and sand tiger sharks. They were so close that Izzy could smell Dominic's aftershave. The scent was so familiar. She focused very hard on the side of his head. He'd actually grown a few grey hairs in the last year. They blended very well into his blond hair and she hadn't noticed them before. Oh God, she was literally welling up over the sadness that she now knew so little about Ruby's father's hair colour.

'Bath time, gorgeous girl,' she said, pulling backwards out of the hug.

'Bye, Ruby. Iz.' Dominic blew a kiss to his daughter from the gate at the end of the short path from the front door to the pavement. Izzy's heart clenched some more.

*

The next morning, like every first day back after a school holiday, was hell.

Izzy and Ruby both overslept, despite the early morning June sunshine, after being up in the night when Ruby wet her bed. The bed wetting was definitely due to Ruby's day out with Dominic – a distinct correlation between his visits and night-time accidents had emerged.

Izzy started thinking about Dominic as soon as she peeled her eyes open on the third snooze of her alarm. Maybe she should have invited him in yesterday. Maybe then Ruby wouldn't have wet the bed. Maybe he should have stayed until after Ruby's bedtime. Maybe they should have moved to Milan with him. So many maybes.

Shit, she'd been lying in bed thinking for far too long. Better check her emails and get into the shower.

There was a reply from Sam.

No time to read it now; they were very late for school.

Izzy had forgotten until just before they were leaving that Ruby needed a packed lunch for a school trip, and Ruby had had a nicely timed meltdown about having lost her favourite hair scrunchie and because Izzy wouldn't let her take white-bread jam sandwiches and cake for lunch.

Izzy wasn't proud of the fact that the only reason she hadn't given in to Ruby for an easy life was that Ruby's teacher was already extremely patronisingly kind about how they all understood, of *course* they did, how *hard* it was to be a single mother. *Piss off, Mrs Blake*, Izzy had thought as she slathered hummus onto brown, seeded bread from the freezer and sliced carrots as fast as she could, while Ruby shouted, 'I hate carrots.'

They'd both won the argument in the end. The carrots had stayed in, but they'd had a four-fingered KitKat each in the car on the way to school. Mrs Blake could deal with Ruby on a sugar high at a museum, ha. And then Izzy had dashed straight from school to work.

She finally read Sam's email between her first two appointments. She still felt a bit weird about talking to him, especially today when she was thinking a lot about Dominic, and wondering whether she'd been right to separate from him; she just didn't want the feeling of going back in time. But if she was going to attempt to help his son properly, she was going to *have* to have a phone conversation with him. Or maybe not. Maybe she could just describe a couple of strategies in writing. Or even not describe them. Just send some bumph. Yep. She banged an email out.

Sam had replied by the time Izzy's next appointment had finished, which must have been the crack of dawn New York time. Did everyone in New York get up that early or was it just him?

Hi Izzy,

Very kind of you to send that document through, thanks.

Do you do private consultations and would you consider taking Barney on as a client?

Best,
Sam

Bloody hell, the man was tenacious. Although, to be fair, who wouldn't be when they were worried about their child?

Izzy took a large bite of the almond croissant she'd snaffled from the bakery round the corner on her way in. Maybe next week she'd start getting up early enough to have a healthy breakfast at home.

Right. She didn't really have a choice about speaking to Sam. She'd suggest Wednesday, her work from home day.

*

It wasn't a surprise that Sam was an extremely punctual caller. At 2 p.m. on the dot, Izzy's phone rang. She was under the tree in her garden, taking advantage of an unusually sunny first week of June, ploughing through work on her laptop, only closing her eyes for a gentle snooze very occasionally.

'Izzy Castle.' Really? Was she really behaving like a teenager pretending that she wasn't expecting Sam to ring? Like another US number would have called her at exactly the same time. Why hadn't she just said *Hi*?

'Hey, Izzy, it's Sam. Thanks for taking the time to speak to me.' His voice, with its lovely New York accent, was still shiver-down-spine-inducing gravelly, and he still sounded as though he was smiling as he spoke. He could make a fortune doing sex-god voiceovers. Obviously, now that Izzy was no longer twenty-two years old and completely un-cynical about the world, gorgeous voices no longer had the same effect on her, but still. Nice to listen to.

Actually, thinking about it, he could do pretty well in sex-god film roles too, not just the voice.

'Hello,' she said. *Ooh, snappy dialogue.*

'How've you been?'

'Good, thank you. I'm working while sitting in my garden and it's beautiful weather and there are lots of birds cheeping, the flowers are in full bloom, there are lots of bees buzzing around and it's the perfect temperature. Basically your perfect work day.' Total verbal diarrhoea. What was wrong with her? This was worse than being over-formal. She needed a happy medium. 'How are you?'

'Also good, but not also sitting in a garden. I'm high up in my office in a skyscraper, far, far from anything that could be described as fresh air or cheeping birds. The closest things to nature I can see are tiny people running around ant-like on the sidewalks. It's great that you get to work from home one day a week. And great that you managed to carry on working after you had your baby. I remember we talked about that.'

Flattering that he remembered the details of their conversation. Izzy remembered it very well, but being heavily pregnant and going to a café with the biggest crush you'd ever had was presumably a lot more memorable than gathering up someone's spilled groceries and going for coffee with them. For all she knew, Sam regularly got taken for coffees after performing spilled-food, knight-in-shining-armour duties.

'Yep, I'm very lucky. I'm very busy, obviously, like a lot of people, but my daughter's seven now, and it's getting easier, to the extent that, not joking, I occasionally even manage to get enough sleep. And I do love my job.'

'I'm impressed. And pleased for you. And a little jealous on the sleep front.'

'I can imagine. You must be even busier than I am.' Did Izzy sound stalker-like knowing that he had a busy life? Hopefully not. It would have been strange if she *hadn't* googled him.

'Yep, busy is right. And not loving my job as much as you love yours probably. Well, I say the job, I actually do like my job, I could just take or leave some of my clients.'

'But sadly the clients are kind of integral to the job?'

'Exactly.'

'Always a bugger.'

'Indeed. And I've stupidly developed a reputation for getting things done quickly, which is great for business, but not so great for work-life balance. Speaking of which, I shouldn't take up too much of your time. Thank you so much for speaking to me today.'

'No problem. So how many other therapists have you spoken to?'

'We've seen twelve. You're the thirteenth.'

'Twelve. That's a lot.' Crikey. There had to be a reason that twelve therapists had tried and failed, for a want of a better word.

'Yep. Hoping thirteen's our lucky number.' Eek. This was starting to feel like a huge responsibility.

'Let's hope so. Does Barney know we're speaking?'

'No. I thought I'd check in with you first. I wanted to find out whether you were happy to try to help him. I know that kids in the UK carry on with school until July, but here they're just starting their summer vacation. I was hoping to make strides with Barney's stuttering during that time, away from the pressures of school. If you do feel able to take him on, it will obviously have to be mainly via video call or telephone, presumably, although we might visit the UK over the summer to see my in-laws, and could meet up then if you could fit us in.' In-laws. Ridiculously, it hadn't occurred to Izzy that Sam might have re-married. Way more ridiculously, she felt mildly disappointed, like it had *anything* to do with her or her life. 'And, if you're happy to take him on, I'll very happily pay whatever your private rates are, plus any costs. Obviously. As you can tell, I'm, frankly, a little desperate. It's affecting his confidence hugely, and has had a negative effect on his friendships, and I think he's got into a vicious circle that I need to get him out of.' Sam's voice cracked slightly as he spoke. No-one would have been able to resist him sounding like that. Izzy certainly couldn't.

'I'd be very happy to work with him if I think I might be able to help. I really hope I can. Why don't you tell me some more about his stutter? Let's start with how it sounds.'

Izzy watched two greenish white butterflies, maybe cabbage whites, fluttering around each other a few feet in front of her while Sam spoke. It seemed that Barney's stammer increased under stress and that he'd suffered some bullying because of it, and that his confidence had taken a nosedive as a result.

Sam really did have a lovely voice. Good job she was taking notes, or she might have ended up not concentrating and just enjoying listening to him talk. Lucky that she was an experienced professional, and therefore in no way fantasising about a prospective client's married father.

'Okay,' she said. 'I think you've painted a pretty full picture there of Barney himself, thank you. Now could I ask some questions about your home life, if that's okay? Some of them might sound quite personal.'

'Not a problem.'

'Could you tell me first who lives at home?' Maybe Sam and his new wife had had more children.

'Barney; his twin sister, Liv; me; and our live-in housekeeper, who's middle-aged and extremely strict and dour but adores the kids.'

'She sounds perfect. I think we could all do with an adoring live-in housekeeper.' If Izzy had one, her kitchen probably wouldn't currently contain a very full ironing basket and a very empty fridge. She needed to remember to buy groceries on the way home from school with Ruby today. 'And anyone else?'

'Nope.'

'You don't have a partner?' There were reasons that people generally used strangers as therapists. This was just embarrassing.

'Not one who features in the kids' lives.'

'Okay. Great.' Did she sound too enthusiastic about his single, or near-single status? Why did he have in-laws? 'And, sorry to ask, do you ever have a partner staying over, or have you done so over the years? And, if it was before the accident, how did Barney react to that at the time and does he react worse now?'

'I doubt that you'll want to hear my entire dating history—'

He was right there. Izzy really didn't. What did you *say* when someone you'd had a mega crush on years ago talked you through the many stunning women he'd shagged? Nothing? Something witty (but what?)? Something cool? *Yeah, yeah, me too. I have a very lively sex life, no embarrassment here when my mother and her wife gave me sex manuals for my birthday, different date with a gorgeous man every week.* Actually, what was she thinking, no need to say *anything*.

'—but, in summary, I don't have partners to stay over, and only stay over myself with someone if the kids are both away. And I don't introduce them to my dates, so I don't think that's a problem. I mean,

I'm not saying Barney *likes* the idea of my dating, but he doesn't like my working either. I do have my in-laws, my late wife's parents, to stay from time to time, but I think that's stress-free for Barney. In fact, better than stress-free; he loves having them to stay.'

Ah, so that was what he'd meant about in-laws. Though nothing to do with Izzy, of course.

'Okay.' Izzy felt it was time to move on. 'And are there any arguments at home?'

'Not really. I mean, no more than the usual. Maybe fewer than usual in that I have no significant other to argue with in front of the kids. Liv's—' he paused '—quite easy. As I mentioned, Barney gets upset when I have to work late, and then he stutters a lot. I don't have a lot of opportunity to reduce my workload, but I figure that that isn't the problem, in that most kids don't stutter when they're upset.'

'Great. I have a fairly full picture now, so I think the next step would be for me to chat to Barney, if he'd like to.'

'Fantastic. I'm hugely grateful.'

Izzy could hear the relief in Sam's voice. He was clearly a very devoted father. Endearing, and more than a little attractive.

Chapter Nine

Sam

'I appreciate that we might be intruding on family time, but would you be able to chat to Barney at the weekend? Probably work better that way because of the time difference.' Sam definitely needed to be home when Barney was scheduled to make the call, to make sure that he did actually make it. Barney had met Therapist Twelve literally once, on his school premises, and hated her. He had then pretended that he was still talking to her regularly for the next three weeks until Sam discovered that he'd been paying for the woman's time but not her actual services. To be fair to Barney, it hadn't sounded as though her services were worth a lot, even if you actually took advantage of them.

'Yes, no problem.' Izzy had a very attractive voice. Almost musical. 'I'll email you if I may, once I've checked my diary.'

'Of course. Thank you. I'm very grateful. I should probably let you get back to your garden solitude now before you have to return to the fray.'

'Yep, I'm going to have to drag myself off for the school run in a minute. I'll email you later.'

'Great, thank you. Goodbye.'

'Bye.'

It had been a good conversation, although Sam wondered if he should have given Izzy more details about the accident. Maybe, except he couldn't bear to talk about it. And he wasn't going to think about it now.

He caught himself doing a jaunty whistle as he walked across his office to get his third coffee of the morning. He was pretty hopeful that thirteen was indeed going to prove to be their lucky number.

Izzy was true to her word. The email came through mid-afternoon. It was very specific. She could do the call in one of two narrow time slots on Sunday.

Clearly a woman with structured weekends. There was married life for you. Sam did feel a little guilty about the additional pressure he was putting on her, but if there was even the smallest chance she could help Barney, he had to do it.

Hey Izzy,

2 p.m. your time Sunday will be great—I'll make sure I haul Barney's teenage butt out of bed in good time for it. Apologies in advance if he's grumpy!

Best,
Sam

Obviously now he was going to have to clear the whole Therapist Thirteen situation with Barney, but at least Barney had indicated a couple times recently that he was getting pretty desperate to be able to speak 'normally' again. It was likely that he'd make the first call to Izzy, even if it didn't go well and he refused to continue with her.

Hi Sam,

Ha, I'm with Barney on not liking an early start.
   Great – I'll speak to him Sunday.

All best,
Izzy

She sent through some details about where the call should take place, like somewhere Barney felt comfortable in but not violating a safe haven, and not his bedroom for child protection reasons. Good points. Which previous therapists with whom they'd consulted by phone had not made. Sam was liking Izzy's therapy style a lot so far.

*

Sam wished the barman would turn the music down. A quiet evening would be nice. He spread his shoulders and leaned back in his chair, watching Melissa as she strutted towards him back from the restroom. She didn't move like a regular woman. Everything she did was a performance, as if this venue were her personal catwalk.

She came to a halt in front of him, posed for a moment so that he could admire her, and then arranged herself, slowly, in the chair next to his, sitting just a little closer to him than she needed to, resting a hand just a little too high up his thigh for polite company. He couldn't decide whether it was a turn-on or actually slightly annoying. Slightly over-proprietorial. Or slightly over-slutty on both their parts, given that they were out in public.

'How would you like to stay over at mine tonight?' she purred. Literally. Like a cat. A moderately terrifying cat. Maybe a panther.

Sam covered her hand with his own, having to make quite an effort not to push it down his leg towards his knee, and smiled at her. 'You know I'd love to, but you know I can't. The kids.' His housekeeper was in the apartment overnight but, apart from anything else, he needed to be home to get Barney out of bed tomorrow morning and ready for his call with Izzy. He only ever stayed away from the kids overnight for work, never for pleasure, and now, with the way the twins were at the moment, was not the time to change that. 'I have stuff to do with the kids in the morning.' He and Melissa had been, loosely, together for, what, three or four months now? He should probably feel ready to tell her more about his children. Although, really, what was the point? Their relationship was never going to be serious, and, yes, she was great company, but he hadn't yet uncovered a lot of evidence of empathy or sympathy in her. He smiled at her again. 'Sorry.'

She pouted. 'You always choose them over me.' Well, of course.

'I'm their father. They only have one parent. They deserve the best I can give them.' Which obviously included his time. Even if they had two parents, they would still deserve for both their parents to choose them over anything or anyone else.

Melissa was looking up at him from under her impressively long lashes (were they real?), giving her lower lip a delicate chew. Sam was fairly sure that it was a look she'd mirror-practised at length. To good effect. If he were a lot younger and had known fewer women, he'd probably be feeling a little guilty right now. Maybe turned on as well. As it was, he just felt somewhat impatient. She gave the long eyelashes a flutter.

'Let's dance,' he said. He wasn't having whatever conversation she wanted to have.

'And then back to mine for an hour or two?' She was purring again. Couldn't hurt, he supposed.

*

It was a good job that at no point had Sam been tempted to stay the night with Melissa, because getting Barney out of bed and alert and docile enough to call Izzy at 9 a.m. on Sunday morning had required the tenacity of a pit bull and the patience of a saint.

'So how was that?' Sam dared to ask as Barney headed past him toward the fridge after the call.

'Cool. Izzy was nice. We just chatted.' Barney was smiling.

Hey Izzy,

Thanks so much for the conversation with Barney. He said it was good—a major victory. He also said that it was great that you didn't ask him his name. Hates saying it; never gets it out in one go.

Sam
P.S. He told me that you're a big baker. Your husband's a lucky man.

He should re-read his emails before he pressed Send. Why had he mentioned her husband? Did it sound sexist? Over familiar? What an idiot. If she was going to be lucky therapist number thirteen, he wanted to make sure that she stuck around therapy-wise.

She replied within a couple of hours.

Hi,

Not a problem. He was lovely. When would be best for our next call, assuming Barney would like to continue? I could do Saturday

3 p.m. UK time, while daughter at bucket-decorating (?!?) party,
or Sunday 8.30 p.m. UK time (daughter in bed, I hope).

Izzy

P.S. For a lot of people with a stutter, their name's the hardest
word of all. And I already knew his name… Pointlessly sadistic
if I'd asked him to say it!

P.P.S. Separated from husband. Much cake eaten by self
therefore, to severe detriment of waistline.

Separated. Crap. Sam could give a masterclass in tactlessness.

Hey Izzy,

Serious apologies—foot in mouth. So sorry to hear about your
separation.

Am sure your waistline still looks great.

I want to ask if you're okay, but clearly none of my business.

Saturday 3 p.m. your time would be great.

Sam

The moment he pressed Send, he realised what he'd just written.
What? What was he thinking? He'd just said he thought her waistline
looked great. Way to improve on his tactless comment. This was making
all the blathering he'd done on the phone about his dating history seem
like relatively competent social interaction.

She replied almost immediately.

Hi.

All good, thank you. Sometimes relationships just get worn out...
I'll look forward to speaking to Barney on Saturday.

Izzy

Hey.

With you on worn-out relationships.
    Saturday fantastic.

Sam

Again, what? What did he even mean, '*with you on worn-out relationships*'? Officially losing it. He should stop emailing and get on with his day and behave like a person with normal levels of tact. And think before he pressed Send.

'More chowder?' Sam attempted an upbeat tone for the twins.

'No. I wanted to go to Granny and Gramps' for proper Sunday lunch.' Liv pushed her chair back and stomped out of the room. Yeah, their housekeeper's chowder was good but not up there with the pork dish and creamy dessert Sam's mother had promised. The company at his parents' would have been a lot more interesting, too. Sam was going to have to get back to his work soon, which was why they hadn't been able to go over to New Jersey; and Barney had been pretty monosyllabic throughout the meal.

Sam looked at the door still vibrating slightly from Liv's slam and at the top of Barney's head. Who to tackle first in the limited time he had?

Barney.

He'd let Liv cool off and speak to her this evening. This was one of the times where he missed Lana. It seemed like Liv needed a mother. Someone who'd be able to get through to her better than Sam could, anyway.

'I arranged another session with Izzy,' he said.

Barney actually looked up. 'Can I do two sessions a week?'

Wow.

'Fine by me. I'll ask Izzy.' He'd better email her immediately. This felt like a big step forward. It was an imposition, but, if it would help Barney, Sam had no choice but to ask. He suspected she would say yes. She seemed like one of those people who couldn't help being nice.

She replied to his email within minutes, and, yes, she could do it – metaphorical punching of the air on behalf of Barney – she had painting on Wednesday, but would these times work? Sam was only too happy to confirm.

Hey,

Tuesday 9.30 p.m. UK time great. Thank you.
   Painting—intriguing. Naked person? Bowl of fruit?

Sam

Hi,

I'm perfectly copying a famous painting in under three hours, apparently.

All my friends clubbed together to buy me a series of 'experiences' for my birthday. Painting sessions are the first one.

Trying to reserve judgement, and be extremely grateful for the lovely present, but hard not to remember that was truly atrocious at art at school and did not enjoy.

Izzy

Ha. Look forward to hearing how it went!
S

Chapter Ten

Izzy

Izzy turned the steering wheel with her right hand while she passed two cereal bars back to Ruby with her left. They should have got up in time for a proper breakfast. Although cereal bars were a big improvement on last Monday's KitKat car-breakfast. And she'd got Ruby to speed-eat a banana and some blueberries before they left the house. Could be a lot worse.

She was *so* tired.

Adding two Barney sessions and one painting session a week into her life wasn't going to help her sleep levels. But she couldn't say no to Barney, and Emma and Rohan had gone to a lot of trouble to book the painting. She was just going to have to make the time.

Her phone rang several times and then pinged as she turned into the road Ruby's school was on. No parking spaces anywhere near the gate, obviously. She parked right at the end of the road, and checked her messages while Ruby got out of the car unbelievably slowly. All the calls were from Dominic. Must be something urgent.

Hi Iz, Just tried to call you. Could we get together soon to discuss where we go from here? This weekend? You said Ruby had party?

Meet at the Carter at 3? My treat. I could pick up from party and take Ruby out? Dom

Not urgent, then. Odd, though. They hadn't been out anywhere together since they split up. Maybe he wanted to meet to formalise their divorce. Maybe he'd met someone else. How would Izzy feel about that? And how would Ruby feel about it?

'Is that from Daddy?' Ruby was standing on tiptoes peering at the phone's screen. Izzy's heart squeezed as she looked at her daughter's beautiful, innocent, little-girl face. It would be awful if Dominic re-married. Ruby would be so upset. Izzy would have to be very grown-up about things, even if she hated the other woman, for Ruby's sake.

'Yes, it is. Let's run. We're late.' She put her phone in her bag and took Ruby's hand.

'Is he coming again soon?'

'I think so.'

'Yay.' Ruby's beam nearly broke Izzy's heart. Their split had been so bad for Ruby.

She hassled Ruby through the school gates as fast as she could, gave her a big, squishy hug, sprinted back to the car, drove like a maniac to work, arrived four minutes late and did three one-hour appointments back to back before she had time to think and reply.

No surprise that Dominic wanted to meet at the Carter. Izzy had never been but she knew that it was a very smart hotel in town, and Dominic liked a smart venue. She was obviously going to say yes. Ruby would of course love to see Dominic at the weekend. Izzy could think of a lot of things she'd rather do than have the Divorce Conversation, anything really, even cleaning the bathroom, but obviously at some point they were going to have to talk, and it would be too emotive having the talk in the house they'd once shared. So posh coffee at the Carter it was.

It was only during her call with Barney the next evening that Izzy linked meeting Dominic on Saturday to the fact that she'd already agreed their next speech therapy session then. Sam replied immediately to her email suggesting they make it later in the day. Efficiency was a very attractive quality, in Izzy's view.

Hey Izzy,

Thank you for this evening's session. It was another success from our side and I'm very grateful that you've fitted Barney into your busy life. I'm still at work (and likely to be here for the whole evening unfortunately) but have spoken to Barney by phone, and he repeated your statistic that over 1% of the population stutter and that Ed Sheeran is part of that number. Obviously he said Ed S is lame but probably some cool people stutter too.

And yes he can do midday Saturday for the next session, thank you so much.

Sam
P.S. Enjoy tomorrow's painting!

Hi Sam,

Great thank you – I'll speak to Barney on Saturday.

Ed Sheeran is not lame. He's Perfect (song title pun intended – drawing to your attention as proud of self and not sure Ed big in the US and therefore you might not have registered my incredibly clever joke).

Not convinced about painting…

Hope you don't have to work too late tonight.

Izzy

Hey.

You don't have to Take Me Back to London to make Ed song title puns. We Beautiful People in the US know him too.

S

Izzy spent a good three minutes trying and failing to match Sam's pun compilation speed but then decided that she'd missed her moment. Best not to reply and walk away with her punning dignity intact.

*

'Dominic's found someone else. Obviously. He wants to tell you in person.' Emma looked at what the artist had done on the demonstration easel and then did a massive streak of canary yellow across the middle of her canvas. 'Christ, that's bright.'

'I think maybe if you put some water on your biggest brush and pull it across it'll dull the brightness.' Izzy mixed a bit of white into her yellow. 'Yes, that's what I thought. Another woman.'

'I put too much water on. The yellow's all dripping down into the blue now.'

'Dab it with your paper towel. Quick. Dab harder. Okay, I'm doing mine now.' Izzy's big yellow streak was also very bright. She added some water to her brush and pulled it across. Not bad. No drippage.

'You're a yellow paint natural. This is a lot harder than I was expecting.' Emma started mixing black, white and a tiny bit of red, to paint riverside railings onto her picture. 'How are you feeling about the other woman?'

'I don't know.' Izzy genuinely didn't. It was like her mind couldn't process the concept. Would she have wanted to get back together with Dominic given the option? Maybe. At the end, they'd been more like slightly irritable housemates than lovers. They hadn't done much together, both too busy, separately. When he'd said he wanted to move to Milan for work and Izzy had pointed out that Ruby was happy at school and she wouldn't be able to work in Italy, they'd barely even discussed things further. And then he'd gone and Izzy had been miserable at first. But, with Ruby and her job, she'd been very busy, and when she didn't think about Dominic she didn't get upset. So it was simple. No thinking and all was well.

And him with another woman was definitely too huge to think about. 'I'm going in with the top of the railings.' It was a lot more difficult than she'd have expected to do a very long smooth swoosh.

'A lot of people would say that you should think about dating again.' Emma did her own, really wobbly, swoosh.

'I know that. Some of those people might buy me the *Kama Sutra* for my birthday. But those people would be wrong. I don't think I'm ready. I'm not sure I'll ever be ready. It's a lot easier being by myself.' Izzy steeled herself, made sure there was definitely enough paint on her brush, but not too much, and went for the bottom of the railings. Hmm. Not brilliant, but could have been worse. 'I don't think I'd ever have the guts to move in with someone again. Now I *know*.'

'What do you mean "now I know"? What do you know? Maybe this'll look better when I've painted in all the actual railings.' Nope.

'Now I know that successful long-term relationships are all about whether you can live together practically. Love, passion, all of that, they don't mean you can actually be great housemates. I like living with Ruby, just the two of us. I really don't want another relationship break-up, ever. I don't want to fall in love with someone, move in together, discover that we can't actually live together because, for example, one of us wants to be in Milan and the other in London, or because we like different food or music, and then have to split up. And it was awful for Ruby having to come to terms with us living separately and I don't want her to experience anything like that again. So I'm going to stay single. Simple.'

'Simple as painting lots of straight railings closer and closer together for perspective.' Emma had unfortunately started her railings on a slight tilt, and the tilt was getting more pronounced as she went backwards up the canvas.

'Simpler, I think.' Izzy was awestruck by Emma's painting. This was literally the first thing Emma had done badly in the entire time they'd known each other.

'I think you might be wrong. I think that maybe the whole point is that if you really love each other, all the toothpaste-squeezing stuff shouldn't matter.' Emma put her head on one side. 'I've *totally* messed up my railings. Bugger me, I'm bad at this.'

'I loved Dominic,' Izzy pointed out. 'And the toothpaste stuff *did* matter. You aren't bad at this. We haven't finished yet. Remember, she said at the beginning that we might doubt ourselves along the way.'

'It'll take a miracle to sort my railings out. Anyway. What are you going to wear on Saturday?'

'That's a tricky one. Obviously, if he is with another woman, I would like to look as though I've made no effort to impress him, but I would also like to look good on principle as the spurned and still-single ex. And also to remind him that the mother of his daughter is someone he used to be in love with. But that in itself is difficult in that what I like and what Dominic likes can be two different things.' Dominic's tastes were a lot more conservative than Izzy's. She'd always suspected that he might only have started talking to her the first time they met because she'd been wearing a dress of Emma's. Emma had had an Audrey Hepburn kind of vibe going since they were about twenty. Izzy and Audrey Hepburn shared pale skin and a liking of the lipstick colour Audrey had worn in *Breakfast at Tiffany's* and that was pretty much it.

Emma nodded as she painted vertical grey rectangles that were supposedly going to metamorphose into recognisable constituents of Tower Bridge. 'That's true. Remember the navy dress he bought you for that party. It was like a strange kind of *Through the Looking-Glass* experience. You looked amazing, like a film star, but you'd never have chosen it yourself, so you also looked all wrong. You'd have looked a lot more like yourself in bright red velvet or something. And equally good.'

'Thank you.' Izzy smiled at Emma. She was a very good friend. She mixed some water in with her grey and started tracing triangles at the top of her two rectangles. 'And, yes, exactly. So do I wear something that I think I look good in, or do I wear something that Dominic will think I look good in, which will involve shopping for something that I'll never wear again? And would be pandering to the taste of a man I am separated from?'

'I think you have your answer right there. Don't waste any shopping time or money. Also, you look amazing, all the time, in your own choice of clothing. Maybe decide what you'd wear if you were going out for afternoon tea with some close friends this Saturday and wear that?'

'Mmm, think you're right.' Izzy concentrated hard on painting little dots on top of her triangle roofs. Then she put her brush down. 'God. I can't bear the thought of having to tell Ruby that Daddy has a new partner.'

'I'm so sorry that it's all been so hard for her. But young children are very adaptable. Better to split up when they're her age than when they're older, I think.' Emma put her brush down and gave Izzy a quick hug. Then she squinted at Izzy's painting. 'Izzy. Your roofs. Now I've seen it I can't un-see it. They look like boobs with very *Well-hello-there* nipples.'

'*Emma.*' Yep, she was right.

'What about if you just slap some more sky colour on top of the curved bits and the nipples?'

It was a shame that the after-effects of an unravelled marriage couldn't be solved as easily as boob-shaped roofs.

*

'Wow. They're amazing. You're real-life artists.' Rohan was looking genuinely impressed. They'd waltzed into Izzy's kitchen holding their – not as identical as they should have been – paintings up for him to admire, both on a high from the evening.

'It was so good. Thank you both so much for booking this. And thank you, Rohan, for babysitting Ruby. Honestly one of the best evenings I've had in a really long time. Even better than my birthday.' Izzy tried to imagine how it would have been coming home to Dominic with her painting. It would probably have been a bit flat because he wouldn't have got why she'd loved it. She was definitely going to put the painting up somewhere. Maybe in the kitchen. It wouldn't go well in the hall or sitting room where some of Dominic's investment art pieces still hung.

'Pleasure.' Emma propped her canvas up on Izzy's work surface and hugged her. 'Shame there were no men there. But you can't have everything.'

Izzy hugged her back. 'It was fab. No interest in having men there.' She pulled back and looked closely at Emma. When they'd arranged all these experiences, were Emma and Rohan, or maybe just Emma, trying to get her to meet someone as well as branch out activity-wise? Well, whatever. No-one could actually make her start dating. 'I'm really looking forward to the next one. We're previously undiscovered art geniuses. So cool.'

Cups of tea drunk, Rohan stood up. 'Drop you home on my way, Emma?'

'Great, thanks.'

Izzy hugged them both and watched them out of the door. She felt a little lonely, but that was ridiculous. It was just nostalgia for her marriage, because of all the Dominic chat. She was fine.

*

Izzy dolloped their Saturday lunch fish pie and broccoli onto plates and told Ruby to sit down at the table.

'Mummy, are you sad?'

'No, munchkin, I am *fine*.' Damn, had Ruby had seen her frowning at the thought of her impending conversation with Dominic?

'You look sad.'

A ping from Izzy's phone was a welcome distraction. It was an email from Sam confirming Barney's session later, and asking about her evening. One of those emails that made you feel fuzzy inside because someone was interested in your life. Even though she hardly knew him, really. As she pressed Send on a reply attaching a photo of the picture, she was hit by a sudden, heart-lurching memory of Sam smiling lopsidedly at something she'd said when they'd had coffee, and how warm that had made her feel.

Hey,

Ruby's right about the genius—that's seriously impressive! Can see why you enjoyed. I'll be interested to hear about the next one.

S

'Mummy, now you're smiling at the fish pie,' Ruby said.

*

Izzy hated revolving doors. They brought back memories of a GCSE museum visit when her skirt had got caught in some and exposed her over-large knickers to at least half her class. The only saving grace had been that she'd successfully done a full-leg fake tan for the first time the weekend before. The Carter's revolving doors were particularly speedy ones, so it took her some time to summon the courage to take the plunge.

Safely inside and her heart rate returning to normal, she looked around and saw Dominic a few feet in front of her, dressed in a suit and tie. He was such a familiar sight. Her throat felt a bit lumpy when she thought about the end of their marriage.

'You look nice.' He looked as though he meant it, even though Izzy was wearing a sundress with yellow sunflowers on deep purple fabric, accessorised with a large gold tote and gold flip-flops and big yellow jewellery, all brighter than his choice would be. The other women here were mainly middle-aged-to-elderly women, who'd ignored the heat today and were dressed in sombre-coloured, Chanel-style suits, accessorised by pearls, neat handbags and neater court shoes, and elderly, retired-military type men.

'Thank you. You too. And hello.' She held her hand out to him just as he went in for a kiss on the cheek. He took her hand and carried on with the cheek kiss, as though they were barely more than acquaintances. Really quite awkward considering that they used to have sex a lot, at the beginning of their relationship anyway, and had a child together.

'I booked afternoon tea for us.' Dominic nodded to one of the livery-clad waiters and said, 'The Green Room.'

'This way, sir.'

'Thank you.' Dominic put his hand in the small of Izzy's back and started to usher her towards the Green Room. It was strange, having him behave in a husbandly way. They hadn't been out together anywhere like this for such a long time. It was kind of nice, in a weird way.

A couple of women seated at tables they passed on their way across the room smiled at Dominic as he walked behind Izzy. Women did like the wholesome handsomeness he had going. Handsome. Sam popped into Izzy's head. Although he was more rugged than wholesome.

'Everything alright?' Dominic asked after the waiter had seated them.

'Yes, lovely, thank you.' Izzy was going to be the perfect ex-wife this afternoon, however much what he was about to say might hurt. She looked round the room. Very classically tasteful, very high-end, very full of more well-dressed and well-jacketed people. 'It's very nice here.'

'Yes, I think so. I've been several times and it's always a good experience.'

'Have you?' Now Izzy was staring at Dominic. Had he been back in London several times without telling her or seeing his own daughter? Or did he mean that he used to meet people here before they split up and he moved to Milan? If that was the case, there was a lot they'd ended up not talking about. Izzy tried to remember if she'd told Dominic about her own favourite cafés. Or when the last time they'd been for coffee together had been.

'Yes. My mother likes it here, very much.' Dominic caught the eye of one of the waiters, who started walking towards them. Izzy nodded. That made sense. Dominic was a devoted only child. And his mother was nearly always Chanel-suited and pearl-necklaced, so she'd be in her element here. 'And clients.'

'So how long have you been coming here?'

'Years. I don't know why I never brought you here.' Wow. Was she hurt that he hadn't told her? She wasn't sure.

Dominic put his menu down on the table without opening it. 'I think we should both have the summer tea. You'll love it.' He was well meaning, but he'd always had a tendency to think he knew what she'd like. Sometimes he was right; sometimes he was wrong.

'Just something small for me and maybe a cappuccino. I'm not hugely hungry.'

They ordered one afternoon tea to share. Their waiter reappeared remarkably quickly with a tiered stand containing delectable-looking sandwiches and patisseries and their coffee pots, and embarked on a detailed description of all the food.

By the time he'd finished, Izzy had almost bitten through her lip, she was trying so hard not to laugh.

'Every time.' Dominic shook his head at her, smiling, as the waiter left and Izzy sniggered out loud.

'I know. Sorry. It's because it's supposed to be serious.'

'Like standing in a lift.'

'Exactly.' She smiled at him. They'd had the same conversation about Izzy's compunction to laugh in certain situations *many* times, in the earlier days of their relationship, when they still went places together.

Her smile dropped. Dominic and she didn't always find the same things funny, but they knew each other very well, and she liked him, and she was pretty sure he liked her too. It was *really* sad. They had a lot of history.

'Why did you ask to meet?' she asked. They should get the chat over and done with now, rather than making things feel worse with trips down memory lane.

'I've been missing Ruby, and you, and London life, so I'm moving back from Milan in a few weeks' time.' Woah. Not what she'd been expecting to hear. Did this mean that he was going to want to share custody of Ruby now? Was that what he wanted to talk about? 'I thought that we could maybe start spending some time together again?' What?

'The three of us?'

'Yes, the three of us, but also the two of us.'

'Oh.' Again, what? So not what she'd been expecting. Did he mean that he didn't want a formal divorce at this point? Why did he want to spend time together just the two of them? Izzy had been thinking about this in a very theoretical way, but it hadn't seemed at all likely that he'd actually move back to London in the near future. What would this mean in practice?

She loved seeing her friends, but it was already tricky to squish them in round Ruby and work. And Izzy had begun to really value those two or three hours to herself in the evening when Ruby was in bed. Did she actually have *time* for Dominic in her life right now?

Maybe that had been the problem with their marriage. Maybe they should have *made* time for each other. Izzy was making time for painting and Barney, after all, because she *wanted* to. Maybe they should both have made a bigger effort.

'So what do you think?' Dominic held the sandwich plate out for Izzy. She took a crab salad one and a smashed avocado one. It would be criminal to leave them uneaten. Also, chewing was handy when you weren't sure what to say. Ruby. Izzy needed to think about Ruby and what would be good for her.

Having parents on good terms was what would be good for her. Modern, amicably separated, consciously uncoupled co-parents.

'Sounds nice.'

'Great. So maybe we could have dinner next time I'm over? And perhaps spend time together with Ruby as well?'

'Lovely.' It *would* be good, actually. This was good, now. Comfortable.

'Excellent. So what have you been up to recently?' Dominic poured coffee for her.

'Well, I've been quite busy with Ruby and work, obviously. And chores. They're never-ending.'

'Why don't you re-hire a cleaner?'

'Yes, maybe.' Izzy couldn't afford a cleaner. Dominic was very generous with money and she knew he'd happily pay but she didn't want to be financially dependent on him. 'I had a nice birthday. I went out with a few friends and then Emma stayed over. And Emma and I went to this painting event on Wednesday, which we both *loved*.'

'Painting?' Dominic didn't look up. He was busy taking another sandwich.

'Yes. There's an artist with two canvases on easels. They've already done a copy of a famous painting on one and then they replicate it on the other easel, in stages, and you copy them on your own canvas. It's kind of confusing to start off with, but *so* cool, and…' And he wasn't paying attention at all. No point talking. To be fair, Izzy had often tended to zone out when Dominic talked about multi-million-euro deals and carbon fibre golf clubs, which he did quite a lot. They did have fairly separate interests. They'd been too busy. Going back to the point that they should have made more of a conscious effort to spend time together.

'I thought you meant you'd been to a gallery. Sounds unusual.'

'It was great. I've put it on the wall in the kitchen.' Now she had his attention. His head had shot up.

'You've put the adult version of children's artwork on our kitchen wall?'

'Ruby and I *like* it,' she said, possibly with a snap. *So* rude. And it was Izzy and Ruby's kitchen wall. She and Dominic had agreed that. They'd split things informally so that Izzy had the house but got no maintenance from him, and they'd agreed that if and when they got formally divorced, that's how they'd carry on.

Dominic looked at her, properly. 'Sorry. That was rude. Maybe a bit pompous.' He smiled slightly. Possibly he'd remembered the word *pompous* from occasional arguments in the past. 'I'm glad you had fun.' Patronising, but he was clearly making an effort to be nice, so Izzy should too. She smiled back at him.

'What have you been up to?' she asked.

She made herself focus while he talked, and, actually, he did have some good anecdotes. Not laugh-out-loud funny, but listening to him was a pleasant way to spend the afternoon. They could absolutely be friends. Ideal for their own sakes as well as Ruby's.

That crab sandwich was *amazing*. Izzy took another one. They were only small. Mmm, the *flavours*.

'This is a delicious sandwich,' she said. 'I want to recreate this filling at home. Like one of those *MasterChef* challenges. It'd make an amazing salad with baby spinach.'

'You've always been a good cook.' Dominic took another couple of sandwiches. 'Try one of these mackerel and gooseberry ones. They're very good, too. What time would you like me to bring Ruby home this evening after the party? I thought I might take her to the cinema.'

'Eight-ish? Eight thirty? I'm sure one late night will be okay. She'll be very excited to see you.' And then probably have an accident later tonight like last time. Poor Ruby; it was all so confusing for her.

They finished their – much more enjoyable than expected – afternoon tea just in time for Dominic to jump in a cab to go and pick Ruby up while Izzy took the Tube home. She nearly missed her stop because her mind was full of her next Barney session and chores and how lovely the tea with Dominic had been. It had felt almost date-like, in a good way. She'd enjoyed their conversation. Although Dominic hadn't made her laugh as much as the email that had just arrived from Sam did.

Honestly, now she was smiling away to herself thinking of Sam. Ridiculous; she barely knew him. If anyone, Dominic was the one who should make her smile. They weren't divorced yet, and maybe they wouldn't ever be.

Chapter Eleven

Sam

'Cheers.' Sam nudged beer glasses with Luke and tried to relax. This was great. Him and Luke, the twins, Luke's wife, Nadia, and their three little girls, a barbecue and a beautiful, still, warm evening, sitting in the garden of Luke and Nadia's new family home upstate, enveloped in the sound of cicadas, the scent of clematis and milkweed. Perfect really.

For someone who didn't have at least another sixteen hours of work to get through before Monday morning, anyway. Sam was going to be working extremely late both tonight and tomorrow night because his mother might actually kill him with disappointment if he pulled out of their extended family lunch again tomorrow, but the Buck contract wasn't going to review itself, plus it looked as though his Mexico deal was blowing up.

'You look a little stressed. Kids okay? Barney's looking happy. Liv's walking better.' Luke indicated to a corner of the garden, where the twins were laughing at Luke's four-year-old, dressed this evening in Halloween ghost garb for no apparent reason.

'Yeah. The physio's pleased with her progress. Other than that, teenage girls are complicated. You know. But all good.' Not true. Maybe one day he'd be able to talk to Luke about the guilt and how difficult his relationship with Liv was becoming, but he couldn't get the words out yet. 'Barney has a new speech therapist. She's good.' He wasn't going to mention how he'd found Izzy, or their frequent email exchanges, which were fast becoming the best moments of his day. What would he say? I'm a thirty-nine-year-old man with a new penfriend? Yeah, no.

Also, how would he explain how he'd met Izzy in the first place? Luke had been his best man at his wedding and Sam hadn't mentioned their earlier encounter, despite it being just the kind of anecdote he would have loved. Truth was, it had shaken him so much that he couldn't tell anyone about it. *So this woman asked me out this morning and a big part of me wanted to say yes.* Yeah, again, no. And he'd never mentioned their subsequent meeting, because, really, how to explain that it had felt a big deal? He'd felt pretty conflicted after that coffee. He hadn't been able to shake the feeling that he'd met the right one, just at the wrong time. Again.

Now, several short-term relationships down the line, and with the knowledge that if you loved too much you could just get hurt, Sam knew that friendships were what you focused on if you had any sense, not romance. He had a new friend in Izzy, but he wasn't ready to talk about that friendship with Luke.

'And work?' Luke's broad face was creased in concern.

'Yeah, the usual nightmare of trying to fit in a twenty-hour day around family time, sleep, food, exercise.' Sam knew he was sounding bitter and he didn't like the worry in Luke's eyes. 'But tell me more about your new job.' Luke worked in AI and had just joined a very hip tech company. 'And let me get another look at your gorgeous new addition.' Sam took Baby Ellie from Luke. 'Did she just poop?' Excellent timing to deflect Luke's attention well away from talking about Sam's problems. Sam watched Luke take Ellie inside for a diaper change.

He was too good a friend to let the subject of Sam's misery drop, but Sam didn't have the emotional capacity to talk right now. There was no point. He couldn't change anything.

'Bedtime,' Sam said as soon as he and the twins got back to the apartment. If he didn't start his work right now he'd be up half the night. 'That was a good evening, wasn't it?' Sam had enjoyed it, although considerably less than he would have done without the constant niggle that work was calling.

'Yes. Baby Ellie's sooo cute and Nadia's really cool. She's a really nice mom,' Liv said.

Liv had been mentioning other people's mothers a lot recently. It didn't take a genius to work out that she was probably thinking more about her own mother as she grew up.

'Yeah, it was fun.' Barney had seemed noticeably more outgoing this evening. His sessions with Izzy were definitely helping. Maybe Sam would take a couple minutes to email her before he started going through the contract.

Hey,

Gotta say, you're a miracle worker. Barney's much happier. Thank you!

He and I shot a few hoops together this afternoon. He passed on what you said about stuttering being a different way of talking, not worse, not better, just different. I think that way of looking at things gave him a real boost and he now understands that the strategies are there to help him cope with speaking in stressful situations but not to change him. Thank you. He's grateful that you treat him 'a lot more like an adult than Therapists One to Twelve did'. Calls you Izzy, too (not 'Thirteen')—serious compliment.

He also told me that you said you were planning to email over a cake recipe that he'd like to try. I can only say: Recipe? Baking!? Barney!?!

Looking forward to tasting (I think?!).

Hope the meeting with your ex went well.

S

He'd look forward to her reply in the morning.

*

Sunday lunch the next day was more difficult to get through, firstly because Sam had only managed four hours' sleep and secondly because his mother cornered him in the kitchen when they went in together to get the egg tarts she'd baked for dessert.

'Honey, you seem distant.' She opened the freezer and took ice cubes out. 'Is everything alright?' She plopped cubes into water jugs.

'Everything is *great*,' Sam lied. 'Just a little tired. Those look heavy.' He took the jugs from her and escaped to the garden, and made sure to take Barney back with him to collect the food, so that his mother wouldn't pursue the conversation.

'I worry about you,' his mother mouthed at him from behind Barney's back.

'Thank you. I love you.' Sam hugged her, picked up a large tart and a big bowl of raspberries and left the room, and to avoid his mother sent Liv back in his place to help with the rest of the dessert and crockery.

Sam left shortly after the last of the egg tarts was demolished so that he could get some work done. Ignoring side-eye from Liv, and Barney refusing to meet his eye at all, he accepted the offer of a lift home for the twins from one of his brothers-in-law, so that they could continue to hang out with their cousins for the rest of the day while he worked.

The twins got back straight before dinner. Sam discovered quickly that for the third meal running he was going to have to endure a conversation he didn't want to have.

'Dad, I was thinking.' Barney, sounding awkward, twisted spaghetti round his fork and piled on more of Sam's bolognese sauce, his signature – and only – dish. 'Could we meet your girlfriend?'

Liv said, 'Woah.'

Sam nearly choked on his spaghetti and said, 'Not my girlfriend.'

'What is she then?' Liv had her head tilted to one side and a completely non-judgemental look on her face, covering, Sam was sure, a lot of internal judging. Only thirteen and she could give most attorneys Sam knew an extremely good run for their money. She was currently reminding him, which didn't feel good, of when he'd been about seventeen and he'd had a very brief but sexually outstandingly gratifying 'relationship' with a woman in her early thirties who he'd met when he was out running, and his mother had got wind of their affair – she'd done the same head tilt, non-confrontational, non-judgemental questioning. It had worked a lot better than his father's yelling had.

'A friend.' He took a big mouthful of spaghetti, buying thinking time. Rude to talk with your mouth full.

'Good friend?' Liv asked, still with the head tilting and the lack of visible judgement. All very conversational. That was actually a very good question. On balance, no, Melissa probably wasn't a good friend. Not probably, definitely. She had some great conversation, she was excellent company for an evening, they had fun in bed. Would he confide in her? No. Would he trust her? No. Would he introduce his children to her? Absolutely not.

Sam kept on chewing, so that he didn't have to speak. No danger of indigestion after this mouthful. He imagined for a moment Barney stuttering in front of Melissa. She'd probably raise a beautifully arched eyebrow, just a fraction, and smile just a fraction too un-warmly, and the stutter would seem huge. And get a lot more marked, instantaneously.

When they'd met a man with Tourette's in a bar on Friday evening, Melissa had been an intolerant asshole – no other word for it. Zero understanding or compassion.

In that moment, Sam realised that he wasn't going to see her again. Funny how it could take an innocent question from one of your children to make you nail down what had been hiding from you in plain sight. Once your kids had asked to meet a *friend* of yours and you'd realised that never in a million years would you want them to meet that friend, you realised that the friendship had kind of run its course. And had never been a great friendship in the first place.

Decision made, he swallowed the last bit of his now extremely mushy mouthful.

'Not really,' he told Liv. 'I'm probably not going to see her much any more. Eat your pasta and then you can have another slice of Barney's cake.'

'Are you going out with her this evening?' Barney's stutter was even more pronounced now. Sam shook his head. He'd seen Melissa a handful of times for a Sunday evening drink and now he thought about it he'd much rather spend the time at home, with his family. In fact, now that the kids were older and went to bed later, he should probably socialise less in the evenings. He'd meet Melissa for a weekday coffee or lunch to tell her in person that things were over between them. He wasn't going to sacrifice an evening with the kids.

'Nope,' he said. 'Rather hang out with you guys. Maybe catch a TV show together?'

'Okay, cool.' Barney's smile was a joy to see. And his easy speech was a joy to hear.

*

A week later and Sam still hadn't managed to speak to Melissa. To be fair, he'd barely had time to speak to anyone. Three o'clock in the afternoon on a glorious summer's day in the Hamptons, and he was sitting at a table in the north-facing dining room of the beach house they were renting for the week with his parents and one of his sisters and her family, battling with unreliable Wi-Fi and stupid amounts of work, while the others hung out on the beach.

The hell with it. He was going to go and join them. He'd work during the night. Maybe the Wi-Fi would be better then, with less competition for it.

Within ten minutes, he was changed and jogging toward a family game of beach volleyball, the white sand warm and soft under his toes, the sounds of seagulls and lapping waves mingling with laughter and chatter. This was what life should be about.

After some serious high-fiving between him, the twins and his father following a resounding underdog victory over his sister, her husband and their older teen sons, Sam suggested a walk to Barney. He'd promised himself before this holiday that he was going to take some time alone with each twin.

They walked parallel to the ocean through warm, shallow water, gentle incoming waves tickling their ankles. Barney's in-depth and very fluent analysis of the last few, crucial points of their volleyball match was a joy to hear.

The conversation moved on through other sports and then to school and Barney's sessions with Izzy.

'I like them,' Barney said simply. 'Izzy's nicer than all the other therapists. That's why it's working. Her strategies aren't that different. It's her.'

Sam nodded. 'Yeah, she's great.' And then his phone rang and he made the mistake of glancing at it, and Barney clammed up even though Sam didn't actually answer it. More great parenting. Good job Liv wasn't there to sneer and his mother to look concerned; they'd both been doing a lot of that this week.

*

It was another week before Sam was able to see Melissa in person. The Buck deal was turning out to be a complete nightmare and work was busy anyway with clients trying to finalise projects before they exited the city for summer vacations. So it wasn't just Melissa that Sam didn't have time to see; he also barely saw the twins, other than some snatched phone conversations with a superficially understanding Liv and a stuttering Barney.

Sam hadn't even suggested summer camps for this year. Liv needed to be completely recovered from her physical injuries and to continue to attend her physio appointments regularly, and Barney clearly wasn't in the right place for it emotionally. They had both agreed to attend some day camps in the city, and the rest of the time they were mainly hanging out in the apartment, with Mrs H, Sam's housekeeper.

And now it was Thursday evening and he was finally on his way to a bar to meet Melissa for the last time. He was emailing Izzy as he walked. He hadn't really had time for it, but he'd nonetheless exchanged a few emails with her that week.

He'd mentioned to her that he'd be going to London next month for work and taking the kids, so maybe she and Barney could meet then. Sam wouldn't mind meeting Izzy in person again himself. Izzy, Ruby and Emma had a weekend break in New York in August already arranged, so they could meet up then too. Which, if he was honest, he was really looking forward to. He was loving Izzy being in their lives, and not just because she was a great therapist for Barney; she was enriching Sam's life too.

It was amazing how well you could get to know a person without actually seeing them. Recently they'd talked on email about their ideal jobs (Izzy, jockey; Sam, professional hockey player or inventor). They traded recipes (just the bolognese one in Sam's case), and shared anecdotes about their real jobs. They'd even talked about their kids – not just from a client/therapist perspective, but as two parents doing their best. Izzy was clearly devoted to Ruby, and it was nice to be able to talk openly with someone who understood.

The emails had been a comforting thread through the otherwise shitty fabric of the past few weeks.

Sam laughed out loud at an anecdote in Izzy's last email and noticed only just in time a taxi bearing down on him as he crossed the road. He typed out a quick reply before going inside.

'You're late.' Melissa was standing unsmilingly at the bar holding a glass of red wine. 'Ten minutes late but also two weeks late.'

'Sorry. I've been busy.' Maybe, if he was lucky, *she'd* dump *him*, right now.

He bought himself a beer and they found a table in the corner.

'Sorry I snapped. I missed you.' Melissa moved her stool closer to Sam's. Damn.

He should just get on with it.

'Melissa, I'm so sorry. As you alluded to, I'm incredibly busy in my life right now, I don't think I have time for a relationship. Work's insane. The kids. It isn't fair to you. You deserve better.' Really? Why hadn't he planned this better? Any minute he'd literally be saying, *It isn't you, it's me.*

'Your kids are teenagers. They must want their own lives.'

'I'm sorry. They need me. More, actually, as they get older.'

Melissa's eyes narrowed. 'Is there someone else?'

'No. There really isn't.' Sam's phone buzzed and he wondered if it was Izzy replying to his pun. It had been a good one, if he said it himself. He really wanted to read her reaction.

'You know what? Screw you. You keep me waiting to tell me this?' Melissa pushed her stool back so violently that it fell over, and stalked over to the bar. She spoke to the barman and then went into the restroom.

Sam was trying very hard not to smile too much at Izzy's reply to him when the barman that Melissa had spoken to came over with an open bottle and two glasses.

'Your fiancée asked for a bottle of our finest champagne, sir.' The barman indicated the fancy bottle. 'Armand de Brignac Brut Gold, Ace of Spades.' Holy crap. Sam didn't need to google to know that this was going to have been a very expensive break-up. Melissa waved at him on her way out of the bar.

Sam should probably at the very least drink one glass but actually he just wanted to get home to the twins. 'We aren't going to drink this after all,' he told the jaw-dropped barman, getting out his credit card. 'Why don't you and your co-workers share it?'

His first thought was to tell Izzy about this, except he'd never mentioned Melissa to her in the first place.

After a long night working, a short night at home in bed, and a very long morning in the office, Sam got an exceedingly foully worded message from Melissa, so over the top that it almost made him laugh, and an email from Izzy which made him smile.

Hi,

Made your bolognese yesterday evening. The chocolate's genius. Ruby said YUM and she was right.

Izzy

Two very different women.

Chapter Twelve

Izzy

Izzy blinked her eyes open with difficulty.

Ruby was silhouetted in the bedroom doorway.

'Mmm?' Izzy said. She had no strength for actual words.

'I've had an accident.' Bloody hell. Izzy fumbled for her phone.

Three thirty-seven. She was going to have to drag her heavy limbs out of bed and sort Ruby out. Torture.

'Give me minute,' she mumbled.

'Mummy, I'm wet.'

'Yep. Sorry. Love you. Coming. Don't move.'

Izzy counted to ten. Four times. And then, in one superwoman move, swung her legs out of bed. Okay. She could do this.

'I weed on the duvet and on the pillow too.' Ruby sounded very tearful.

'It's okay. Let's give you a very quick shower and get some clean pyjamas and then you can get into bed with me.' No way was Izzy doing a full bed change now.

Izzy should have done the full bed change. Four forty-nine. She was wide, wide awake with Ruby pressed right up against her. Cuddles were *so* lovely. But briefly. Not all night. There had to be a good four foot of empty bed on Ruby's other side. Izzy gently prised Ruby's arms away from her neck, got out, tiptoed round the end of the bed, and got back in onto the lovely cool mattress. So nice. She was finally going to go to sleep. So good. *So* nice.

'Mummy, where are you?' Ruby's flailing arm hit Izzy in the face and she rolled over and pressed her hot little body against Izzy's. Bloody *hell.*

'Love you, gorgeous girl.' *Bloody* hell. Izzy was going to die of tiredness tomorrow.

*

Rohan and Emma were already at their agreed picnic spot under a tree on Primrose Hill, and were laying a blanket out.

'Sorry I'm late,' panted Izzy. She plonked herself down on the rug next to them. 'Nodded off on the sofa after Dominic picked Ruby up. Really bad night's sleep. They're going out for lunch but Dominic suggested joining us afterwards. I hope that's alright. Sorry to spring it on you.'

'Of course it's alright.' Emma kicked her ballet pumps off and sat down on one side of the rug with a poker straight back. 'Always a delight to see Ruby.'

'And Dominic.' One of the lovely things about Rohan was his unfailing politeness. 'When's he moving back?'

'In a few weeks. Great for Ruby obviously but he wants to spend more time with her. I miss her when she's with him.'

'Annoying that he can bugger off to Italy for a year and then come back and see Ruby on his terms.' Emma was sitting even straighter. 'How much custody will he want?'

'Well, to give him his due—' which Izzy was going to have to do, because moving to Milan for a fantastic work opportunity wasn't a crime, and he'd made a lot of effort to visit Ruby regularly '—he isn't being that demanding. I mean, it could be worse. A lot worse. He's suggesting one full day every weekend and four weeks a year of the holidays. And today we're going to spend half the day together, so it isn't even a whole day. I know I'm lucky. But it's still quite stressful.' She opened her picnic bag. 'Drink? I have Prosecco and cassis, plus beer. Plus water in Ruby's particularly tasteful unicorn bottles.'

'Beer, thanks,' Rohan said. 'Dominic will be entitled to up to fifty per cent custody, so looking at it from a legal entitlement perspective, you're lucky that he isn't asking for more.'

'Whatever.' Emma added cassis to a mini bottle of Prosecco. 'Basically, you get to combine full-time working with all the school runs and homework and so on and then at the weekends he gets to have one lovely parenting day while you get to fit in all the homework and crap on the other day? And as she gets older there'll be a lot of crap homework.'

'Yes.'

'Although all the homework and other crap is real life, isn't it?' said Rohan. 'And if you think about your own childhood, that's what makes you close to your primary carer, isn't it? Think about your grandmother versus your parents, Iz.'

'Good point.' Izzy nodded. She hadn't seen much of either of them. They'd both been too busy with their new families. Her father had provided occasional, very glamorous, outings, of the yacht, helicopter, Michelin-starred restaurant genre; and her mother had provided occasional sophisticated outings, of the niche fourteenth-century Korean archaeological artefact museum exhibition genre, and sex accoutrements on important dates. Her grandmother had provided constant love and care, shopping and cinema trips, and been there at doctors' appointments, parents' evenings and school sports fixtures, just *been* there. 'Yep, you're right. Granny was always my number one. Thank you, Rohan. Although this shouldn't be a competition.'

'It won't be. You're too nice for that.'

'Thank you.' Izzy smiled at him.

'He's right. You're lovely and you're doing an amazing job at keeping things normal for Ruby.' Emma slurped her Prosecco. 'So you had afternoon tea with Dominic and now you're spending this afternoon together.'

'With Ruby, and you.' It was clear where Emma's mind was going. 'Not just the two of us. Although Dominic did suggest dinner, just us.' Full disclosure. 'Which I thought would be nice. I actually really enjoyed our afternoon tea.'

Emma pursed her lips and then opened them. Rohan gave her a massive nudge. She closed her mouth.

'Dominic's a nice guy,' Rohan said.

Emma bottom-shuffled forwards out of his reach and said, 'I have to say, Izzy, because I love you and I love Ruby, that if you're tempted to get back together with Dominic, it would only be a good thing for Ruby if you could do it happily. Don't you think?'

'Mmm, probably.' Izzy couldn't be bothered to deny that it was crossing her mind ever more frequently that maybe they *should* think about getting back together, if Dominic was keen. Ruby clearly missed him and Izzy did like him. 'But what is being together happily? It's just all about compromise, isn't it?'

'Er, no, it's about being in love and being best friends and fancying each other plus loving each other's company and all of that?' Emma said, with a *duh* shoulder raise.

'Yes, because *you're* the expert.' Rohan almost never said snippy things. Izzy turned to stare at him.

'Because I haven't yet found the perfect man.' Emma tossed her dark hair magnificently, like a Herbal Essences advert. 'I'll know when I do.'

'Course you will,' Rohan almost sneered.

Extraordinary. What was wrong with Rohan?

'So,' said Izzy. 'Salad?'

'So back to Dominic,' Emma said.

'I think for Ruby's sake that I should try to spend some time with him if he wants to, so that we can at the very least be friends.'

'Sounds like a plan,' Rohan said. 'You have to put Ruby first.'

'You don't have to spend time together to put Ruby first.' Emma put a cherry tomato into her mouth. 'The sad fact is that you are separated. So you would expect to make your own lives and, yes, co-parent, but mainly separately. It would be normal, and nice, for you both to be there at birthdays and school events and so on, but it isn't normal for separated people to spend weekends together, is it?'

'That is true.' Izzy took some asparagus and ham. 'But for Ruby's sake, even though we're separated, it would be nice for us all to be able to spend time together more often than birthdays. I don't want to end up like my parents.'

'Yep, fair enough, I can see that.' Emma nodded. 'Remember your wedding.'

'Yes.' On Izzy and Dominic's wedding day, Dominic's happily married parents had been the perfect parents-of-the-groom all day, while Izzy's parents had managed one family photo together before Izzy's mother told her father that he should be ashamed of himself for knocking up someone younger than his own daughter, and he'd yelled 'Stupid bloody woman,' at her, and her mother's wife had chucked a glass of champagne at his crotch and then doubled up laughing. The groom and a lot of the other guests had not laughed. 'I still wonder why she went for his crotch and not his head or chest.'

'I know.' Emma gave a snort of laughter. 'But there's a happy medium between going down the, frankly, weird, "We're still best friends" route, and your parents' route. Surely you can be civil and always be there for birthdays and sports days and things without having to meet Dominic at other times. Unless you want to.'

'I think maybe I *do* want to.'

'Okay. That's great, if it's actually right for you,' Emma said. 'It won't be right for Ruby anyway if it isn't right for you. Not to repeat myself or nag or anything.'

'Thank you for caring.' Izzy smiled at Emma.

'How's it going with Barney and the speech therapy?' Emma asked.

'Yep, great. He's lovely and the coping strategies are already making a difference, I think.'

'You haven't said much about Sam.' Emma took a quiche, plates and a knife out of the picnic basket and did a really bad job of trying to look as though she was interested in the food below her while in fact staring gimlet-eyed at Izzy through her hair, obviously keen to get every detail there could possibly be about Sam. This was a ludicrous amount of interrogation for one picnic. Izzy really hoped that Dominic and Ruby would arrive soon, to stop the inquisition.

'Nothing to say, really. Do you like my new plates?' Izzy handed one each to the others. 'They're very seventies throwback aren't they. I *think* that I really like them. Or maybe they're just spectacularly tasteless.'

'I like them,' Emma said. 'So have you spoken to Sam much? Is he married again?' Bloody hell. Dog with a bone.

This was uncomfortable. Emma's questions were mirroring Izzy's own thoughts. Sam popped into her head far too much.

'I don't think he's married again.' Why had she not just said that he wasn't married? She knew he wasn't. Why didn't she want to mention their email chats? 'I've only really spoken to him to arrange Barney's sessions.' And there she went, not telling the whole truth again. But why? He was just a friend and nothing would ever happen between them. They lived on opposite sides of the Atlantic. She was Barney's speech therapist. It would be rubbish for Ruby. And Sam probably wouldn't be interested in her in that way anyway. If she was going to start a relationship with anyone, it should be with Dominic.

'What, no chat at all?' Emma reached for another slice of quiche. She had the appetite of a horse.

'Not really.' Izzy resisted the siren call of the quiche and took some more salad. She really wanted some of the lemon drizzle cake she'd brought but the scales hadn't been kind to her this morning, possibly due to the crap breakfasts, mainly chocolate bars, she'd had all week. She really needed to start getting up early enough to eat proper food in the mornings.

She didn't want to talk about Sam, even to her two best friends. It felt like he was becoming another close friend, not just a client, except their friendship hung by a delicate thread.

She loved their email exchanges. She knew almost more about Sam's daily life than she did about Emma's at the moment. And she looked forward to writing to him more than she probably should.

But, even though it felt like a long time, probably because they'd been emailing back and forth pretty much every day, in reality it had been less than two months. Izzy didn't want to make a thing of it, and she *certainly* didn't want Emma to make a thing of it when probably she and Sam would stop talking when Barney no longer needed speech therapy. Which, as a caring professional, Izzy had to hope would happen soon.

'I might get to meet Barney soon,' Izzy said. She didn't like being secretive. 'Sam mentioned that he was coming over with the twins, and Barney would like to do a session in person, so if I'm around we're going to meet.'

'How do you feel about that?' Emma was so excited that she was sitting even more bolt upright than before. She was also spraying balsamic onion and cheddar quiche crumbs all over her neatly folded legs, very un-Emma-like.

'I think it would be a good thing. It's a little bit weird doing long distance speech therapy. Although it seems to be working.'

'I'm surprised he can understand your Devon burr over the phone,' Rohan said.

'Skype. And piss off, posh git.' Izzy smiled at him.

'Can we get back to the point?' said Emma. 'Are you looking forward to seeing Sam again?'

Izzy shrugged. Properly shrugged. Total nonchalance. She was an *amazing* actress.

'Yeah, I think it'll be nice.' Excellent answer. A lot more believable than pretending she wasn't that fussed. 'How was your date last night, Emma?'

'Fine.' Emma waved a celery stick dismissively. Izzy really wished she liked celery more than just the idea of losing more calories than she ate.

'End up in bed with him?' Rohan had an eyebrow raised.

What? Unbelievable.

'Sorry, what?' Emma looked seriously unimpressed. Unsurprisingly.

Rohan shrugged, both eyebrows up now. 'You usually do.'

'Right.' Emma physically turned her back on Rohan and said, 'So when are Sam and his kids coming? We need to shop for something for you to wear.'

'You're so persistent,' Rohan said. 'Maybe Izzy doesn't want to tell you every single thing.' What was wrong with Rohan today?

'Thank you for looking out for me but I'm fine to talk about it, honestly,' Izzy said, trying to defuse the tension. 'They're coming in three or four weeks' time, but I don't need anything new to wear for meeting them. It isn't a big deal.' *Big* lie.

'Hey, look.' She stood up and waved. Dominic was walking up the hill towards them with a giggling and waving Ruby on his shoulders. *This* was Izzy's life, not a man who she barely knew who lived in New York. She should be focusing on Dominic and Ruby, not buying clothes to wear to meet Sam, for goodness' sake.

'Hello, gorgeous daughter.' Izzy swung Ruby off Dominic's shoulders for a big hug and smiled at him over Ruby's head. 'What've you been doing?'

Ruby had a lot to say about what she and Daddy had been doing. She was glowing. Spending time with Dominic was obviously good for her and Izzy should be happy that he was going to be a regular feature again in Ruby's life from now on. And she really should consider spending a lot more time with him herself so that they could be a family again.

*

After a lovely afternoon, Izzy couldn't help sneaking a look at her emails on the way home on the Tube with Ruby. Another email from Sam, which made her smile.

He'd tried one of her pasta recipes and by all accounts it had been a success. She replied while Ruby read out the name of every stop on the Piccadilly line from Cockfosters at the northern end to Heathrow at the western end.

Hi,

Impressed by the lemon zesting!

    Had picnic with Emma and Rohan. Nice picnic other than some bickering between E and R (!).

    But lovely weather and a nice day.

I x

As she and Ruby made their way out of the station, it occurred to Izzy that, in only a matter of weeks – or thirteen and a half years, of course – things had changed between her and Sam. She'd discussed Emma and Rohan, her two best friends, with him. Not in detail, but she'd done it. Her relationship with him had definitely moved firmly from professional into friendship territory. Although she hadn't mentioned seeing Dominic to him.

Izzy got into bed early that evening and, propped against her pillows, finished writing a report to a client on practising bump and smooth speech with her three-year-old, before checking her mother's Instagram account ('DoctorDebz: Wife, mother and grandmother. Cardiologist. Training for the North Devon marathon. Proud owner of two rescue donkeys. Baking with herbs and rose water.').

Busy donkey-owning and baking surgeons in training for marathons did not have time to talk to their daughter in person. Izzy had left at least four unanswered messages for her mother in the past fortnight. She should probably give up.

There were several recent posts of her mother and Veronique with their two sons and their other granddaughter, Ella, so they weren't too busy to speak to *all* their family.

She should try to get over her obsession with her mother's Instagram. Every single time she looked, she ended up with boiling blood. At this rate, she was going to be too wide awake from annoyance to be able to get to sleep, despite her tiredness. She should probably read for a while, to try to get her mind off it.

And then an email from Sam arrived. Was it too soon to rant to him about her mother? Either way, her heart lifted, as it always did these days when her inbox pinged.

Good job Emma didn't know.

Chapter Thirteen

Sam

Sam knew that Jim Buck would be able to see him checking his watch over the video conferencing, but he didn't care. This meeting shouldn't even have been in his diary, because he'd had several hours blocked out for the twins. The man was in full flow yet again. Sam was going to be very late at this rate. He needed just to go.

'Sorry.' Sam didn't even wait for the end of Jim's sentence to interrupt him. 'I have an urgent appointment. Let's pick this up later.' He exited the call, grabbed his jacket and ran. If he wasn't on time, Barney was likely to freeze on stage, and Liv was likely to freeze Sam out even further.

He made it about seven or eight minutes late to the function room in the New York Historical Society where the kids' vacation camp drama presentation was taking place, heart pounding and uncomfortably sweaty from his sprint from the office. Running through the park had definitely been the fastest way to get here, but it had not been comfortable in a suit and ninety-degree heat.

Sam could see from the programme that there'd been a group intro, but other than that he hadn't missed anything of note. He struggled to focus on any of the parts of the show that Liv and Barney weren't in, because he could feel his phone vibrating with constant emails, and it was obvious that work was going to be hell later on, so he wasn't completely aware of what was happening plot-wise.

He did know that, when Liv came on, she was poised and very beautiful, moving around effortlessly on stage with no trace of a limp. He was transfixed. His amazing daughter.

And then it was time for Barney to speak. Sam was on the brink of welling up before he'd even started. Barney's face was so anxious and Sam was so desperate for things to go well. He smiled at him as hard as he could. Could you psychically transfer confidence? And memory of words? Sam knew them by rote from Barney practising so hard over the weekend.

Barney stuttered on the first word. He attempted it a few times and then stopped and turned away from the audience. Please, no. He had to carry on. It was bad enough when he felt he had to abandon one-on-one conversations, but there had to be at least eighty people here. Giving up on this would be such a colossal setback. Sam sent him as many 'You can do it' vibes as he could. No. They weren't working. Barney had almost entirely turned his back to the audience now. If a heart could physically break, Sam's was doing it now.

Barney started to walk towards the stage wings. And then Sam saw Liv dart out and say something to Barney. He stood still and she carried on gesturing at him.

And then Barney turned back to face the audience, started speaking, very slowly, with the words of the first sentence rearranged, and carried on, his fluency increasing, looking just above Sam's face the whole time. Fortunate that he wouldn't be able to see that Sam's eyes were moist. He stuttered badly in a few places and gave up on a few sentences and so it didn't all make sense, but he carried on and he got to the end.

Afterwards, Sam was pretty sure that he'd never clapped so hard in his life.

He should email Izzy later. She'd be nearly as proud as he was.

'That was amazing,' he told the twins backstage, hugging them. Amazing was an extremely inadequate word.

'I missed some of it out,' Barney said.

'Hey. We all do that. A word-for-word speech is a boring speech. You were fantastic,' Sam told him. 'I was so proud. And I could see you using some of your strategies.'

'Yeah. I have to tell Izzy I changed the word order and took it slowly,' Barney said. 'And I did the "big fake smile in the restroom" thing beforehand and focused on your eyebrows.'

'You were great. As were you, Liv. Both in your own part and in being there for Barney.' As Sam reached to hug them both again, his phone buzzed and he removed his arm from Liv's shoulders to take it out of his jacket pocket. Liv stepped backwards away from him.

'We have to be there for each other because you aren't,' she said. Woah. Punch to the gut. Sam knew she was right, though he knew she'd said it to hurt him. And damn, it did hurt.

Barney's euphoric smile faded.

'Y-y-y-ou were l-late. You m-m-issed us at the beginning.'

'I'm so sorry. I did my best.' Sam's arms were suddenly empty of Barney, too.

'Bye, Dad. You probably need to catch up on the work that you've missed. Guess we'll be eating with Mrs H this evening?' Liv's smile and tone were so cold Sam almost shivered. Her evident hostility was almost more horrifying than Barney's misery.

'Actually, I'm taking you both out for dinner to celebrate how well this went.' Sam put his phone back in his pocket without looking at it, which cost him a greater effort than it should have done. Neither

Liv nor Barney looked as though they *wanted* him to take them out at this point, but tough. And he'd work through the night.

*

Sam took another few sips of his espresso. He was in danger of yawning while Robert Wade, his firm's senior partner, droned. In Sam's defence, six forty-five was an unusually early start for a breakfast meeting.

'So to summarise, Sam, the other managing partners and I are unanimous in thinking that you're the natural choice to take over from Rutger on his retirement, but there have been questions about your commitment level.' Ironic from a man who'd married four of his PAs, and was just about to move on to the fifth. Of course, Robert *was* fully committed to the firm, but he didn't have a good home life to destroy. Reputedly none of his six children spoke to him unless they wanted money. Would this be what Sam's life was like when he was Robert's age? Minus the serial PA-marriage thing. 'For example, today's meeting was postponed from Monday afternoon after you left the office very abruptly and didn't return.'

Was he joking? To climb the greasy pole to partner, Sam had missed so much of his children's lives, while his mother and sisters and Mrs H babysat in the evenings and on weekends. And now he *was* partner, apparently it wasn't enough. They were considering him for the role of head of their Mergers and Acquisition group. Even more money and kudos, sure. But it meant even more commitment. Even less family time. Also even less time for his pro bono work and lecturing, both so important. And if he didn't go for it, it might ruin his career and then they might not be able to afford their lifestyle. Sure, you didn't need to be rich to be happy; after all, Sam's childhood had been idyllic and his parents weren't rich.

But after the twins had lost their mother, he'd wanted to give them the best that money could buy. Education, lifestyle and the best healthcare insurance. They needed his time but they also needed stability and now wasn't the time for a dramatic lifestyle change. Catch-22.

'Sam?'

'I'd be honoured to be considered and I'm fully committed to the firm. Monday afternoon was unavoidable but it won't happen again.' Nothing else he could say.

The meeting finally at an end, Sam, still reeling, found that his work email inbox was filled, obviously, with a tsunami of annoying messages. He didn't have time to check his personal inbox, but he did anyway. Izzy had emailed. However pissed at life he was, his mood always lifted at the sight of her name.

It was Wednesday. Her work from home day. She was probably in her garden. He checked London on his weather app. Nope. Raining and not warm. Very different from the extreme heat in New York this week. She'd have to be inside today. She was suggesting moving Barney's speech therapy sessions to once a week now that he was doing so well.

He really hoped that, without Barney's sessions, their emailing wouldn't eventually fizzle out. He didn't think it would, actually. They were real email buddies now. In fact, a couple of emails later, Izzy had achieved the near impossible: Sam was smiling.

He didn't smile much again for the rest of the day.

Hey Izzy,

Must be the middle of the night in London now. In fact, nearly morning. I'm up way too late (workload).

Long day. Not a great one. Big and unpalatable meeting first thing. Then, during a working lunch, one of my clients actually made a waitress cry. Swung his arms to demonstrate an amazing golf shot, knocked over a tray of drinks she was carrying, yelled at her for standing too close to him. Client's a big spender in that (very high end) restaurant so the girl nearly lost her job until a couple of us stepped in. Client then called me a pussy and I called him a dick. He told me I was lucky he needed me so wasn't going to fire me. I nearly fired myself but then realized I need him too. Not a great realization.

Liv super pissed at me this evening. I couldn't work out why, but I did learn that she has an impressive line in swearing.

Recipe looks good.

How was painting?

S

That was a little indiscreet but it was Sam's personal email, and he felt a lot better for having told Izzy. This was probably why people liked keeping a diary. It was very therapeutic writing your thoughts down. Except this was better than a diary would be. This was a diary that replied and always wrote exactly the right thing. He looked forward to receiving her emails and he was really looking forward to seeing her next month.

He should go to sleep.

It always kicked the day off nicely having an email from Izzy waiting for him as soon as he took his phone off airplane mode.

Morning.

In mad rush (overslept) – just to say I hope today's better!

Pretty sure restaurant (and other) karma will hit the client eventually. Or maybe sooner rather than later. As you know (!) I used to work in a café. I'm not saying that anyone would do this on purpose (not much anyway) but if there's a choice to be made between whose plate the staff sneeze over I think we all know who's getting the germs.

Hope you're having a better morning!!
xx

Mid-morning, Sam got an email from the hospital who'd been treating Liv for her injuries after the accident.

They'd been waiting to get a date for what was expected to be a definitive scan. Sam could feel a stress headache starting as he read. So much crashing through his mind. Images of the accident, the immediate stress at the time, the short-term worry that Liv might require amputation, the nights in hospital sitting at her bedside bargaining with every god he'd ever heard of that he'd do anything if they'd let his daughter keep her leg and walk again, the longer-term worry and then hope, now the short-term question marks over whether she'd get back to sport at the level she was at before, whether she'd end up with early onset rheumatism. And of course the guilt, always the guilt.

Deep breathing. He needed to practise some deep breathing right now.

He needed to email Izzy. She always said the right thing. He had an urge to call her but she'd probably be busy with work and, besides, they only ever emailed. It was like it was their thing. Maybe chatting by phone would disrupt the balance of their friendship. And with Izzy he didn't want to open the can of worms that was WhatsApp, with its panic-inducing blue ticks and endless emoji requirements.

She replied within minutes.

Hi,

You have a LOT on your plate. Sounds as though Liv's been doing really well and that there's a really good chance that the scan's going to deliver good news? I know nothing about medicine BUT intuitively you'd think that if things look so positive in the way she's walking etc and pain levels (or not) then things inside will be good too? Really sure it will go well.

Xxx

Hey,

You know what, I think you're right. I think if it were anyone else's child I'd be pretty sure the scan was going to be okay. Logically, it will be. Thank you.

S x

Look at that. He'd turned into one of those people who added a kiss to emails. Izzy did the occasional one, but until now he'd always been pretty certain that he'd never, under any circumstances, do any virtual kissing of his own, except possibly to Liv, who was a keen double kisser herself, and his daughter. But here he was, kissing away with abandon. Never say never.

*

'Luke. Ash.' Sam went in for big handshakes and then man hugs. 'It's been too long.' It was months since the three of them had been together. Luke was a busy man, and Sam was even busier. Ash didn't have a family but, as another partner at Sam's firm, he didn't have a lot of spare time. 'What're you drinking?'

When they were all settled with beers at a table, Sam looked around. 'This bar's a lot more down to earth than some I've been frequenting recently.'

'You should stop dating models,' Luke said.

'Yeah.' Sam joined the others in taking long draughts of their drinks. 'So what've you been up to? How are Nadia and the girls?'

As he listened to Luke and then Ash fill him in, Sam reflected that he'd missed this.

In the twenty years since they'd all met at college, Sam and Luke had never gone more than a couple weeks without speaking, by phone if they weren't living in the same place. This time they'd only exchanged a few texts in the time since they'd last seen each other. Sam had far too much going on in his life but so did Luke, with his three young daughters and house move, and Sam shouldn't be too busy to make the effort to spend time with close friends. It felt all wrong not speaking to Luke regularly. He missed Ash too, even though they nominally worked together. In reality, their working paths rarely crossed.

Now he thought about it, though, he hadn't missed either of them as much as he would have done if he hadn't been emailing Izzy.

'So now fill us in on you,' Luke said.

Sam talked them through his family vacation, Liv's progress and the upcoming scan, Barney's progress and baking, courtesy of Therapist Thirteen. He barely touched on how busy work was; it went without saying. He also didn't mention how difficult Liv had become or how silent Barney was becoming, or his ongoing guilt about the accident or his nightmares. And he didn't mention his emails with Izzy.

Obviously it wasn't normal for your son's therapist to have become your penfriend. Also, on his way to the bar this evening, he'd discovered that Izzy's second 'new experience' with Emma was 'singles climbing' and he'd realised that he didn't particularly like the idea of Izzy doing singles activities. Uncomfortable food for thought, which he didn't really want to talk about.

Three beers and an eight-ounce steak each later, Sam checked his watch with reluctance. 'I'm going to have to go. I have work to do before bed plus I want to be up in time tomorrow for a run. Let's do this again a lot sooner.'

'Love you, man.' Luke was always emotional after not that much beer. Sam thumped his shoulder in response, while Ash laughed.

His thoughts returned to Izzy on the way home. *Should* he like her this much? No. Obviously not. She was Barney's lucky Therapist Thirteen, and Sam's buddy, and that was it. He wished her the very best of luck with her singles climbing.

Chapter Fourteen

Izzy

Izzy thumped down into the car, heart thudding after sprinting back from the school gate. Thank God they'd got to the end of July and the last Monday of the school year. They'd been *really* late because she'd forgotten until she woke up to a 'thoughtful reminder' group message from the class rep that their class were doing 'Buns and Biscuit Break-time' today. ('*And no shop-bought buns or biscuits from our class, thank you, ladies!*') Lacking the ability to re-wind the clock and start baking in good time, Izzy had taken a Tupperware cupcake holder from home, done a pitstop cupcake shop in Sainsbury's on the way to school and made the cupcakes look home-made by squishing them. Any more end of term 'fun' and she *would* kill someone.

And in pinged another WhatsApp. '*Dear all, I thought it would be a lovely idea if our children all wrote their own lyrics to their favourite song (between twelve and sixteen lines please!) and we videoed them singing (with the backing music so that the song's recognisable!) as an extra present for Mrs Blake! By Wednesday please! Thank you!*' For goodness' *sake*. Izzy hated the class rep.

Not everyone was a two-parent family with one stay-at-home parent and unlimited cash. How did single parents with more than one child manage? Like Sam. Who had Liv's appointment this morning.

Morning Sam,

Hope the appointment goes well. Thinking of you.

Xxx

His reply didn't come through until Ruby's bath time.

Hey Izzy,

Thanks for your email. It helped. I was a wreck this morning.

The appointment was fantastic. Couldn't have hoped for better. Everything looked good on the scan. No long-term damage. Six months ago, I wouldn't have dared dream of this.

For the second Monday out of three, I nearly cried like a baby. If I'm honest, I think I did let slip a tear. I'm just so happy for my daughter.

S xx

Izzy took the plug out of the bath and hauled Ruby out of the tub so that she could turn her back on her so Ruby wouldn't see her damp eyes and she could safely ignore her for a minute to send a 'So pleased for you' reply.

And then she hugged Ruby so tightly that Ruby squeaked. How did anyone cope with witnessing their children struggle so much?

*

A week later, Izzy was already missing term time. There was a lot to be said for the regularity of school hours. Today she was working as fast as she could through her lunch hour so that she'd be able to get away early and pick Ruby and a friend up from their tennis camp, which finished half an hour earlier than school.

She finished writing up some notes on an initial assessment of an anxious little girl with a developmental stammer with five minutes to go before her first afternoon appointment. She shovelled in a duck wrap while she checked her phone.

There was a message from Dominic.

Hi Iz. I was thinking about taking Ruby to a West End matinee a week on Saturday and thought it would be nice if we all went together? Show's at 2.30. Dom

And also an email from Sam.

Hey,

Good morning I hope?

You free Saturday afternoon next week?? Deal deadline's changed—we're coming to London on the red-eye next Thursday night now. Working Friday and Saturday morning. Obviously we'd love to see Ruby too (not expecting you to get babysitter).
Went for a run this morning. Fry-up at desk now.

S x

Woah. They wanted to meet at exactly the same time. Decisions. And no time to think because the receptionist was buzzing Izzy's next client through.

Her first appointment was with a lovely girl who had had a very serious stammer, and who had made huge progress and wouldn't need any further speech therapy for now. Izzy was delighted for her and her mother. She felt a warm glow like the one she'd had when Sam and Barney had told her about Barney's drama presentation. A lot of things were reminding her of Sam at the moment.

That and another appointment finished, and only five minutes late for tennis pickup, Izzy herded Ruby and her friend into the car and started the engine. The girls were giggling together in the back and thankfully had no interest in boring mummy-conversation. Finally, some time to think.

Izzy really wanted to see Sam. And Barney obviously. But she also wanted to see Dominic. Ruby would enjoy an outing with both her parents together. And Izzy was sure she'd enjoy it too. She'd been appreciating Dominic more each time she saw him recently.

She wanted to see Sam more, though. And Barney, of course.

And Dominic was moving back to London soon and Izzy would be able to see him any time. Whereas she obviously couldn't see Sam, or Barney, any time. And Ruby always had a lovely time on her own with Dominic.

Yep, she was going to see Sam. And who was she kidding? It was so not about meeting Barney in person. It was all about wanting to see Sam again. It would be interesting to meet his children, but that was all. Whereas meeting Sam again felt like an irresistible temptation. She had actual butterflies now.

What would she tell Dominic? On balance, it would probably be easiest just to tell him that she was seeing a client.

*

She heard again from Sam that evening, just before she went to bed.

Hey,

Just got a card (an actual card, in the mail) from my mother after their lunch at the apartment on Sunday. My mother adored the chicken cacciatore and (very well zested) lemon drizzle pudding. She's ecstatic that her son has reached adulthood and learnt to cook by the tender age of nearly forty. Ashamed to say that I didn't immediately tell her that I'd had a little push on the catering front. Then Liv and Barney told her that the recipes came to Barney from his speech therapist. She asked me to extend a big thank you to you for also being my (in her words) "cooking therapist."

How's your day been? Painting good?

Great that you can meet next Saturday.

S x

Izzy smiled all the way through flossing her teeth.

*

Emma already had three dresses ready for Izzy to try on when she and Ruby met her at the shops after school the following Thursday.

'Look at these.' She held them up in turn for Izzy. 'Gorgeous. Nearly as gorgeous as you. Perfect for you to wear on Saturday.' They *were* all gorgeous dresses, but Izzy really wasn't sure.

'I don't know if I want to buy a new dress.' Izzy checked Ruby was engrossed in her new unicorn book. This was all feeling as though she was preparing for a big date, and it shouldn't. This was the exact opposite of when Emma had suggested not buying anything new when she met Dominic at the Carter. Even though Dominic was *lovely* and he was *real life*, and Sam was not part of her normal life. 'I think I'm going to wear jeans.'

'Your navy denim high-waisted wide-leg ones?'

'Yep.' So much better for your averagely shaped woman than skinnies. 'And I've got this new emerald green top.' Which had cost about half her monthly post-bills salary, but she loved it.

'Sounds perfect. How're you going to do your hair? As is?'

'Yep.'

'You're going to look lovely. Very girl next door, in a good way.'

'Middle-aged woman next door.'

'We aren't middle-aged.'

'Emma, we're bloody thirty-six. We aren't spring chickens.'

'But also not old. Our life expectancy's over ninety. We're nowhere near middle age. That's why you shouldn't settle for a relationship that isn't real love. Let's go and get pizza if we aren't shopping?'

*

Izzy's heart was going like the clappers. Honestly, it was surprising that the people closest to her weren't turning to check what was going on and asking what was wrong with her.

She was standing in the middle of the café, near the escalators, on the top floor of the very nice Peter Jones department store in Chelsea's Sloane Square, scanning the moderate crowds round the tills for Sam, while trying to look totally chilled. She should probably have gone with her initial instinct, which had been to be a few minutes late. This was exactly what she would have done if this had just been a social meeting, but actually she was meeting a client, so she couldn't be late. So here she was, like a teenager having arrived far too punctually for a first date.

First date. She should get phrases like that *right* out of her mind. This was so very much not a date. She was meeting her client, and his father, her friend. It was ridiculous that she was physically jittery with anticipation.

'Hey, Izzy.' Sam's voice came from behind her. 'It's good to see you.' That voice. Izzy's heart started to thud so loudly that she was almost deafened, and she got very sudden whole-body goose bumps. It was actually him. Sam McCready was here in the flesh, right behind her.

She spun round to say hello, catching an elderly woman's tray with her elbow as she did so.

'Oh my goodness,' Izzy screamed, doing nothing at all to save the tray. It was going. Everything on it was going. The teapot, the cup and saucer, the slice of carrot cake, the fork, the napkins, they were all sliding to one side. The woman wasn't strong enough to hold the tray now that it had been knocked off balance. There was going to be a huge mess.

Izzy finally unfroze and stuck her hands out just as Sam and Liv dived in together and both caught it. Miraculously, everything stopped sliding.

Izzy couldn't speak. Literally. It was like her tongue was glued in place. In fact, all of her was stunned at the weirdness, and yet utter rightness, of being in the same place as Sam. Who was so much *more* in the flesh. In a really good, gut-punchingly sexy, way. His smile. His strong forearms holding the tray. The humour in his eyes. The thick hair that you'd happily plunge your hands straight into.

'Let me carry that to your table for you.' Sam smiled at the elderly woman and the woman actually simpered at him; there was no other word for it. Did he have this effect on every woman he met? Izzy smiled at Barney and Liv as Sam escorted the woman over to a table and had a short chat with her, which just increased the simpering. Izzy was still too overcome to be able to produce actual words.

Sam had aged very well, as indicated by his work photo. Same dark-blond hair, with a bit of grey in it now, which just made him look even better. He'd be rocking a silver fox look in a decade's time. His olive skin was even darker than she remembered, presumably because it was the summer. And his shoulders and chest and thighs were still gorgeously solid-looking. Total housewife's dream.

Not that *Izzy* was dreaming about him. Not any more.

'Sorry about that.' Sam was back now. The elderly woman was still directing a simpering smile in his direction. Izzy concentrated very hard on not doing any simpering herself. Was she smiling normally? Or did she look as though she was in pain? What was she *doing* with her face now? Once you started thinking about how you were arranging your face, it was very difficult to behave completely naturally. Now all she could think about was whether her eyes, cheeks, mouth, everything, were normally relaxed. 'So I should introduce you. This is Barney, who of course you already recognise from your Skype sessions, and this is Liv. And this is Izzy.'

'Hello.' This was better. Izzy had regained some basic powers of speech and the ability to smile less self-consciously. 'I'm so pleased finally to meet you in person, Barney. And you too, Liv. I've heard a lot about you from your father and brother.'

'Hi,' they said simultaneously.

'Liv, Barney, why don't you go over to the counter and choose yourselves some food. I'll come pay when you've decided.' Sam indicated over to the counter with his head and then turned to Izzy. 'They'll take forever to decide on the perfect café snack. Gives us a chance to say hello properly.'

'The twins are gorgeous!' This was an excellent topic of conversation, because hellos felt awkward. *Izzy* felt awkward. And they really were gorgeous. And fascinating to see together. They were both tall and slim, but Liv's colouring was a surprise. Barney was dark and curly-haired whereas Liv was blonde, straight-haired and fair-skinned.

'They really are, aren't they?' Sam beamed and Izzy felt her heart expand. It was the devoted-father-with-toddler-in-supermarket effect. 'And I love that they're chalk and cheese when it comes to looks, as well as personality. Lana was mixed race, and I'm one quarter Puerto Rican, one quarter Nigerian, one quarter Irish and one quarter Norwegian. Equals two pretty beautiful kids.' He glanced over at the twins adoringly. 'No apologies for the fact that I'm a very proud dad.' And presumably no regrets whatsoever about the fact that he'd married Lana, because he had his perfect kids. Just like she, Izzy, had no regrets about the fact that she'd married Dominic, because they had Ruby.

'The best dads are proud ones.' Bloody hell, she sounded like a Hallmark card. Sappy. Her mind wasn't working properly. She was too distracted by the fact that Sam was here, in the flesh: tall, broad-shouldered, and even more attractive than she'd remembered. And he was standing right next to her, smiling at her.

'Yeah, if only pride was all there was to parenting. Right, what can I get you to drink?'

Chapter Fifteen

Sam

Sam followed Izzy over to the counter, doing his best not to look at her butt as she walked. It was as if he'd swapped life stages with Barney. Barney was being very relaxed and grown-up, which was fantastic to see, while he, Sam, was behaving like a teenage boy with a crush. For example, he should not have had a physical reaction to the sight of Izzy that went right to his stomach and he should not be thinking about how she filled her jeans out very nicely. He was going to be forty this year and he should therefore be more than capable of focusing on things more highbrow than a person's figure, not to mention their gorgeous smile. Especially when the person in question was a friend, because you did not think about your friends in that way.

And it would be nice if he could hold a normal conversation. Why would Izzy have any interest in his heritage? He'd literally just listed all four of his grandparents' ethnicities. Within two minutes of seeing her in person for the first time for several years. Why would anyone with any ability at normal human interaction do such a thing?

'A peppermint tea would be lovely, thank you.' Izzy smiled at Sam. The smile went right to somewhere deep inside him. Such a great smile. Very genuine, which made sense because if there was one thing that he'd found out about her over the past few months, it was that she was a very genuine person. Kind. Great sense of humour. And what was wrong with him now, losing himself in thought? He should smile back at her for Chrissake. He moved his lips into a smile. There. Better.

'Great,' he said, finding words again. 'And I'll get a decaf macchiato. The kids are always nagging me to lower my caffeine intake, which is a difficult thing to do when you're permanently running a twenty-hour-a-week sleep deficit, but it's the weekend and I've finished my work so now we're officially on a mini-break. I slept well last night too.' Fantastic. Now he was talking about his sleep. Great conversational skills. He didn't have these problems when he talked to other people. Or when he was emailing Izzy. Maybe he should have stuck to writing rather than suggesting meeting in person. 'Any cake?'

'I normally would but I promised to take Ruby out for early-evening pizza later, so I'm going to pass. But you go ahead.'

'I'm good. I'm more of a savoury man. Cheese would be a much greater vice for me. Especially here in Europe where you have so many great ones to choose from.'

'What's your favourite European cheese?'

'Beaufort. I think it's from the French Alps. It's very nutty in flavour.'

'Mmm, I like that one too. It's similar to Gruyère.'

However mundane the topic, Sam loved talking to Izzy.

They found a table for four next to a window with a fantastic view over rooftops and the streets below, and sat down with the twins, Sam and Barney on one side of the rectangular table, and Izzy and Liv on the other.

'Look at that.' Izzy was pointing at a colourful rooftop garden. 'This is one of the things I love about London. There's always something new to see. I've sat up here loads of times, and I've never seen that garden before. Look, there's a hammock.'

'That is very cool.' Sam leaned forward to get a better view, which also caused him to catch Izzy's scent: a lovely vanilla/strawberry combination. Was he inhaling too deeply? Fortunately, the twins were talking, so hopefully no-one would have noticed.

'Okay,' said Izzy, 'so what would be in your ideal roof garden?'

'An ice cream machine.' Barney was straight there with his answer.

'Amazing bright flowers that stay in bloom all year round,' said Liv, 'plus, obviously, a hammock like that.'

'We did actually have a hammock when we were kids. It must still be somewhere at your grandparents' house. Maybe in one of the sheds.' Sam couldn't believe that he hadn't thought about it before. Too busy to think about fun activities with the kids.

'Awesome,' breathed Liv, even less like her usual aloof self. 'Can we get it out next weekend?'

'I can't see why not.' Sam prayed that he wouldn't be too flat out with work to head out to his parents' place. It was so refreshing when Liv exhibited child-like enthusiasm for life.

The conversation flowed easily. Barney and Liv, despite living in a fourth-floor apartment close to Central Park, which wasn't short on views, were both fascinated by the London views around them, and by Izzy's local knowledge. Liv was smiling away, her usual cynicism set to one side, and Barney was fully engaged, too. He only stuttered a couple of times. Each time, Izzy behaved as though she didn't notice, and just waited very naturally for him to finish what he was saying, like she had all the time in the world. Sam could have kissed her.

Actually, Sam *could* have kissed her. Now he thought about it, there wasn't much he'd rather do. He shook his head slightly, watching her and the kids chat.

He clearly wasn't going to kiss Izzy, not now or ever. He didn't want serious romance, and he obviously wouldn't have a casual fling with her. Barney might need help from her for years on and off. And he valued their friendship too much to ruin it. Plus, even if he did want a committed relationship, it was hard to imagine a long-distance romance working and he'd never move back to London. The kids' lives and his were in New York.

He needed to get his mind off Izzy's infectious laugh and the way her beautifully shaped lips looked over very nice teeth, and the way her eyes lit up when she was about to say something just the right side of over-bold, so that it was funny and sweet rather than too close to the bone for comfort. When she laughed she had a dimple just to the right of her mouth.

He needed to think instead about how much she'd helped Barney, and how he did not want to have to find a Therapist Fourteen.

Coffee went quickly. In the hour that they had, they talked about a wide variety of things, but also nothing. Sam would have loved to have spent another few hours with Izzy and, if he was honest, however much he adored the kids, he wouldn't have minded spending that time alone with her.

'You know what.' Izzy checked her watch. 'I'm going to have to dash. I have to meet Ruby and her father.' She pushed her chair back and stood up. 'It's been so lovely to meet you both.' She smiled at Liv and Barney. 'And to see you again, Sam.'

'Would you like to come with us to Hyde Park tomorrow afternoon?' Liv blurted out. 'I think Dad's planning for us to hire a boat on the lake there.' And then she went bright red, as she always did when she wasn't sure of herself, and looked at Sam as though for confirmation that it was alright to have asked. Sam himself would have liked to have asked Izzy to spend more time with them but absolutely wouldn't have done, so he had no problem with what Liv had said. In fact, he was delighted. And he wasn't going to be reminding anyone that the original stated reason for them all getting together had been for Izzy and Barney to meet in person.

He'd love to have the opportunity to speak to Izzy alone, enjoy more conversation with her and get to know even more about her. Like, for example, whether she was singles climbing again with Emma last night and whether she'd met anyone she liked. Not that that was anything to do with him.

He smiled at Izzy. 'We'd love to share our outing with you if you're free. But completely understand if you aren't.'

'I'll have Ruby with me.'

'Not a problem,' Sam said.

'Then we'd love to. I've never taken Ruby on the Serpentine, if you can believe it. No-one ever spends quality time visiting places in their own city. It's always the tourists who take proper advantage. I'm going to have to go now but email me the details?' Her smile was slightly uncertain, as though she wasn't sure whether or not he genuinely wanted her to join them.

'Perfect. I'll send you a message later.' Sam pushed his own chair out and stood up to say goodbye. They had a very awkward moment where they combined a slight handshake with a vague air kiss across the table and then Izzy hurried away while Sam tried hard not to follow her with his eyes.

'Izzy's cool,' Liv said. Sam nodded.

'She's great,' he said. An understatement.

Chapter Sixteen

Izzy

Izzy was going to be late. Flip-flops were a nightmare for running in. She couldn't believe that she wasn't on time to meet Dominic and Ruby. She should not have given in to the temptation to grab those extra few minutes' conversation with Sam. Dominic was a big fan of punctuality and would be feeling slightly irritable when she got there. At least Ruby wouldn't notice that she was late. She'd have been having a lovely time with Dominic and she wasn't exactly a time-telling genius.

She picked up her pace, dodging shoppers, tourists, Saturday workers on their way home, and just made it into a carriage between the closing doors of her Tube train. Sitting down, she tripped over a pair of feet wearing stripy green and red socks and bright pink suede loafers. She smiled and apologised to the owner of the feet: a middle-aged man with a mullet and a cap. Izzy loved London. You could wear whatever you liked and no-one ever batted an eyelid. She loved a lot of other things about London too.

Would she ever want to leave? And was she asking herself that question because of Sam? Moving to another city or country for a relationship would probably be madness, just one more factor, along with all the other compromises that any relationship entailed, that would make things difficult in practice. No, Izzy certainly wouldn't do it, because it would be bad for Ruby, especially now that Dominic would be back in London.

The train beeped and it was time to Mind the Gap.

Izzy's heart lurched when she saw Dominic and Ruby standing together in the Earl's Court station ticket hall. Her beautiful daughter standing holding her father's hand.

Ruby's curls were Izzy's, but her lovely colouring, her height and her excellent physical co-ordination were all Dominic. What had Izzy been thinking? Sam was a moment in time and a fun companion, but Dominic was the father of Izzy's child. Fantasy versus reality.

'Hello, gorgeous girl.' Izzy picked Ruby up and gave her a couple of big smackers on each baby-soft cheek. 'Missed you this afternoon. Tell me what you've been doing.'

Izzy watched both Ruby and Dominic while Ruby babbled about their Natural History museum visit and Dominic gazed at her with obvious adoration. Yep. It was a good thing for Ruby that Dominic wanted to spend more time with her, and Izzy was just going to have to get used to it. And she'd probably be joining them on their outings sometimes anyway.

'How was your client meeting?' Dominic asked.

'Good, thanks.' Izzy bent over to put Ruby down, hiding her face so that Dominic wouldn't see her ill-timed blush at the thought of Sam. 'We should get going, Ruby.'

'Bye then, Rubes. Love you. Only a few weeks until I move back. I'll look forward to seeing more of you, Izzy, as well.' Dominic gave Izzy what she could only have described as a meaningful smile as he spoke. Izzy gave him a *non*-meaningful smile. She didn't want to introduce too much meaningfulness quite yet.

*

Izzy saw the email from Sam first thing in the morning, after she'd woken up a lot earlier than she would have liked because Ruby was hungry. At least there'd been no middle-of-the-night wet sheets. He'd sent it at the crack of dawn, probably jetlagged. She loved waking up to emails from him.

Good morning,

Great to see you in person yesterday. Hope we didn't make you late for picking up Ruby.

Liv's suggesting a picnic in Hyde Park followed by boating, and the kids (and I) would love for you and Ruby to join us for lunch too if you're free?

S x

Izzy had just clicked on Reply to say yes, when a message came through from Emma.

So sunny!! Meeting Sarah and Geeta and kids for lunchtime picnic – you and Ruby want to come?? Xx

Okay. So. Dilemma. Sarah and Geeta were university friends of Emma's who Izzy had known for years and really liked. They'd had a lot of excellent drunken nights out dancing together over the years, plus many sober days out. They were part of the fabric of Izzy's ongoing life, some of the constants that had kept her going through rubbish times like when she'd lost her grandmother and when she and Dominic had split up. And she hadn't seen them much recently. Sam and his kids, by contrast, were new in her life. They lived in New York, the kids were a different age from Ruby and they didn't have any other friends in common. It wasn't likely that she was going to see them at all on an ongoing basis.

So obviously they should meet up with Emma and the others for lunch and then meet Sam and the twins afterwards. And yet...

Morning gorgeous Emma. Love to have done but we're already picnic-booked up this lunchtime! Looking forward to seeing you Weds for painting. Xx

Morning Sam.

Love to. Meet outside the Serpentine Gallery in the park and walk somewhere from there to find picnic spot?

Izzy x

Izzy was shampooing her hair in the shower post breakfast with Ruby when she finally admitted to herself that it was a little bit odd that she hadn't told Emma who she was meeting at lunchtime. She always had her biggest moments of self-analysis or brainwaves in the shower. She'd been in the shower fifteen years ago when she'd decided to turn down the accountancy job she'd been offered and train as a speech therapist instead. And last year when she'd realised that she and Dominic were inevitably going to split up. And last week when she'd made her resolution to give up chocolate. Shower flash of clarity every time.

She normally told Emma everything. But she did not want to tell her about meeting Sam, Liv and Barney. Was that because it felt embarrassing or not-quite-right, or because it felt as though Emma would interpret it as one of those things? Or because, maybe, Izzy *really* fancied Sam and she didn't want to admit that to anyone, even to herself, in the shower. Ow, ow, *ow*, shampoo in her eyes, *shit* that hurt. Yes, that was a sign. *Stop thinking.* Or at least only think about things actually relevant to her day, like what she was going to wear for her in-no-way-a-date with Sam and the children.

*

Izzy, dressed in a new pink-and-orange striped top, which had only taken about half an hour to choose from her wardrobe, and purple, high-waisted flares, could see Sam, Liv and Barney waiting outside the Serpentine Gallery as she and Ruby, dressed in her favourite dress, walked along the path towards them. Sam had on well-worn jeans and a slim-fit green-and-white checked shirt and looked very *phwoar*. He was beaming at her and Ruby as they approached, and Izzy could feel herself beaming right back at him. Even the warm and sunny (but not too hot) weather and cloudless sky were joining in to make this feel like the start of a perfect afternoon.

'Hey.' Sam's voice was gorgeous. Listening to it was one advantage of speaking to him rather than emailing. 'You must be Ruby. We're very pleased to meet you. How're you both doing? I hope you're hungry. Liv and Barney found a bakery this morning that they liked and went a little OTT. You name a desirable picnic foodstuff, we almost certainly have it.'

'We did go mad.' It was lovely to hear Barney sounding so confident.

'This looks like a good spot.' Sam, apparently not a man who did picnics by halves, had brought significantly plusher rugs than the one that Izzy had taken to her picnic with Emma and Rohan last weekend and was laying them out while Izzy struggled, and definitely failed, not to ogle the way his muscles flexed across his back as he moved. 'Kids, why don't you get that frisbee out and go play while Izzy and I settle us down here.'

'I'm loving your luxury approach to picnicking.' Izzy snuggled herself onto the very deep pile blanket as the three kids ran off.

'Wait until you see the food we got. I wasn't kidding. It's a feast.' Sam started pulling out bakery box after bakery box. 'We went very global, to cater for all tastes. See?' He started opening the boxes. Izzy was awestruck.

'There are only five of us. We're going to have to find a homeless charity and hope that they can use what we don't get through. Or take them home and live off them for a week.'

'If you're going to do something, do it properly. Teenagers eat a *lot*. So do I.'

'Fair enough.' Izzy smiled at him. He returned the smile but didn't speak. Izzy felt her heart begin to beat faster. Too much tension. 'Beautiful weather,' she said.

'It is. You can't beat a summer's day in London. Even more so when right now our three kids are over there entertaining themselves pretty damn perfectly with that fifteen-dollar frisbee, while we sit here and prepare to gorge ourselves on food cooked by someone else. We should enjoy this.' Sam pulled shades out of his shirt pocket, wedged them on his face, leaned back on his elbows and smiled, one of his long, slow smiles. Izzy had a full body shiver moment, a common occurrence in Sam's presence, apparently, as though the smile had penetrated every nerve in her body.

She took her own shades out. It was bright, and also, with sunglasses on, you could spend a lot more time studying someone without looking like you were staring so much that they needed to get a restraining order against you. Happily, she'd gone cheap, and chosen pitch-black lenses rather than graduated shade ones, so they completely disguised her eyes. She settled back onto her own elbows, alternating between watching the kids and looking at Sam's face.

'Seeing Liv walk and run now, you'd never think she'd had any problems,' she said.

'I know. Every single moment I look at her I'm grateful.'

'It must have been unbelievably stressful.'

'Yeah.' Sam paused. 'I lost it once. In hospital, during the night, sitting next to her bed, desperate, so desperate, for her leg not to be amputated, and absolutely wracked with guilt. The nurse who'd been assigned to Liv came in and caught me at a bad moment. She asked me how I was and next thing I was crying, and then she cried too because she'd seen a lot of tragedy that night. We just held each other for about five minutes. And then I thought "pull yourself together, man", so I said, "Right, that's enough, now give me your most foul sentence about what a pile of shit this all is." And that tiny, demure Puerto Rican nurse came out with the worst swearing I've ever heard – put my own pedestrian cussing to shame. And in the middle of it, Liv woke up, and she started laughing, and then the nurse and I both laughed until we nearly started crying again. Rosita was her name.' Sam looked as though he was fighting to keep his expression completely neutral. Probably a good job he had shades on. It was definitely a good job that Izzy did, because some tears had escaped while Sam was talking.

'Why were you wracked with guilt?' Should she have asked?

Sam didn't speak for a few moments. Then he said, in an unsteady voice, 'Because the accident was my fault.'

'How?' Was that too blunt a question?

'I was driving.' A blunt answer.

'But you can't have crashed on purpose?'

'No. But I think I could have been driving more slowly and reacted better, maybe steered better so that the point of impact was more optimal. We were on a highway, probably pushing the speed limit a little, because we were late for lunch with my parents, because I'm always too busy. Someone turned left from a side road without looking left first, and hit us. I'd had very little sleep and I wonder if my reactions would have been better if I'd been less tired. And if the impact would have been less or if we wouldn't have been hit at all if I'd been driving more slowly.' His voice was bitter.

'Sam.' How awful. Such a burden for him to carry. Izzy wanted to reach out and hug away his pain. 'No. We all drive slightly too fast on occasion. And so many parents are almost permanently too busy and too tired. I certainly am. Most parents I know are.'

'I'm not sure. I let the kids down. Liv called for her mother in the hospital. I didn't think she missed her in that way any more.' The pain in Sam's voice was heartbreaking. 'And, you know, if she still had her mother, I'm sure her life would be a lot better now.' Probably. And Sam and Izzy probably wouldn't be here together like this and that was not relevant at this moment.

'It's incredibly sad that she lost her mother, but very lucky that she has such a caring father. The accident could literally have happened to anyone. And being tired probably made no difference.'

Sam didn't speak for a few moments and then he said, his voice rough, 'We smashed the window but we couldn't get Liv out of the car. We had to wait for the emergency services. A passer-by stood with Barney, and I knelt and held Liv's hand. She was in so much pain. I was scared out of my mind. Like, did she have internal injuries? Was the car going to explode? Would the ambulance arrive soon enough? When they got her out and onto a stretcher and into the ambulance, Barney stuttered for the first time. And he hasn't stopped. I can't shake the feeling that I'm to blame for it all.'

'Oh, Sam. No.' What a terrible experience. Izzy needed not to give in to the tears that were threatening, but to find some helpful words from somewhere. 'You must think about it a lot.'

'Yes. It's always there. I have nightmares.'

'I'm not surprised.' Izzy paused. 'Would you swap places with Liv if you could?'

'Of course I would. I'd do anything to rewrite the history of that day.'

'Exactly. Of course you would. You're an amazing father. It's so obvious. It was bad luck, not your fault. Bad luck happens.'

Sam stared straight ahead for a long time, and then he said, 'Thank you. That helps.'

His voice sounded like it was clogged with un-cried tears. Izzy had to blink back her own tears again. She wanted so much to be able to hug him.

'Maybe you should try talking to the twins about it, if you haven't already?' That had to help. They couldn't possibly blame him.

'I can't.'

Well, that was understandable.

'Look at your beautiful daughter now.' Izzy pointed at Liv, who was chasing Barney down, almost as fast as him despite the accident and the extra inch or two he had on her. 'Amazing.'

'Yeah.' Sam's voice was still thick. 'Thank you, again.'

They lay in silence for a few moments, a good silence.

And now it was like they were completely alone, just the two of them, on their blanket on the daisy-scattered grass, warm from the afternoon sun. Sam was only in the periphery of Izzy's vision, but she knew exactly how he was lying, his right leg, the one closer to her, straight, his left one bent at the knee, so that the denim fabric strained over his very firm thigh, his body angled a little towards her as he leaned on his elbows and *gorgeous* forearms. If she turned her head very slightly, she could see him better. The top two buttons of his shirt were open, giving her a glimpse of dusky chest hair. It was a miracle that she wasn't dribbling with desire.

Sam shifted a little, so that he was turned more towards her. His smile was smaller, more intimate than his usual broad grin, like it was just for her, like not a lot of other people would ever get to see him look like that. Izzy swallowed. He moved a little closer again. Now their hands were nearly touching. And their legs. Izzy was aware of every part of her body, desperate, frankly, to touch him and for him to touch her. He leaned even closer. It was just the two of them. All that would have to happen for them to be touching arms, legs, would be for one of them to move a little. Sam's smile grew. Izzy was going to *choke* from lust. Was he moving his head towards hers? Their mouths were so close.

'Dad,' Liv yelled. 'Barney threw the frisbee onto that roof.'

Sam remained completely stationary for a moment and then heaved a big sigh.

'And?' he called.

'Can you get it?'

'More trouble than you're worth,' he shouted back. 'Coming.' He sat up, slowly. 'Right. Sorry. Got to go try be a frisbee superhero.'

Izzy was sorry too. She'd been so unbelievably ready for something to happen. For no good reason. They'd just been leaning back on a blanket in a busy London park, not even touching. Her heart was still

thudding away as he jogged towards the kids. He moved very athleti-
cally. Her brain and body were going to be going *phwoar* all afternoon.

The upside of there being so much food was that, even though the kids
had persuaded Izzy that they should start eating immediately, there
was still a lot left for Sam when he'd finished borrowing a ladder from
the museum staff and climbing up onto the flat roof of the ground
floor to retrieve the frisbee.

'Sorry about that.' He lowered himself to the blanket between
the twins. Izzy smiled at him, completely in control of her lust now,
courtesy of the kids and the food.

'I have to be honest—' she gestured at all their plates '—we've
had a lovely time eating all your delicious food.' And watching his
shoulder and arm muscles and bum through her pitch-black lenses
while he climbed.

It was a lovely lunch. Great food and even better conversation.
When they'd all finally recovered from their immense over-eating, Sam
re-packed the picnic basket, refusing to let Izzy help on the grounds
that he was hosting this picnic and it was the least he could do after
she'd provided them with so many amazing recipes and thus so many
fantastic family meal experiences over the past few weeks. Then they
started to walk over to the boating lake, the girls in front, and Barney,
Sam and Izzy a couple of paces behind.

Ruby was in complete older-girl-adoration mode now and Liv was
wonderfully good-humoured with her. There was something really
lovely about Ruby getting on so well with Sam's children. And there
was always something relaxing about being *with* Ruby but not having
to do full-on parenting. It was like this when she and Ruby were with

Emma and Rohan. Really, it felt as though Sam and the twins were old family friends.

When they got to the lake, Barney and Liv had an energetic argument over hiring a pedal boat versus a rowboat. Liv won, because Barney had to concede that they had been in a rowing boat before but they had not been on a pedalo before.

'So, would Emma approve of this as a new experience?' Sam asked, once they were all settled on the pedalo, only slightly wet.

He'd had to repeat his question because Izzy hadn't heard him the first time, too occupied thinking about his shoulders.

'Yes.' Of course Emma would approve. Although it wouldn't be the pedalo experience, it would be the 'on the pedalo with Sam' experience that she'd approve of. Now Izzy was feeling very hot. Any minute she was going to blush. She pointed at a biggish bird with a long neck and surprising colouring and tufts on its head. 'Look at those birds.' Saved by unrecognisable wildlife.

'The kids and I read up on the Serpentine this morning, in true tourist style. I think that bird was mentioned. Can't remember its name.'

'Great-crested grebe And, yes, thank you, I do have an amazing memory. Unlike you.' Liv grinned at her father.

'And the lake attracts a lot of insects, which means that there are a lot of bats here at dusk,' Barney joined in.

This was nice. More than nice; it was *fun*.

The afternoon went quickly, and no-one fell in. The easy chat continued afterwards as they meandered along the path by the side of the lake.

Izzy was laughing at a joke of Liv's when she noticed an elderly couple in a rowing boat, close to them, the old man half standing, wielding one oar only, and sending the boat round in circles. His oar caught on something and he started to fall.

'Oh no,' Izzy yelped. The old man reappeared from under the water and then went under again.

Izzy said, 'Hold Ruby,' to Liv and started to run. And then Sam powered past her and was jumping. A few seconds later, he'd emerged from the water holding the flailing old man in his arms. As it turned out, the water was only about five-foot deep, not even up to Sam's shoulders. Sam spoke to the man and then set him down on his feet, holding him under his arms. With a lot of help from Sam the man made it to the edge, and Izzy and Barney pulled him out while Sam turned and front crawled – *nice* action – over to the old lady in the boat. She had thankfully stopped all the screaming and hand-wringing she'd been doing, and Sam pulled the boat over to the edge.

Izzy struggled to concentrate on helping the old lady out, because she was having a serious Elizabeth Bennet moment. Colin Firth as Mr Darcy had nothing on Sam as he jumped out of the lake. He had *excellent* chest, shoulder, stomach, thigh muscles. Very good proportions. Thank God for her sunglasses and the commotion now surrounding the soaking elderly man so no-one could see her ogling. Although, to be fair, she suspected she wasn't going to be in the minority. Objectively speaking, Sam looked amazing.

Sam finished shaking the water out of his hair and looked up, catching Izzy's stare. A slow grin spread across his face, like he knew exactly what she was thinking. There wasn't a lot Izzy could do other than grin right back.

When they'd made sure that the boat owners had blankets for the old man and he was comfortable, Sam said, 'So I should probably dry off a little in the sun before we walk back. Good job it's so hot now.'

Which was ideal, because on top of the Mr Darcy moment, Izzy then got to ogle Sam again when he took his shirt off for it to dry over a branch in the sun and they all sat down on the blanket again. And yes, his naked chest and stomach and back were as expected. Muscly. Gorgeous light-brown skin. Very ogle-worthy. Never had a pair of dark sunglasses served a woman so well.

Until she realised that Liv was staring at her, with a hard, appraising look on her face, that was like nothing Izzy had seen from her before.

Liv had clearly realised that Izzy had the hots for her father; there could be no other explanation.

And then Ruby said, 'Mummy, look, there's Emma.' Emma, Sarah and Geeta and their kids were waving manically at them from the path on the other side of the lake. Suddenly, on top of the glare from Liv, meeting Sam today felt almost sordid, or pathetically teenage. Like blowing out good friends for a date with the school heartthrob. Even though her friends definitely wouldn't have minded and Emma's text had been very last minute anyway.

Izzy's phoned pinged. Emma, of course. Izzy couldn't help looking at the message.

Is that Sam?? With no shirt and mega pecs and a six pack?? I need binoculars. Call me when Ruby in bed. Just a client, EH??

Marvellous. Definitely time to go.

'Lovely to meet you, Barney and Liv.' Izzy didn't dare move to hug them. 'And lovely to see you, Sam.'

'Great to see you too. We'll look forward to seeing you in New York next week,' Sam said. Barney was smiling and Liv was looking daggers. 'Why don't you come over to the apartment for lunch or dinner?'

'Great,' Izzy said. Although maybe it wouldn't be such a good idea given Liv's evident antipathy.

'Cool,' Barney said.

'Yay,' Ruby said.

Looked like they were going.

Sam and Izzy kind of hovered in front of each other for a second, neither of them raising their arms for a hug, the awkwardness magnified hugely for Izzy knowing that Liv was watching, and then Izzy grabbed Ruby's hand and pulled her away, calling, 'Bye,' over her shoulder.

'I had a really nice time,' Ruby told Izzy when they were sitting on the Tube on their way home.

'Me too,' Izzy said. She had, though some things could have been better. Liv. The Emma, Sarah and Geeta sighting – little bit embarrassing. The conflict she felt between her undeniable feelings for Sam and loyalty to Ruby and Dominic. The feeling of things left unsaid – she'd have loved to have spent more time talking to Sam. And the feeling of things left un*done*. As wrong as she knew it was, part of her – a very significant part of her, if she was honest – would have loved for that kiss on the rug to have just *happened*.

Chapter Seventeen

Sam

Sam settled back into his airplane seat and looked at the twins. They were laughing together over something on Barney's phone, probably incomprehensible to anyone over the age of twenty. Their weekend in London, nicely rounded off by an evening river cruise and a trip on the London Eye this morning with the twins' grandparents, had been great for family bonding.

The only thing that had marred it had been a teenage tantrum from Liv yesterday when they were leaving Hyde Park. Giving no reason, she'd told Sam in impressive language that she really disliked Izzy, in direct contrast to what she'd said on Saturday. When he'd asked her why, she'd gotten very angry and refused to say any more. Maybe he'd talk to her again about it when he was alone with her.

Other than Liv's strange behaviour, the only downside about the weekend had been that he and Izzy hadn't had enough time to talk. She was the first person he'd told about his guilt over the accident and his shoulders felt a little lighter now. Incredible, really, how good it had been to talk to her. He should have opened up about his feelings before now. Somehow, though, it had felt easier with Izzy than with anyone else.

He wanted to find out more about her too.

And in that moment, on the rug, he would have liked to have done something a lot more intimate than talking. In retrospect, it was obviously a good thing that he'd had to go get the frisbee.

It was probably silly, given that they shouldn't and wouldn't be more than friends, but he was very much looking forward to seeing Izzy again on Saturday in New York.

Anyway, overall, London had been a great weekend. He needed to make more time for quality experiences with the twins.

'Let's all watch the same two films now,' he said to them on impulse. 'One of Liv's choice and one of Barney's choice. As though we're going to the movies together.' His work could wait. Well, he could maybe skim through some documents while he was watching the films, but he wasn't going to go back to his full schedule until tomorrow morning.

'Yes and then we can compare notes.' Liv looked genuinely enthusiastic.

Sam was actually somewhat grateful to have documents to read when he discovered that Barney's choice was a Marvel Avengers film and Liv's was a teenage high school screaming girl thing. But it was still good to be sharing experiences with them.

He was going to text Luke when they landed. Squeeze in a beer or lunch in the next week. Taking a long weekend away from work was a good reminder of what was most important in life. Family and friends.

He had an email from Izzy waiting for him on his phone when they landed early evening New York time, just a chatty one. It felt as though the London trip had very much cemented their friendship. But had it also left him wanting more than that? He didn't want to think too much about that.

*

Sam's sense of wellbeing from the weekend had almost entirely dissipated by the end of the evening. When they'd arrived back at the apartment, Barney had gone straight to his bedroom and Liv had followed Sam into the kitchen.

'Nice weekend, huh?' He was concentrating on pouring juice for the two of them, so he wasn't looking at Liv's face.

'Really?' Her tone of voice was bizarrely hostile, so he looked up. Her stare was unnerving in the extreme. Piercing. Like she could see into his soul and she didn't like what she saw. Except Sam had no idea *what* she'd seen. Hadn't they just had a fantastic weekend away together?

'Um.' Should he mention her meltdown on Sunday afternoon about Izzy? Was this a continuation of that? Or was it something else entirely? Jesus, he missed Lana. He was so out of his depth here.

'Forget it.' She did a magnificent head toss, slammed her glass down on the table so hard that juice splattered out and stamped her way out of the room.

Right.

He should probably go after her.

She didn't answer any of his knocks on her bedroom door, or his cajoling.

Right. She clearly needed his time. He thought she did, anyway. But she was also clearly angry right now. He'd go and check his work emails and come back to knock on her door every so often to see if she wanted to talk. He wrote a note telling her he loved her and put it under her door.

In his office, he ploughed steadily through some work. He addressed a query from their Houston office, dealt with a point on a contract, agreed to give a lecture to Harvard alumni next month. All fine.

Until, woah, a big email. He needed to put his pitch in by the end of this week for the head of department role. Hours of extra work putting the pitch together. So he'd have zero time for the kids and they were on vacation. And, again, was it what he wanted? Maybe he should try to discuss it with Ash. If he had time.

Shit. It was late. He'd forgotten to go back and knock on Liv's door. When he got there, he saw his note, pushed back under the door. She'd written that she wanted to talk. He knocked. No answer. He checked his watch. Midnight. He pushed open the door, very cautiously. And she was asleep. *Shit*. He'd really messed up.

It looked like it was going to be a really crappy week.

At least he'd get to see Izzy again, on Saturday. Hopefully that wouldn't involve further fall-out from Liv.

Chapter Eighteen

Izzy

'Maybe the socks and the scarf?' Izzy held them both up.

'Yes, Mummy.' Ruby clapped. 'Can we phone him and show him?' They'd already phoned Dominic three times today. Ruby had a lot to tell him. Her New York excitement levels were *high*.

'No, sweet pea. Let's make them a lovely surprise for him.'

'That's a lot of cashmere for a soon-to-be-ex-husband,' Emma murmured when they'd paid and gone to Macy's toy section and Ruby was fully occupied comparing Barbies.

'They were a very good price. Can't ignore a bargain,' Izzy said. She also couldn't ignore her slight feeling of guilt about how much she was looking forward to seeing Sam this evening. Dominic was Ruby's father and, if there was a chance they might get back together, he should be the man who made her heart beat faster and who she wanted to save all her anecdotes for. But, honestly, just thinking about Sam she was getting hot and flustered and bordering on giggly. And she kept seeing and thinking of things that she wanted to tell him because she knew he'd appreciate them in the same way she had. The, yes, far too expensive cashmere for Dominic had been a definite guilt purchase.

Ruby skipped up, holding a truly hideous doll. 'Mummy, can I have this?' Excellent distraction.

'Yes, munchkin.' Bloody hell. It was an expensive doll. Always check the price tag before saying yes. 'Shall we go to the zoo in the park now?' They needed to get away from the temptation of the shops, although maybe they could just have a quick look at the sales… it would be nice to have something new to wear this evening.

'So Sam invited the three of us over later, for dinner.' Izzy said it as airily as she could manage. They were standing in the queue for the Rockefeller Center, the three of them squished together, Ruby's ears on stalks for whatever the adults said, so it was unlikely that Emma would start an awkward conversation. Izzy had been putting off mentioning the dinner all week. After last weekend, she didn't need any more 'Sam's *gorgeous*, how do you feel about him?' type comments from Emma.

'Wow. *Wow.*' Emma looked down at Ruby, whose little face was angled up to theirs, and visibly changed her mind about what to say next. 'Where does he live?'

'Upper East Side, near the park.'

'Wow again. Fancy location.' Emma attempted a subtle wink at Izzy as they shuffled forwards in the queue. 'You should go alone. Why don't I babysit Ruby?' This was why Izzy hadn't wanted to mention it to Emma. It was not a date of any kind. In fact, bearing in mind the looks Liv had directed at Izzy last week, the whole thing felt pretty awkward. And it was hugely embarrassing at her age to have a crush on someone. Which of course she did. Despite all the awkwardness, she was really looking forward to seeing Sam.

'No, no, no need. And no reason for me to go alone. The twins will be there. Really, it's for me to see Barney.' *This* was why she'd put off mentioning it to Emma.

'You and Ruby go. I'll chill at the hotel with some room service.' Emma had a definite match-making look in her eye.

*

Emma had refused to budge on her fake 'I'm tired and I want to stay in the room by myself' position, so now Izzy and Ruby were standing outside Sam's very swish apartment block without her. Liv's disembodied voice came over the intercom and they were buzzed inside. Everything was remarkably smart in the foyer. Lots of marble, stainless steel and mirrors and huge vases of well-arranged, brightly coloured flowers.

Liv was waiting for them at the front door of the apartment when they stepped out of the lift.

'I'm so sorry we're a bit late,' Izzy said. 'I know it's ridiculous to get lost in Manhattan, with the grid system, but we managed it.' Plus she'd spent too long deciding which of her two new sale-purchased outfits to wear.

Liv took the wine and chocolates that Izzy was holding, without looking at them. 'No problem. Daddy's a very punctual person but please don't worry. I think the food can survive waiting for twenty minutes.' Woah. Okay.

Thank goodness Sam had replied to her email saying that Emma wasn't coming, so that he'd known not to cater for her. Really, she should have just texted or WhatsApped. She had his number from when he'd phoned her to discuss Barney the first time, but emailing was what they did.

Sam rounded the corner at the end of the hall and came towards the door, his hands held out, saying, 'Thank you so much for the gift. And it's a lot less than twenty minutes, more like five, the perfect time to arrive. No-one appreciates an early guest.' Eek. He obviously thought they were over-late too. Or maybe he was just trying to compensate for Liv's teenage hostility. Slash full-on hatred.

Sam leaned down and kissed Izzy's cheek and her insides melted. Oh, God. She should not be experiencing this in front of Liv and Ruby. At all, actually.

He looked further down. 'How are you, Ruby? Are you enjoying New York?'

'Yes. We went to the zoo in Central Park this afternoon. I liked the penguins.'

'Liv and Barney have always loved the zoo. We're still members.' Sam smiled at them all.

'Yeah, although we did a project at school about whether it's okay to keep penguins in New York,' Liv said. Izzy snuck a look at her. Wow. Such a sneer.

Sam looked a little startled. 'Why don't you come into the kitchen and get something cold to drink?' he said. 'We have orange, apple and pineapple juice, Ruby. I'm hoping you like one of those?' He started walking down the hall with Ruby, leaving Izzy to Liv.

'Why don't I show you round the apartment while Daddy gets the drinks? The living room, anyway. Would you like Daddy to bring you water to drink, Izzy?' Liv's smile was, frankly, terrifying. Was it normal to be intimidated by a thirteen-year-old? Liv was a *child*.

'Great.' Izzy overshot on the fake enthusiasm factor and ended up sounding ridiculous. Liv smiled at her as though she was weird, fair enough, and then led the way through the wide hall and into the first room on the right, a sitting room.

'Wow.' This time Izzy didn't have to fake the enthusiasm. 'This is a beautiful room.' It had to be nearly thirty foot square and very high ceilinged. The walls were painted navy and the woodwork cream, and the soft furnishings were navy and lime velvet. Whoever had designed it had an excellent eye; they'd managed to create a feeling of both opulence and cosiness. She walked forwards towards the huge windows overlooking Central Park. 'What a wonderful view.'

'Yes.' Liv moved close to her, effectively nudging her towards a side table with a number of photos on it. A *large* number of photos. Some of the photos were of a single subject, some of groups, but they all had one person in common. A stunning woman. Obviously Lana. In one photo she was in a wedding dress, next to the young Sam, suave in a suit, obviously a few hours after Izzy had asked him out on his wedding day. In others, she was holding the twins, as babies, then as toddlers. There were family photos. There were photos of Lana on her own, laughing, smiling, in action.

Liv was a bit taller than Izzy and she was standing quite close to her, looking at her hard. Izzy swallowed. The vibes coming off Liv were not friendly. How long were Sam and Ruby going to *be* in the kitchen? She really hoped he hadn't given her too many drinks choices. They could be there for several minutes if so. Liv wasn't speaking. She was just looking at Izzy. Bad.

'So these are photos of your mother?' Izzy ventured.

'Yes.' And then Liv started talking, at great length, about her mother. Izzy smiled and nodded and felt desperately sorry for Liv and desperately awkward.

Chapter Nineteen

Sam

It had been a strategic error asking Ruby what juice she'd like. Sam had ended up walking to the kitchen with Ruby and leaving Izzy with Liv. This was not panning out how he'd planned.

Sam wasn't a nervous person but he'd been almost pacing the apartment in anticipation of Izzy and Ruby's arrival. Izzy had said that Emma wouldn't be joining them after all. Sam was pleased. While he would have liked to have met Izzy's best friend, he was hoping for the opportunity to talk more to Izzy alone.

When Izzy and Ruby had been due to arrive, Barney was in his room, not surprising, while Liv was flitting around the apartment, adjusting photos, cushions, flowers towards ever greater heights of perfection. Mrs H kept the place immaculate, but apparently that wasn't good enough for Liv today, which was odd, because Sam would have sworn from her behaviour at the weekend and a couple things she'd said during the week that she had no desire whatsoever to impress Izzy – quite the reverse. Something had happened on Sunday afternoon to change Liv's view of Izzy, and Sam couldn't work out what that was.

Maybe, given how anxious she seemed for everything to be just right, she'd mellowed. Or, if not, maybe today she'd realise how great

Izzy actually was. Although, really, it was irrelevant. Your kids didn't have to like your friends, although it would be nice if they did. And realistically they might never see her again. He didn't take them to London that often and this sounded like a once-in-a-decade trip for Izzy, plus the twins were getting older and within a few years would be more independent. He and Izzy could meet up in future without the kids.

Sam had returned to the kitchen after checking on the kids, and re-checked the table. Yep. All good. He'd looked at his watch. Ten minutes late. Only polite – no-one ever liked when someone arrived exactly on time for a dinner party, formal or informal – but he couldn't help worrying that for some reason she wouldn't turn up.

He'd checked the bolognese again. Had he definitely added the oregano? Yes, he was sure he had.

And the doorbell had gone.

Liv had got there before him. Had she run there to beat him to it?

By the time Sam made it into the lobby, Liv had accepted wine and chocolates from Izzy with no audible thank you, and was ushering Izzy and Ruby inside, pointing out that they were late. Was she saying it on purpose? She was smiling like an angel, but she had to know how unfriendly it sounded.

Sam rushed to thank Izzy for the gift and to say that they'd arrived at the perfect time. And he'd over-compensated and probably made it sound as though he too thought they were late. Izzy was wearing a bright green skirt and a purple top, which looked great against her reddy-gold curls. In fact, she looked amazing. He leaned down and kissed her cheek. She smelled amazing too.

He'd caught a narrow-eyed look from Liv as he turned to speak to Ruby and then, after some sneery passive aggression from Liv, he'd decided that the safest thing to do was get drinks for everyone.

But it had backfired and now Liv was talking to Izzy in the living room, and Sam was in the kitchen with Ruby.

Ruby took her time choosing her drink. Should she have pineapple, which she'd never tried before, or should she have apple, which she knew she liked? Sam worked very hard at keeping an interested smile on his face the whole time while also trying hard, with zero success, to hear what was going on in the living room. Eventually, literally minutes later, Ruby had her apple juice, with three ice cubes, not two, or four. Sam should not have asked her how many cubes she wanted.

When they got into the living room, having called Barney from his bedroom on the way, Izzy was standing with Liv, holding a photo of Lana.

'Hey again.' Sam handed Izzy her iced water.

'I was just telling Izzy about Mom,' Liv said. 'Izzy wanted to look at the photos.'

'She was beautiful,' Izzy said. Not much else anyone could say in the circumstances.

'She was.' Sam nodded. Not much else he could say, either.

'We all miss her, don't we, Dad?' The look Liv threw him was shockingly challenging. Chin up, eyes hard. Sam snuck a look at Izzy. Her smile was a little wobbly. Unsurprisingly.

'Yes, we do. Very much.' The only possible answer. Did Sam actually miss Lana? Very much so, as the twins' mother. Personally? Less so now. It had been a long time and, yes, they'd become good friends and he'd cared about her; but they hadn't been true soulmates. 'She was great. Obviously. Like her children. Why don't we all sit down?' He took the photo out of Izzy's hands and put it back on the sideboard. Was it completely wrong that, at the same time as he was handling his late wife's photo, he felt the brush of Izzy's fingers against his own right to his core?

He turned round from replacing the framed photo very carefully amongst the other pictures and caught Liv looking at him again in an odd way, as though she was puzzling over something. Someone had rearranged things so that the sideboard was covered in photos of Lana. No prizes for guessing who. Liv was clearly keen to send a strong message to Izzy that her mother was very important. Sam wanted to throttle her and he wanted to hug her. He'd obviously made a huge mistake in inviting Izzy and Ruby here to the apartment. Liv blatantly felt threatened, presumably worried that he was planning to introduce Izzy into their lives in some kind of bigger way. Sam's first loyalty would always be to his children and he needed to demonstrate that to Liv. Later, he was also going to mention to her that it was completely unacceptable to be rude to guests, but only once she understood that he would always put her and Barney first. He needed to keep the conversation with Izzy very light this evening.

Right now, he needed to make Izzy feel comfortable, without upsetting Liv further. Izzy was holding Ruby's hand and studying a painting on the wall with a fixed, unnatural smile.

'I bought that painting in London. Fond memories. Why don't we all sit down?' Sam suggested, leading the way over to the sofas and taking care to sit next to Liv. 'Ruby, have you been anywhere other than the park and the zoo?'

He watched as Ruby chattered about the Children's Museum of Manhattan, the Statue of Liberty, the Rockefeller Center, the shops. Liv, his amazing, infuriating, apparently insecure daughter, seemed to thaw as Ruby talked and was soon engaging with her, although avoiding Izzy's eye, telling Ruby nicely about the Bronx Zoo. Izzy and Emma were planning to take Ruby there on Monday. Barney joined in as well. Izzy seemed to be consciously not catching Sam's eye, instead focusing on the kids and making occasional very uncontroversial input to the conversation, mainly to clarify what Ruby was talking about when she got confused over the places they'd visited.

When Ruby had finished her drink, Sam stood up and said, 'Why don't we all go through to the kitchen?'

Liv and Barney cut bread and handed olives, marinated artichokes and Italian ham from the local Italian deli to Izzy and Ruby, while Sam cooked spaghetti and heated his bolognese sauce up.

'The famous spag bol,' Izzy said, laughing, as he handed steaming bowls out.

'Yep. Barney chose a new cake recipe for dessert but I decided to play it safe. It's not exactly fancy, but it never fails.' He'd wanted to make a special meal for Izzy and at one point had genuinely toyed with the idea of making a beef Wellington, until he'd googled it and discovered that it looked both hard and very time consuming. On the rare occasions that he had guests over to the apartment for dinner, he used caterers, but he'd wanted to cook himself for Izzy.

'Dad's bolognese is the best.' Liv did what Sam could only describe as a proprietorial smile. 'My mom was a great cook too.' Could she really remember Lana's cooking? The twins had been only five when she died.

'Great,' said Izzy, brightly.

This was excruciating. Good job Sam never invited his dates to the apartment.

Dinner was hard work. Liv made several dozen references to her mother, while Izzy maintained forced-seeming cheeriness. Barney caught the tension and clammed up. Only Ruby seemed unaffected, chattering away.

All in all, against all his expectations, because he'd been really looking forward to this evening, Sam was heartily relieved when Izzy put her napkin on the table and pushed her chair back.

He'd never have expected that he'd be keen for her to leave. She was funny, kind-hearted, beautiful, basically wonderful. If Liv suspected that he had feelings for Izzy, she'd be right. Liv was also wonderful, in many of the same ways as Izzy. The crucial difference between Sam's relationship with Izzy and his relationship with Liv was that Izzy had other friends, but Liv had only one father, and if there were ever a choice to be made, he would of course choose his kids. So it was best that Izzy leave now. He'd apologise by email somehow.

'Thank you so much for the lovely evening,' she said. 'We should go. Ruby's going to be very tired and we have some serious sightseeing to do tomorrow.' Before this evening, Sam had vaguely considered suggesting that they meet up tomorrow afternoon, so that he and the twins could give a natives' tour of New York City. He absolutely wasn't going to do that now.

'Hey.' He infused his voice with as much warmth as he could. 'It's been a pleasure. Really. Great to see you. Hope you enjoy the rest of your stay.'

By the time they got to the front door, the relief that they were done with the torture was mingled with real disappointment. He'd really wanted to get the opportunity to talk more with Izzy. And now she was leaving.

He leaned down to kiss her cheek. His arms itched to hug her. He kept them firmly by his side, which probably looked quite odd. 'Goodbye then.'

'Bye.' Izzy smiled up at him and his breath caught a little. Damn, he wished they could have had some time alone.

'Byeeeee.' Ruby danced off towards the elevator. Izzy gave a small laugh, raised a hand, and followed her.

Sam turned around. Barney had already disappeared. Liv was leaning against the wall, arms folded across her chest. Sam couldn't face talking to her right now, other than a bit of basic reassurance. He needed some time to work out what to say.

'I love you, Liv,' he said. She snorted. He reached out to her, but she moved sideways, away from him. Alright. 'I'm going to clear the kitchen up and then I have work to do.' Completely avoiding the issue. Fantastic parenting.

*

Sam had intended to speak properly to Liv on Sunday but in the end she and Barney were out with his parents all day while he finalised the application for the senior role that he did and did not want. He wouldn't have had time for sightseeing, in the end. And then, as so often, the week slipped away from him. He knew that he should talk to Liv, but he couldn't do it by email or by phone, and he was still too incredibly busy to get home in good time.

He did have some email correspondence with Izzy. He composed a lengthy apology for Liv's hostility and then deleted what he'd written and replaced it with a one-liner about teenage girls being very difficult at times. Any more of an apology and he might have ended up in 'She's worked out that I have feelings for you' territory, and he wasn't going there.

Izzy's emails, about the rest of their New York sightseeing, their flight home, Wednesday's painting (*Girl with a Pearl Earring*; apparently Izzy was not a gifted portraitist), how Emma and Rohan were bickering a little again, were somewhat stilted at first but settled back to normal. In his turn, Sam ranted as usual to Izzy about his job and told her how pleased he was that Luke had asked him – by text because Sam had had to cancel evening drinks – to be godfather to one of his children for the third time.

The good news, which he certainly wasn't going to mention to Liv, was that he might be able to get to see Izzy again soon, and alone finally.

Hey Izzy,

And FINALLY we get to Friday night. A very long week.

No time for a run today so did push-ups in my office—temp secretary barely in her twenties walked in as I was doing some with claps. She giggled for hours.

Question: I'll be back in London on business Weds—Fri week after next. Kids at school and staying home with Mrs H. Can you fit me in for dinner that Thursday evening between art and climbing? Love to catch up if so. Fully understand if not.

Climbing good this evening?

Hope you're over your jetlag.

S x

He'd caught Izzy's capitalisation habit. She liked to stress words when she was speaking. Look at that, he was smiling just thinking about her.

He was pretty much desperate for Izzy to say yes to dinner, which was why he was doing the trip the week after next, instead of this coming week when she and Ruby were going to be away in Dorset. Obviously the twins still took precedent, but after Saturday's awkwardness it would be great to see Izzy and clear the air. At least that's what he was telling himself.

He finally managed to catch Liv for a conversation over pancakes on Saturday morning while Barney was at basketball training. He made a few attempts to move the conversation naturally in that direction before just going straight in there, because no natural segue was happening.

'Liv. Honey. You know how much I love you and Barney. I got the impression that you were unhappy when Izzy and Ruby came over last weekend. There's no need to be unhappy.' He should say more, but it was difficult.

Liv turned her mug round a few times and then said, 'I really don't like her. I don't think you should see her any more.' Oh-kay. Sam needed to choose his words carefully.

'Izzy lives in London and we live in New York. She and I are friends and nothing more. I'm sorry if you got a different impression and that upset you. I would never want to hurt you in any way. You and Barney are more important to me than anyone or anything else.' That was absolutely true, even though, if he was honest, Izzy had also become very important to him. Maybe he shouldn't see her for dinner.

'Do you miss Mom?' Liv looked at her plate, spearing some pancake on her fork and putting it in her mouth slowly, before finally looking up into Sam's eyes. There was only one possible answer.

'Yes, I do. Very much. She was my best friend.'

'And no-one could ever replace her?'

'Correct. She was your mother.' True. 'I loved her like I'll never love anyone else.' Which was also true. He and Lana had become parents for the first time together; that was pretty irreplaceable. And he had loved her.

Liv smiled at him for the first time in a week.

*

At the movies with Liv and Barney that afternoon, sitting on the back row, which he'd booked so that he could surreptitiously use his phone during the film, Sam found two new emails.

There was, very unusually, one from his mother.

Dearest Sam,

I'm resorting to writing to you because I've been trying to speak to you alone for months, but you never seem to have time to talk.

I'm worried about you, and I'm worried about Liv and Barney.

You appear to be so busy and so stressed. You don't seem to have the time to enjoy your children, your family and friends, sport, all the things you've always loved.

I don't think it can be good for Liv and Barney either.

Your father and I love you so much and we'd love to help in any way we can.

Your mom

Jesus. It was lovely that they cared, obviously, but it wasn't like he could do anything about his shitty work-life balance. And now his mother had just made him even busier, because he was going to have to spend time fashioning a reply to her.

He had an email from Izzy, too, which, given the conversation he'd had with Liv this morning, wasn't as welcome as it would normally be.

Good morning.

Quick one.

Press-ups – head or bottom facing towards door?

I can do Thursday after next for dinner! Have booked babysitter!

Climbing good. Emma might have met someone! There was a new man. Very attractive in a young Tom Cruise kind of way. They were flirting outrageously.

THEN we got home and were chatting with Rohan, and I mentioned that Emma might have exchanged numbers with someone and next thing he'd gone very stand-offish. And normally he gives her a lift but they went home separately. Good day today?

I xx

Izzy had gone to the trouble of arranging a babysitter. He couldn't pull out of dinner now. And he was going to be in London anyway, after all. He'd just be meeting a friend. And he ought really to apologise in person to Izzy for Liv's rudeness. No need to mention it to the kids.

Hey.

I'm starting to think that Rohan has a thing for Emma? Only possible explanation?

Push-ups: My (obviously manly and clenched) buttocks were facing the door.

I'll look forward to next Thursday—eight fifteen? I'll book us a restaurant somewhere near your house. And I'll say right now that it's my treat.

Cooking your prawn pasta and apple crumble recipes tomorrow. Kids shopping for ingredients later.

If you're still sure about doing it while in Dorset, Barney will look forward to your session as always.

S x

And he was looking forward to dinner with Izzy.

Chapter Twenty

Izzy

Izzy looked at the three dresses on her bed. Okay, calm. Decision time. She had seven minutes until she needed to leave the house. Lucky that she'd decided to do her hair and make-up before she did Ruby's bath. This was what going out for dinner with someone you had a massive crush on did to you. Normally it didn't take her that long to decide what to wear. Now she was making Ruby in a unicorn shop look decisive.

It was an unusual situation, though. This evening felt strangely illicit. Dinner last weekend at Sam's had been excruciating. Firstly, it had been awkward telling Emma about it, and unpleasant feeling that she was going behind Dominic's back in some way. Which was utterly ridiculous. She'd been wondering if she and Dominic might become close again, but so far nothing had actually happened between them. She was single. Still uncomfortable, though.

Secondly, Liv had clearly not wanted her there, and both she and Sam had been at pains to emphasise how missed Lana was. Understandably. Sam had briefly mentioned Liv's behaviour in an email, and had attributed it to her being a teenager, but it had felt to Izzy as though it was personal.

So having dinner now felt odd. Irresistible, though, to finally to get the chance to talk properly, alone, with Sam. And it wasn't like it would be more than a one-off.

Okay. Time to focus. Five minutes. The shimmery gold dress and the red heels.

No. Too glitzy.

Four minutes. But down to two dresses.

The green one.

Or maybe she should check her wardrobe again.

No, she shouldn't. She and Ruby had been all the way through it already. These were her best options. She was going with the green one. Except she'd been wearing a green top when she met Sam and the twins in Peter Jones and a green skirt in New York. Okay, the blue one. But she *loved* the green one.

The green one it was. Only one minute until she needed to leave the house.

Fourteen minutes later, she was on her way through the hall, in the green dress.

'You look amazing.' Lily, Izzy's next-door neighbour's seventeen-year-old daughter was babysitting. Izzy could have asked one of her friends, but then she'd have had to tell someone where she was going.

'Thank you.' Izzy beamed at Lily. She did love this dress. The top half was fitted, the waist was cinched in and the knee-length skirt was full, so it didn't just flatter a generously boobed and hipped woman, it *required* generous boobage and hippage. She had her gold Anya Hindmarch clutch, a present a couple of years ago from Dominic, and was wearing gold mega heels, which she couldn't really walk in but which she knew from her mirror made her calves look a lot more defined and her legs a lot longer than they actually were. The elegance gain was very much worth the foot pain.

Her phone pinged while she was in the cab on the way to the restaurant. It was Sam.

Hey,

Looking forward to seeing you soon.

S xx

Stomach-droppingly date-like. They were going to spend the whole evening together. Now her throat was getting dry. Too much anticipation. Honestly, she was being ridiculous. It was not a date.

She should let him know that she was running late. She typed out a quick 'Me too, there in ten, xx' reply to his email and pressed Send.

'You on a date?' The taxi driver looked at her in his rear-view mirror and winked. 'Messaging the boyfriend?' To be fair, Izzy had just been smiling at her phone.

'No, just meeting a friend.' She shook her head and tried to arrange her features into an I'm-not-going-on-a-date look. It totally felt like a date. But it wasn't. She *was* just meeting a friend. Who she *totally* fancied, but anyone would, in the same way that anyone would fancy George Clooney.

The restaurant was a Sicilian trattoria, in a quiet, residential street about a mile from Izzy's house, sandwiched between a florist's and a vintage comic shop, and otherwise surrounded by narrow terraced houses. Izzy had never noticed it before.

Izzy's non-date was waiting outside the restaurant, wearing smart navy jeans and a black shirt with a tailored jacket. There was something about a very handsome man in a dark shirt. And the way Sam wore his thick, wavy hair slightly long with no apparent regard to styling added a bit of a devil-may-care attitude to whatever he was wearing, which, obviously, just made him even more gorgeous.

As Izzy's cab drew up, Sam moved forwards, opened the door and put his hand out to her. His slow smile was spreading across his face as though he'd developed that smile just for her. Izzy literally got a stomach tingle as she took his hand. She hoiked herself out of the cab, caught one of her heels in a crack in the kerb and wobbled spectacularly, while Sam held her up with no apparent effort. His arm had to be strong, because she was not tiny.

'Good to see you,' Sam said when she'd finished wobbling and had two feet stable on the pavement. He leaned down towards her, still holding her hand, and they exchanged a cheek-kiss. The tiny scratch of his stubble against Izzy's face massively upped her stomach-tingling. 'You look beautiful. Lovely dress.'

'Thank you. Not looking so shabby yourself.' Understatement.

'Why, thank you.' His smile widened. Possibly the most attractive man she'd ever seen in her entire life. 'We're in here.' Sam let go of her hand to push open the door to the restaurant and then held it so that Izzy could walk in ahead of him.

She loved his natural chivalry. Like when he'd scrabbled around on the pavement on his hands and knees for several minutes picking up her scattered groceries. She knew he'd have done it for anyone – man, woman, young, old, someone he fancied, someone he didn't – and he wouldn't be expecting any kind of gratitude in return.

Sam placed a hand lightly in the small of her back as a smiling waiter directed them towards a table for two at the back of the restaurant. The room was small, very busy and full of the sounds of happiness and the smells of Mediterranean cooking.

From Sam's one little touch, Izzy's whole body was on high alert, even her shoulders, even her feet. Even her *ear lobes*. All of her. Like if he touched her anywhere else she might explode in fireworks. What she needed was a glass of water with a lot of ice in it. When Dominic had put his hand on her back when they went for their tea at the Carter, it hadn't felt more than comfortable, familiar. Now, as she walked, she was fantasising about leaning right back into Sam, feeling him behind her, his hand sliding round her waist, moving across her body.

And now, right now, she needed to stop comparing Sam and Dominic. Firstly there was no reason to since this was *not* a date, and secondly it *was* a lovely dinner with a friend, which might not happen again, so she should enjoy it.

Sam visibly had his full attention on her, so much so that she couldn't stop smiling idiotically at him.

'This is lovely,' she said, gesturing. They'd been seated at a small square table at ninety degrees to each other on cushioned benches along the walls so that they both had a great view of the whole restaurant. It had to be the best table. Maybe Sam was well-known here. Maybe he used to come here with Lana.

'Yeah, I've always liked it. Off the beaten track, but perfect. What would you like to drink? They do a mean cocktail.' Every time Sam spoke, Izzy got butterflies, even when she was wondering if he'd come here with Lana. It was like she had a full-blown case of teenage-style hormonal lust. Any minute she'd start batting her eyelashes at him.

'I think I'm going to go for a Kir royale. Always my favourite.'

'Sounds like a good choice. I'm going to go for a screwdriver, also always a winner.'

While the waiter gave them menus and took their drinks order, Izzy spent a couple of minutes openly admiring Sam. He had very capable hands. And a very square jaw. Chiselled. He really should have become a film star. Irrespective of whether or not he could act. Some of them definitely only played one part, Handsome Heartthrob. You'd think he'd have a much better work-life balance as a rich megastar. It didn't sound like George Clooney had many problems getting to see *his* twins.

By the time they had their drinks and some truly delicious antipasti, Izzy had herself a lot more under control, mainly because Sam had been making her laugh so much about some of his no-name clients' demands that she couldn't think about anything else.

'So not all bad then.' She took another mouthful of stuffed artichoke. 'Mmm, that is *so* good. At least you can laugh about your job.'

'You know, if I didn't laugh, I might almost be crying.' Sam's smile dropped suddenly and Izzy saw the tiredness round his eyes. 'I'm aware that I've vented about this far too much already, but my workload's continuing to increase ridiculously and now I'm likely to get a bigger role, and at the same time, the kids seem to be getting ever more demanding emotionally. Maybe they blame me for the accident. Maybe it's just that they've woken up to the fact that I'm never there. Maybe all teenagers are like this. Maybe this is when not having a mother is really going to hit home. Maybe it's a combination of all of that. I don't know. I do know that it's hard. And I feel like a failure.' Sam clearly missed Lana a lot.

'I'm so sorry. You're doing your best. You are so not a failure.' She wanted to reach out and squeeze his arm, or hug him, comfort him physically, like she would with one of her girlfriends, or Rohan. Well, maybe not in exactly the same way. 'I'm sure they know how much you love them and everything you do for them and that you have no choice about working long hours. And, honestly, I think pretty much every teenager goes through a tricky phase. I definitely went through an evil witch from hell phase.'

'You? Really?'

'Yup. And took it all out on my lovely grandmother, who I lived with from the age of ten, because my parents split up and they were both basically too busy with their new partners to look after me, so I moved in with her. You know how she dealt with it? I was being awful, I mean *really* awful, and she'd been so lovely throughout about a week of me ranting at her, on top of months and months of horribleness, and then one Saturday early evening, we were in the kitchen and she turned round and said to me, in a really calm, quiet voice, "I do love you, but if I'm honest you're being a real bitch at the moment and it's pissing me off." Her exact words. The kind of thing you remember. It was literally the one and only time I ever heard her swear. I was so shocked that I looked at her, properly, and a little switch went inside me, and I told her I loved her. And then we both nearly cried with laughter, for a really long time and then we went out for a curry. And after that I was a lot nicer. I'm not really recommending you do that with Liv, though. Not yet, anyway. I think it's a high-risk strategy.'

'Wow. Your grandmother sounds awesome.'

'Yes, she was.'

'When did you lose her?'

'Three years ago.'

'Still miss her I'm sure.'

'Yep. But, you know, I was lucky to spend as much time with her as I did and she was a good old age, eighty-eight.'

'Someone having lived a good long life is little consolation when you miss them.'

'Yep.'

'I'm sorry.'

And then Sam reached across the table and squeezed Izzy's fingers. She'd been right. It wasn't like squeezing her girlfriends' or Rohan's hand. None of her friends caused her to wonder whether you could actually dissolve with lust and longing for closer physical contact. She was going to be able to feel where they'd touched long after he let her fingers go when the waiter came over with their main courses.

They talked through a lot of exceedingly good food about films, cooking, fantasy holiday destinations, worst birthday presents ever (Izzy being a clear winner with her mother and her wife's sex manuals).

'Yes, climbing again tomorrow evening,' Izzy said in response to a question from Sam, as they ate too many *delicious* cassatelle, fried crescents of dough filled with sweetened ricotta.

'I haven't asked you how painting was last night.'

'Well. Interesting question. Painting was a lot of fun. We did the *Mona Lisa*. Badly.' Izzy got her phone out to show him a photo of the finished disaster. 'But it was a strange evening, and a bit worrying, because Rohan didn't babysit. Emma brought our friend Geeta instead.'

'For the first time since you and Emma started painting?'

'Exactly. And I don't think it was because Rohan had anything else on. I think he'd blocked out Wednesdays for us. He didn't say last week that he wouldn't be coming, and Ruby loves seeing him. They play Harry Potter Dobble every Wednesday before she goes to sleep. I think that if he'd been planning not to come he would have said, and I think if something last minute had come up he would have said. I think the reason he didn't come is this coldness between him and Emma. They'd already been at each other's throats for a while, but since Ruby and I came back from Dorset they've barely been talking.'

'After she talked about meeting someone else.'

'Yep. Very weird. She's single, so she's obviously free to do what she wants.' Izzy wondered if Sam slept with a lot of people. Nothing to do with her, clearly. 'And Rohan's really nice, never judgy, never sexist, really laidback. I don't know what's happening and I'm worried that it's the end of our friendship, the three of us.'

'You know what I think?' Sam poured more wine into both their glasses. 'I think that Rohan has a thing for Emma. I think that's what's happened.'

'You said that before. And normally I would agree, given the signs. But we've all been friends for eighteen years. No-one's friends for this many years before starting to *like* each other.'

'Maybe he's always liked her. Or – you mentioned that they shared a flat for a few months – maybe something happened then.'

'No, surely not.' Although. That would make some sense. That was when the bickering had started. 'Nooooo.' Woah. Izzy's mind was boggling. 'They *have* always got on very well. Like they just get each other.'

'And.' Sam filled their water glasses. 'How often are straight men and women just close platonic friends?'

'A lot. I will prove it to you. Rohan and me. I love him but I have genuinely never fancied him and I'm sure he's never fancied me. Ever.'

'But is your relationship, in fact, more like that you might have with your best girlfriend's boyfriend or husband? As if, for example, he were Emma's partner?' Sam raised his eyebrows like he'd made a very clever point.

'Nope. We met at university and we became close friends almost immediately, before he met Emma. Totally platonically.' Izzy took her final mouthful of pudding. *So* delicious.

'Hmm. I realise as I say this that it sounds very old-fashioned, and maybe it's just the way my life has panned out, but I don't have close, straight, female platonic friends. Can't think of a single one. Friends' partners, yes, women I know less well, yes, but, no.' Their gazes caught. For ages. 'I mean, other than you,' Sam said eventually. 'You're a good friend. I probably just haven't been meeting the right women. Women like you.' They were still looking at each other. Izzy swallowed, super-aware of Sam's face, shoulders and chest, and of her own body. Sam's eyes moved to her mouth. And back to her eyes. And then back to her mouth.

Izzy swallowed again. Apparently she'd lost all power of speech or saliva control.

'Why don't we skip coffee here and find a pub to have a drink? I miss your London pubs.' His voice sounded a bit croaky, even deeper than usual, which did all sorts of things to Izzy's insides.

'Good idea.' If his voice sounded odd, hers sounded ridiculous. Squeaky. Not a voice that would do anything sexual to anyone's insides. She focused hard on speaking normally, and said, 'I'll have to be home by midnight. My neighbour's seventeen-year-old daughter's babysitting and she has school tomorrow.'

'So you're on a Cinderella schedule.' Sam was already nodding to the waiter. He had his credit card out by the time the bill was on the table, and they were out of the restaurant very quickly.

It was one of those London evenings where the day had been warm but as night had descended the temperature had fallen too, even though it was still August. Izzy was shivering within a minute or two of leaving the restaurant. And also tottering in her shoes. She hadn't factored in a walk anywhere. These were strictly house-to-venue-in-a-taxi-and-straight-back-home-again shoes, and her dress wasn't made for a freezing evening.

'You're shivering.' Sam was already taking his jacket off. 'And those shoes don't look totally practical.' He put the jacket round her shoulders and held his arm out for her to take. 'Want some support?' The jacket smelled of Sam's aftershave, something foresty and masculine. The same scent that he'd had every time she'd met him. She took his arm. If she didn't, she was genuinely at risk of falling over.

'Thank you.' She put her arm through his. She *loved* his forearms. 'I have history on the falling-off-high-heels front. I ran across a road once in platforms, tripped over and tore ligaments in my ankle.'

'Ouch.'

'Yep. Took ages to get back to normal.' She looked up. 'It's a lovely evening.' There was a full moon, and a lot more stars were visible than usual in the London sky. They were both looking heavenward now. Sam pointed to a couple of constellations and they stopped walking.

And then he stopped looking at the sky and looked down at Izzy. Their arms were still linked.

Slowly, very slowly, Sam let go of Izzy's arm and encircled her waist with both his arms instead, and pulled her very gently towards him. Izzy had her hands on his chest, his splendidly solid chest. He bent his head towards hers and she raised hers. They paused for a moment with their lips not touching, but so close that their breath mingled. It was a long moment. Izzy looked at his face, his lovely, kind eyes, his beautiful mouth. The very bones of him were amazing.

Something was going to happen.

And then, suddenly, somehow, they were kissing, very gently at first, and then ridiculously urgently, like this might be the only kissing left until the end of time. Izzy's arms were round Sam's neck now, her hands in his hair. He had one arm still round her waist, under the jacket, and the other on the back of her head, his fingers in her hair too. Their bodies were pressed against each other, Izzy's legs against Sam's hard thighs. It was the most amazing kiss she'd ever had, as though everything she'd felt for Sam from the moment she saw him in the greasy spoon was encapsulated in that kiss.

Chapter Twenty-One

Sam

The kiss went on for a very long time. Probably the best kiss of Sam's life. Fully clothed, hands not really going anywhere they shouldn't, really very chaste, and yet so damn erotic.

When they eventually stopped kissing, after who knew how long, they stood together for a while longer, not speaking, Sam's arms round Izzy's waist and her arms round his neck. She was smiling gorgeously at him. And he was smiling foolishly back at her, he was fairly sure.

'So, wow,' he said. Yeah, he was sounding pretty foolish, too.

'Yes.' Izzy's voice was at whisper-quiet level.

He couldn't suggest that she come back to his hotel because she had to get home to Ruby and her teenage babysitter. She clearly wasn't going to ask him to go back to her house because of Ruby and the babysitter and the possible neighbour gossip. He really didn't want the evening to end though.

'Shall we get that drink?' He indicated with his head the pub on the corner of the road.

'Good idea.' Her voice was still pretty quiet, as if she was a bit stunned. Understandable. He was in shock himself.

He held his arm out again, Izzy took it and they started walking.

The pub was one of those olde worlde traditional English ones, that looked as though it had been there for hundreds of years. Probably had. It was one he'd been to a few times when he lived in London. It had never felt like this before. It was as if this was one of the most special, significant evenings of his life.

There was a table free in a corner.

'Why don't you sit down and give your feet a rest, and I'll get the drinks?' he said.

'Thank you.' Izzy was already settled on the two-seater sofa next to the table, and had slipped her shoes off. 'I'd love a lime and soda.' Sam would probably be wise to join her in something non-alcoholic, after what had just happened. It felt huge.

Too huge, actually. This evening shouldn't have been this special. Sam started walking over to the bar. He didn't want to lose Izzy's friendship. It was so important to him. He honestly loved talking to her as much as he loved talking to Luke, and he cared about her as much as he cared about his other close friends. Although with Izzy there was this intense sexual attraction thrown in. Yeah. It was pretty obvious that Sam would struggle to be just platonic friends with Izzy. But romance? No. He wasn't doing serious romance, for so many reasons. And obviously a fling was out of the question. Liv. Barney. And they'd lose their friendship afterwards and Sam would be bereft.

So he *was* going to be just friends. Starting right now.

Sam put Izzy's lime and soda down in front of her and his own drink on the table and sat down next to her awkwardly. The sofa was really too small for two people. In a furniture store, they'd probably describe it as a 'love seat'. Not a phrase that sat well with him right now.

'What are you drinking?' Izzy seemed keen not to talk about what had happened. She inched herself sideways, away from him, right against the arm of the sofa, maybe also regretting the kiss. Their thighs were still touching though. He loved the softness of her.

'Virgin Mary. Bloody Mary without the vodka.' Definitely not a time to be drinking alcohol.

'Sounds good. Thank you so much for dinner.' Izzy sipped her drink. 'The food was amazing.'

Sam opened his mouth to thank her for her company but it sounded too odd, given what had just happened.

'Yeah,' he said. 'I really like that restaurant. One of those hidden gems.' Yes, this was good. A restaurant conversation. Very uncontroversial.

'I love eating great food in restaurants,' Izzy continued. 'Obviously it's lovely in the moment, and it's nice afterwards, for ideas for things to cook at home.'

'That does not happen to me. It is lovely in the moment, yes, but there's literally zero chance that I could create anything at home that would be inspired by food as good as that.'

'Not true.' Izzy shook her head and her beautiful auburn hair shimmered in the light. 'You could totally have made that pudding. You successfully made profiteroles, so you could definitely make those.'

'Yes, you're right. I am an incredible baker now.' Sam nodded. 'I mean those chocolate profiteroles only took the three of us about five times as long as you said they'd take one person. And while they tasted fantastic, they were a little oddly shaped. Now, would you agree that those ham and cheese pastry things were essentially puffy cheese and bacon crisps?'

'Yes, I would. And yes, I do remember you saying that if they existed they'd be a bestselling savoury confectionery item. Very good flavour-predicting skills.'

'Yep. That time we had coffee.' Sam was strangely pleased that Izzy remembered their long-ago conversation as well as he did. 'That seems like almost a lifetime ago.'

'Yeah. A lot's happened since then.' Izzy wasn't wrong. 'Big things and small.'

'If you had to sum up your life since then in one paragraph what would you say? The headlines.' As he said it, Sam regretted his question, because it was taking the subject matter right back towards the personal, but he couldn't really immediately say *No, scrap that, don't answer*.

'Good question.' Izzy took a long drink. 'Okay. Headlines. In no particular order. Gave birth to the most amazing daughter. Lost my wonderful grandmother. Successfully combining fulfilling career and parenthood. Separated from husband. Great friends. And, almost up there with the big things, discovered that even though I hated Art at school, I love painting. You?'

'Okay.' Why had he started this? This was what happened when you kissed the woman who you used to think was The One, until you realised that life was complicated and there was no One. It addled your brain and caused you to start really stupid conversations. Because where was this going? 'Moved back to the States. Took a great job. In car accident.' Sam's voice wobbled and he swallowed. Now he really wished he hadn't started this. He should lighten things. Maybe go for a joke. 'Discovered that I'm severely lacking in the social media, gaming and fashion skills required to parent teenagers. Who probably just really need their mother right now.' He paused. This was ridiculous. He'd sounded bitter, not remotely jokey. Why had he mentioned Lana? That kiss had shaken him far too much. 'And dated a succession of beautiful women with whom I have little in common.' Why in hell had he said *that*? Was it because the expression of sympathy and understanding on Izzy's face had had him wanting both to punch something really hard and cry? Her expression had changed now. He'd seen hurt in her eyes before she smiled, a bland, fake-looking smile. There was a long, uncomfortable pause.

'I'm sorry,' Izzy said eventually. Sam wanted to say sorry too, but he didn't.

'Yeah, you know, we all have our crosses,' he said. He couldn't keep the bitterness out of his voice.

'Could I say something? As a friend?' Izzy always looked and sounded confident. But not now. She looked hesitant.

'Sure.' He flattened his voice to try to discourage her from continuing.

She waited a few seconds, and then said, 'You seem completely overwhelmed by everything in your life at the moment. You don't get to see the twins as much as you'd like to, you don't get to exercise as much as you want to, you've mentioned that you don't get to see your friends, you have to sacrifice sleep to fit things in, and it all seems to be because of your job. Have you ever considered just… leaving? Taking a career break for a couple of years?' She was right. His life was a shitshow at the moment. Totally messed up. But there was nothing he could do about it.

'My job pays the bills. It's a bit of an all-or-nothing career. People don't take career breaks.'

'But, at the risk of being too personal, do you need the money to pay those bills? Someone like you, with your CV and at your age and, just, *you*, surely could get a different kind of job in due course, maybe full-time lecturing, or something else, one that would give you more time to live the rest of your life? More time with the kids?' She thought he was a bad parent. He *was* a bad parent. Although, she wasn't a judgemental person. Nonetheless.

'You think I don't spend enough time with the kids.' She was right. He didn't.

'No. I think that you're an amazing dad who's doing his best in really difficult circumstances but who would benefit from having more time in his life both to spend time with his kids and do other things.' Of course he would, but there was no way that he could see to get off the treadmill of his life. And it would be ridiculous. The hours he'd put in, the sacrifices he'd made. Now he and the kids were supposed to be reaping the rewards of his hard work.

And she was wrong on the first point. He was not an amazing dad. A lot of the time at the moment, the twins effectively had no parental input. Recently, there'd been many weeks where he didn't see them from Sunday evening to Saturday morning. Mrs H was fantastic, but teenagers needed a parent to talk to, and he was letting them down. In fact, right at this moment, they'd be arriving home from school, and instead of video calling them, he was here with Izzy, a real betrayal of Liv's trust, in particular.

'You think I'm letting my kids down.' He knew that she didn't think that but she *should* think it, because it was true.

'No.' She shook her head. 'I don't. I think you're always there for them emotionally but sometimes it's really hard to be there for them physically. I think you're a wonderful father. I mean, so much more devoted than both my parents, to name but two examples.' She shifted her position and her eyes didn't hold his, like she regretted making the comparison. She should regret it. Sam didn't want to be compared to her parents. She'd told him enough that he knew that they'd both been physically and emotionally absent from her life and, frankly, very uncaring.

'So now you're comparing me to your uninvolved parents.' Wow. That sounded too vicious out loud. He couldn't apologise, though. He had too many emotions warring inside him to be able to find the words.

'No. I'm not. I'm saying that you're clearly an amazing, loving, caring dad but that circumstances are against you and that maybe there's something you can do about that. Maybe you can walk away from your job. For your sanity and happiness. Make some kind of fundamental change in your life.' She'd repeated some of the comments his mother had made in her letter but she'd gone a lot further than his mother had. They were both completely right, in theory. Except, in practice, it just wasn't possible. Apart from anything else, he was too busy to think, at all, ever. Change required thought, energy, time. He had none of those commodities. He was just going to have to carry on the way he was, screwing up his kids' lives.

'You're wrong.' Sam knew that his voice sounded hard and angry. Damn right. He was suddenly furious with life and furious that they were having this conversation. His heart was beating uncomfortably fast and he realised that he'd made fists with his hands.

'I don't think I am.' What was she? On a death mission?

'I thought I was paying you for speech therapy, not life therapy.' As Sam spoke, Izzy flinched, almost as though he'd raised a hand to her. Understandable. He'd been a complete asshole. Two nasty comments for the price of one.

He could apologise. Or he could not apologise. He picked up his drink and took a large slug. Yep, apparently he was going to go with not apologising. The drink tasted very bitter.

'Sorry.' Izzy stood up, almost falling over on top of him as she did so, because of her haste. Those ridiculous, cute heels. And what the hell was wrong with him, noticing *now* how beautifully that dress clung to her body and wondering if that was the edge of a black lace bra that he saw? 'Here's your jacket. Thank you. I need to get going. Thanks for a lovely evening.'

'How are you getting home?' He shouldn't let her go like this. He should apologise, right now. Again, though, he couldn't squeeze the words out through the red mist. It was like, after the kiss, he'd almost been seeking an argument, and he couldn't reverse his way out of it now.

'I'll get a black cab. There are always lots on this road. Good night.' She was right, there were always a lot of cabs on this road, so she'd be safe to get home.

She did an excellent job of stalking towards the door on those wobbly heels, with her hips swaying and her hair rippling down her back.

She didn't look round and Sam didn't make any attempt to stop her going. Maybe the end of their friendship. Apparently he'd just destroyed one of the few uncomplicated great things in his life. Except it wasn't uncomplicated, was it? Because he'd clearly fallen head over heels for Izzy but a) Liv hated her, so he couldn't do anything about it, and b) he didn't want to do anything about it because there was too great a risk of getting hurt. He'd have liked very much to have remained friends with Izzy, though. And yet now he'd driven her away. Really, what was wrong with him? The kiss had been a disaster and the way he'd spoken to her even worse.

He went over to the bar and ordered an extra-large Bloody Mary, with the vodka.

Chapter Twenty-Two

Izzy

Just over three hours ago, Izzy had been sitting in a taxi on her way to the restaurant, full of anticipation, trying really hard not to think of the evening as a date. Now she was sitting in a taxi on her way home, full of food and immense misery, trying really hard not to cry, because she did not want one of those 'Cheer up, love, it might never happen' taxi-driver conversations. Honestly one of the worst evenings of her life. She couldn't remember a time when someone she'd liked so much had spoken to her so unpleasantly. Just awful.

How it had ended felt even worse because the rest of the evening had been so wonderful. Dinner had been lovely. She and Sam had connected in the way they had the last time it had been just the two of them, all those years ago in the café. But this time they were both single, and Izzy wasn't a pissed-off heavily pregnant woman. There'd been tension sizzling between them from the moment she'd stepped out of the taxi, all the way through dinner. She'd laughed, smiled, confided, been confided in. And the food had been delicious.

Had it been inevitable that they'd kiss? It was when the conversation had turned to the question of straight men and women being friends that the tension had reached almost boiling point, like from that point on they'd both known that something was going to happen.

Or maybe they'd both known even before the evening started that something might happen. Izzy had, anyway, if she was honest. She'd happened to place an online order earlier in the week, and was wearing a considerably fancier bra and knickers than her usual M&S cotton comfort, all about the boob support and tummy flattening, no-sex-here-thank-you underwear. This evening she was wearing matching underwear. Black lace, silk. *Lingerie*.

She definitely hadn't been intending or expecting that Sam would see the underwear. In fact, there'd been no way that he'd see it. She couldn't possibly have taken him home, because Ruby was there and so was Lily. She couldn't possibly have gone back to his hotel with him because she had to be home on time for Lily to be in bed by midnight. And aged thirty-six and wearing very hard-to-balance-on shoes, she wasn't exactly going to have been doing stuff al fresco in a doorway. She'd still worn the black lace, though.

The kiss had been earth shattering. The best of Izzy's life. And she was sure that Sam had felt the same way. Afterwards, he'd had a look in his eyes, a look that she was pretty sure mirrored the one in her own eyes. Glazed, astonished, but yet not astonished, and, above all, completely besotted. At that moment she'd known something, which had crept up on her over the past couple of months but which she hadn't acknowledged. And she wasn't going to acknowledge it now. She needed to move her thoughts on.

Except she couldn't. Their kiss had probably been way better than it would have been if they'd kissed all those years ago, when they first met, because now they properly *knew* each other. Except. Did she know

Sam? Did she really? Could you know someone properly via only the written word and a couple of meetings? Would the Sam she'd thought she'd known have been capable of speaking as harshly as he did in the pub? No. So apparently she didn't know him at all.

She'd obviously overstepped the mark. Obviously mistaken how close they were. Although did you share a kiss like that if you weren't close?

Maybe she'd worded what she'd said awkwardly. Or maybe she'd been right and struck a nerve and he'd been lashing out. Whichever, it must have been obvious that she'd said it because she cared, and he'd been a complete bastard in response.

'And there you go, young lady.' The taxi driver pulled up outside her house. Young. Ha. Izzy felt about a hundred. She switched on a smile, paid him and went inside.

'Hi, Izzy.' Lily was so bubbly, so teenage, so bloody happy. Not a clue about real, adult life. Izzy had been like that once. In Izzy's case, when she was twenty-two, an idiot who'd asked a complete stranger out, genuinely believing that she'd been struck by love at first sight. For God's sake. 'Did you have a lovely evening?'

'Hi, Lily. Yes, thank you, really nice. I hope you've had a good evening. How was Ruby's bedtime story?' Izzy was struggling to remember how to hold a normal conversation. Now that she was home, she just wanted to sit in the kitchen, by herself, and howl. And swear. Again, bastard. Who spoke to people like that? 'Nearly midnight. I mustn't keep you. Here's your cash. Thank you so much.'

Obviously, Lily had mislaid her shoes somewhere in Izzy's tiny house. Izzy just wanted to scream, 'Go in your socks then, we live in a bloody terrace of minute houses, it's only about ten feet to your front door, just *go*.' She didn't, she managed to stand and smile and not stamp her foot, while Lily searched and eventually found them next to the front door under her bloody coat. Why did she even *need* a coat when it was *summer* and she lived next door? Teenagers weren't supposed to feel the cold; what was wrong with her?

And, obviously, Lily's shoes were in fact DM boots, and she had to sit on the bottom stair and put her feet in really slowly. That's right, Lily, so important to make sure there are no wrinkles on the bottom of your socks when you're walking *ten feet*, and yes, Lily, make sure you do the laces *just bloody right*. Who'd have thought a person could be bubbly all the way through putting boots on? Bubble, bubble, chat, chat, bubble. And Izzy had to chat right back because otherwise Lily would tell her mother and Izzy would have a concerned neighbour asking her in the morning what was wrong.

Eventually, Lily bubbled her way out of the front door. Bubble, smile, bubble. Good *night*.

Izzy put the bolts on the door and went and sat down at the kitchen table, put her arms on top of the table, and her head on top of her arms, and wailed. Quietly, so that she wouldn't wake Ruby up.

She felt as if she'd lost her best friend. Which she hadn't, because Emma and Rohan were her best friends. Except she didn't fancy them, or love them the way she loved Sam. The way she *had* loved him, anyway, the Sam she'd thought she'd known.

And she'd acknowledged The Thing. The L word.

Her phone pinged. An email. From Sam. Maybe he was apologising. Maybe he was going to say that the reason he'd reacted like that was that he knew that Izzy was right and that he needed to sort his work-life balance out and he'd been stressed and he was sorry, and everything would be okay, they could be friends again. And ignore the kiss, because that was too big to deal with.

Hi Izzy,

I just wanted to check that you got home safely.

Best,
Sam

Best. He was *Besting* her. After everything they'd talked about over the past few months, everything they'd shared. And their *kiss*. He'd stepped back from two kisses to a Best, his whole name and no kiss. Fuck him. *Fuck* him.

She'd discussed her two best friends with him, for God's sake, while barely discussing him with them. She'd literally put him above them in the confidences stakes and now he was Besting her and *not* apologising. Okay, then.

Hello Sam,

Yes, thank you. I got a taxi immediately and am now home, sitting in my kitchen.

Thank you for a lovely evening.
Izzy

Good job the recipient of an email couldn't tell if you were crying when you wrote it.

Bastard. The Sam she'd thought she'd fallen in love with was a nice, decent, lovely person. The Sam who'd spoken to her like that in the pub was unfair, unpleasant and rude. Maybe he'd regretted the kiss.

Maybe it had been too intense for him. Maybe he was still mourning Lana. He'd paused for ages after he'd mentioned her in the pub. Maybe he'd created the argument on purpose because he didn't want anything serious to happen with Izzy because he still missed her.

Whichever, he'd still been unacceptably unpleasant.

Again, fuck him.

She started to trudge upstairs.

One thing this evening had underlined was that successful relationships weren't about passion and stars and all of that crap. They were about being able to find a common ground, talk about things, work together. Share the toothpaste, actually and metaphorically.

Probably the way this evening had ended had been a good thing. Stop any stupid daydreams of Izzy's once and for all.

She went into the bathroom and scrubbed off all her carefully applied make-up, her pathetic new lash-enhancing mascara and the remains of her glossy Charlotte Tilbury lipstick, until her face hurt. And then she went into her bedroom and threw her stupid, lovely, black silk underwear viciously towards the laundry bin, where *obviously*, because that was the kind of evening this had been, it landed on the floor, so she had to walk over and pick it up.

Chapter Twenty-Three

Sam

Sam knocked back three painkillers and a pint of water before he stepped into the shower. Your two-tablet dose, suitable for anyone over twelve, wouldn't get close to tackling this hangover. The way he felt physically this morning exactly matched his mood: black as hell.

He turned the shower as hot as he could take it. No. The steam was going to make his headache worse. He turned the temperature knob to cold. He really needed an extreme shower today. And, jeez, that was extreme. He did feel a little better when he stepped out of the shower, though. Physically, anyway.

Mentally, not so much. Izzy had forced him to confront the fact that he had zero work-life balance and should do something about it. And then he'd been an asshole to her and ruined their friendship. Although maybe their kiss had already ruined it. It had been awkward in the pub even before he'd been so snarky to her. Snarky was an understatement. He'd been outright nasty.

He wrapped his towel round his waist and looked at himself in the bathroom mirror. And there was the face of someone who'd messed up big time. The only thing in his life that he was succeeding in was his job. And for what?

All of his relationships were heading towards disaster in one way or another. Kids, family, friends. He had no time for any of them and it was really starting to show. Liv and Barney, his mother, Izzy. And who had to be asked by text by someone who lived in the same state to be godfather?

He should probably apologise to Izzy. He'd hurt her, he knew that, and it felt terrible. But he couldn't. He should have followed her out of the pub, said sorry, explained to her that the reason he'd rounded on her like that was that everything she'd told him was true, and he couldn't deal with it. And that he probably wouldn't have lost it so much if he hadn't been freaked out by their kiss.

But since – even if he hadn't been betraying Liv – he couldn't deal with the way he felt about Izzy, because if there was one thing he'd learned in the past fourteen or so years, it was that love hurt, and he didn't want any more hurt, he hadn't gone after her. And when he'd worried that she might not have gotten home safely, he'd sent her a really shitty, over-formal email to check in on her. From her response, and from common sense, he was fairly sure that his email had hurt her too.

He started brushing his teeth. He was thinking about his relationship with Lana now, the first time he'd properly thought about it for years. He hadn't been *in* love with her, but during their short marriage he'd grown to love her, because she was a nice person and a good mother. When she'd died, despite the fact that theirs hadn't been a passionate love and maybe they wouldn't have stayed together forever, he'd been devastated. And with the twins, seeing everything they'd been through after the accident, watching them hurting in different ways had nearly killed him. Loving someone was basically a special kind of torture. One that you'd be insane to choose.

Yesterday evening, dinner with Izzy and then their kiss had been mind-blowing. He was right on the brink of falling deeply in love with her. Maybe he'd already fallen. Whatever, he needed to haul himself back up to the precipice and out of the trough that love was. And get on with his life.

He rinsed his mouth.

Better get dressed and go to his breakfast meeting, since work was the only thing that was going well in his life. And it was low risk emotionally. No love involved.

PART THREE

Chapter Twenty-Four

Izzy

'Hello, hello.' Emma burst into Izzy's hall in a flurry of hugs and chirpiness. She was followed by a smiling Rohan. Okay, good, so they'd obviously got over their argument. Although if Izzy was honest, cheerful people were really pissing her off today. She'd been tempted all day to pull a sickie to get out of climbing this evening, but Emma had sent several texts of the 'Yay, it's climbing tonight' genre, so she'd felt too guilty. Plus, a physical workout would probably be a good thing. 'You look tired. Are you okay?' Emma had pulled out of their hug and was holding Izzy's shoulders and studying her face.

'Yes, fine.' Izzy did her best 'I am very much looking forward to climbing' smile. She was *so* glad now that she hadn't told Emma that she was going out for dinner with Sam. It had been bad enough avoiding questions about him before. Now she *really* didn't want to talk about him. 'How's your day been?'

'Good,' Emma and Rohan both said at the same time, and then looked at each other and smirked. What? Weird. Whatever. Izzy didn't have the emotional energy to think about why other people were in good moods.

Emma was on fine form all evening, producing some great one-liners. She even summoned up some tolerance from somewhere when a new single, who was sweet but very unfunny and very much not Emma's type, asked her for her number at the end. She seemed to have lost interest in the Tom Cruise-alike, but she was nice to him.

While Emma was buckling up in the passenger seat of Izzy's car after climbing, Izzy snuck a look at her phone. And no, no email from Sam. Although there wouldn't be, because he'd probably be somewhere over the Atlantic now.

He hadn't emailed all day. Maybe he was never going to email again.

Emma turned the radio on and started singing along to Pharrell Williams' 'Happy', making the song her own, as Simon Cowell might say. Bloody *hell*. Izzy truly loved Emma, but she wasn't really up for this level of happiness in anyone. She just wanted to be miserable alone.

'Are you definitely okay?' Emma asked over the mint teas that Rohan had very kindly made for them when they got back, while Izzy screamed *Just go home* in her mind.

'Yes, sorry, just really tired. Been a busy week. You know. Work. Ruby.'

'We should let you get to bed then.' Rohan stood up, fast, and carried his and Emma's barely touched cups of tea over to the sink. He was blatantly eager to get away. Obviously he'd just been being polite in making the tea. Good.

And finally they'd gone, after what felt like only about a hundred more happy hugs from Emma, to a background of nice smiles and a couple of back pats from Rohan.

Normally, Izzy might well have told Sam about Emma and Rohan getting on again, but obviously she wasn't going to be emailing him this evening.

She did hear from him late afternoon on Saturday, after a miserable day trying to be a happy mother for Ruby and then a happy therapist for Barney while Ruby watched *Frozen 2*.

Hi Izzy,

Thank you for Barney's session. He enjoyed it as always.
    He said that he forgot to ask you for another cake recipe and
asked me if I could remind you on his behalf.

Best,
Sam

Yep. She should send a recipe. The kids shouldn't suffer in this.

It occurred to her that she'd had exactly the same thought about
Ruby when she and Dominic had split. This argument with Sam
literally felt like a break-up, which was utterly ridiculous. She counted
on her fingers. Yes. They'd met precisely six times ever. It didn't exactly
compare to a marriage. She should stop being so pathetic.

Hi.

Courgette and sultana loaf recipe attached. You might be scepti-
cal initially but you'll love it.

Izzy

There. Good email. Rising very well above the situation, dignity intact.

She checked her emails at least fifty times, not so dignified, before
a reply came through a couple of hours later, a boring one, containing
extremely mild humour. Izzy didn't bother to reply.

Sam sent another email, on Sunday evening, as Izzy was getting
into bed after a very dull day. Ruby had been out with Dominic, while

Izzy did chores and tried not to cry. On the upside, she wasn't going to need to do any housework for the rest of the week.

Just more recipe talk; nothing to get excited about. Like, say, an apology.

Izzy could barely be bothered to lift her typing finger to reply. But she shouldn't be petty and Sam was clearly making an effort, albeit a small one, presumably for Barney's sake, and she should too. She sent some brief-but-friendly recipe chat.

Sam pinged straight back. Apparently he was intrigued by her recipe suggestion.

Whatever.

*

Izzy's phone started ringing as she dolloped a portion of their regular Tuesday veggie lasagne onto Ruby's plate. Nobody she wanted to speak to ever called at five thirty in the afternoon. Probably someone to tell her that they *knew* she'd been involved in a car accident and could definitely help her sue someone for many thousands of pounds. She ignored it and started to load the dishwasher.

The phone started ringing again. She glanced over at it. It was actually Dominic. Odd.

'Hi, Dominic.' She wedged the phone between her cheek and shoulder and picked up two dirty saucepans.

'Iz, hello. I'm calling with bad news, I'm afraid. There's no good way to say this. My father died this afternoon.'

'Oh my goodness. I'm so sorry.' Izzy put the pans down to hold onto her phone properly and sat down hard on a chair at the table, opposite Ruby. 'What happened?' Dominic's father was, or had been, she should say, in his late sixties and in seemingly very good health.

'Heart attack.'

'I'm so, so sorry.' Dominic was an only child and very close to his parents. He was going to be distraught. 'How's your mother and where are you now?'

'A neighbour's with her. I'm at work, just finishing things up, because I'll probably be out of the office for at least a week, and then I'm coming back. Could you tell Ruby for me?'

'Of course.'

'And could you bring Ruby for the weekend? To my parents' house? And could you stay?'

'Of course.'

Izzy finally sat down on the sofa to watch some mood-lifting junk TV at about 10 p.m., after explaining to a thankfully uncomprehending Ruby that her grandfather had died, and then, after much hesitation about whether or not she should, phoning Dominic's mother Helena to say how sorry she was. She'd expected to be on the phone to Helena only very briefly, or perhaps not at all, if the neighbour was screening her calls for her, but in fact Helena had wanted to talk, and cry, to Izzy for a good forty-five minutes. It was, obviously, deeply sad speaking to someone who'd just lost their life partner. Helena had been only twenty when she'd met David, Dominic's father. She was now sixty-five, with maybe another twenty or thirty years ahead of her, and it was hard to imagine how she was going to cope with all those years.

Izzy needed some sharp and vulgar TV humour before she went to bed. As she pressed Menu on the remote, her phone pinged. So selfish, but *please* let it not be Dominic.

It was an email from Sam. Izzy put her phone down without reading it and focused on the television.

Okay, this was supposed to be cheering her up but she couldn't concentrate. She might as well just read whatever the arse had to say.

Izzy. Hi.

I wanted to apologise for the way I spoke to you in the pub on Thursday evening.

Sam

Izzy clicked off his message, very carefully, and leaned her head against the back of the sofa. Her eyes were stinging. One tear escaped and then another. That was a crap apology.

An actual, proper, apology would have been something along the lines of '*Hey*' (not Hi, because before he'd always Hey-ed her) *I'm so sorry about Thursday, I don't know what came over me, I think it's because you hit the nail on the head, I took out my stress on you, and I'm really sorry. Here are a few lovely, caring questions about what you've been up to and now here are some little stories and jokes about what I've been doing. Sam xx. And P.S. That kiss was out-of-this-world amazing and it definitely meant something but it won't impact on our friendship in a negative way at all because neither of us will let it, will we?*

For heaven's sake. She could hardly see now because of the tears. So stupid. She was going to sniff hard, not reply, watch some great TV for an hour, not think about Sam any more and get a good night's sleep so that she'd be on good form for Dominic this week.

*

She realised mid-week that she'd have to email Sam to let him know that she couldn't do Barney's session at the weekend. She stuck in an acknowledgement of his apology, and an apology of her own for having interfered. He replied within minutes.

Hey Izzy,

No apology necessary.

I'm so sorry to hear about the passing of Dominic's father.

We completely understand, and Barney will look forward to his next session with you whenever you're ready.

I agree that it would be great for him if we could start to reduce the frequency of the sessions.

He tells me that the recipe looks "weird but awesome." Thank you.

Our very best,
Sam

Once Barney didn't need any further sessions, there'd be no reason for Izzy and Sam to stay in touch. This would have been like a silly holiday romance that had slightly broken her heart. Honestly, pathetic. Actually, it was a good thing that she and Sam had argued. Now she could get over her childish crush once and for all and get on with real life.

*

Sometimes one day could drag on for an incredibly long time.

By the time Izzy was reading Ruby's bedtime story on Saturday evening, breakfast that morning seemed like a far distant memory. And there were at least another two or three hours to get through before she could reasonably go to bed herself.

Breakfast had been as normal and then things had gone downhill.

Packing for the weekend had been difficult – should you wear sombre clothing when it was going to be a funereal atmosphere? Izzy didn't own a lot of sombre clothes. She hadn't felt as though she should wear her normal bright colours; it felt disrespectful to David's memory and to Helena's grief. Helena was very big on people dressing appropriately for the occasion and Izzy suspected that, even when suddenly bereaved, she'd notice what her ex-daughter-in-law was wearing.

In the end, Izzy had worn navy trousers and bought a navy top on a dash with Ruby in and out of a Whistles she'd spotted en route to the M4 on their way to Oxfordshire. The only parking space had been on a double yellow, so she'd shopped as fast as she could, without trying the top on, or looking at the label, which had caused her two nasty surprises. Three, if you counted the fact that it had turned out to be dry clean only.

The first nasty surprise had been the price (huge) and the second, during her service station car park change, had been that the top was more cropped than she'd thought, so unless she breathed in uncomfortably hard and hunched a bit, she was flashing an embarrassing amount of untanned slight tummy roll above her, thankfully, very high-waisted cigarette trousers. Unfortunately, the top she'd swapped it with was a primrose yellow t-shirt with the word HAPPY printed on the front in rainbow colours – what had she been *thinking* when she got dressed – so she had no choice but to go with the navy one.

The traffic had been bad, which would have been fine, because self-ishly Izzy had no wish to arrive early and see Helena and Dominic for longer, except Ruby had whinged non-stop from literally before they'd even got onto the motorway about the fact that Izzy had forgotten to charge her iPad or bring a charger.

The rest of the day had been worse. Helena and Dominic were both, unsurprisingly, wearing their grief very visibly, Helena in pretty much permanent tears, and Dominic looking drawn and much older, haggard really.

Helena had snapped out of her tears for long enough to say, 'Interesting choice of top, Isobel,' and that was it. Straight back to the tears. Understandably.

They'd spent the whole day together. The rest of the morning. Lunch. The afternoon. Early dinner with Ruby. Crying. Talking. Crying. Reminiscing. Crying. Panicking about a future with no David in it. Crying. And now it was 8 p.m. and when Izzy went downstairs she was going to have to endure more of it. Obviously, she was evil incarnate but she *really* wanted a break from Helena and Dominic.

She decided to read another chapter of *The Magic Faraway Tree* to Ruby.

Eventually, Ruby nodded off and Izzy was reading to herself. She was going to have to gird her loins and re-join the others.

Maybe she'd be lucky and Helena and Dominic would like to have some time to themselves. Maybe she could just go and read in her room and leave them to it.

'Isobel, darling.' Helena had obviously been weeping a lot more while Izzy was upstairs. She had new tear streaks through the powder on her cheeks, underneath the panda rings a mixture of all-day-crying and non-waterproof mascara had given her. Izzy hugged her, again.

She'd hugged her a lot today. However annoying someone had been as a mother-in-law, you could only feel sympathy for them when you saw them in this state. 'I thought that it would be good for Dominic to be able to talk, get things off his chest. Why don't I babysit Ruby while you and he go for a walk, or to the pub?'

Really?

Izzy turned to Dominic, wondering which of them should tell Helena that, honestly, he'd rather stay at the house with her.

Dominic was nodding and smiling at her.

Okay. Izzy was going to have to go with it.

'Absolutely,' she said. 'Great.'

'Pub?' Dominic said when they got outside.

'If you like?' Izzy had a very clear memory of the day her grand-mother had died. She definitely wouldn't have wanted to go to the pub, and Dominic had loved his father a lot. But everyone was different.

'Yes, I think so.'

The pub was one of those very old ones, with a lot of tiny rooms. They sat in one of the two booths in a miniature room, where no-one could see them, and Dominic talked and talked about his father and his loss, and how worried he was about his mother, and Izzy listened and felt very sad for him. Basically, an extension of how the day had been, minus Helena.

'We should probably go back.' Dominic looked at his watch, with obvious and understandable reluctance. 'It's eleven o'clock.' He had to deal with the stress of seeing his mother like that on top of his own grief. Awful.

It was dark now. Outside the pub, Dominic flicked the torch on his phone on. The village had no street lights and a lot of potholes.

'Could we go the long way round?' he asked.

'Of course.' This was clearly not the moment to mention that she was wearing suede pumps, which would probably be ruined by walking over the field on the long way. Izzy shouldn't even be *thinking* about her shoes at a time like this.

As they walked, Dominic took Izzy's hand. She nearly jumped when their hands first touched. It was such a surprise. It was okay, though. Familiar, and clearly for comfort.

In the middle of the field, he stopped, turned to face her and put his arms out. Izzy hesitated for a moment and then stepped forwards and hugged him.

He just stood there, hugging her really tightly. And, actually, it was quite pleasant. His body was, or had been, so familiar to Izzy. She wasn't completely comfortable, because her feet were getting wet and she *knew* that her shoes were getting more ruined by the second, although obviously she should so one hundred per cent not be thinking about footwear. She should just focus on comforting Dominic. It *was* comfortable.

Until he reached his hand out to cup her chin.

Did he want to kiss her?

No, no, no. Not the moment for it. If anything was ever going to happen between them again, she needed to be prepared for it and it needed not to be when his father had just died.

She moved her chin away from his hand and shook her head. 'I don't think it's the right time. For you. Now. This week. With your father.'

Dominic looked at her for ages, and then said, 'You're probably right. Thank you. Always wise. I've missed you, Iz.' She smiled at him. When she thought about it, she'd definitely missed him too in certain ways. He was a nice man.

He put his hand out again for her to hold. She took it, and they started walking. This time it felt quite normal and companionable.

Her shoes were completely and utterly soaked and mud-stained beyond repair by the time they got back to the house.

Helena, in the midst of more crying, nonetheless looked at them and said, 'Oh dear.' Really, Izzy should be proud that her inappropriate top and footwear had provided Helena with brief respite from full-on grief.

Izzy left the shoes at the back door and she and Dominic went into the sitting room with Helena. They sat with her for another hour of crying and comforting, at which point Helena said that she thought they should all go to bed. Yessssss. *Finally*. A break from the crying.

'You two are in the blue room,' Helena told Izzy and Dominic. What? No. Surely not. If in the midst of her grief Helena could function sufficiently to register what Izzy was wearing, surely she could function enough to remember that Izzy and Dominic were *separated* and therefore put them in *separate* rooms. Her house was large, six-bedroomed and several-bathroomed. There was definitely no need for them to share. Izzy would happily make a bed up for herself if necessary.

Standing behind Helena, she shook her head and did some you-tell-her eye signalling at Dominic.

Dominic, standing in front of Helena, twitched his head a very small amount at Izzy, smiled at his mother and said, 'Great, thank you.'

This was unbelievable. It would be like a clichéd scene from a rom-com *if* Dominic were the hero in Izzy's life.

And maybe he was. Maybe it had been a mistake splitting up, maybe they'd just needed to find a way to rub along more comfortably. Maybe they'd just needed to make a conscious effort to spend quality time together. And, sure, it was a long time since she'd really fancied him. But maybe that was the same with all couples, the familiarity-breeds-contempt thing. Although, could she ever stop fancying Sam? Christ. Why was he in her head now?

Anyway, whatever. She and Dominic *had* split up and they should not be sharing a bedroom.

But Dominic was in the hall, picking up Izzy's bag and walking up the stairs with it. Which meant that Izzy could either point out to Helena herself that they shouldn't be sharing, or just follow Dominic.

She looked at the quietly crying Helena and couldn't do it. 'Good night,' she said. 'I hope you manage to sleep.'

In the blue room, door closed behind them, Izzy whispered, 'Why did she put us in here together and why didn't you say anything about it to her? She does *know* we're separated, surely?'

'I think she thinks it might have been temporary.' Dominic was screwing his face up, like a small child lying.

'What?'

'I think I might have told my parents that. Not to upset them. People in our family don't get divorced.'

Izzy made a very big effort and didn't shout *What the hell were you thinking?* She could see why he'd done it. His parents would obviously have wanted a long and successful marriage like their own for their only son. And, like many people, Dominic didn't like difficult conversations. And being in Milan he could easily have explained away not seeing them together all year.

'Right. Well, we can't share a bed, can we? We're separated,' she said, still managing not to shout.

'Of course we can. We were married for eight years. We know everything about each other.'

'Everything?' Izzy couldn't help asking. Something made her say it. Even though it was so very much neither the time nor the place. Dominic's eyes shifted sideways and back again and he looked her very carefully in the eye.

'Yes.' And then his eyes shifted *again* and then he made a clear effort to re-look her in the eye. Wow. Blatantly lying. *Wow*. He must have slept with someone – maybe several people – since they split. Or maybe even before. No, she was sure he hadn't been unfaithful before they split. Wow. Did it hurt? Yes, it did. But should it? They *were* separated, currently, even if they might get back together in the future. It wasn't like she hadn't snogged the face off Sam, and, if she was honest with herself, of course she'd have slept with him at that point, if they'd been in a room with a bed in it, or no bed actually, she'd have totally done it on a sofa or on the floor.

Suddenly she was really tired, and she just didn't care about the inappropriate bed sharing. She just wanted to sleep.

'I'll get changed in the bathroom.' Thank goodness she'd brought modesty-maintaining, high-necked, very comfortable pyjamas. Her one clothing success of the weekend. She'd wear her bra under them to prevent any jiggling of the sort you wouldn't do for someone you weren't shagging. 'And we can put a pillow down the middle of the bed.'

Izzy was *really* tired. She started nodding off to sleep very quickly.

And then a snuffle from Dominic's side of the bed pinged her into wide awakeness.

'Dominic?'

He said nothing, just snuffled a bit more. Izzy moved her head closer to his. He was crying, his face buried in the pillow, like a little boy. She couldn't ignore it. He was a human being and Ruby's dad and, as he'd said, they were married for eight years. She wasn't *in* love with him now but she did still care about him. She put her arms round him from behind, and he turned towards her and hugged her in tightly to him and cried and cried. Izzy cried a bit too, and eventually they rolled over and went to sleep, back to back. Comfortably.

And it was actually comfortable when they woke up in the morning. Izzy got fully dressed in the bathroom before she came out and left the room, with her suitcase packed, just as Dominic came out of the shower, still damp, with a towel round his waist. He was actually a very attractive man. Maybe not as attractive as Sam, but, unlike Sam, he'd never been unpleasant to her. They'd had the odd minor argument and that was it. You were probably better off with someone who might not make you feel good fireworks, but also didn't make you feel bad ones.

Sunday was pretty much a repeat of Saturday, minus the near kiss with Dominic. Izzy was extremely thankful late on Sunday afternoon that she had to go to work on Monday, so that she and Ruby *had* to leave. She got an email from Sam just before she went to bed, hugely relieved to be in her own bedroom at home in London. A polite one, about their latest cake, and asking about her weekend. Signed 'S'.

Izzy started to tap out a reply describing the awfulness of the weekend, and then she deleted it because, despite the thawing in his tone, she and Sam weren't actually that close. He'd shown a side of himself she didn't recognise at all and, really, how well did she *actually* know him? A lot less well than she knew Dominic.

Chapter Twenty-Five

Sam

This was new. Sam was thumb twiddling while the kids were busy in their bedrooms, doing homework in Barney's case and who knew what in Liv's. He pressed the button on the remote a few times. There was nothing he wanted to watch in real time right now and he couldn't be bothered to hunt through Netflix. Really, what was the point of his having taken a break from his work?

Izzy probably wasn't going to reply to his email today. She'd probably be going to bed in the next hour or two. Normally, that would mean that he'd get a response from her in the morning, but he wasn't holding his breath for tomorrow. Basically, it looked as though he'd ruined their friendship. He flicked through a few more channels. Really. Nothing. Maybe he'd text Luke or Ash. Call his mother. Go for a run. Read something.

All quite unappealing. What he *wanted* was an email from Izzy.

He should not have spoken to her like that in the pub. He'd clearly hurt her badly, when she'd just been trying to help, as a great, caring friend. He'd lashed out, partly because he didn't know how to change his life and partly because he just couldn't do romance with someone he might actually love. Who lived in London.

And then he'd sent a really crappy apology. And now they weren't really talking.

So he'd completely destroyed their friendship.

Or had it already been destroyed by their kiss? Was it inevitable that it would have been destroyed eventually, because the attraction between them was too great?

Love.

If two people were in love, could they ever happily just be friends?

He turned the TV off and threw the remote to the other end of the sofa. Really, there was nothing on that any person with a brain could stand to watch.

Whether or not he and Izzy could be friends again, he'd hurt her and he shouldn't have done that. Maybe he should break with the tradition they'd established and call her. No. Easier to write so that he could make sure he said everything he needed to. It had to be a proper apology. Maybe they could be penfriends again, maybe they couldn't, but he was going to do the right thing.

He needed to get the email right, including the title, to make sure she read it.

To: Izzy Castle
From: Sam McCready

Proper apology—I'm very sorry—please read?

Hey Izzy,

No preamble.

This, I hope, is going to be a proper apology for the way I spoke to you in the pub on Thursday evening.

The first thing to say is that you were absolutely right. I do have a work-life balance problem.

The twins are the most important thing in my life. I need to spend more time with them, particularly now as they, and I, navigate their teenage years, but I don't know how to do it without leaving my job, and I don't think I can leave my job. In short, I'm stressed.

But none of that excuses how I spoke to you. You were just trying to help and I lashed out. I was a complete asshole to you and for that I am truly sorry. I hope that I haven't destroyed our friendship, because I value it more than you know.

I hope that you can accept my apology.

I hope also that your weekend with your ex-husband and his mother wasn't too difficult, and that Ruby isn't struggling too much with the loss of her grandfather.

Sam xx

That had taken a long time. He'd considered mentioning their kiss in some way but hadn't managed to find the words. *That was literally the most perfect, amazing kiss of my life and immediately afterward I was forced to admit to myself that the reason that it was so good is that I love you, a lot, and have done for some time, and that freaked me out because I'm scared of getting hurt. Plus, my daughter hates you, and my first loyalty has to be to her.*

No. Obviously not. You didn't declare love if you weren't going to act on it. And he wasn't going to lie to her and tell her that the kiss didn't mean anything, because that would be really shitty of him. So he hadn't mentioned it at all, hadn't given that additional background to why he'd lashed out so hard. She'd just have to think that his stress had been the entire factor behind his behaviour. Or maybe she'd know already that the kiss had played a part in it.

He re-read the email, pressed Send and dropped his phone on the sofa next to him. Done.

And now he was going to haul the kids out of their rooms and spend some quality time with them.

'Liv, Barney,' he hollered. And again.

'What?' Liv said, when Sam had got himself off the sofa and was knocking on her door.

'Come to the kitchen?' he asked. 'And hang out? Cook bolognese with me? And then maybe watch TV together? Or play a game?'

'Maybe.' Eventually she opened the door. 'We could watch TV after dinner. And we could make a cake for dessert. If you don't think it's boring.'

'Never boring. That sounds great.' Sam smiled at his daughter, delighted, and she smiled back, a proper smile. He knocked on Barney's door. 'Barney? Come and join us?'

So this was nice. The three of them in the kitchen together. Alright, anyway. Barney had been pretty silent the whole time, but Liv had been chattering away.

'We need music,' Liv said. 'I left my phone upstairs. Can I use your phone, Dad?'

'Sure.' Sam. 'It's on the sofa.'

Sam, busy getting onions and carrots out to start chopping, didn't register immediately that she'd gone quiet, until she said, voice shaking, 'You lied. I *hate* you. You saw her in London.'

Liv was holding his phone towards him, her arm completely straight. He'd left it open on his emails and Izzy had replied while he'd been upstairs.

'You *lied*.' Liv had upped the volume of her voice. 'I hate you.'

'You read my email. That's unacceptable.' And not what he should be focusing on right now. 'Liv. Listen.'

'Listen?' Liv screeched. 'You want me to listen to you telling me that it's unacceptable for me to read your emails?' She drew a deep breath and then said, so quietly that Sam had to lean in to hear her words, 'You're trying to tell me that it's more unacceptable for me to read your emails than it is for you to lie to me and tell me you love me and that you won't see that woman any more? Insane.' And then she threw his phone on the floor and the screen shattered.

'You broke my phone.' Christ. What was wrong with him? Again, not exactly the most important issue here.

'And *you* broke my *trust*.' Liv turned and marched out of the kitchen, slamming the door behind her.

Barney was looking at Sam in silence, eyebrows almost meeting his hair.

Sam decided to follow Liv. She already had her bedroom door firmly closed behind her when he got there. He knocked. Nothing.

'Liv. I love you so much. There's nothing between me and Izzy.' He wished he could remember exactly what he'd said in the email, and that he knew what Izzy's reply had said. How bad had it looked to Liv?

Liv turned her music up. At that volume it could damage her ears.

'Turn it down,' Sam yelled. She turned it up higher. 'Okay, I'm going,' he yelled harder. She turned it up even more. Clearly, this was not the way to talk to her.

Barney had gone when Sam got back to the kitchen, presumably holed up in his bedroom again.

Sam Scotch-taped his phone screen and read Izzy's reply.

Hi Sam

Thank you so much for your email.

I'm sure that I could have phrased things a LOT better in the pub, and I'm sure also that if I hadn't left so quickly, maybe we'd both have felt better at the time; I'm sorry on both counts. Your apology is completely accepted and I hope that you can accept mine in return.

The weekend was not fun, obviously. Dominic and his mother are both incredibly upset. His parents were happily married for a long time and I'm not sure how Helena, his mother, is going to cope on her own.

Ruby's okay.

Hope you're having a good day today.

Izzy x

Under any other circumstances, he'd be trying to work out if this meant he and Izzy were friends again, but now he was trying to work out how bad her reply – and his own email – had sounded to Liv. Very fortunate that neither he nor Izzy had mentioned the kiss. If he replied, he'd better remember to delete the email. Cover his tracks. From his own daughter.

This was a ridiculous situation to be in.

He typed out a WhatsApp to Liv explaining that he loved her and that he'd met Izzy for dinner because it had already been arranged, and that they'd had an argument about nothing in particular and he'd thought that he should apologise, but that that was all.

His message got two grey ticks which did not turn blue.

Liv did turn her music off eventually but she wouldn't open her bedroom door before Sam went to bed, and didn't reply when he knocked on the door and WhatsApped again to say good night.

After a terrible night during which Sam had a nightmare – for the first time since talking to Izzy in Hyde Park – about Liv and the aftermath of the accident, he was up early and off to a breakfast meeting with Jim Buck at the Waldorf Astoria.

Back in the office, he was ploughing through a large pile of documents when his secretary buzzed him with an urgent call. It was Penny Ellis, the school secretary. Not again. She'd called him three times already this trimester to arrange calls to discuss Liv's behaviour. So different from the younger, angelic Liv.

'Good morning, Mr McCready. This is Penny Ellis calling. Olivia hasn't arrived at school today. Could you confirm that she's ill?'

Everything about Sam froze in that moment. Face, body, ability to think, ability to speak.

'Mr McCready?'

'I don't know,' he managed. 'I'll call you back.'

She wasn't answering her cell phone.

Mrs H was in the apartment. 'She was fine this morning. She left at her normal time and said she was meeting her friends. Barney left early, obviously.'

'Obviously?'

'He has basketball practice before school on Mondays.' If Mrs H knew that, Sam should. He was their father.

'Which friends does she normally meet?' Sam should know that too.

Sam tried tracing her on the family app they shared. Her location permission had been turned off. He called the school back and asked them to ask her friends if she'd met them. And then he sat at his desk and tried not to panic. It would be okay. It had to be. She'd probably just forgotten to sign in or whatever it was that they did when they arrived at school. Another thing he didn't know and should do.

Penny Ellis called back after seven minutes. 'Liv didn't meet her friends, I'm afraid.'

The terror that washed over him was physically paralysing. Where *was* she? His beautiful, stroppy, innocent, vulnerable daughter. What had happened? He needed to pull himself together immediately and *do* something. The police. CCTV. He needed to *act*. Had she run away on purpose? Had she been abducted?

The police were great. Mrs H was great. School was great. His apartment building security team were great. They all had ideas about how to search for her and they were all going to start that search immediately. But none of them actually knew where she was. They were all just going to *try* to find her. They might all fail. It might already be too late.

Sam was on his feet, running through the office. He took the stairs because he couldn't wait for the elevator. He kept on running when he got to the sidewalk.

This was insane. He was jogging now, checking every above-average height, slim, blonde young woman he passed. Of course none of them were Liv. Better to be doing something than nothing, though.

His phone was ringing.

'Joshua from Security. We've found her on CCTV. She crossed the road and we think she went into the park.'

Sam upped his pace. Was she still there? What would she be doing? Had she gone in by one exit and left by another? Did she have secrets from him? Was she being groomed online? Or was this because of their argument last night?

His phone again. Mrs H.

'She left you a letter. I've taken the liberty of opening it.' Mrs H read it to him. It confirmed that Liv had run away because of their argument. She hadn't said where she was going.

Sam ran into the park. Liv loved the park. Maybe she was in here, just hiding out, needing to calm down. Maybe he'd jog down all their favourite paths. Maybe he'd find her here.

He didn't find her anywhere. His temples were pounding, and he could taste bile in his throat. What if they never found her? Or what if it was bad news when they did? No. If she'd run away on purpose, she'd have a plan. She was a great kid, a sensible kid.

His phone rang. His secretary. He was missing an important meeting. Whatever.

And then it rang again. The police.

So much bile in his throat.

They'd found her. On a train. Completely safe.

Sam leaned his forehead against a tree and cried.

'So.' They were sitting on the sofa in the kitchen and they'd both been crying. 'I love you, Olivia McCready. You took a lot of years off my life today.'

'I love you too, Daddy.' Liv's usual bravado was absent. She'd scared herself today, coming across some unsavoury characters who'd freaked her out. Sam had wanted to kill them when she told him what they'd said, but at least she'd learned a valuable lesson. Hopefully.

'I should have told you that I was meeting Izzy. She and I are friends. Nothing more. You don't have to like my friends. She's important to us because she's great for Barney. And you shouldn't have read my emails.

Although if you did read them carefully you will know that I told Izzy that you and Barney are the most important thing in my life.' Thank God he'd said that.

'Yeah, I did see that.'

'Right. Again, I love you. Is that a good summary of where we're at?'

'I think so. Yeah. It is. I'm sorry for scaring you. Sorry I broke your phone.'

'Hey. Phones can be repaired. I'm sorry I upset you so much and that we haven't been spending enough time together. Things are going to change.' He was serious about that.

Chapter Twenty-Six

Izzy

Shit, shit, shit, shit, *shit*, she was going to be late. There were sheep everywhere. Behind her, in front of her, on both sides of her. Izzy edged the car slowly forward and came very close to touching a couple of them. They didn't notice and they didn't move, at all. How did sheepdogs manage? A dog couldn't do as much damage as a car, could it? So why did sheep respond to dogs?

How dreadful to be late for a funeral. She needed to do something, fast.

Maybe if she got out. Maybe they responded better to people or animals than they did to vehicles.

No.

Sheep were surprisingly large when you saw them up close. She couldn't get out. There was one right up against the car and she couldn't get the door open. Again, *shit*. She'd been sitting here for minutes already, and she'd already been on a tight schedule, having left London later than she'd intended.

She rolled the window down and shouted, 'Shoo.' Nothing happened, obviously.

Maybe she could call the police and they could move the sheep.

Maybe the funeral cortege would be held up by the same sheep so she wouldn't be late.

Both unlikely.

And then she saw a shepherd at the front of the herd. A man dressed in a lot of brown and carrying a stick and surrounded by the sheep, anyway. He was definitely the person in charge of them, if anyone was.

'Excuse me,' she called. Nothing. She put her hands round her mouth and called again. Still nothing. She was actually going to miss Dominic's father's funeral. This was *awful*. Really, really awful. Dominic wanted her support, and whatever might or might not happen between them in the future, she did care about him and, if he wanted her there, she should be there. 'Move your bloody sheep,' she screamed. 'I'm missing a *funeral*.'

Miraculously, the man in brown turned round. He looked at her and then turned back round again. What the actual…? Izzy undid her seatbelt, and with a lot of effort and some pain, pulled herself up and out so that she was balanced half out of the car, through the open window.

'It's my father-in-law's funeral *right now*,' she yelled, so hard that it hurt her throat. 'I am *begging* you. Please. Move. The. Sheep.'

The man turned round, again, stared at her for a while, and then raised his stick at her. Then he turned back round and Izzy's eyes filled. What was she going to *do*? Could she *run* the rest of the way?

And then the man did some stuff with the stick and the sheep, and within a couple of minutes there was a path through the herd, thank the Lord.

She was still late. The vicar had started the service when she arrived out of breath at the back of the church. There was an empty pew at the back, thank goodness, ideal.

But no.

'Isobel?' The elderly man speaking was vaguely familiar to Izzy. Some distant family member perhaps. Maybe she'd met him at her wedding. 'Front pew.'

Walk of shame completed, in total silence, the vicar having obligingly paused for her while the entire congregation watched, Izzy was wedged between Dominic and his aunt, staring at the coffin in front of them.

As the vicar talked, Helena – sitting on the other side of Dominic – wept into a black-edged handkerchief, and Dominic sat very still. His shoulders started to move a little against Izzy at the same moment that Izzy herself was battling a very large lump in her throat. The vicar's mention of David's love of golf had conjured up an image of him lying in his coffin in a pale yellow V-neck jumper, golf slacks, stupid golf shoes and a big, infectious smile. Izzy reached her hand out to find Dominic's, and squeezed hard. He squeezed back and sniffed. Izzy rummaged in her bag with her other hand and then passed him a tissue. He carried on clinging onto her hand. Poor, poor Dominic. And Helena.

Izzy had known that Dominic was going to give a eulogy, because he'd run it past her on the phone, but she hadn't bargained for how affecting it would be as part of the service. Dominic looked so dignified, and his words hit exactly the right note between grief, pride in the man his father had been, and anecdote. Izzy's heart broke for him as he spoke, and tears trickled down her cheeks.

When he sat back down, he put his hand straight back into hers and it felt like the most natural thing in the world.

'Stay by my side all day?' Dominic whispered to her at the end of the service.

'Of course,' Izzy said.

Dominic and Helena had walked from Helena's house to the church, so Izzy drove them to the country house hotel where the wake was taking place.

'Such a comfort, dear Isobel.' Helena was sitting in the front seat. She was wearing black Chanel and pearls and looked a lot smaller than usual. Fragile. Her hair had always seemed blonde but suddenly it was all silver, like she'd aged significantly in a fortnight.

'Izzy's been wonderful,' Dominic said, doing nothing at all to dispel Helena's evident belief that Izzy and he were properly back together.

Maybe they *should* be.

'Family photo, family photo,' bossed Helena's cousin Annie, ushering them into a family grouping on the grand stately-home-esque steps of the hotel when they arrived. 'So nice to get everyone together for once.'

'It isn't nice, is it,' Dominic muttered. 'It's a bloody funeral.'

'Is that everyone?' the waiter who Annie had commandeered to take the photo asked.

'Stop.' Dominic's querulous and extremely elderly Great-Aunt Margaret lifted her walking stick to wave, and stumbled. 'David isn't here. He should be in the photo. Where's David?'

Helena moaned.

'Aunt Margaret has dementia,' Dominic explained unnecessarily to Izzy. He put his arm round Helena and took her inside while Annie called, 'We haven't finished taking the photo.'

'I'm so sorry,' Izzy told Margaret. 'David's passed away.'

'That's terrible.' A big fat tear rolled down Margaret's cheek. Izzy shouldn't have told her. If she couldn't remember, she was going to experience the shock a lot of times. Awful.

'Let me find you a chair and a drink of water.' She held out her arm for Margaret to lean on as they went inside.

'It's a complete bloody nightmare,' Dominic said to Izzy. Helena was with her sister and Margaret was with some other elderly relatives. 'I wish I could just walk out.'

'I'm so sorry.' Izzy reached up and gave him a hug. 'I'm here and I'm not going anywhere.'

'Thank you.' Dominic hugged her back, hard.

For the duration of the meal, Izzy stood with Dominic while he received condolence after condolence.

'Where's David?' Margaret shouted, at least three more times. She had an excellent set of lungs for such an old and infirm-looking woman. Helena cried each time.

Finally, a couple of people started to make moves to leave.

'Goodbye, dear. You've been very brave.' Dominic's Great-Aunt Laura, Margaret's younger sister, was the first to get to the door. She was hunched very oddly. Maybe she had a back problem or something.

'Thief,' shouted a waiter. Laura dived for the door. The waiter was a lot younger and a lot faster and got to her before she was completely through the door.

Izzy was the closest to them and gasped as he reached down Laura's blouse.

Laura was batting at his hand and screeching. Two of her buttons popped off and the blouse opened over a gilt candlestick, nestling between her beige all-in-one corseted bosoms.

'You can't arrest an old lady,' Izzy said.

'Sorry,' the waiter said, 'but they'd have taken it out of my wages.'

'Fair enough.' Dominic nodded. 'Could you?' He indicated sideways with his head. 'Given that it's a wake?'

'Yes, okay.' The waiter took the candlestick and returned inside while Dominic averted his gaze and Laura pulled her blouse closed.

An unrepentant Laura gave Izzy a hug and whispered in her ear, 'Still got an egg mayo sandwich and a pepper pot in my pocket,' and shuffled off.

'Once a kleptomaniac always a kleptomaniac, apparently,' Dominic said. 'For God's *sake*.'

Margaret was one of the last to leave.

'Where's David?' she asked on her way out.

Dominic and Izzy sat on a bench outside, holding hands, while Helena finished talking to David's siblings.

'If I'm honest,' Izzy said, 'I think that's the worst wake I've ever been to.'

'Yeah.' Dominic nodded. 'Total madhouse. Awful. Poor Margaret. Poor Laura. Poor bloody all of us.' He took his hand out of Izzy's and put his arm round her shoulders instead. 'Thank you so much for being here today. I don't think I could have coped without you.'

'Hey. Not a problem. Obviously.' Izzy meant it. Dominic was a big part of her life and always would be, whatever happened in the future, and when he needed her, she should obviously be there for him. She looked up at him. He was smiling down at her, his eyes doing their creasing thing. And now he was looking at her lips and moving his head closer. It didn't seem to Izzy as though there were about to be any fireworks, but this felt right nonetheless. He moved even closer and she inched towards him too.

And then Helena called, 'Are you ready, Dominic?' and they moved apart.

*

Izzy got home very late that evening. After she'd checked on a sleeping Ruby and thanked Lily from next door for minding her, she found a polite email from Sam asking how the funeral had been.

Emma and Rohan were both out and she really wanted to vent about her day from hell. Except she and Sam weren't that close any more. Since his second apology a couple of weeks ago, she'd barely heard from him. She should probably be polite, though. Nice of him to ask. She should probably send a quick one-liner.

Half an hour later, she had, somehow, in a moment of weakness, given him an exhaustive account of the hideousness of the day.

Hey,

Wow. Don't know how to reply to that other than to say I'm so sorry and please tell me you're home now and away from the madness, with Ruby in bed, and having a large glass of something. And again, wow. That's one hell of a bad day. Does this limerick (attached) help?

S Xxx

Izzy laughed so hard she snorted rosé. He was clearly a very skilled and fast composer of dirty limericks. She was tempted to reply with one of her own. Except it already felt strangely disloyal to Dominic to be talking to Sam about Dominic's father's funeral. She just sent a two-word 'Thank you' in the end.

*

Painting on Wednesday was a welcome relief from everything that had been going on. They did *The Scream*.

Surprisingly, given that apparently it symbolised the anxiety of the human condition, and Izzy wasn't exactly at her best emotionally, and Emma was beyond annoyingly chirpy tonight, Emma's was very good and Izzy's was truly rubbish.

'Great paintings.' Rohan was nodding earnestly.

'Yeah, mine's crap.' Izzy hoped they were going to go home soon. She'd been feeling permanently knackered since the argument with Sam, and David's death.

'So, we have news.' Emma was practically bouncing up and down.

'Do we?' Rohan said.

'Who does?' Izzy said.

'Don't we?' Emma said.

Rohan smiled at her. 'Yes, I think we do.'

'What?' Izzy said. '*What?*' The two of them were standing next to each other, beaming away, almost shoulder to shoulder, Emma being nearly six foot in her heeled boots. Izzy's gaze travelled down to where her two best friends were holding hands.

Yes, Emma and Rohan were holding hands. Their fingers were linked. Izzy stared. They were doing funny things with their hands, like they were having hand *sex*. Was that a *thing*? Izzy's gaze travelled back up. Emma's eyes were only about an inch below Rohan's and they were looking at each other in a nauseatingly soppy way.

'Oh my gosh, oh my gosh, oh my gosh,' Izzy said. 'No way, no way, no *way*. No bloody way.'

'Yes way.' Emma reached out to pull Izzy in for a three-way hug.

'No actual way,' Izzy screamed. 'Tell me everything. *Now.*'

'Firstly,' said Emma, 'sorry about the timing. It doesn't feel right to tell you now when Dominic's dad's just died and you had the funeral on Monday. But I wanted to explain why we've both been out at the same time quite a lot. I'm really sorry we were both busy on Monday. We were meeting Rohan's parents together and it was the only evening they could do for the next few weeks because they've got work and they're going away.' Rohan's parents were both very high powered in indescribable jobs, and travelled a lot. 'And obviously we really wanted to tell them but we felt terrible that neither of us were around to chat after the funeral.'

'Don't be silly.' Izzy did not want to admit that she felt ridiculously happy about the fact that there was an excellent reason for the fact that they'd both been busy on Monday evening. She'd tried really hard not to feel hurt but she hadn't totally succeeded. 'So what *happened*? *When* did it happen?' Now she was starting to think about it, so much made sense. And Sam had been right. No. Stop thinking about Sam. *Why* was he in her head when he shouldn't be? This was all about Rohan and Emma. 'So. Details. Now. No, actually, not *all* the details.'

'To cut a long story short,' Rohan said, smiling soppily again, 'we've been involved on and off for a long time but only recently admitted our feelings.'

'Oh, please.' Izzy shook her head. 'I'm prepared to stay up all night if necessary. That's far too short a long story. I'll get wine.'

'So basically,' Emma said, while Izzy poured, 'we slept together once after uni. Which was amazing. But nothing else happened for a while. I'm not really sure why. When you and Dominic were in Seattle we slept together quite a lot. Then when we were living together for those few months we shagged all the time. It was like we were together. Except neither of us said anything, so we weren't officially together and we never went out together, it was all just at home. And then it was time for Rohan to move out and I was too nervous to say anything because I'd realised that I loved him and I was scared he didn't feel the same way.'

'And I felt exactly the same,' Rohan said.

'So basically we pissed about for a while, no longer sleeping together, just arguing and getting pissed off and Rohan being an arse.'

'With good reason. When you saw other people.' Rohan smiled at Emma and dropped a kiss on her lips, which seemed to start as a quick affectionate peck, but carried on for a good few seconds longer than it should have done in front of Izzy.

'Sorry,' said Emma, a huge just-been-kissed smile on her face. 'And then we had a big argument after I nearly went out with that guy from climbing and stopped speaking, until Rohan phoned me up and told me he loved me. Honestly it was the best conversation of my life. Followed by the best sex of my life. And Rohan's, he tells me.'

'No, no, no,' said Izzy. 'I am *so* happy for you, I really am, but please, never talk to me about sex ever again. I really mean it.'

'And I'm so sorry about having had a secret from you.' Emma was screwing her face up like she was worried about Izzy's reaction.

'Don't be *silly*. I totally understand,' Izzy said. Which, actually, she did. She hadn't told Emma about kissing Sam. Sometimes, you just couldn't talk about enormous things.

'We've got a question for you,' Rohan said.

'Is it about sex?'

'No,' Emma said. 'Will you be my matron of honour?'

Izzy looked between the two of them. 'You mean…?'

Rohan nodded. 'We're getting married.'

Izzy screamed and screamed and hugged and hugged them, and then Ruby woke up because of the noise and joined in with the hugging.

'I'm so honoured,' Izzy said. 'Thank you for asking.' She felt an uncomfortable twinge of envy. Their love was so huge and so passionate and, now at least, so straightforward. She forced the feeling away. She was over the moon for them, of course she was. 'My two best friends. Love you both. I'm so happy that you're happy together.'

Chapter Twenty-Seven

Sam

'Many congratulations, Sam.' Robert Wade was finally winding up his unnecessarily lengthy monologue. 'And I have great news for you. As you step up to head up the M&A group, we'd like also to invite you to become a managing partner.' Good grief. Sam had not seen that one coming. 'Congratulations again.' Robert reached across the table to pump Sam's hand. 'You'll be the youngest managing partner in the history of the firm.' Exactly. Sam had thought he had at least another three or four years proving himself in the group head role before they'd offer him managing partner. Maybe even longer, so that the twins would have been at college.

He smiled. No option. This should be the best day of his career. Except if he took on the roles, he'd probably actually die. He'd certainly never see daylight again until he was about fifty. At which point the twins would be well into their twenties and he and they would hardly recognise each other. And he could kiss goodbye to any further personal involvement in lecturing or pro bono work.

'Thank you,' he said.

Robert drew his monobrow into a frown. 'You seem under-whelmed.'

'Overwhelmed,' Sam told him. 'It's hard to take in.' He needed to find some enthusiastic words. 'I'm hugely grateful for the trust you're placing in me and very excited about the future.'

'Excellent. Drinks with your fellow managing partners this evening to celebrate. We have a room at The Vine booked.'

'Perfect,' Sam said, keeping his smile going.

Disaster. After Liv's running away incident a couple weeks ago, he'd promised her that he'd set one weekday evening a week aside to spend with her and Barney. They'd had two great weekends together, but that had involved Sam surviving on minimal sleep because he'd had work to do.

This evening he was supposed to be going to a school presentation with them and then taking them out for dinner.

He'd worked so hard for his career to hit this point. And he'd worked so hard to parent the twins. It was obvious which one he was better at. And it was obvious what he was going to have to do now.

He got his phone out as soon as he left the meeting.

'Mom. Hi. I have news.'

When he told her, she sounded about as excited as he felt. 'Honey, I'm so proud of you but how are you going to cope?'

'I am going to cope *fine*,' he said. 'It's an honour. But I do have a favour. Could you and Dad go to the twins' school presentation for me this evening? And take them out for dinner?'

'Of course, honey.'

Liv was a harder sell than his mother. 'You promised,' she said.

'Yes, I did. I know that I'm letting you down. But this is huge. This is the biggest moment of my career other than making partner in the first place. And I'd love to take you two out on Saturday evening to celebrate with me.'

She ended the call while he was still saying 'me'.

His phone pinged with a message from Barney. 'Congratulations Dad.' That was something. But not enough. He needed Liv to be onside too. Assuming Barney even meant it.

He knew he wasn't going to enjoy the drinks this evening. He was going to spend the entire time worrying that Liv would think about running away again. Or worse.

Sam's mother was the best. She forwarded a video of the presentation so that he could watch it on his way to the drinks, and she sent regular messages during the evening telling him that the twins were doing *great*. In the end, he did enjoy the evening.

On his way home in a cab, watching couples strolling home under the street lights, he suddenly really wanted to talk to Izzy. Screw it, even if they weren't on the best of terms, he could send her an email. He wouldn't talk to her about Liv – it didn't feel like they were in the right place yet – but he could tell her about work.

It was late, middle of the night UK time, so Sam didn't get a reply from Izzy until he woke up on Friday morning.

Hi Sam,

Congratulations!! I'm so pleased for you and so impressed.

Well done!

Izzy x

P.S. I have a confession: you were right… EMMA AND ROHAN ARE TOGETHER! And getting married! Seems I was the last to guess. Even Dominic suspected (or so he says)! X

So she was spending time with Dominic. Natural, probably, because he'd just lost his father and they'd had the funeral. It still felt a bit off, though. Kind of Izzy, anyway, to congratulate him and not to mention that his new role was blatantly the exact opposite of the better work-life balance that he'd admitted he needed.

Maybe he'd just ask how Dominic was when he replied to her.

Hey,

Thank you!
    Your two best friends getting married—huge! When are they planning the wedding for?
    Obviously, I'm not going to say "I told you so." Although, I did.
    How's Dominic doing?

S x

By Friday evening, she'd replied and Sam had found out that she was going out for dinner with Dominic this weekend. Right. No reason that she shouldn't, of course. But was it a good idea to go out with your ex?

Sam really didn't like Dominic's name. It sounded stupid. As did the man himself. If you were married to Izzy, why would you separate from her? Why would you move to Milan without her? Or behave in a way that caused her to want to separate from you? And that thought reminded him uncomfortably of his own behaviour.

Back to Izzy. Why had she told Sam that she was going for dinner with Dominic? Did she want him to comment? He was not going to do that.

Sam's mood wasn't improved by the fact that he was working late and Liv was ignoring him. His last message had received two blue ticks and she was online but she wasn't replying. Your basic 'If you're busy, I'll be busy too' ploy. It was working. He wasn't happy. And he was yet again WhatsApp stalking his daughter, not cool.

And then he got an email from Barney's account. His own children had emailed him at work.

Hi.

We'd like to go and live with Granny and Gramps. They love us. You have no time for us.

We'd tell you in person except we never see you.

Liv and Barney

Sam dropped the slice of pizza he was holding back into the box. It was very difficult to swallow the mouthful that he was chewing.

It had to have been written by Liv. Damn, that girl would make a fine attorney. Clearly, he wasn't a parenting expert. But he was sure that thirteen-year-olds didn't normally write emails like this.

He was their only parent. And he wasn't going to have any more children. He didn't want to become that fifty-year-old who no longer recognised his own kids or sunlight.

His stomach and throat were pinching. He really couldn't eat this pizza.

He called Liv's number. She actually answered.

'Liv. Hi. I got your email. I'm on my way home right now.'

'Whatever.' She ended the call.

When he strode into the kitchen twenty-five minutes later, Liv was leaning against the wall, her arms folded across her body and her lips clamped shut. Barney was lounging on the sofa at the end of the room.

'Liv, Barney.' Sam placed himself in the middle of the long wall behind the dining table, where he could see both of them. He'd thought and he'd planned during his journey home. This was a conversation that he really needed to get right. 'I love you both so much. I've made vague promises of spending more time with you and I've let you down. Now I have a concrete suggestion for you and I'd like to discuss that with you.'

There was a long silence and then Liv said, 'I don't think we trust you.'

Sam waited but Barney continued to say nothing.

'Understandable,' Sam said eventually. 'No reason that you should trust me, obviously. Actions do speak more loudly than words. But I'd be very grateful if you would listen.'

Neither of them spoke.

Sam looked at the table. 'Shall we sit down?'

'Nope.' Liv still wasn't looking at him. Barney still wasn't speaking.

'Okay. Alright. My suggestion is that from now on I block out in my diary one day a week, every week, to work from home. And in the evening on that day I will not do any work of any kind including important meetings or client dinners or drinks. Nothing. Non-negotiable. All my previous attempts at carving out time have failed because I haven't been specific enough.'

Neither of them replied.

'I love you both so much and I don't want to fail you. I know that I could do more than what I've suggested, but I think it could be a good start.' It would be very difficult to operate workwise, but he was going to do it. It felt like this was a last chance to develop a good relationship with his children.

Barney suddenly spoke out of the blue. 'It should be Wednesday.' Like Izzy. She worked from home on Wednesdays.

Liv nodded. 'He's right. Then we would only have two days in a row where we don't see you. *If* you stick to it.' *Yes.*

'I promise you I will.' Sam couldn't remember ever being so serious about a promise. He was so serious that he wasn't even slightly worried about how it would go down at work. It would just have to. Maybe he could sell it as their firm being trailblazers for modern working practices in the world of corporate law.

'Let's start blocking your diary out now,' Liv said. She walked over to the table and sat down. 'Come on.' Yes. This felt like such a victory.

Sam took his phone out and flicked his calendar on and started the blocking. His secretary was going to be unimpressed by how many appointments were going to have to be switched around.

'Keep going,' Liv said. 'For the entire next decade.' And then she smiled at him. And so did Barney.

Such an enormous relief. Baby steps, but maybe he could pull this back.

For a mad moment, Sam considered talking to them about the accident. No. They were both still smiling at him. He didn't want to ruin this evening.

The twins went to bed about ten thirty on Saturday evening and Sam poured himself a glass of Scotch and sat down on the sofa in the snug. All things considered, it had been a good day.

Barney was still pretty monosyllabic and Liv was still prickly, but Sam had devoted the entire time to them and they were definitely making progress as a family. Tomorrow they were going out to New Jersey for a family lunch and he was going to stay there all day. Sure, he'd need to stay up most of tomorrow night to catch up on work, but the twins were more important. This was the first time in a long time that he'd really acted in anything other than a short-term, reactive way on putting them first, and it felt very right.

His mother had been right to nag him, and Izzy had been right in the pub. Maybe not completely right, because was he really going to sack off his whole career? But she was right about him improving his work-life balance. He should tell her. He would also like to ask her how her dinner with Dominic had been. And, if he could do it tactfully, ask her how close she and Dominic were getting. He'd email her now.

Izzy had replied by the time he woke up in the morning.

Hi Sam,

Great news that you're having a good weekend with the twins and I'm sure that you'll all enjoy your Wednesdays!

I did have an enjoyable dinner with Dominic, thank you. Yes, we have been spending more time together. We have a child together and he is still my husband, after all!

I hope that you enjoy your family day today.

Izzy

There was a nice symmetry to the fact that she was evidently annoyed with him, because he was annoyed with her, too.

'Still my husband'? As in, she was planning to go back to him? Maybe already had last night? Was she insane?

Clearly, she didn't love Dominic. No-one was in love with two people at once. And he was sure she loved Sam in the same way that he loved her. He knew this from their kiss and from her eyes and from a lot of small, indescribable, but absolutely definite, things. Which was to say, she loved

Sam with a passion so strong it was physically stunning, a visceral passion that went right through you. He knew she did. He felt the same way.

And Sam knew, because he'd done it, that marrying someone you didn't love like that wasn't the best idea. But he also knew that he couldn't tell Izzy that he loved her. Too risky. Even in five or ten years' time when the twins were adults and could cope better emotionally if he met someone, and it might be feasible to manage a trans-Atlantic relationship or move, he'd never do it.

And he also knew that if he had his time again he wouldn't change things with Lana. They'd had the twins together. And he had loved her; not in the 'rug being pulled from under you' kind of way he was experiencing with Izzy, but his feelings for her had grown into a genuine, steady love. Would he give the twins back their mother if he could? Yes. Of course he would. Would he still be with her? He didn't know. He wasn't sure if the relationship would have lasted without the kind of passion he had for Izzy.

What he did know was that, if he'd got to know Izzy as well as he knew her now, while married to Lana, he'd have struggled.

But he wasn't going to tell Izzy that. This was clearly one of those pivotal moments in a relationship, and he was going to pivot right away from her. Clearly, in retrospect, this had been going to happen once they'd locked eyes in the restaurant and both known that their kiss was going to happen at some point. You couldn't, in fact, carry on being just good friends with someone you were deeply in love with. Of course you couldn't.

Why *had* she called Dominic her husband in her email when they were separated? Was she trying to provoke a response? A declaration of love maybe?

He couldn't do that, but he should say something. He'd do it right now, before he hopped in the shower.

Hi Izzy,

I'd call you a good friend.

And, as a good friend, I'd have to ask you if you think it's the right move to get back together with someone just because you share a child. I think that most people would agree that a successful marriage needs a more solid foundation than co-parenting. It needs romance.

Sam x

He could have told her that he knew all that from experience, but he couldn't be disloyal to Lana's memory.

She'd replied before he was out of the shower.

Sam,

Marriage is real life.

Real life isn't about romance.

Izzy

Well, yes, she was right there. When he thought about it now, he'd been in love with Izzy since pretty much the moment their eyes met in the café nearly fourteen years ago. That was romantic. And was he going to act on it? No. He didn't want a relationship, and certainly not when he was finally making progress with the twins.

Another email pinged in. Izzy again.

Unless you can convince me otherwise?

Wow. From Izzy, that was huge. Was she encouraging him to tell her he loved her? Part of him – a big part of him – wanted to do it. Maybe say something along the lines of *Real life should be about romance. I love you and I think you love me too and because we love each other we'll make it work, so please don't go back to him. Be with me.*

He couldn't do it. He could not tell her that he loved her. Even though he did. He knew that she'd be hurt, but he really couldn't say it. Allowing yourself to love people was too high risk a strategy; there was too much pain involved when bad things happened to them.

Izzy,

Yeah. You're right. Real life is not about romance. Personally, I gave up on it a long time ago.

My bad.
Sam x

Sam hoped the kiss would soften the blow of his rejection, but he knew it probably wouldn't. He suspected this might be the end of their emails for a while.

Chapter Twenty-Eight

Izzy

There was only so much loved-up-ness you could happily be around when you yourself were not loved-up and were never going to be because the person you loved had basically ignored you when you put yourself right out there.

Bastard Sam for his bastarding email. 'My bad.' Arse.

Why had she said what she'd said? She might as well have written, 'Tell me you love me and that it's real.' She might as well also have written, 'I love you.' And he hadn't attempted to convince her. He might as well have written, 'I do have some feelings for you but I will not act on them.' Or maybe, 'I have no feelings beyond friendship so please leave me alone, you deluded woman.' She should have written him off the night of their disastrous non-date.

She shouldn't be angry with him, not really. She was being unreasonable. If he didn't love her, that was just the way it was. Her misfortune. He had probably never got over Lana. That was probably what he'd meant when he said he'd given up on romance a long time ago.

And it wasn't as though they could actually have a relationship, given the kids and where they lived. But she'd have liked him to have told her he loved her, and he hadn't. And it really, really hurt.

And now she was surrounded by love, love, love.

Last night, after climbing, Emma and Rohan had been so bloody smiley and cuddly and clearly desperate to get away from Izzy and into bed for a serious session. Izzy was so, so pleased for them, but not so keen on the gooseberry experience.

And now this evening, this.

Izzy took her seventh truffle arancino from a passing waiter and raised a big smile and her champagne glass in the direction of her mother and Veronique, who were standing holding hands on the stage at the end of the room. They were both fantastic adverts for 'Life Begins at Sixty Plus', both rocking their evening dresses, lots of good jewellery, great make-up and intricate hairstyles. They must both have been doing a *lot* of exercise recently. Surely it wasn't normal to look so in shape at their age. They looked more toned than most women Izzy knew of her own age. And they obviously had a *great* hairdresser. Or hairdressers. It would probably be weird to go to the same one. Amazing colours.

Izzy was very happy for them both. It was a little bit galling, if she was honest, that she'd had to organise a sleepover with Dominic for Ruby, her mother's granddaughter, while her half-brother Nat, her mother and Veronique's younger son, had got to bring his five-year-old daughter Ella, also their granddaughter, with him to the party. His mothers were both ludicrously bad at hiding their pride in his Jack-the-lad-ness – neither of them had been remotely upset that he'd got someone pregnant at seventeen, where a lot of parents would have worried that it was far too young – but that was a very bad reason for all the favouritism towards Ella.

Izzy's mother had the mic.

'Thank you so much, everyone, for coming today. We're so pleased to have the opportunity to celebrate our love with you. As you know, this is our twenty-fifth anniversary party. It isn't the twenty-fifth anniversary of our civil partnership or our marriage, because neither of those options were available to us when we got together. It *is* the twenty-fifth anniversary, a huge but wonderful quarter of a century, of our personal commitment to each other.' She turned and gave Veronique a saucy smile. Veronique did a bit of eyebrow waggling and pouting.

Really? *Really*? Were they talking about *that* kind of commitment? Probably. No worse than giving your daughter a lot of sex presents for her birthday.

Izzy looked round at Nat. He was smiling and laughing like everyone else. Surely most normal people didn't like listening to their parents making innuendos about sex?

'My turn for the mic.' Veronique planted a big smacker on Izzy's mother's lips and then turned to address everyone. 'I just want to say how lucky I was to meet Deborah. She's the love of my life. Funny, kind, beautiful.'

It was nice, of course it was, not just nice, truly wonderful, that they were still so in love after so long. And properly in love. On the occasions she saw them, Izzy always witnessed smaller signs of mutual affection, a bit of surreptitious shoulder-squeezing, and hugs, belly laughs at in-jokes that no-one else would find remotely funny, stolen kisses when they thought no-one was looking. It was lovely.

And Izzy was a bad, bad person, because she felt a tiny bit envious. She'd never had this kind of relationship, and she was never going to. If she got back together with Dominic, it would never be like this, because it never had been. There was only one person she thought she could have this with, and that was never going to happen.

She should focus on some positives. Dominic would never truly break her heart. And he was lovely and familiar, and now they were putting more effort in, they were having a good time together. Who needed fireworks, actually? And in time, Emma and Rohan's passion would probably fade. Maybe she and Dominic had been like that once, and she'd just forgotten.

Izzy did a quick scan of the room while she listened to Veronique's speech. She couldn't see Emma and Rohan anywhere. Not having an official plus one to bring, she'd decided to bring plus two. One minute they'd been next to her, the next her mother had started talking and they'd snuck off. She wouldn't mind having them here so that she could share a bit of eye rolling with them.

Now Nat and her other half-brother, his older brother Max, were on the stage to give speeches. Shit, was Izzy going to have to go up there and speak too? She should have prepared something. She started planning some words. She wouldn't mind doing a speech, actually. She could definitely think of some funny anecdotes off the top of her head. Probably not the sex books one, though, on balance.

And then Max got some cards with notes on out of his pocket. Which meant that he had obviously *known* that he was going to give this speech. Which meant that either the boys had volunteered and her mother and Veronique had said yes without thinking of mentioning it to Izzy, or they'd asked him. Whichever, Izzy was pissed off. She was her mother's child too. And they clearly weren't going to ask her to do a speech.

Also, if she was feeling uncharitable, which, yes, she was, she'd have to say that Max's speech was crap. Wooden. Humourless. Okay, she should not have thought that. Now she felt terrible. Max was lovely. So was Nat. It was one hundred per cent not their fault that Izzy's mother preferred her other children to Izzy. Izzy could really do with getting a smile of sympathy or something from a good friend at this point, though. She looked harder for Emma and Rohan. No, she couldn't see them anywhere.

When the speeches finished, after Ella, or as Izzy's mother and Veronique described her, 'our beautiful granddaughter' – did they even *remember* their older granddaughter – had sung the entire first three verses of 'Let It Go' down the mic, very tunelessly but, to be fair, very cutely, everyone moved into groups and Izzy finally saw Emma and Rohan.

They were in an alcove at the end of the room opposite the stage, in a very Get-a-Room position, Emma up against the wall, both arms round Rohan's neck, while he leaned into her, cradling her face in his hands, full-on canoodling. Tremendous.

Izzy grabbed another glass of champagne from yet another passing waiter – there were a *lot* of them, thank *goodness* – and downed it. Not good enough yet. Champagne was supposed to make you feel happy. She was still short on happiness and long on serious pissed-off-ness. She took another glass. Nope, still pissed off. Bloody Sam. And bloody loved-up bloody everybody bloody else. She needed more champagne.

'Hi, I'm Tom.' Tom was a nice-looking man, dressed in skinny jeans, a slim-fit blue and green floral shirt and pale-blue suede brogues. 'Your mother's a friend of mine.'

'Nice shoes.' Izzy smiled at him, accidentally slopping champagne onto the shoes. Oops. To give him his due, Tom kept on smiling.

'Like to dance?' he asked.

'Love to.' Better than standing by herself and he seemed nice enough. 'I think we both need another drink first, though.'

Tom was a very good dancer and a very good procurer of champagne.

By the time Izzy's mother came over to talk to them, towards the end of the evening. Izzy's feet were sore from dancing, she was feeling sick, and she was seriously impressed by both Tom's footwork skills and his knowledge of the words of *all* songs *ever*.

'Izzy, darling.' Her mother gave her a hug. 'So nice to see you. Thank you for coming. And Tom.' She hugged him too. 'I hope you and Izzy have been having a nice time together.' She winked. She actually bloody winked. She was bloody trying to set Izzy and Tom up for *sex*. Izzy could tell. Izzy decided that her mother could piss off with her winking and her sex books and her not inviting her own granddaughter or asking her own daughter to give a speech.

'You should have invited Ruby,' she stated.

'Darling, we haven't invited any children.'

'Ella's here.'

'She's our granddaughter and Nat didn't have a babysitter.'

'Ruby's your granddaughter and I had some babysitter issues, because Devon's a long way from London.'

'Darling, Ella's *our* granddaughter.'

Izzy looked at her mother and wondered whether this was the moment where she was finally going to say 'I'm your actual daughter and I've been second best in your life ever since you met Veronique and then had the boys, and sending me advice about the pill when I was sixteen and a vibrator when I was twenty-five and crotchless bloody underwear on my wedding day and sex books on the one-year anniversary of my marriage break-up *is not sufficient to make you a good parent*. Good parenting involves more than advice on sex. Maybe advice on sex is not involved *at all* in being a good parent.'

'Deborah, Izzy, I've got us more champagne,' Tom interrupted as Izzy opened her mouth.

'Thank you so much.' Deborah beamed at him. 'Now, you two have a *great night*. I've booked you into a *very nice room* upstairs, Izzy.' And then she sashayed off and Tom put his hands on Izzy's waist.

She knocked back the champagne he'd just given her and smiled at him. Why not?

It was very peculiar when he started kissing her, because he wasn't Sam, and there were no fireworks, and he wasn't Dominic, who she knew so well. He was just a nice man in sharp middle-aged clothes and stained shoes fastening his lips to hers and going for a bit of over-sloppy tongue action.

*

Izzy was woken by a muffled ringing phone sound coming from quite close to her head. It was a very annoying sound. It stopped, result. And then it started again. Stopped. Started.

She finally found it under one of the three pillows that her head wasn't on, on the other side of the bed, ringing again. Emma.

'Hi,' Izzy said.

'Morning. You in bed with someone?'

'Er, no. Obviously not.'

'What about the man in the floral shirt?'

'What? No.' Izzy looked round the room. Big. Classic furnishing. Large and very comfortable bed. Hard to remember how she'd got here but all the signs were telling her that no-one else had been here with her. She had a flash of memory. 'Tom,' she said. 'We were dancing.'

'And practically having sex on the dance floor. Have you decided not to get back with Dominic then?'

Oh yes. There'd been a lot of kissing and some groping. Eeurgh, in the cold light of day. There'd also been some actual cat calls from her mother when they'd left. And then Izzy had binned Tom in the lift. Thank the Lord for that. Good decision. Izzy's head felt terrible and she was going to have to get showered and dressed very fast and straight back to London to pick Ruby up from Dominic at two, and she was incredibly glad that she wasn't sharing a room with a man she didn't know who kissed like a blubber-lipped fish. And that she hadn't slept with someone else while Dominic – who definitely seemed to be hoping that they might get back together – looked after Ruby.

She really hoped she hadn't said anything rude to her mother last night. There was no point and it would be awful if she'd ruined her party in any way. *Shit.* Had she sent her an email? She'd definitely done some emailing when she'd got into bed. She could remember feeling very angry and very determined and full of decision and jabbing her phone. She'd *definitely* done some decisive emailing. Shit shit shit.

'Got to go. Speak later,' she told Emma.

She clicked into her emails and went straight to the Sent folder.

On the upside, she hadn't sent an email to her mother last night.

On the downside, she'd sent one to Sam and one to Dominic.

Hi Sam,

Screw you.

Izzy
P.S. Just nearly shagged someone called Tom (blue shoes) and I'm going back to Dominic.

Hi Dominic,

Dinner next weekend would be lovely.

Izzy

Bloody *hell*. Izzy was a mother, a professional and knocking on
the door of forty, and yet give her a bottle or two of champagne and
not enough food and *this* was how she behaved. This was almost up
there in the mortification stakes with proposing to someone on their
wedding day.

She went to her inbox.

Hi Iz,

Great. I'd already booked a restaurant.

Dom

Sigh.

Hi Izzy,

Congratulations on both Tom and Dominic.

Sam

Yep. Fair enough. Izzy nodded on her pillow; *ow*, that hurt her
head. Not much anyone could add to that. She'd been outrageously
rude. It wasn't Sam's fault that he didn't love her.

Bloody, bloody hell.

Obviously, she should apologise to Sam. Except, to say what? *I'm
so besotted with you that I was gutted you wouldn't declare undying love
for me, a declaration which I would have rejected anyway, because I
don't* want *more from you than being friends. Except that's clearly a lie,*

because clearly I love you. So I got drunk and sent a 'screw you' email. Obviously not.

She needed to think about it before she replied.

*

Dominic liked his moonlit strolls nowadays, it seemed. They were taking an after-dinner walk through autumnal trees in Kensington Gardens, a week on from the anniversary party. At least there was no danger here of Izzy ruining her shoes. Lily was babysitting again because Izzy did not want to discuss Dominic with any of her friends. Emma clearly didn't think she should get back together with him, and her silent disapproval was pissing Izzy off.

They were walking hand-in-hand. Dominic tugged on Izzy's hand slightly and pulled her closer to him.

'Why don't we sit down on that bench?' He was already walking over to it.

They sat down together, and he put one arm round her shoulders and his other hand gently on her neck, in her hair. He drew her towards him and kissed her.

It was nice. Pleasant. Not earth-shattering, but very familiar and definitely better than kissing Tom.

It seemed kisses were like buses in Izzy's life. None for a very long time and then in the space of only a few weeks, Sam, Tom and Dominic. Sublime to ridiculous to alright.

Dominic stopped kissing her and smiled at her. Was it awful that Izzy was pleased that the kiss had stopped? She really wanted to get to bed on time tonight. It was never great going out on a Sunday evening; it always ruined Monday morning.

'So I've been offered a promotion if I move back to Milan…'

Izzy pulled away from him. What was he *thinking*, implying that he was moving back permanently to London and that he wanted to get back together, kissing her and then telling her he was buggering off again to Italy?

'…I've got a few weeks to decide, but I'm not going to take it.' His smile grew. Oh. Okay. She relaxed a little back towards him. 'I've loved being back here with Ruby. With you. I want to make us work, if that's what you want. Maybe I could even move back in?'

Wow. Was workaholic Dominic Castle really suggesting he give up a promotion? His eyes looked very twinkly in the moonlight. He was such a nice man. Really, his only fault was a bit of dishwasher laziness. He was kind, he was generous, he was decent. And he was putting her and Ruby first. Could you ask for more in a husband?

She needed a bit more time to think, though. It was too big a decision for this evening. She was too tired. It had to be the *right* decision, for all their sakes. She put her arm round his waist and hugged him.

'That's… wow. I've loved having you here too. But I think we should think about it and not rush into anything,' she said. 'Because of Ruby. Maybe dinner again later in the week?'

'Can't wait.'

*

Izzy was back in her car after school drop-off literally ten minutes earlier than usual the next day. Ruby had been an angel the whole morning. Izzy was sure it was because of how much she'd enjoyed yesterday with both Izzy and Dominic. Another point for Dominic.

She got her phone out. If she was really getting back with Dominic, she couldn't, even if they hadn't just had an argument, carry on emailing Sam, even as friends. It would be like having an emotional affair while married, from her side, anyway. It would in fact *be* having an emotional affair while married. But Barney shouldn't suffer. If the speech therapy was still doing him good, they should continue, and Izzy was a professional.

Hi Sam,

I'd like to apologise for my drunken rudeness last weekend.

On another note, could you confirm that you're happy for me to make arrangements directly with Barney for his speech therapy sessions over email, just copying you in? I need written permission from you for child protection purposes.

Best wishes,
Izzy

He replied with the confirmation during Izzy's lunch hour. So that was fine. Great.

Chapter Twenty-Nine

Sam

Damn, he missed Izzy. It was two weeks since they'd had any communication at all. Sam wanted to email her right now, with a photo of the mac and cheese dinner that he and the twins had just cooked.

He also wanted to yell at her about Dominic and Tom, whoever Tom was. He wanted her to apologise properly for the email she'd sent. And he wanted to apologise for having upset her. He couldn't say any of that, though, because that would involve a conversation about love.

He pointed his phone at the kitchen table and took a photo anyway. His mother would be pleased to see their culinary efforts. Obviously, writing to his mother was not like writing to Izzy. Writing to Izzy was actually like sending and receiving love letters, but not overt ones: perfect, subtle ones. Shit, he really wanted to write to her now.

But, he couldn't. Given how he felt about her, it wasn't appropriate if she was going back to Dominic.

Liv had posted some Insta-perfect photos of their dinner and already had a deluge of likes and emoji-filled comments.

'Can we just eat it?' Barney said.

'Yeah, I'm with you.' Sam sat down at the table and started to serve.

'Daddy, you can actually cook now. This is so good.' Liv was chewing, talking and smiling at the same time.

Things had been so much better between them recently.

Sam suddenly decided. It was time. He'd been searching for this moment.

'Liv. Barney. I need to apologise for the accident.'

'Why?' Liv was always straight to the point.

'It was my fault. I was driving too fast and I was tired.'

'N-n-n-o.' Barney was shaking his head, frowning. It took some time for him to get his words out. 'It wasn't your fault. It was the other car. He was a really bad driver.'

'Yeah.' Liv took more salad. 'You were really cool. Like, no-one could have avoided crashing.'

'No. If I'd been concentrating better, driving more slowly, I think I *could* maybe have avoided the other car,' Sam said.

Liv looked up and straight at him. She shook her head. 'No. I think you're wrong. The other guy was going too fast, not you. And you turned the wheel really quickly and we didn't hit them as hard as it looked like we were going to.'

'Yeah.' Barney was looking at him too. 'And you braked the right amount. Like, hard, but not enough to skid.'

'And you were awesome afterward,' Liv said. 'Cool swearing in the hospital.' She grinned at him.

Barney was smiling at him too.

They really didn't blame him.

Oh, crap. Tears were coming. Sam put his fork down and his hand over his eyes.

And then Liv came round the table and hugged him. He felt the burden lift.

If only he could tell Izzy.

*

After the kids had finished their homework and he'd read up on some meeting notes, Sam called them both into the snug and suggested playing a board game. It was the evening for it.

'I don't like board games,' Barney said.

'And we never play them,' Liv said.

'Well, it's time we started.' Sam had very clear memories of his mother insisting throughout his childhood that they play Sunday evening board games, when all he'd wanted was to be outside with a ball when he was younger and hang out with his friends when he was older, but, actually, the board games had been good. 'If I can work from home one day a week, the two of you can indulge me in playing Clue right now.'

'Lame,' Liv said. She was smiling, though.

'But we're doing it.'

'*Fine*, but prepare to lose big, because girls are way better than boys at everything.' Liv suddenly grinned properly and launched herself at him and gave him an enormous hug. Sam hugged her back with one arm and held out his other arm to Barney. Barney held back a little and then put his arms round both of them.

Sam held onto them for as long as the kids would let him. He was choking up yet again. This moment alone was worth the difficult conversations he'd had about his new working arrangements.

Izzy would be proud of him if she knew.

'Dad,' screeched Liv.

'Mmph.' He had a momentary suffocating sensation. Oh, okay. She'd whacked him around the face with a cushion.

'You keep going to sleep,' she said. Well, of course he did. He'd been working even later and sleeping even less since he'd been making more time for the twins. Absolutely the right thing to do, but he was exhausted.

Liv was jumping up and down, crowing, 'Two games in a row. Losers.' Sam grinned. It was great to see her showing genuine enthusiasm.

*

'This is a great deal for us,' Robert said. The other managing partners in the breakfast meeting all nodded in agreement. Sam was too stunned to find the energy to bend his head and neck to join in with the nodding. It might be a great deal for the firm, but it was a terrible deal for him.

Merging with an M&A boutique firm in Buenos Aires was 'ideal timing' coinciding with Sam taking up his new role. Robert had made the 'suggestion' – aka command – that Sam alternate weeks in Argentina and in New York 'for the next year or so' to oversee the merging of the two businesses. Just when things had started to improve with the kids.

He couldn't commute between countries. It would be life ruining. Could he row back on accepting the role? Or suggest sharing it with someone else? He was going to have to think of something. He couldn't do any more of the 'short-term pain, long-term gain' thing. He and the kids needed their better life *now*. He looked down at the smoked salmon and eggs in front of him and pushed his plate away. He really couldn't stomach eating right now.

He managed a tight smile eventually, and no-one seemed to notice his quietness amongst all the braying and self-congratulation.

*

Twelve hours later and Sam had himself better under control. He threw his head back and roared with fake laughter. Looking around, he was fairly sure that everyone else was genuinely amused. There was some back slapping, some words of appreciation and some hand shaking, and then he moved himself backwards out of the group and towards Ash, at the bar.

'Hey. What're you drinking?' Ash ran a finger round the inside of his collar. 'Hot in here, or I'm overworked and out of shape?' In college, Ash had been an outstanding athlete and nearly two decades on he was still a great basketball player. He was wasted in law.

'Both. I'm going to have a glass of water.'

'Really?'

'Trying to live more healthily. You ever think events like this are a waste of your life?' Sam gestured round the room. Their partners and their most important clients were eating mouth-wateringly delicious bowl food and drinking nectar-like champagne cocktails in one of the function rooms at The Fifty-First Floor, one of New York's most exclusive venues, with extraordinary views over Manhattan.

Ash shook his head. 'You're getting too philosophical. You stop appreciating these events, why are you still doing the job? I mean, I'd rather be here than at an event in a church hall somewhere. You know?'

'Yeah. But, you know, I'd rather be in my apartment with the twins.' Or in an amazing but off-the-radar local restaurant, or, actually, a greasy spoon, with Izzy. Not going to happen.

Ash nodded. 'I can see that. If I had, or wanted, kids, I can imagine that I'd feel differently.'

'I think I'm actually just going to leave.' Maybe Sam *would* rather be in a church hall, if it meant he had a regular job and a regular family life. His father had been that 'man in a church hall' equivalent and his family had been very happy. His father's salary had meant that they hadn't always had access to luxury, but Sam had done a good job of proving that a luxurious lifestyle was not enough to make either him or the kids happy.

Suddenly, he knew. He wasn't just going to leave these drinks now; he was going to leave his job next week. Resign from the partnership. Literally, walk away.

Everyone in this room would be astonished. So would Izzy, if she ever found out.

'Yeah, good night. Have a great weekend,' he told Ash.

'Too late.' Ash spoke into Sam's ear. 'Someone very determined would like to speak to you.' Fiona, the senior in-house attorney at a large investment bank, was heading straight towards Sam, a big smile on her very beautiful face.

'Hey.' She leaned in for an air kiss. 'Good to see you.' She addressed them both but her smile was only for Sam.

Ash left them to it.

'Shall we get out of here? Maybe have a nightcap?' How was Fiona doing that? With a smile and her eyes indicating that they would *definitely* be ending up in bed together later? It just made Sam think about how much he liked Izzy's lovely grey eyes. Christ. Talk about sentimental. He should go with Fiona. The kids were safe at home with Mrs H and he wasn't expected back until late. He needed to get Izzy out of his head.

They decided to go back to Fiona's apartment. In the cab, Fiona flirted. Sam responded, but it was an effort. Which did not make sense. Fiona was witty, she was a successful attorney, she was gorgeous, tall, vivacious, probably as great in bed as she was great at everything else in life: exactly Sam's type. And she didn't look as though she'd waste time on being tied down romantically: even more his type.

Except doing this was actually getting old. Or Sam was getting old. One or the other. He was going to be forty soon. Maybe that was it. Whichever, rather than think about the woman he was with, he was thinking about a smallish, creamy skinned, red-headed woman, who was abnormally nice to be around. And if he couldn't be with her, he'd like to be home with his kids.

He finished paying the taxi driver and followed Fiona out of the cab. 'I'm so sorry, Fiona. I think I'm actually going to go straight home.'

She stared at him for a long moment and then said, 'Right. Thanks for nothing.' She turned her back on him and took a key out of her bag. Yeah. He should have made this decision before they left the drinks.

'Sorry,' he said again.

No reply. Fair enough.

Objectively speaking, Fiona was great. But she wasn't Izzy. Standing alone in the middle of the sidewalk, Sam felt a sudden sense of extreme loss like a blow to the stomach. He wanted to tell Izzy everything about these past few weeks. And he wanted to know how Ruby was. Most of all, he wanted to know how *she* was.

Okay. Enough. He was going to go home, see the twins, and try to forget about Izzy for one night.

Chapter Thirty

Izzy

Izzy looked at herself in the mirror and nodded. She looked as perfect as she could for her big Getting Back Together With Dominic evening, if she said so herself. She'd survived a particularly stressful YouTube 'Chignon Hair Tutorial' experience and had Helena-like hair and the beginning of a bad headache because of the extra hair pins she'd jammed into her head, but hopefully nothing two paracetamol and a couple of glasses of wine wouldn't fix. As a handy side-effect of doing the chignon, her hair looked duller than usual because of all the hair spray she'd had to use. She was wearing nude, slightly shiny tights and the navy dress that Dominic had once bought her, with the pearls he'd given her on their wedding day and nude court shoes. And she was wearing barely there make-up, with light-pink lipstick. Demure. That's how she looked. Perfect for Dominic's conservative taste.

The doorbell rang. This was it. She was going to go downstairs and Dominic was going to tell her that she looked lovely, and they were going to go out for dinner to a Michelin-starred, many-waitered restaurant, they were going to have a nice evening and then he would stay over, and tomorrow they'd spend all day with Ruby, as a family. And then they'd be a family forever.

'I'll get it,' Lily shouted from downstairs.

'Thank you.' Izzy's voice sounded odd, possibly because she was trying not to cry.

'Mummy, you look weird. You don't look like you. I don't like you like that. You look like when you went to the funeral.' Ruby was standing in the doorway of Izzy's bedroom, which after tonight was going to be Izzy and Dominic's bedroom again, and she sounded as tearful as Izzy felt.

Izzy looked back at her reflection. She didn't love looking like this either.

She was going to get changed. Yes, you should make an effort in a relationship but no, you should not compromise your own taste, unless it was truly offensive.

She went out to the landing and called, 'I'll be ready in about three minutes.'

'No problem,' Dominic called back in the voice of a very punctual man who would normally be seriously stressed about her not being ready *right now*, but who was pretty sure he was getting sex tonight, so could very magnanimously let those three minutes go.

Sixteen minutes later, Izzy had changed into a red dress that she really liked, because when you were rekindling your marriage you *should* wear one of your favourite dresses, and lipstick to match, and had taken her pearls, tights and shoes off and replaced them with silver hoop earrings and black suede wedge ankle boots, *so* much more comfortable, and, joy and bliss, had taken the chignon out and shaken her head upside down.

Evening.' She walked down the stairs, smiling at Dominic. He looked good in his product-of-an-English-boarding-school way. Chinos, shirt, blazer, tasselled loafers.

'Good evening.' He smiled at her very warmly. Izzy waited for a little fizz of sex-anticipation excitement. And, yes, there was a small fizz.

Ruby had followed Izzy down the stairs. Izzy turned round and hoiked her up into her arms for a big hug.

'Love you, gorgeous girl.' Izzy swung Ruby round and Dominic landed a smacker on her cheek. Ruby beamed. That gave Izzy a bigger fizz of pleasure.

'Daddy, can I come to your flat for lunch again tomorrow after the museum?'

'Of course. Mummy might come too.'

'Why? It's your flat.' Ruby's head swivelled between the two of them, her face suspicious. Huh. Did Ruby even *want* them to spend time together? Maybe she was used to them living separately now. Now Izzy thought about it, she hadn't wet her bed at all since Dominic had moved back to London.

'We'll think about it tomorrow,' Izzy said. 'Good night, munchkin.'

Dinner was pleasant. No belly laughs but definitely some chuckles. Izzy and Dominic had a lot of history together. It felt comfortable, two old friends catching up. Not incredibly romantic, but it was a long time since they'd been newly-weds. Would Emma and Rohan's mega-passion last? Had Sam and Lana's? Maybe it had, actually. Sam clearly still missed her hugely.

'Will you be having dessert?' The waiter was holding the pudding menus out.

'Mango parfait, Izzy?'

This was the time to say it, when they were re-starting their marriage. 'Actually, raspberry pavlova, please.'

Dominic's eyebrows shot up. 'Two pavlovas, please,' he said to the waiter and then turned back to Izzy, the picture of Astonished Man.

Izzy leaned forward and said, 'I can't *stand* mango.'

'When did that happen?' Dominic was still open mouthed.

'Always. You misheard me the first time. I said I *didn't* like mango.' It had been on their first ever date. 'And I didn't want to hurt your feelings and it just went from there.'

'Wow. *Wow.*' He'd bought her so many mango-related presents over the years. He'd hunted down mango yoghurt when she was pregnant and she'd flushed it down the loo when he was at work. Mango chocolates. Mango notelets. A bracelet with a mango charm. A mango-wood stool as a nod to her mango love. Almost every romantic gesture he'd made during their marriage had been mango-based.

'Yup.' Izzy screwed her face up, waiting to see how Dominic would take it. He seemed stunned still.

And then he started laughing. Proper, huge roars. And then she did too. They were still wiping their eyes when the waiter brought their puddings.

'We haven't laughed like that for a long time,' Dominic said. He was right. Izzy had laughed like that with Sam quite a few times, though. In person and because of his emails. Bloody Sam, in her thoughts again, and on this most crucial of evenings with Dominic.

'So what else don't I know about you?' Dominic asked. 'Please don't tell me you don't like baking or Kir royales. I don't think I could cope with the shock.'

Izzy arranged her face into a smile, which was the right thing to do, but her mind was doing the wrong thing. She was thinking that one huge thing that Dominic did not know about was her friendship with Sam. Or what used to be a friendship anyway. No need to mention it now.

'I've started drinking peppermint tea instead of coffee,' she said.

'Already noticed that a few weeks ago.'

'Nothing, then.' Izzy fiddled with her cutlery. It was hard to meet Dominic's eye. She needed to get Sam out of her head.

The waiter swooped in to refill their wine glasses, thank goodness.

'This is delicious wine,' Izzy said. 'Which region of France is it from?'

While they ate, Dominic talked about wine-making and told Izzy about his weekend ski trips last winter while he was in Milan. The pavlovas had reminded him of snow. He did actually have some very good stories.

When they'd finished their pudding and the waiter had taken their plates away, Dominic reached across and took Izzy's hands.

'Could I come home with you this evening?' He was stroking her hands with his thumbs, which did give her a minor stomach flutter.

She looked hard at his face, so very Ruby-like. He really was a nice man. She did love him. Not in a fireworks way, but who wanted their life to be a series of Catherine wheels and sparklers. She could grow old with Dominic. She could already imagine him in slippers. Embroidered, tasselled ones. Maybe velvet.

'Yes.' She disengaged her right hand and picked up her glass of wine and downed it.

*

'Mummy, wake up.' Ruby's voice and the eyelid-piercing light were both far too penetrating. Izzy was never drinking again.

'In a minute.' Izzy really didn't want to open her eyes. She stretched. And her foot hit a hairy leg.

Dominic's.

'Morning.' He sounded as though he was smiling. She felt him reach out for her and his arm came into contact with her boob. Her naked boob.

They were both naked and Ruby was in the room.

'Ruby's here,' she hissed, wriggling away from Dominic and pulling the duvet right up round her neck.

'Why's Daddy here?' Ruby's voice was coming from right above Izzy's head.

Izzy scrunched open her eyes and looked up. Ruby's face was drooping, like it did when she watched something she didn't like on TV.

'I stayed the night,' Dominic said, still sounding remarkably happy.

'Why?' Ruby repeated. Good question. So that your parents could have sex.

'Because he was tired,' Izzy said. 'Now it's time to go downstairs and I'll be there in two seconds to get your breakfast.'

'Come now.' Ruby wasn't moving.

No *way* was Izzy getting out of bed naked. 'Please go now and I'll follow.'

'I want you to come with me.'

'I'll give you chocolate if you go now.'

Ruby started trudging towards the door. 'Are you coming soon?'

'*Yes.*'

As soon as Ruby was out of the room, Dominic reached out for Izzy again and nuzzled into her neck.

The sex had been nice but this felt all wrong. Izzy pulled away from him.

'Ruby's expecting me now,' she said.

'Yeah. Later?'

'Mmm.' That thought should probably be making Izzy a lot happier than it was.

*

Telling Emma and Rohan that she couldn't make brunch because she was going to be spending the day with Dominic and Ruby was going to be awkward given the effort Emma had been to point Izzy in the direction of *any* man other than Dominic since they split.

So sorry – am going to have to pull out of brunch – big news – Dominic and I spending the weekend together! Xx

It felt like it would be easier to drip-feed the back-together-with-Dominic news to Emma.

Emma's message came through over ten minutes after the two blue ticks appeared.

No worries, have a lovely time! Xx

Very un-Emma-like. If she thought Izzy was doing the right thing she'd have been extremely effusive. Her message could be translated as 'What the hell are you thinking, you idiot'. This was actually really annoying. Emma should just be happy for her.

Izzy was going to ignore Emma and have a nice family Sunday putting up their Christmas tree and decorations with her daughter and husband.

Chapter Thirty-One

Sam

Sam picked his phone up from the kitchen worktop and re-read the message from Barney's teacher.

It was a month since he'd resigned, and the kids were doing so well.

Barney had been selected for his junior high school debating team. This was incredible. Fantastic. There weren't actually enough superlatives to describe it. He wished he could tell Izzy. She'd be so proud.

It was eight weeks now since they'd last spoken by email. Izzy copied Sam on her emails to Barney but he didn't open them.

It wasn't just Barney. There were other things he'd like to tell her too. A lot had changed in the past few weeks.

He recalled this phase of bereavement from when Lana had died. He remembered when they moved back to New York, realising that if she'd somehow returned then, she'd have slotted right back into his and the twins' lives, but further down the line, he'd have had to explain to her what had been happening. If Lana came back now, eight years on, there'd be *so much* to tell her.

And with Izzy, he'd already got to the point where he'd have to fill her in on stuff. The big news, that he'd turned down an amazing role and instead resigned, and was now handing his clients over to other partners. Plus all the drama there'd been with Liv when she ran away and the conversation about the accident. Izzy also didn't know that he could now cook a variety of non-pasta dishes, unaided. Or that he and the twins had been to a one-off painting session and adored it.

It was really sad. And it was as though he'd always have an Izzy-shaped hole in his life. And he'd done it to himself.

Why had he never told her he loved her again?

He could have tried talking to Liv, explained to her how he felt about Izzy, told her that no-one would ever replace her and Barney in his affections but that he also loved Izzy. There was also the New York/London issue but maybe they could have worked that out. They could at least have tried.

Really, the reason that he hadn't tried to work those things out was that he'd been scared. He hadn't wanted to expose himself further to the hurt that came with loving people, hurting when they hurt, or hurting when you lost them.

So that had worked out well. He was hurting like hell now.

And he was going to carry on hurting. It was possible that if he'd told her how he felt, they'd have got together. And now he'd be happy. And yes, maybe he'd get sad somewhere down the line, if something happened to her, but *now* he'd be happy.

What a dumbass.

It was too late even to try now. She was with Dominic. Stupid name.

He'd really like Izzy to know about Barney's debating success, though. She and Barney were down to monthly sessions but their next one was coming up. Barney should tell her.

Sam turned the gas down under the sauce, another thing he'd like to tell Izzy about; he'd just made some sauce, what she would call gravy, from scratch, for a proper British roast dinner. And then realised that it was disgusting and had to make some from a packet, but he'd tried. A few months ago, he wouldn't have attempted any kind of sauce, even packet-based.

Once they were seated with their roasts, Sam said to Barney, 'Congratulations on making the debating team. I'm so proud of you.'

'Hey, Barney, that's amazing.' Liv smiled at her brother and Barney smiled back at her.

Barney started to stutter a word out and then he stopped for a second and then said, 'It's cool, yes. Thank you.' Clearly using one of Izzy's suggested strategies.

'Izzy would be really pleased to hear about it. Maybe you could tell her?' Sam concentrated on loading chicken, potato and broccoli onto his fork. He sensed Liv looking at him.

'Sure.' Barney shrugged, like it was no big deal. Sam put his forkful into his mouth.

'You still hung up on her?' Liv asked. Sam nearly choked on his chicken. Barney started to whack him energetically on the back. Sam waved him away and took a drink of water.

When his eyes had stopped watering and his throat had stopped burning, he said, 'No.'

'Oh, please,' Liv said. 'What are we, children?' *Uh, yeah*? Sam didn't reply. What was there to say? 'I know Izzy told you to work less.' Sam nodded, because still no words.

Silence stretched between them, not a comfortable one.

Then Barney said, 'I like Izzy.' Sam nodded.

More silence.

'Liv likes her too.' Barney nudged Liv.

'She's okay,' Liv said eventually, staring at her chicken.

'If you like her you should tell her.' Barney's words had come out in a rush. 'Liv?' Wow. Barney never did this.

After a few seconds, Liv looked up. 'Yes.'

'And?' Barney nudged her.

'Okay.' Liv put her cutlery down. 'I hated her because I knew she liked you and you liked her, a lot, and I was worried that it meant that you'd have even less time for us and that you'd forget about Mom. But, yeah, I know that isn't true, because you gave up work for us. And, yeah...'

'We know you miss her,' said Barney. 'And she's really nice.'

'Wow,' Sam said. 'You do know how much I love you both? And how much I loved your mother?'

'Yeah. We do,' Liv said. 'Did you ever tell Izzy you were in love with her?'

Sam didn't choke this time, because he'd had the common sense to stop eating.

'No,' he said.

'Why not?'

'Just, you know, because.' Was it normal for a forty-year-old man to be sounding like a petulant teenager while his teenage daughter questioned him?

'You should tell her now,' Liv said. Wow again. It was kind of a relief to be having this conversation. And kind of all wrong, because Sam was supposed to be the grown-up here.

'She's married. You don't tell a married woman you love her.'

'Don't think she is,' Barney mumbled through a large mouthful of his own.

'Yes, she is.'

'No,' Barney said. 'She isn't. She still calls him her ex-husband in emails.'

'Are you sure?' Sam looked up from his plate.

'Yep. I'll show you.' Barney reached for his phone. On this occasion, Sam was pleased that teenagers were never more than a yard or two away from a device.

Barney swiped for a few seconds and then held the screen out to Sam.

Wow. Sam's heart rate actually quickened when he saw the open email with Izzy's name in it. A rush of memory back to when they were emailing all the time and the little thrill of happiness, excitement, he didn't know what to call it, maybe, just, *love*, when he used to see a message come in from her.

Hi Barney,

Apologies, but are you free to change the time of our session this weekend? My ex-husband has changed the day he's seeing Ruby.
  Would 10 a.m. New York time on Sunday work for you?
  Pleased that you're still enjoying the baking!

Best wishes,
Izzy

Liv had stood up and was craning over Sam's shoulder to read the email.

'She totally isn't back with him,' she said. 'Barney's right.' Sam wasn't so sure. You could interpret that email in different ways. 'I'm pretty sure she's in love with you.' Sam should rise above this conversation and not ask Liv why she thought that.

'Why?' he asked.

'Little things. The way she looked at you when we met her in the café. The expression on her face when you rescued the old man from the lake. She laughed at all your lame jokes. She looked really sad when I showed her the photos of Mom. She's totally into you.'

Sam should stop this conversation right now. It was ridiculous to discuss important adult life matters with your own child, who used expressions like 'she's totally into you'.

'So are you going to tell her you love her?' Liv said. Annoyingly persistent.

'No,' he said. Maybe.

'Why not?' Seriously. His daughter had turned into a very scary woman. Sam had a strong urge to whine *Leave me alone*, like a miserable teen.

'You know, I'm going to think about it. Now leave me alone.'

'Love you, Dad.'

'Love you too, Liv. And you, Barney.' He was a very lucky man. He knew he was. His kids were amazing.

The question was, was he going to try to get even luckier?

Later, when the twins had gone to bed, Sam sat down at his laptop. He'd made the decision. He was going to write to Izzy. It would be the early hours of Monday morning now in London.

What exactly was he going to write?

Hey Izzy, I hope you're well. I'm just writing to say that I love you and I should have told you that before. One of the reasons I was holding back was that Liv hated you but turns out she doesn't any more. So would you like a trans-Atlantic relationship with me? I mean, obviously, that isn't likely to work, is it? But I'd love to go back to best-buddy-emailing. Exclusive best buddies. No best-buddying other people. No dating either, actually, because, as I just said, and should have said weeks, months, ago, I love you, and I don't want to date anyone except you and I don't want you to date anyone else either. And when I'm in London we could kiss again, because that was incredible. We could do other stuff too, because I'm pretty sure that would be even more incredible than the kiss, if that were possible. I couldn't come to London too often, because of the twins. And we couldn't really stay in a hotel together very often, because of all the kids. And you probably couldn't come to New York much, so, again, that would make sex and in fact any one-on-one time at all difficult. So, yes, we can't possibly have a relationship. But, Jesus, I love you so much, Izzy.

No. He absolutely was not going to write that. Hard to think of an alternative, though.

Right. Think of it like work. He'd never had a problem there. Break it down into clauses. A thank you for everything she'd done for Barney, obviously. And for them as a family, with her pep talks in the park and in the pub. Tell her about the life changes he'd made and thank her for her input. Address their kiss. Say he loved her. Or was that too much?

Okay. Time to start a draft. He flexed his fingers, rolled his shoulders and his neck, and started typing.

Hey Izzy,

Long time no mail.

Was that a lame way to start? Trite?
He should just push on and edit it afterwards.

I've missed you.

Wow. This was hard.

Eventually, he had his draft.

That had taken a seriously long time to write. It had taken about twenty minutes just to compose the title. And he'd ended up with 'Hello and thank you'. Punchy.

He wondered if she'd agree to his suggestion that they see each other in London next week. He was pretty sure that after Liv's one-eighty on his relationship with Izzy, there'd be minimal objections from the twins if he said he was going to London. Would he go even if Izzy didn't reply to the email, or said that she was busy? Maybe. And try to engineer a meeting. Or would that be a bit stalkerish?

Was it too much that he'd told her he loved her, in writing, out of the blue? Was it too little? Should he have mentioned their kiss? What if she actually *was* with Dominic? Would she even read the email? He needed to think of a better title for it.

He should sleep on it, re-read it in the morning, edit it and then send it.

He couldn't sleep. He sent the email, unedited, at 1.30 a.m.

PART FOUR

Chapter Thirty-Two

Izzy

Izzy was in a deep, dreamless sleep when the alarm on her phone went off. Ruby had had an accident in the middle of the night, and Dominic had got up in the dark at about five fifteen, to go back to his flat and get changed for work after two nights with Izzy. After being disturbed by Ruby, Izzy had managed to get back to sleep; but she'd struggled to after Dominic had crept loudly round the room for several minutes. She'd lain wide awake for a while, worrying about whether their reconciliation was right for Ruby, about work, about the cod in the fridge that needed to be cooked today except she had no time to make a fish pie but pie was the only way Ruby would eat fish. She'd finally gone back to sleep, too close to her getting-up time.

She turned the alarm off, buried her face in her pillow and went back to sleep. Five minutes later it beeped again. She turned it off and re-buried her face. And woke up to more beeping five minutes later. Okay, now she was in that state where your body was incredibly heavy-limbed, basically still asleep, but your mind had pinged awake. Her mind was telling her that Ruby would have been watching Disney films for too long already this morning and that if she didn't get out of bed and into the shower *now* they were going to be late for school *again*, and her body was telling her *Piss off*, she wasn't moving.

At least – now that it was proper daytime rather than still the middle of the night – the things she'd been worrying about seemed a lot smaller. Except the 'was it right to have got back with Dominic' one, but she was pretty sure that if she worked hard at ignoring that thought all would be well. And once he moved properly back in, next weekend, she'd have no time to think.

She reached her outside arm down and picked up her phone, to get on with her usual morning 'blue light from screen dragging herself into physical action' routine. Chin on mattress, she looked at the headlines on her BBC news app first. Yep, all good, no major tragedies had occurred overnight. She read a heart-warming story about ninety-year-old twins who'd been separated when they were fourteen and had finally met up again. It was a long story and now she and Ruby were *really* going to be late.

Izzy was nearly ready to get out of bed. She wiped a sentimental tear from her eye and pressed the email icon on her phone to see how many annoying, crack-of-dawn messages she'd had from Ruby's school or work. There was one from school, about swimming kit. There were three from colleagues. There were quite a lot of the usual shopping ones. One from an early-rising girlfriend who lived in Dublin, sent at 6 a.m.

And there was an email from Sam. Its title was '*Hello and thank you*'. Woah.

Izzy rolled onto her back, holding her phone to her chest, and looked up at the ceiling. Just seeing Sam's name brought back so many emotions. Ones that a happily married woman shouldn't – and surely wouldn't – feel about another man.

Should she read the email? Should she read it now?

No. She should have her shower now. Maybe she'd read it later, maybe she wouldn't.

They were later than usual for school. That twins-reunited story had been very long. The upside of the lateness was that Izzy got a parking space right outside school, so she was back in her car in time to read Sam's email before she set off for work. If she wanted to.

Actually, she didn't. She'd rather arrive at work in good time. She probably wouldn't read the email at all.

The morning was busy, as always, back-to-back appointments. She found herself a number of times losing focus and thinking about Sam and having to force her thoughts back to the matters in hand, *really* bad, really unprofessional.

At lunchtime, she smiled her last client of the morning out of the room and then looked at her phone. Nope. She wasn't going to read the email. She was *fine*, totally over Sam, and she didn't want to become un-fine again.

She went to the café round the corner and bought a salad and a packet of salt and vinegar Hula Hoops. It was drizzling and December-cold. Not pleasant for sitting or walking outside in. The best idea would be to eat in her consulting room, while she went through her admin.

She sat down at her desk, put her phone down next to her and started eating.

It was like the phone was signalling to her. Read me, *read me*.

No.

At first, when she and Sam had stopped emailing, it had been awful, like an actual break-up. Properly painful. She'd kept thinking about Sam, wondering every time she looked at her phone if there'd be an email from him, imagining what he might be doing. She'd even sometimes thought that she saw him out and about. And, even though she knew that he was almost certainly in New York, when whichever tall, broad-shouldered man she'd noticed turned round and she saw that they looked similar – but nowhere near as perfectly, gorgeously Sam-like as actual Sam – she felt another stab of misery, every time.

Now, she was a lot better. The pain was more like a diminishing, dull ache. She didn't expect emails from him any more and she thought about him less. Sometimes things reminded her of him and she'd feel a sharp pang again, but, basically, she was recovering from her ridiculous infatuation, and that was a good thing, given that she and Dominic were back together.

Clearly, reading his email wouldn't help. Although, she'd seen that it was there. If she didn't read it, she was just going to wonder. So, actually, reading it probably wouldn't make any difference. In fact, on the evidence, *not* reading it was going to make her go mad with wondering.

Bugger it, she was going to read it. She was going to read it and then ignore it and carry on moving on from him.

She picked her phone up and button-pressed it into life.

No, she couldn't read it. She couldn't go there.

And, oh God. There it was. The other thing she couldn't do. She couldn't go through with getting back together with Dominic. Not when she hadn't felt that happy all weekend, and when just seeing an email from another man made her feel like this. And it was clear that Ruby was now happy with them living separately as long as she saw Dominic regularly.

She should tell him immediately. This evening. Before he started packing for the weekend's move. And before he turned down the promotion he'd been offered in Milan.

*

'It just doesn't feel right. And so, I'm so, so sorry, but this is it.' She and Dominic were sitting on the kitchen sofa holding hands. Izzy could see tears on Dominic's cheeks and feel hot tears on her own. 'I'm sorry,' she whispered again.

'Better now than in a year or two,' he said eventually.

God, it was horrible when something that felt so right was also so painful.

'Listen,' Dominic said, his mouth and chin squeezed in an 'I will not cry any more' way, 'we won't be like your parents. We'll always put Ruby first.' He was such a nice man. He just wasn't Izzy's One.

'Thank you,' she said. And then they both bawled their eyes out, and held each other for a long time.

*

Forty-eight hours since she'd resolved to finally split from Dominic, and Izzy still hadn't read Sam's email. It didn't feel right. She was about to start formal divorce proceedings with her husband; her mind should not be on Sam. But that email was burning a hole in her inbox. For the third day running she'd spent the whole of her lunch hour wondering what it said.

It probably said nothing interesting. She should just read it, and then move on.

Right.

Hey Izzy,

Long time no email.
    I've missed you.

If you and Dominic are back together and happy, I wish you all the very best.

If not, I hope you'll read the following. There are a number of things that I think I should have said to you but never did.

Firstly, I have a lot to thank you for.

I'm incredibly grateful for everything you've done for Barney. You've been a fantastic speech therapist for him. Thirteen was very much our lucky number. You know how badly his stutter was impacting on his confidence when you first started working with him. Today I got an email from his school saying that he'd been selected for their debating team. On merit. I think that sums up exactly how far he's come. Thank you.

I also need to thank you for your advice with regard to my work-life balance. I reacted badly at the time. And I'm sorry for that; your words hit straight to the core of my dilemma, and I felt too trapped to be able to do anything about it. But it got me thinking. Eventually, I took the decision to resign. Best thing I've done for years (other than getting in touch with you way back in May. Can't believe that was nearly seven months ago).

Secondly, I should say again that I've missed you.

I'd very much like to know how you've been. I'd love to hear more about how Ruby's doing, Emma and Rohan, your "new experiences." Are you still painting and climbing? Have you tried anything else? I'd love more recipe conversations.

I'd like to tell you how Liv's doing, about my coaching Barney's basketball team (and realizing that if he wants to be an artist when he grows up—his latest thing—that's cool), about my fortieth birthday (yup, old), about my cooking expertise (poor but improving—last week the kids and I cooked Thanksgiving Dinner for fourteen with only minimal input from my mother), about my friends, my running.

Basically, I'd like to hear everything about your life and I'd like to tell you everything about mine.

Also, and very importantly, there's something that I never told you.

I love you.

I'm going to be in London next week and I wondered if you would be free to meet?

S x

Woah.

Woah.

She'd been wrong. It was going to take a long time to move on from that.

She needed to read it again, paragraph by paragraph.

She needed to think about it, paragraph by paragraph. And sentence by sentence. Especially that tiny but momentous second-to-last sentence.

It was actually too big to take in now.

She opened her salad and got cutlery out of her desk drawer. The salad was too poncy. Pomegranate seeds were really hard to fork up.

Sam had said he loved her. And he missed her.

The salad was tasty, and she was getting the knack with the seeds now. She munched and thought, and munched and thought. Her mind was working very slowly.

It was wonderful news about Barney. She obviously wanted to reply to that. But she could email Barney directly.

She munched some more.

Sam wanted to meet her next week. She couldn't. It was too much. What if he told her he loved her in person? What if she admitted she loved him too? How would she get over that? It wasn't like they could have an actual relationship. For practical reasons as well as the fact that she couldn't compete with Lana.

He obviously still missed her. There were all the photos in the apartment, and all the times he'd mentioned how much he'd cared about her. It was bad enough being second-best as a daughter; Izzy definitely didn't want to be second-best as a lover.

Her desk phone buzzed. Damn. One thirty. She wasn't ready at all for her next appointment. She'd been sitting with her fork suspended in mid-air and hadn't finished her salad or even started her Hula Hoops.

'Sorry, sorry, give me two minutes,' she told the receptionist, hoovering food into her mouth. She'd re-read the email later. And do some more thinking. Her head was already aching.

*

Izzy still had the headache when Emma and Rohan arrived that evening. She really wasn't pleased to see them. If there was one thing she did not need tonight, it was choir practice, or for Emma to ask about her love life.

This was Emma and Izzy's third new experience. Last week had been their first choir session, and it had not matched up to painting or climbing. They'd signed up long-term to monthly painting now, and they both still loved it; and they were going fortnightly to climbing, to a non-singles session, which was great too.

Choir was different.

'Ready to sing?' Emma walked into the kitchen with what had to be fake bounciness given the frostiness there'd been between them recently. Emma had made it very clear that she didn't think Izzy should be getting back with Dominic, and Izzy had not appreciated that, even if Emma had been right in the end.

'Yes, I am!' Izzy tried really hard to smile and sound exclamation-mark-happy.

'You alright?' Rohan asked.

'Yes, just a bit of a headache after helping to supervise school swim club. You know how you always feel fluey when you've been in a jumper at boiling hot baths.'

'Yes, supervising school swimming's shit,' Emma said, totally buying it, hoorah. 'So screamy as well, with all their voices echoing off the walls. I haven't had to do swim club at all since I became deputy head, thank God. Awful. Right. Ready to go?'

'So how are you?' Emma asked when they were sitting in the car on the way to the church hall where their *Messiah* practice was taking place. Unusually, they hadn't seen each other for a couple of weeks. 'How's Dominic?'

'Okay,' Izzy lied. She turned her windscreen wipers on to clear away the sleet that was falling.

Emma left a big silence, obviously wanting Izzy to fill it with facts about Dominic and the weekend. Izzy said nothing.

Emma started burbling about how much fun choir practice was going to be. Bullshit. It was not.

The other 'choristers' – as the choirmaster, a very annoying thin and brown-suited man called Mr Daniels, called them – were all apparently in jovial mood, keen to get going on some warm-up arpeggios.

'Izzy, not putting enough welly in, on your own now, please,' Mr Daniels said. Why did he use their Christian names while they had to Mister him? Were they twelve years old?

Izzy thought about walking out and decided that that would be rude to Emma, so she had a go at belting some notes out.

'Better,' Mr Daniels said. 'I'd like a bit more enthusiasm, though, please, Izzy.' Izzy glared at him.

Many, many vocal exercises and boring, *boring* repetitions of bits of the *Messiah*, and extreme, *extreme* enthusiasm from Mr Daniels and the other choristers later, they'd reached their half-time break.

'Are you sure you're okay?' Emma asked. They'd snuck round the back of the hall, away from everyone else. Like being at school and sneaking off for an illicit smoke or a snog, minus the cigarettes and the boys. Izzy looked at Emma's lovely, familiar, beautifully scarlet-lipsticked, un-chorister-like face and thought about telling her about everything. It would be a relief to be back on best-friend terms and it would be a relief to talk – a problem shared. But it would also be hard to say things out loud. And Mr Daniels had been very strict about their break being fifteen minutes only.

'Izzy,' roared Mr Daniels, ten minutes later. His skinny frame apparently concealed exceedingly powerful lungs. 'Please. Put. More. Effort. In.'

'Mr Daniels,' Izzy said. 'I am doing my best.'

'Really?'

Izzy picked her coat up. 'Goodbye.' She was pleased to see Mr Daniels' mouth hanging open and his very prominent Adam's apple bobbing up and down like nobody's business as she left.

Emma was in the car passenger seat next to her within two minutes.

'Izzy. I don't have time to talk about how much I enjoyed the look on Mr Daniels' face. I want to know what's wrong. Please tell me. It can't be good for you to be bottling whatever it is up and I *know* there's something wrong and it isn't just a headache. I've known you very, very well for twenty-six years and I know you're miserable. What's happened?'

'Emma. People don't have to tell each other everything. Did you tell me about shagging Rohan on the side for years and years? No, you did not. I do not have to share every single thing in my life with you.' Wow. She'd lost it with Mr Daniels and now Emma. And, no, definitely not, she wasn't going to apologise.

Emma didn't say anything for a minute or two. They both sat staring out of the windscreen at the church car park wall.

'You're right,' Emma said eventually, still looking straight ahead. 'I'm sorry. And I'm sorry for nagging you. Of course you don't have to talk to me about anything if you don't want to. I think best friends should always be there for each other and they should also give each other space if they want it. Sorry, Izzy.'

'I'm sorry too. Really sorry.' Izzy turned round and put her arms out. 'Can we have a hug?'

'No need to apologise and yes please.' They squished into a big hug.

'Ow,' said Emma after a while. 'Is that the gear stick or are you just really turned on by me?'

And then they both honked with laughter, for ages, at one of the worst jokes ever made.

When they'd stopped laughing and she could see straight again, Izzy put her keys into the ignition but didn't turn the engine on. Then she took the keys out again.

'So, Sam sent me an email telling me he loves me.'

'*Izzy*. Oh. My. God. Sam loves you. Oh, Izzy. That's huge. I'm so happy for you. Oh my goodness.' Emma flung her arms round Izzy again.

'I'm not sure it's something to be happy about.'

'But he's The One! *Your* One.' Emma's arms dropped a little.

'Oh, please.'

'What happened?'

'Basically, we kissed and then we argued and stopped speaking, then I got back together with Dominic, we split up on Monday and Sam emailed and said he loved me.'

'*What*? You never told me any of this.' Emma held her hands up as Izzy glanced sharply at her. '*Which* I obviously cannot complain about. I'm just sorry if you haven't had anyone to talk to and if I haven't seemed supportive. How are you feeling about Dominic?'

'Yes, it was the right thing to separate for good. Which I know you agree with.'

'So you're okay about breaking up with him? Are you sure?'

'Yes. It's sad because it's the end of an era and in a perfect world we'd be together forever because of Ruby, but I'm not in love with him.'

'Okay, well, firstly, congratulations on making a very difficult – but I think sensible – decision. That can't have been easy. And Sam? Do you love him?'

'Yes. I do.' It was a relief to say it out loud.

'So now what?'

'Well. He's coming to London next week and he wants to meet.'

'And?'

'Well, it's ridiculous isn't it? He lives in New York. I live here. So we can't have a relationship. How would it work? Would we just carry on emailing? Or Skype or Zoom each other? Watch the same Netflix show and message each other at the same time?' Plus the second-best-to-Lana thing.

'People do manage long-distance relationships, though, don't they?' Emma gave Izzy another hug.

'Well, even if we lived in the same place I don't think it would be a good idea for us to get together, for various reasons. So there's no point meeting.'

'So don't meet him then?'

'I think I want closure, though.'

'So meet him then?'

'Maybe I will.' Closure was very important.

Chapter Thirty-Three

Sam

'You seem distracted.' Ash was apparently unaffected by the sprint finish to their lunchtime run.

When Sam had stopped panting and straightened up, he said, 'Always something going on.' He couldn't talk about Izzy. It felt too raw still. And, really, what to say? Met a woman, fell in love, missed several opportunities, told her I loved her too late.

He wished that she had at least replied to the email he'd sent a few days ago.

He looked behind Ash at the Christmas lights twinkling in the large tree outside their office building. Offensively cheerful, really.

Sam wasn't feeling a lot of seasonal joy this week.

Showered and back in his suit, he checked his personal emails automatically.

Izzy had finally replied.

Hi Sam,

That's lovely news about Barney – thank you for letting me know. I'm so proud of him – he's done brilliantly.

And congratulations on your resignation!
I should be free to meet next week if you'd like to?

Izzy

Yes. He was going to take that as a win.

Hey,

Great to hear from you.
I'm very flexible next week. When would be good for you?

S

Hi,

Would you be able to meet during the day on Wednesday?

Izzy

He didn't know exactly what he was going to say when he saw Izzy but he did know that he was going to be counting down the days until Wednesday.

*

Sam checked the weather app on his phone again. It was definitely going to rain, heavily, for the whole of the time that he and Izzy were supposed to be walking in the park this morning. That was London in December for you. He didn't want to try to switch their meeting place, though. There was a risk that Izzy might call it off altogether. What he needed was a large umbrella. They could both shelter under it. That would be nice. Romantic, even.

There was a department store across the road from his hotel. Fortunately, they sold golf umbrellas. Sam bought the largest one he could find, a very expensive novelty Christmas one, which was sixty-two inches in diameter, so there would definitely be space for both of them under it without it looking as though he was purposely trying to stand too close to Izzy.

Umbrellas had to be great for kissing under, actually. You wouldn't have both your hands free, unless you could balance the umbrella between you – no, that wouldn't work, so, no, you wouldn't have both your hands – but you'd still have one arm free for a hug, and it would be nice, because you'd be cocooned in your own little blue-and-green-striped Santa world, just the two of you.

Actually, now he thought about it, it was pretty good news that it was going to be raining. He'd very happily spend a lot of time under this umbrella with Izzy. It was going to have been seventy-five pounds very well spent.

Sam was early for their meeting just inside Holland Park, near a remarkably rain-resistant, very attractively tinsel-and-bauble-bedecked fir.

There were no rain surprises this morning; the weather forecasters had been spot on with their predictions. It was coming down in sheets, as though the heavens were throwing skip load after skip load of water over everyone.

Sam was wearing a suit, an overcoat and brogues, because he had some meetings – catching up with London contacts – arranged for the afternoon, although if by any chance his meeting with Izzy went well this morning, and she had time, he would absolutely cancel this afternoon's meetings to spend more time with her. Or this evening's dinner. Anything. Everything. His shoes were quite new, and surprisingly waterproof so far, and the enormous umbrella was doing its job, so he was pretty dry all over.

Izzy arrived a couple of minutes late, hurrying towards him along the path from the Kensington High Street gate, wearing a long, jade green coat, belted tightly, and dark-brown leather, long, slim boots, and carrying a red umbrella. Quite a small red umbrella, not really big enough for two people, unless they were standing very close to each other.

Also not really big enough to keep one average-sized woman dry in rain of this nature, especially given the periodic gusts of wind that caused the rain to drive sideways; she was already really quite wet. Her hair was beautifully mussed by the wind and her pale cheeks were slightly flushed, as though she'd been hurrying.

Sam felt himself break into a spontaneous grin as she approached. He wanted to drop his own umbrella, knock hers out of the way, pick her up and swing her round and round, press her against him, hold her, feel her warmth and her hair, touch her face, and kiss her for a long, long time.

Instead, a lot more appropriately for the situation, he just said, 'Hey.'

Would it be alright to kiss her cheek?

It would be awkward, given their umbrellas. Now it didn't seem quite so clever to have bought such an enormous one. He held his higher, so that it went above Izzy's, so that she could come closer to him. She didn't move.

'Hello,' she said. He loved her voice. It was at exactly the right pitch. Very musical.

'Thank you for agreeing to meet.'

She didn't reply. Stupidly, he hadn't thought that it would be difficult to get this conversation going. He took a step sideways and tilted his neck to get the right angle to see her under her umbrella. Izzy still didn't say anything; she just looked at him.

'How's your morning been?' he asked.

'Very wet, actually. Yours?'

'Also wet. I didn't bring an umbrella with me, so I was very lucky that the store opposite the hotel was selling these.'

'It's certainly got all umbrella bases covered. I think it might be the biggest one I've ever seen.'

'Yeah, no-one's going to get wet under here. So how's Ruby?'

'Very well, thank you. Very keen on ballet and netball at the moment. And stationery.'

'All great things to be keen on.'

'Indeed. And how are Liv and Barney?'

'They're doing great, thanks. Barney, you know about. His debating anyway. Things have got a lot better for him socially as a result of his improved speaking confidence, and he's reconnected with old friends and made new ones. I can't tell you how delighted I am, and how grateful. And Liv, physically all's good, and I'm navigating our relationship better now that we have more quality time together.'

'I'm so pleased for all three of you. And congratulations again on resigning.'

'Yeah, it was a good decision. Huge, but it felt great once I'd done it. I have you to thank for that too.'

Izzy shook her head. 'I'm sure you'd have made the decision without my input. I'm sorry again for how I phrased things that evening.'

'Hey, no, you were absolutely right.' Sam reached his left hand out towards Izzy. She didn't take it. After a moment he put it in his pocket. And then on the umbrella handle, to join his right hand. The umbrella was astonishingly heavy. He worked out and usually thought of himself as pretty strong. How would a small, unfit person even hold this umbrella? It was heavy and it was a very annoying physical barrier between the two of them. It was starting to feel like seventy-five pounds very badly spent. Although he was at least still dry.

Maybe he should take the opportunity now to raise the matter of their kiss? And how much he had loved it and how much that had freaked him out? No, she wasn't looking receptive to that kind of talk. Better work up to it gradually.

'Shall we walk?' he suggested. Izzy nodded and they started to stroll. Terrible idea. He was never going to be able to hear what she said, given the umbrella situation. He lifted his one very high so that he could inch in closer to her. Although now he couldn't see her face at all.

'How are things with Dominic?' He leaned down so that he'd be able to hear her response. Awkward question but he had to ask.

'We're getting divorced, formally.'

'I'm so sorry to hear that.' He hoped he sounded less insincere than he felt.

'Thank you. It's for the best.'

'I hope you're okay.'

'Yes, thank you.' Maybe he should change the subject.

'So Emma and Rohan got together. As you said, wow.'

'I know. Amazing. They're actually perfect together. It's lovely.' This was not going well. Open, chatty, always friendly Izzy had been replaced by a woman who looked as though she really didn't want to be here and was going to give blood-letting from a stone a run for its money.

'And how are your activities with Emma going? Still painting and climbing?'

'Yes, but not as often. But both still regular. We did two – well, one and a half – choir sessions and then we left. It wasn't for us.'

'Why not?'

'Well…' *Yes.* Sam sensed one of Izzy's anecdotes coming. He'd missed her stories. He'd missed everything about her. 'Everyone else was a lot more keen. The choirmaster was very strict and gave us homework. It was the *Messiah*, which is really hard. The rehearsals were in a freezing church hall but we weren't allowed to wear our coats because coat-wearing might have hampered our singing. And they gave us orange squash and fig rolls in our exactly fifteen-minute break. There was literally nothing good about it unless you like a fig roll, which I do not.'

'Wow. That's making singles climbing sound much more attractive. So who decided that you weren't going any more?'

'Me. But Emma gave in really easily.' She looked up at him and smiled. Sam *loved* when she got that cheeky look in her eye. In the whole of history, there could barely have been a time between two humans when one person had more wanted to tell the other that he loved her and wanted to spend the rest of his life with her.

Sure, little bit impractical, given that he lived in New York and she lived in London, but they could sort something out. From the moment he'd got on that plane, he'd known the course the rest of his life – their lives – should take. In fact, he'd probably known from the moment he'd seen her in the greasy spoon. It was amazing how *right* it felt to finally admit this to himself. Obviously there was now the slight glitch of broaching it with Izzy and convincing her that they could make it work. If she wanted to, of course. God, he hoped she wanted to.

He was smiling down at her very foolishly and his mind had gone blank. He really needed some witty banter at this point. No, no words. He just kept on smiling. He really wanted to put his arm round her.

Kiss her. But obviously he couldn't just do that. He needed to know that she'd *like* him to.

And then something fantastic happened. The wind kicked up, Izzy gasped as her coat skirts whipped round, and then her umbrella popped inside out and two of the spokes snapped. She looked at it.

'Bugger,' she said. 'I need a bin.' Excellent. Sam's giant umbrella was finally going to come into its own.

'Let me. Why don't you come under here?' Sam asked, taking her broken umbrella.

'Honestly, I'm fine, thank you.' She actually took a step backward. She obviously did not have the same 'snuggle under the umbrella' instinct that he did. She was absolutely soaked, the wind slapping her wet hair across her face and raindrops dripping off her nose. And she was shivering.

'Take this one.' He held it out.

'No, I couldn't.'

'I insist. Please? I'm the one who dragged you out here in this weather. And you need to hold it for me so that I can bundle this one up and get it into that bin.' He handed the umbrella to her and pointed at the bin further along the path.

'Okay, thank you very much.' She took it from him and he saw a small smile on her face before the top half of her disappeared under it.

Seriously. How dumb was he? If he'd just *held* it over her, it was so big that she'd probably have moved inside without thinking. But instead he'd invited her under, like he was inviting her on an under-umbrella *date* or something, she'd *obviously* said no, and now she was under the umbrella and he was outside it and she was so much shorter that he could pretty much only see her boots and there was no way they were going to be able to converse properly.

He squelched over to the bin to put her umbrella inside. It took an unexpectedly long time. The hole was small and the umbrella kept popping back up.

Izzy turned up next to him just as he'd finally got it in.

'We're going to have to share this umbrella,' she said. 'You're soaked.'

'You absolutely sure?' Okay, what was wrong with him? He was making it sound like they were going to be sharing a *bed* or something.

'Yep. You could fit a whole family in here. And also, it's really, really heavy. It's killing my arms.' She smiled at him as he stepped under.

And finally, yes, they were indeed in a little cocoon away from the world. They were also soaking wet and had a very heavy umbrella to hold, on an angle, to accommodate their height difference. But he'd take all of that.

She'd stopped smiling at him. She seemed to be studying the ground. Sam looked down at the top of her head and the side of her cheek and decided that awkward small talk wasn't going to get them anywhere. He cleared his throat. Didn't help. Right. He should just get on with it. This was not a comfortable silence. It wasn't a silence, either. It was very loud.

'The raindrops are very noisy, aren't they?' he observed. Much like a young child with few social skills might do.

'Yes, very,' said Izzy. Yup, they were going to get nowhere with light conversation. He was just going to go for it right now.

'I've really missed you. It's great to see you.' He paused but Izzy didn't speak. Or move. Right. Plough on. He should really have planned what he was going to say. 'Look. Part of the reason I reacted so badly that night in the pub was because of our kiss. It was...' How to describe it? 'It was an extraordinary moment for me. It made me realise how much I love you and I don't think I was ready for that realisation.'

Izzy still didn't move. Sam was holding the umbrella with both hands, looking down at her, and she was standing a few inches away from him, staring at the ground. They were together in their own little umbrella world, and yet entirely separate.

And then she looked up at him. Her beautiful grey eyes were misted with tears and had rings of evidently non-waterproof black make-up underneath and her mouth was a little twisted. The picture of misery. Sam's heart twisted like her mouth, and he reached his left hand to touch her cheek. She didn't move away. Instead she closed her eyes. A tear squeezed out of her right eye. Sam wiped it carefully away with his thumb.

She re-opened her eyes and parted her lips a little. And Sam lost any remaining ability he had to think and moved his hand round so that it was in her gorgeous, thick, tangled hair, now dark with water, and lowered his mouth to hers. And then they were kissing, and it was everything he'd remembered and more.

Sam's umbrella arm was now around Izzy. The umbrella dropped to the ground, and still they kissed, Sam barely registering the torrent of rainwater pouring down on them.

They kissed for a very long time. Deep, urgent kissing, interspersed with softer, caressing, exploratory kisses. All of it was perfect. Life affirming. And *love* affirming.

When they finally stopped, they were drenched. Sam had water inside his collar, soaking across his shoulders, down his back. His shoes had some time ago given up any pretence of holding up against the mini lake they were now standing in. The umbrella had rolled a little down the path and was upside down and already, despite its size, half-filled with water. The bottoms of his trousers were wet and muddy. Izzy was in much the same state.

And Sam felt good, very, very good. This was the moment. From nowhere, words came.

'Izzy, beautiful, amazing, wonderful, kind, funny, perfect Izzy, will you marry me?'

Chapter Thirty-Four

Izzy

Izzy's day had not started well.

Their post had arrived unusually early and it had consisted of two catalogues and a postcard for Ruby from her cousin Ella. The picture was one of those photo ones. It was of Izzy's mother, Veronique, Max, Nat and Ella in front of the Eiffel Tower and it was captioned '65th birthday family trip to Paris'. Izzy had been seriously pissed off by it. Anyone normal would think she and Ruby were part of Izzy's mother's family. But apparently Izzy's mother and Veronique did not. So much so that they'd presumably thought she'd *appreciate* the postcard.

Second best, always. Obviously Izzy was happy that they were happy. But she was not happy that they hadn't included her and Ruby, *again*.

So then she'd checked DoctorDebz on Instagram and there were several Paris photos, with a lot of gushing comments about how fab it was to be surrounded by her whole, *whole*, family on her birthday.

Izzy reading all the posts had made them late for school.

Then she'd spent ages doing her hair and make-up and worn her favourite new coat and boots for meeting Sam, and been half-soaked by the bloody rain before she'd even arrived, a bit late, to meet him.

And now she felt like a drowned rat, although that was clearly not her biggest problem right now.

Most of their conversation had been unpleasantly stilted, monosyllabic on Izzy's side, because she'd felt too overcome with emotion and too unsure about what she wanted from this meeting to speak. And that never happened to her, and it wasn't enjoyable.

And then, somehow, probably because she'd stupidly looked up at him, huge mistake, they'd kissed, in the most amazing way, for an incredibly long time. She hadn't felt cold or wet when the kiss had stopped, she'd felt in utter physical bliss.

And then Sam had asked her to *marry* him.

He had *proposed* to her.

And now she was standing in the pouring rain, holding onto the lapels of his coat, like some heroine in a Regency romance, completely sodden and freezing cold, and her lovely new coat and boots were probably ruined, which was nothing compared to the fact that if felt like her whole *life* was ruined.

Of course she wasn't going to marry him. She let go of his lapels and looked up at his handsome, gorgeous, perfect, rugged, Hollywood heart-throb face. She couldn't see amazingly well because her mascara had clogged together in blobs on her lashes because of the rain. She could see, though, his crooked smile that without fail did something to her insides. And that as she looked at him, the smile was diminishing a little. Probably because she was very much not smiling.

'Sam,' she said. She didn't know what else to say. Had he *meant* it?

'I would be truly honoured if you would become my wife,' he said, taking her hands in his. His hands were lovely and big and warm. His gorgeous dark-brown eyes were very serious. Yes, he'd meant it. Izzy closed her eyes for a moment. If only, if *only* this had happened the day they first met, nearly fourteen years ago. If only he hadn't been marrying someone else that day. Although, of course, Ruby, and the twins.

Could she marry him?

There were a lot of practical obstacles between them. The kids. They lived in different countries. She got up late, he got up early. She hated running, he loved it. She liked chocolate, he'd always go for cheese. Basically, she said tomato, he said tomayto. Although they could probably resolve all of that. In reality, it wasn't practical issues that had caused her split with Dominic, it was that she hadn't ever really fallen hard enough in love with him. And he with her, she thought. Whereas Sam was perfect for her.

Except for one huge thing. She loved Sam so indescribably much that she couldn't be second best in his life. The pain would torture her. And if Lana hadn't died, he'd still be happily with her and would never have given Izzy a second thought.

'I can't,' she said. Sam's head jerked back slightly, as though she'd slapped him. Yep, he'd been serious about his proposal. 'Thank you so much for the compliment.'

'Not at all,' he said, really quietly.

'I should go.' There was obviously nothing else to say and Izzy needed to get home and wallow in misery, alone.

'Of course. One question. Please.' His voice sounded scratchy. Izzy nodded. 'Do you love me?'

There was no point denying it. She'd started their relationship, if you could call it that, just under fourteen years ago, by humiliating herself when she asked him out on his wedding day. There was a symmetry to rounding things off by being fully honest.

'Yes, I do. I really, really love you. And now I need to say goodbye.'

Sam put his hands out to her but Izzy didn't take them. She stepped round him and started walking, towards the really bloody annoyingly cheerfully decorated Christmas tree at the end of the path.

'Take the umbrella,' he said.

'Too heavy,' she said without turning round, and carried on walking, fast.

When he called, 'Izzy,' she ignored him.

She cried all the way home but no-one she passed would have known because of all the rain pouring down her face.

Chapter Thirty-Five

Izzy

Izzy couldn't bear the thought of going painting with Emma this evening. She had the headache from hell from letting herself cry instead of doing her admin, and she just wanted to pick Ruby up, come home, stick her in front of the TV, listen on autopilot to her reading homework, get her into bed as soon as possible, and cry again. It was still raining heavily, which was ideal, because no-one ever tried to chat mid-school-run when it was pissing it down like this. So she could easily avoid talking to any adults this afternoon.

Except, if she pulled a painting sickie, Emma would probably come round anyway to check on her, either because she believed that Izzy was ill and was worried, or because she didn't believe she was ill and was worried. And, it wasn't like Izzy wasn't going to have to start living the rest of her life and try to be happy at some point. Maybe she should just go to painting. Maybe it would take her mind off things a bit.

'What's happened?' Emma asked, literally the second she'd closed the car door on their way to painting. What was she, some kind of misery detective? 'Your face is all puffy, you have no lipstick on, and you're struggling to smile.' Okay, not much detective work required.

'Bad day,' Izzy said, putting the car into reverse.

'Want to talk about it?'

'No. Thank you.' Maybe she did. She put the car into drive and set off.

Neither of them said anything for a minute or two and then Izzy said, 'I met Sam this morning.' Turned out she did want to talk.

'So closure didn't go well?'

'Nope.' Because it had turned out that closure wasn't easily attainable if you were head over heels in love with someone.

'I'm so sorry.'

'Thank you.' Izzy carried on driving for a bit. She stopped at a red light, looked at Emma and said, 'He asked me to marry him.'

'Oh my goodness. Oh, Izzy. But why are you miserable? What happened?'

'Well, obviously I said no.'

'But why?' Emma waited, but Izzy couldn't speak. 'I could be wrong and I could also be overstepping the mark *but* from where I'm standing you jumped straight into a relationship and marriage with Dominic, who really wasn't the love of your life, but you're holding back on a relationship with Sam, who *is* the love of your life, for nearly fourteen years and counting? Why would you do that?'

'Too high risk.' Oh, for God's sake. Izzy was crying again and her make-up was going to be ruined for the second time in one day. She'd already had to have a second shower and hair wash this morning after she'd got so soaked in the park.

'Why don't you pull in for a minute?' Good idea. Izzy couldn't really see to drive; she was crying so much. 'Because?' Emma asked again after Izzy had parked diagonally between a van and a skip opposite a pub.

'Well. There are all the practical reasons. You know, like we live several thousand miles apart. And we're very different. How does that even work in a marriage? It didn't work for Dominic and me. But those are small things compared to the biggest thing, which is that I don't think I can get over the fact that he'd still be married to his first wife if he hadn't lost her. And I've spent my whole life being second best. You know my mother and Veronique barely even remember that I'm my mother's daughter. And my father's the same. I mean, I literally only hear from him about once a year. I can't be second best in my marriage. I actually think I could have been second best in a marriage to someone like Dominic because I wouldn't have cared so deeply. But I can't be second best married to Sam, because it would kill me, because I love him too much.'

'Oh, Izzy. Come here.' Emma hauled Izzy into a hug.

'Mascara all over your shoulder,' Izzy said eventually.

'Doesn't matter, *obviously*. Listen, let's bin painting and go to that pub instead and get very drunk.'

'The car.'

'We're only a couple of miles from your house. We can cab it back to yours and Rohan can walk over here and drive it back for us.'

'That's a lot to ask of him. He's already babysitting for me.'

'Izzy. I will make it up to him with very good and slightly kinky sex later. He really won't mind.'

'Eeurgh.'

Chapter Thirty-Six

Sam

Sam glared at his phone screen. So many pointless emails from people he did not want to hear from. He exited the airport and headed for the taxi rank. Drizzle. Of course. He should be pleased to be arriving home to see the twins, and he was, of course he was. But it was hard not to be sick to the stomach miserable about Izzy.

He did at least get straight into a cab.

There was an email he wasn't expecting in his work inbox. From an E. Brooks, entitled 'From Emma, Izzy's best friend – please read'.

Dear Sam,

Please ignore this email if you don't know my best friend, Izzy Castle, i.e. if you aren't the Sam McCready, although I'm pretty sure you are. If you are him, I wonder if you could give me a call on the number below.

Izzy's deeply in love with you and deeply miserable and has a deeply spurious, but strongly held, belief that she can't marry you. I think she's wrong. I think it's fixable.

I'd love to hear from you.

Yours,
Emma Brooks

Yes, he was going to be calling Emma. Couldn't hurt.

He asked the taxi driver to drop him a couple of blocks from the apartment. He wanted to make this call now, and he did not want to make it in front of the twins. Liv had ears as long as a hare's. And since he now knew that she wasn't shy about asking him about his private life and she was already going to be grilling him on yesterday's disastrous meeting with Izzy, he didn't want her to hear this conversation too.

Chapter Thirty-Seven

Izzy

'Your Christmas party is *here*?' Izzy hadn't set foot inside Terry's Greasy Spoon since her last shift here, over thirteen years ago, the weekend before she started her full-time social work job. The outside hadn't changed at *all*, so there was a more than fighting chance that inside was still fairly similar to how it had been a decade and a half before. No-one sane would ever mistake it for a nice party spot.

Fortunately, Izzy didn't really have any festive spirit to *be* diminished by the bizarre venue choice.

Emma, having recommended that Izzy dress smartly, had turned up to pick Izzy up wearing a very low-cut midnight blue jumpsuit, which looked stunning on her tall, lean frame, and fancy jewellery, shoes and handbag. When she'd seen her, Izzy had gone back upstairs and blinged herself up a bit more before coming back down. Emma had been unusually tolerant about the fact that they'd then set off fifteen minutes later than planned. And *now* they were walking into Terry's. *So* bizarre to be holding a Christmas party in a complete dive, and not a cool one. Was this some kind of trendy ironic thing that Izzy didn't get?

Emma mumbled something that Izzy couldn't hear properly, opened the door and said, 'You go first.'

'Thank you,' Izzy was still saying as her eyes took in the interior of the café and her brain started to compute stuff. Slowly. She felt her forehead stretch into a confused frown.

The layout of the café was exactly the same as it had been when Izzy had worked there. Counter along the back wall, facing the door, with the kitchen behind. This evening, the counter was festooned in Christmas décor: holly, berries, twigs, silver tinsel, silver baubles, all sorts. All very normal for a Christmas party. Very tasteful, actually. It looked as though the walls were still covered in the same foot-square, greyish white tiles they'd worn in Izzy's day, but you couldn't really tell because some decorations had been hung around the room plus the strip lights in the ceiling weren't on. With the lights this low and all the Christmas décor, the café looked genuinely appealing. There were fairy lights on a Christmas tree in the corner and candles on the only table in the room. It was a four-person one, and was in the middle of the room, covered in a bottle green tablecloth, fabric not paper, and laid for two, for what looked like a multi-course meal.

Izzy heard the door close behind her and looked round to ask Emma what was happening and where everyone else was. Given that they were late, surely at least a few other people should have arrived by now.

Emma had gone.

And then she heard a voice from the direction of the counter. Sam's voice. What?

'Good evening. Could I take your coat?' He was dressed in a very nice dark-grey suit, with a sparkling white shirt and red tie. So handsome.

Izzy was so confused that she shrugged out of her coat without saying anything and just stood, lemon-like, next to the table, as Sam took it from her and hung it up in the corner, on a very nice, modern chrome coat stand, very much not something that would normally feature in

Terry's café, and in fact very similar to the one that Emma had in her hall. A man's overcoat was already hanging there, presumably Sam's.

'I have a Kir royale for you, but also a glass of tap water if you'd prefer.'

'Um, water please.' She should stay sober. Before she walked out. Although, a couple of alcoholic sips wouldn't go amiss. The sugar might get her brain working. 'And the Kir royale too. Thank you very much.'

'Not a problem.' Sam moved over to the counter to get the drinks. 'Now, first of all, I obviously have to apologise for having brought you here by subterfuge.' Sam looked like a nervous little boy. In an extremely gorgeous man's body. 'I'd be incredibly grateful if you'd allow me the opportunity to have another attempt at explaining things to you, but I completely understand if you'd rather leave now, and I'll walk you home, or call a cab for you.' Maybe she should stay just for a few minutes. He'd obviously gone to a lot of effort for this evening.

'Would you like to sit down?' Sam pulled the chair on the door side of the table out.

'Thank you.' Izzy sat. These shoe boots had been comfortable when she tried them on but now the left one was really pinching her little toe. And it was weird standing up, just the two of them, for too long. Sam sat down opposite her.

'The reason that I wanted to meet here is that this is where our story started,' he said. Their story, if that was how he wanted to describe it, had indeed started here, and Izzy did not really need to think about that day *again*. It hadn't been good.

'Mm-hm,' she said, hoping that he'd shut up. Nope. He looked like a man with a lot to say and who was planning to say it pretty much no matter what. He'd placed his hands on the table in front of him, in a braced position, and his shoulders and jaw both looked tense, almost a bit muscle-twitchy.

'The day we first met,' he said, 'I loved how you burned the bacon but gave me extra sausages, and I loved your smile. And how cute you were in your ridiculous elf costume that you were clearly furious about wearing. And the cheeky look in your eye. And if I'd been single I would have leapt on your suggestion of a date in a heartbeat. In fact, I'd have been asking you out myself, first. You know, I wanted to say yes. I wished in that moment that I could walk away from my wedding and go out with you that evening.' Wow. There was something about the way Sam spoke that told Izzy it was the truth. 'I knew, somehow, that you'd make me laugh, make me think, make me happy. And I was right.'

'Oh,' Izzy said. While this was mind-blowingly confusing to listen to, it was also nice to know. Like in a few sentences Sam had finally put the mortification of the memory to bed. Maybe she was going to get closure on her relationship with him after all. Maybe he wanted closure too. Maybe that's why he was doing this. He probably didn't propose very often. He'd looked as though he'd meant it in the park last week. Probably he'd found that upsetting. Probably she should stay and listen to everything he had to say.

'On that day fourteen years ago, I knew, *knew*, that you were The One,' Sam continued. 'Which I found ridiculous, for two reasons. One, I did not believe in love at first sight, or that there was one The One for anybody. And two, I was, as you know, marrying someone else that day. Something that I have never said out loud before, to anyone, is that the reason that I proposed to Lana is that I got stupidly drunk following her revelation that she was pregnant with our baby, who turned out to be the twins, of course, and proposing seemed like the right thing to do. Being pregnant, she was sober, and she accepted my proposal, so I couldn't tell her that I hadn't really meant it and wasn't in love with her. And so we got married. I feel incredibly disloyal to her memory in telling you that. But it's important, I think.'

Izzy nodded. Speech was eluding her. All her brain could come up with was *Woah*.

'I don't know whether Lana and I would have stayed together forever. I don't know whether she was really in love with me. I did come to love her, although I don't think I was ever *in* love with her, and the time we had together was good. I was truly devastated by her death, on behalf of the twins, of course, and also on my own behalf, as my companion, and as one would be by that of any close friend or family member who lost their life far too soon. She was a great person and there's a lot she would have done if she'd had the opportunity to live longer.' Sam's voice wobbled and Izzy put her hand out to take his.

'I saw you once, and I think you saw me. I was on the Chelsea Library steps and you were on the pavement. I was going inside to research breast cancer prognoses. We'd literally just found out about Lana's illness. I wanted so much to speak to you and that made me feel incredibly guilty, because it was a moment when I should have been thinking only about her.'

'I'm sorry,' Izzy said. Bit of a stupid thing to say but in her defence this was huge and she'd been completely unprepared. 'I saw you too.'

'Can I offer you an olive? Or a miniature cheese and onion toastie? Or a bacon and Beaufort tuile?' Sam had the air of a man who needed a break from emotional chat. He stood up and moved over to the counter and returned with two plates. 'I'm hoping that your grilled cheese and caramelised onion thing wasn't just a pregnancy fetish.' He smiled. 'I think I remember almost every word of our conversation that day.' Izzy took a mini toastie. It was definitely easier to eat than to speak at this point.

'This is delicious,' she said, pleased that she could formulate some words, even if they really weren't up to the kind of narrative Sam had been producing. He smiled at her, his slow, lopsided smile. Izzy was pretty certain that it was a smile that you could live with for a lot of decades without going bored.

'We both have excellent taste in savoury snacks. I got this very nice restaurant, The Circle, round the corner, to cater for us this evening. My cooking skills have improved, as you know, but they aren't up to producing a gourmet meal in Terry's kitchen. Which I doubt has changed since you worked here.'

'I don't think anyone has ever produced gourmet cuisine from that kitchen. The odd bit of food poisoning, maybe.'

'Are you…?' Sam cleared his throat very thoroughly. 'Are you happy to stay and eat dinner with me?'

'I'd like that.' Izzy really couldn't have said no. He'd gone to so much effort. Plus she was liking what he'd been saying.

'Thank you.' Sam beamed at her. 'Could I say one more thing before I bring our starters out?' Izzy nodded. So far, he'd said a lot of good things. 'You're the only woman I've ever been truly, deeply in love with. However, even if that weren't the case, even if I'd been passionately in love with Lana, or with someone else since we lost her, that would be the past, and now is the present, and the future is the future. One sec, I think that's the timer.' He stood up and went into the kitchen. And Izzy's mind started to work. She wasn't second best. She was the only woman he'd ever properly fallen in love with. And, even if that hadn't been the case, he was in love with her *now* and for the future, and that was all that counted.

In a perfect world, anyway.

'One more thing,' said Sam, poking his head out of the kitchen. 'I know that I'm incredibly lucky with my family. You had bad luck with your parents and they sound spectacularly selfish and it sounds as though they never put you first, but your grandmother did, didn't she? *You* aren't second best. It isn't about you; it was about your parents being self-centred. Anyway. I think I'm expressing myself badly.' He withdrew his head and there was some muffled clattering. He hadn't expressed himself badly. What he'd said actually made enormous sense.

'Our starter is scallops with a cauliflower puree and something to do with truffle and prosciutto.' Sam placed Izzy's plate in front of her. Their hands brushed as he put the plate down and she nearly jumped through the ceiling. The tingle was extraordinary. Another one of those things that, really, did anyone actually believe in? Electricity between two people who were attracted to each other? Really? Well, *yes*. It was like that small touch had ignited lots of flares inside her, all over her body. Okay, time to focus on the food before she spontaneously combusted.

'I love scallops.'

'Yup. Little bird told me.' Sam grinned at her. Izzy decided she'd save having a go about Emma's obvious collusion in this until tomorrow.

Sam held off on any more deep and meaningful chat during their starter and main course, a very nice, Christmassy venison Wellington with roasted chestnuts and purple sprouting broccoli. They talked about the kids, their favourite Christmas customs, Christmas jumpers, skipping ropes, salsa dancing and whether they'd rather be a peacock farmer or an emu farmer. They could have talked for a long time, about absolutely nothing.

As they talked, Izzy drank in Sam's smile, his laugh, his voice, his hands, the way his shoulder muscles strained against his shirt, the way his eyes crinkled at the corners when he was about to say something that he thought would make her giggle.

When they'd finished their main courses, Izzy made to clear the plates.

'No, no,' Sam said, standing up. 'I'm doing this.' He started to carry them into the kitchen.

Watching him work, Izzy felt herself smiling away. This was probably the best meal she'd ever had in her life. Top three, anyway. The other two having been their lunch all those years ago and their dinner in August. Although that had really not ended well. Thinking about it, Izzy felt her smile drop.

'Hey.' Sam sat back down. 'What's wrong?'

'Nothing.' Izzy switched a smile on.

'Fake smile.' Sam reached out and took her hands. Izzy let him. Their hands felt so right together. She could sit like this forever. 'At the risk of sounding either horribly conceited, or just way off the mark, I hope that you weren't remembering the way our last dinner ended.' He was bloody psychic. 'I'd like to hope that this dinner won't end like that. And, in the interests of openness and honesty, I'd like to say that that was the best kiss of my entire life, and the reason that the evening ended the way it did, from my side anyway, was basically that I wasn't ready to admit to myself and certainly not to you that I was deeply, irrevocably in love with you, and had been for a long time.'

'Oh.' Not what she'd thought he was going to say, again.

'I love the way that you try really hard to be on time for things but you're frequently late. I love your recipes. I love that you get relatively easily annoyed but that you rarely lose it with people because just as you're about to say something your mind makes an excuse for them. I love your beautiful face. I won't mention your gorgeous body because I don't want to sound like your average Terry's frequenter. Although, wow, in that dress. But, basically, I love *you*. And I love the way you make me feel. Complete.'

'I love you too,' Izzy said. 'I love you so much.' She could feel her lip going wobbly and her throat tightening up. Any minute now she was going to cry. It was all so sad.

'It doesn't look like you're on the brink of happy tears.' Sam tightened his grip on her hands.

'No.'

'Could you tell me why?'

'Because we live on opposite sides of the Atlantic.'

'Yeah, I agree that's an issue, but I'm pretty sure that we can come up with a solution.' Like what? Please, please help this not be like when Dominic had suggested that she and Ruby move to Milan. Obviously she could work a lot more easily in New York than in Italy, but even so. She had her job and her practice, and Ruby was happy at school and seeing Dominic every weekend, and they both had a lot of local friends. And she couldn't possibly expect Sam and, in particular, the twins, to move to London.

'Mmm?' she said. He was rubbing his thumb on the insides of her wrists now, and it felt amazing. Were wrists one of the seven erogenous zones that Monica and Rachel had been talking about in that *Friends* episode? Must have been. His touch was sending signals to faraway parts of her body. She wanted him *so much*.

'Maybe we could move to London? The twins are very keen for you and Ruby to join our family. And it would be great for them to spend more time with their maternal grandparents. We could keep an apartment in New York and commute a little?' He sounded like a desperate puppy. Desperate being the operative word.

'But they're at such a critical age and they've been through so much, and now they're doing so much better. I mean, Barney and the debate team. And Liv's much happier now and still seeing her physio, isn't she?' Izzy was struggling to concentrate because Sam was continuing the wrist thing with his thumbs. 'You can't leave New York.'

'Izzy. I'll do anything to make this work. I can't ask you to take Ruby away from Dominic or leave your job.' Sam's gorgeous voice was cracking. And, suddenly, Izzy knew. This wasn't like when Dominic had suggested that she and Ruby move to Milan. For the very simple reason that she loved Sam with all her heart, and home would always be where he was. She could work in the US. Ruby was still very young and adaptable. Maybe they could commute a little. They could spend the school holidays in the UK or Italy, to be close to Dominic. She was pretty sure that, now they weren't going to get back together, Dominic would like to move permanently to Milan. He'd got his promotion and Ruby could visit him there as she got older. And maybe they could move back to London when the twins were old enough for college.

She smiled at Sam. 'We'll work it out together,' she said.

His slow smile started. Then his eyes moved to Izzy's lips, further down, back to her lips, back to her eyes.

Izzy's heart was going like the clappers now.

Sam let go of her hands and wrists and walked round the table. He knelt on the floor in front of her and picked up her hands again.

'Izzy Castle, will you do me the very great honour of becoming my wife?' He was looking right into her eyes, immobile other than a small muscle movement near his jaw.

'Sam McCready, I would love to.' Izzy could barely get the words out she was so excited, happy, over the moon, just *ecstatic*.

Sam's face creased into a very wide smile. He took a ring box out of his pocket and opened it for her.

'Oh, wow,' Izzy breathed. 'I *love* emeralds.'

Sam took it out and slid it onto her finger.

'How did you manage to get the right size?' How was that possible?

'Emma. The woman's a genius. Scary. But hugely gifted.' Sam stood up and drew Izzy to her feet. 'Could we have a dance before we eat dessert? Which, by the way, is a lemon drizzle pudding.'

'Yum and, yes, I'd love to.'

'Hold on a second. Forgot to put my elf hat on.' He took the hat out of his pocket and stuck it on his head. 'In memory of the first time we met. I didn't get one for you because I didn't think you'd like to wear one again.' He pressed a button on his phone and Slade's Christmas song started.

'This was playing when I turned my back on The One and walked out of the café that day.' He put his left arm round her waist and took her right hand and moved in close for a waltz position. 'It's always reminded me of you.' They started moving together, slowly, to the music. Who knew that 'Merry Xmas Everybody' was the sexiest song ever written? 'Fourteen years, and finally our stars are in alignment. Meant to be.'

When the song ended, they kissed for a very long time before they ate their lemon pudding, in a very schmaltzy and spoon-sharing, but absolutely perfect way.

Epilogue

One year later

'This is all so gorgeous,' Emma told Izzy, gesturing round the room. 'Such a nice hotel. And the decorations are amazing. I mean, the perfect Christmas wedding. We've done such a good job.'

'I know.' Izzy beamed at her. 'I couldn't feel more smug if I tried.' Coming back to London to hold the wedding had worked out so well. Even the weather had been on their side; there'd been a shimmery-white dusting of snow on the ground this morning, followed by dry, frosty brightness all day.

'Got your milkshake.' Rohan, back from the bar, handed the glass carefully to Emma.

'Thank you. Slow bar service.' Emma was already downing it. She'd been obsessed with full fat chocolate milkshakes throughout her entire pregnancy. She and Izzy had sent a *lot* of messages and emails backwards and forwards between London and New York since Izzy had moved, and for the last few months pretty much every one of Emma's had mentioned milkshakes.

Being Emma, she'd developed excellently large boobs and a textbook beautiful bump while seeming to have put on no weight anywhere else at all. Today, at seven months pregnant, she was looking absolutely stunning in a jade-green silk ballgown, taking her matron-of-honour duties very seriously.

'Not your usual wedding reception drink,' Rohan said and kissed Emma's forehead. It was lovely the way he was so adoring.

'Hey. Haven't seen you for a few minutes. I missed you.' Sam put his arm round Izzy's waist and moved her hair out of the way to kiss her neck. Izzy shivered, deliciously. It had been a year and you'd have thought she'd have got used to the sheer sex-godness of him, but still, every time he touched her, it was *good*.

'Dude. Get a room.' Luke slapped Sam on the back.

'It's my wedding day. If I want to kiss my bride in public, I'll kiss her.' Sam grinned at his best man, his arm still tight round Izzy's waist. Izzy didn't think she could get any happier. Her heart wouldn't take it. It had already expanded to a ridiculous point.

'We have some extra speeches before the dancing gets going,' Luke said. Sam narrowed his eyes.

'Really? I'd like to think you've already done your worst.'

Luke was ignoring him, striding towards the stage where the band were sitting.

'Want me to get up there and stop him?' While pregnant, Emma had been extremely assertive. Izzy had been guiltily pleased to have the Atlantic between the two of them during the wedding planning, although she'd *loved* the very rude email that Emma had sent to Izzy's father when he'd said that he was too busy to come to his oldest daughter's wedding. Her mother and Veronique had, surprisingly, made it, accompanied by what Izzy's mother had stage-whispered to her was a *naughty* present. Izzy didn't *ever* want to open it.

'Grateful but no thanks,' she told Emma.

While Luke was sound-checking the mic, Dominic came over, holding his Italian girlfriend Gabriella's hand. 'Congratulations, Izzy.' He kissed her cheek.

'Thank you.' She smiled at him. 'And thank you for having Ruby.' Ruby was going to be staying with Dominic and Gabriella in Milan, and the twins with their English grandparents, while Izzy and Sam had a few days' honeymoon in Paris before a family skiing holiday. 'So nice to have you here.' She meant it.

Luke banged the mic. 'And now we have a surprise for the bride and groom,' he told the room. And Ruby, Liv and Barney stepped up onto the stage, Barney handsome and very cool in his linen suit and trainers, and Liv and Ruby a gorgeous picture in their matching Christmassy dark green and red bridesmaid dresses.

Liv took the mic from Luke and said, 'Good evening, everyone. We just wanted to say how happy we are that our parents have got married. Let's go, Ruby.' She smiled at Ruby and turned and nodded at the band. 'Our parents have a thing for some movie from the nineties,' she said, like she was talking about the Middle Ages, '*You've Got Mail*, so we're going to sing the song from the last scene of that film.'

And Ruby and Liv sang 'Over the Rainbow', and Izzy realised that she'd been wrong when she thought she couldn't get any happier.

Then Liv gave an excellent speech. Poised, polished, perfect. And funny. She actually alluded to her *own* evil thirteen-year-old self from the year before, with some jokes. She was right. She'd grown up a lot since then. Izzy's heart expanded even more.

And then, Liv handed the mic to Barney.

He took it. He focused on Izzy and Sam. He gave them a big smile. And he started speaking, nice and slowly, and very clearly.

'I'd like to say a big congratulations to my father and to my new stepmother. Liv, Ruby and I are so happy that you two have got married. Izzy, you'll be pleased to hear that I just did a big fake smile to myself in the bathroom.' He had a big smile, just for her. And a barely discernible stammer. And when he *did* stammer, he picked himself up and carried on. Okay, this was it, Izzy's heart *was* now going to break. There was no happiness bigger than this.

Sam held her the whole the way through Barney's speech.

While everyone was clapping and whistling at the end, Sam led Izzy over to the stage and took the mic from Barney.

'Our first dance is Slade's "Merry Xmas Everybody",' he told everyone. 'It's our song. And I think my wife would like to say something.' He handed the mic to Izzy while all their guests cheered.

'Thank you, husband.' Izzy beamed at Sam while everyone cheered again. 'After "Merry Xmas Everybody" we'd love you all to join us on the dance floor.'

'Fifteen years since we first met,' Sam said as they danced very slowly to Noddy Holder. 'That's some journey.'

'Worth every single step,' said Izzy.

A Letter from Jo

Thank you so much for reading *The First Time We Met*. I really hope that you enjoyed it!

If you did enjoy it, and would like to keep up to date with all my latest releases, just sign up at the following link. Your email address will never be shared and you can unsubscribe at any time.

www.bookouture.com/jo-lovett

I had a lot of fun writing Izzy and Sam's story. I love the big 'What if you meet the right one at the wrong time' question. I hope that the story made you smile or laugh.

Izzy's a speech therapist. I wanted to mention here that I'm particularly grateful to the speech therapists I've met. My youngest son has been having speech therapy recently for a stammer (or 'stutter' for US readers) and one of his brothers had speech and language therapy a few years ago because he had difficulty in forming consonants. Their therapy made a huge difference to their ability to communicate and their confidence. And the understanding that there's nothing at all *wrong* in stammering (or stuttering) – it's just a slightly different way of talking, not better, not worse – is also huge.

I hope that you loved Izzy, Sam and their children as much as I did!

If you enjoyed the story, I would be so pleased if you could leave a short review. I'd love to hear what you think.

Thank you for reading.

Love, Jo xx

@JoLovettWrites

Acknowledgements

Thank you so much to everyone at Bookouture – so many truly lovely people. Many of the authors describe it as a family, and I think that's the perfect description. I'm particularly grateful to my editor, the wonderful Lucy Dauman, for seeing something in my writing and for working with me on this story in such a positive and supportive way. All her suggestions seem so right as soon as she makes them, and she sends lovely emails!

Thank you also to Claire Torrance, a friend who is a speech and language therapist and very generous with the passing on of her knowledge. Any mistakes in the book in relation to speech therapy are mine! And thank you very much to Sarah Buckingham, a solicitor friend who provided very helpful advice about lawyerly working practices. Again, any mistakes are mine.

Thank you to *Good Housekeeping* magazine and Orion. I entered their First Novel Competition in 2018 (with a different story) and was runner-up (and won a laptop – exciting!). And thank you to the Comedy Women in Print Award, set up by Helen Lederer in 2019. I entered that year (also with a different story) and was shortlisted. Those competitions really do give aspiring authors a huge boost.

Finally, I have to thank my family. Thank you to my sister Liz for always being so supportive and basically an amazing best friend (and remarkably brave in adversity). And thank you to my husband and children. A lot of the book was written during lockdown. There were many occasions when I should have been engaging a lot more fully with home schooling than I did. My youngest son summed things up nicely when his Year One teacher asked him if he'd been doing any English and he said, 'We've been too busy.' So thank you all for being so understanding about my manic writing over the past few months and for putting up with eating so much pasta (no time for actual cooking).

Printed in Great Britain
by Amazon

26654703R00198